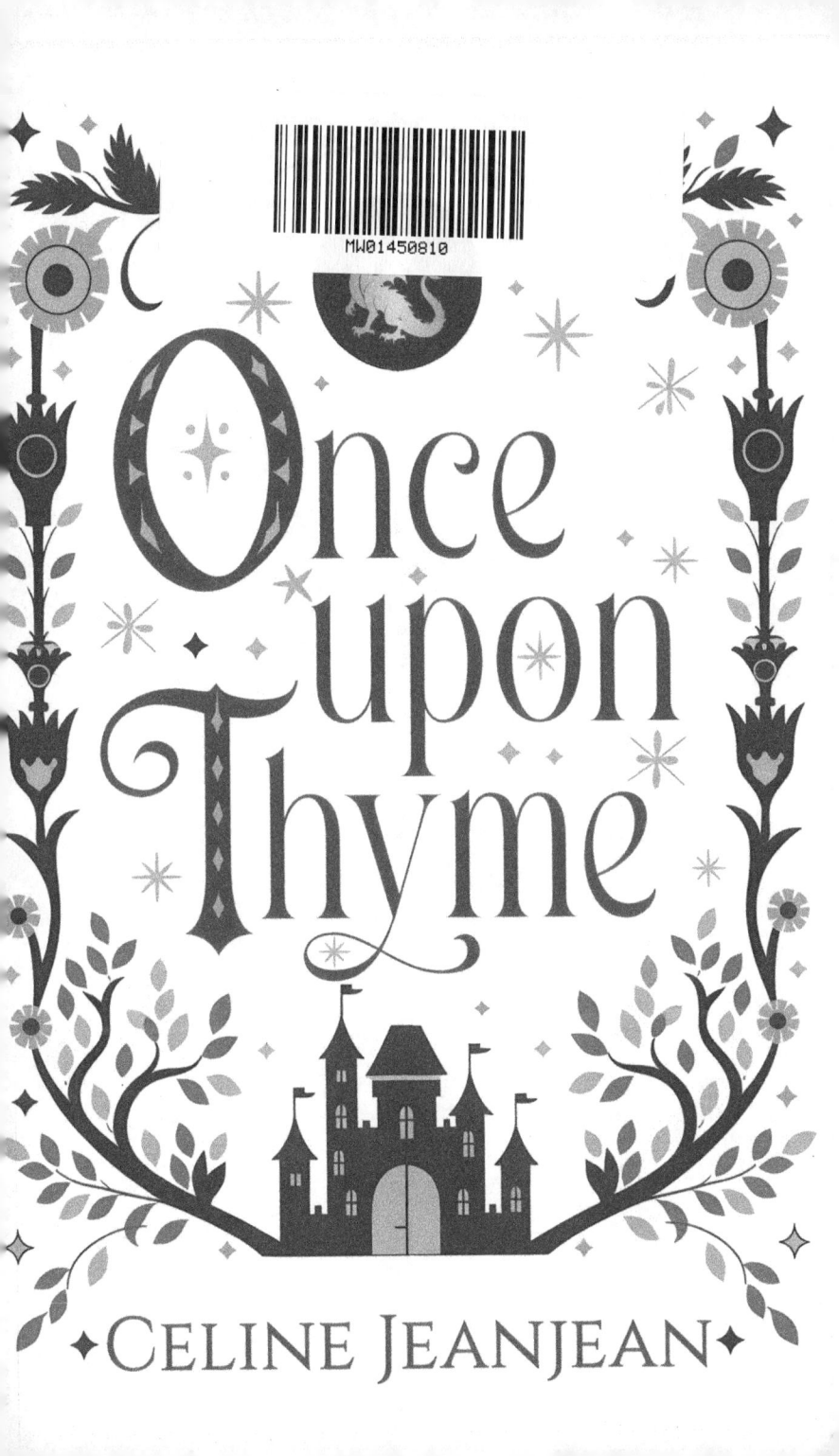

Once upon Thyme

CELINE JEANJEAN

Dear Reader,

I hope you have fun in Once-Upon-Thyme, and that you find a place in this quirky little world.

This book is a work of fiction. The characters, incidents and dialogue are drawn from the author's imagination and are not to be construed as real. Any resemblance to actual events or persons, living or dead, is coincidental.

Once-Upon-Thyme
Copyright © 2024 Celine Jeanjean. All rights reserved
http://celinejeanjean.com

The right of Celine Jeanjean to be identified as the author of this work has been asserted by the author in accordance with the Copyright, Designs and Patents Act, 1988. All rights reserved. No part of this publication may be reproduced, stored in a retrieval system, or transmitted, in any form, or by any means, electronic, mechanical, photocopying, recording or otherwise, without prior permission of the author.

Editing by: copybykath.com
Exterior cover: Elona Bezooshko from Psycat Covers

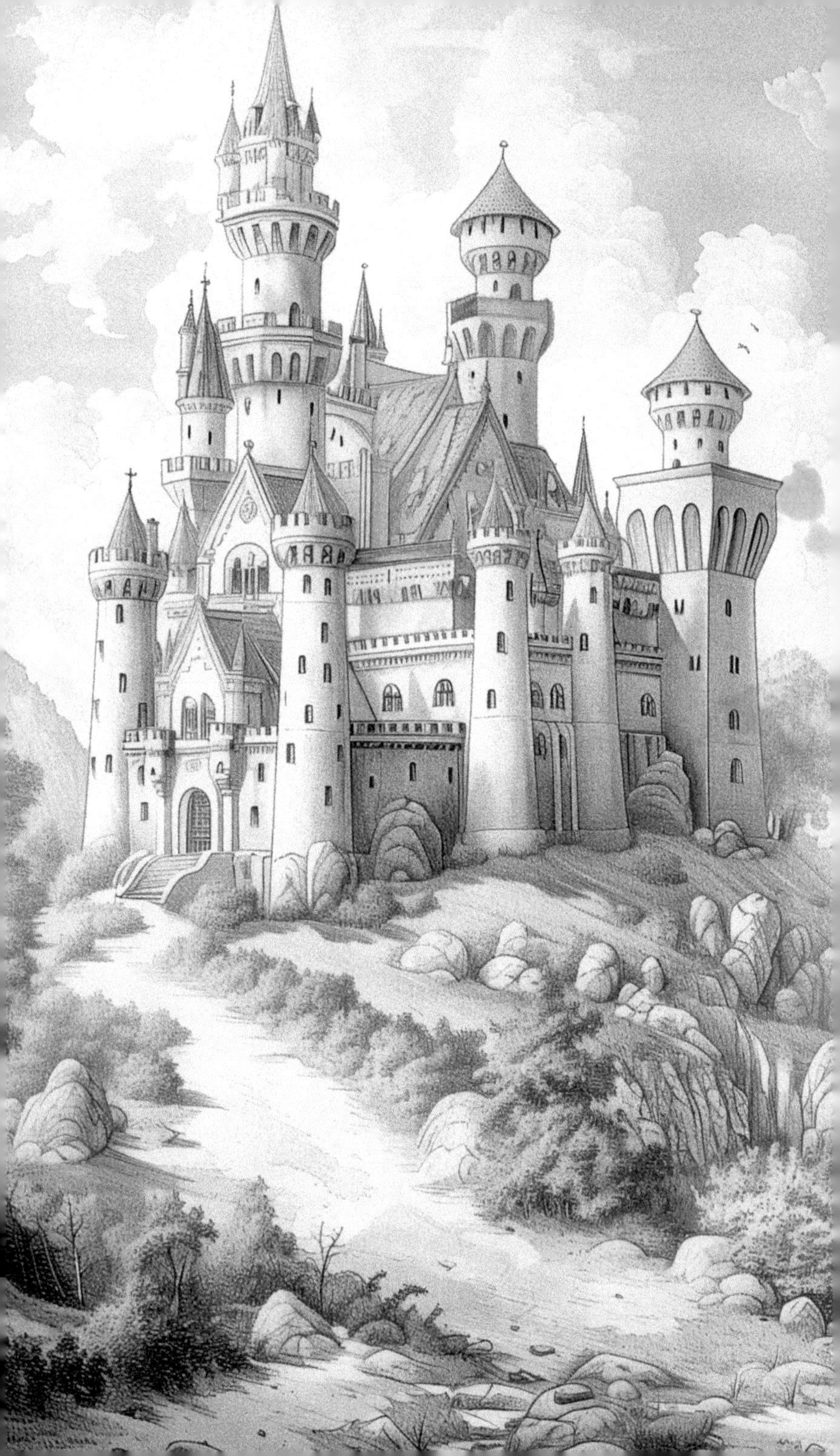

PROLOGUE

Our tale begins quite normally as so many tales do, in Once-Upon-Thyme, that tiny and unusual country. Just like most women's handbags, it was bigger inside than it appeared to be from the outside. So, while on a map Once-Upon-Thyme was barely the size of a large city, cross its borders and you could lose yourself in an incredible vastness that was riddled with royals, fairies, witches, pretty milkmaids, and courageous shepherds.

Perhaps because its very existence defied logic, attempting to apply reason to Once-Upon-Thyme could only result in the kind of headache normally encountered when disentangling a knotted ball of yarn.

This was a place where shepherds were regularly crowned king, in spite of being utterly unqualified to rule, where medicine was actively discouraged from progressing, because queens were supposed to die in childbirth, and where curses were more prevalent than the common cold.

Our tale therefore begins here, in this odd little country, and specifically within the walls of one of its more lavish palaces. Traditions being incredibly important in Once-Upon-Thyme, certain phrases must always be used when beginning a new story. And it goes something like this.

In Once-Upon-Thyme, there was a prince who had an ardent wish. You could be forgiven for thinking that there was nothing unusual in this—princes are, after all, forever wishing ardently for things—but you'd be mistaken. This is no ordinary tale of princely wishing....

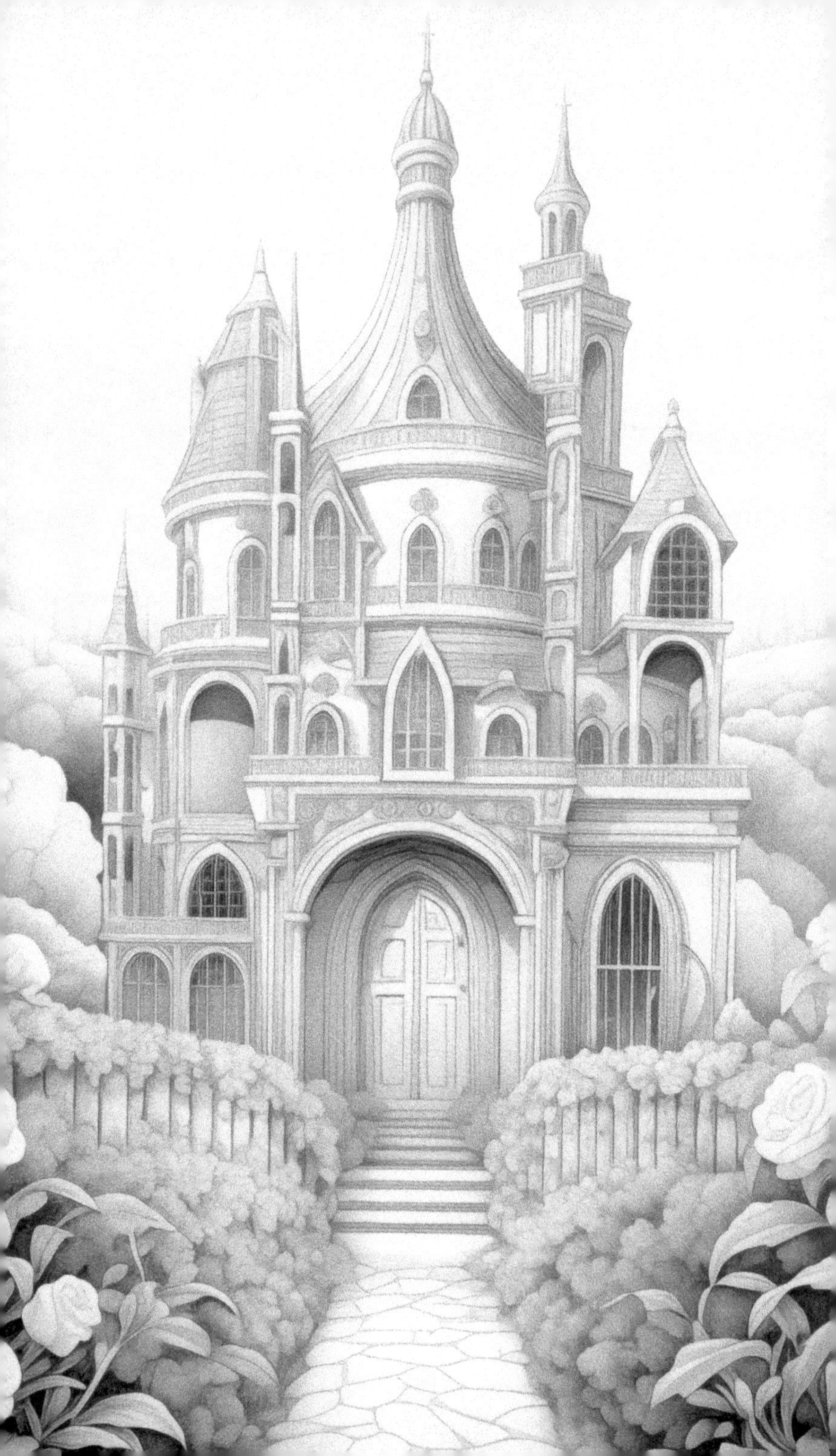

CHAPTER 1

In one of the largest palaces of Once-Upon-Thyme, Prince Charming (for that was, in fact, his name) was in the middle of an embittered battle. Struggling for air amongst the crush of chiffon and tulle, knocking tiaras off heads and setting wigs askew, Prince Charming was attempting as valiantly as he could to find an exit from the hell in which he found himself. Everywhere he turned, another princess, another set of batting eyelashes, another flirtatious smile. Hands reached out for him from every corner, insidiously slipping lace handkerchiefs and favours up his sleeves or down his collar.

Charming ignored the handkerchief assault, for he had now almost reached his salvation: the doors that led out of the ballroom to the balcony that overlooked the garden. With a final and desperate shove of a rotund woman, he managed to expel himself through the double doors and into the cool night air.

The rotund person he had so manfully removed from his way had let out an indignant squawk and was now making such a fuss as to distract and confuse the gaggle of females. Not wanting to waste this opportunity, he hurried down the steps that led to the garden and hid behind a hedge trimmed to resemble a rabbit. He crouched in the darkness, panting, his clothing in disarray.

What Prince Charming desired above all else was to be left in peace. Unfortunately, he was well acquainted with the particular craze that took hold of women when in the presence of a prince—Prince Fever, as he dubbed it to himself—but that didn't make him any less uncomfortable when confronted with the phenomenon. The affected women went into frenzies of flirting, laughing, mad twiddling of hair, and for some reason he had never been able to fathom, they all went to great lengths to bat him on the arm.

The latter was most troublesome since Charming bruised like a peach.

Worse was the fact that the merest flirtatious look threw him into paroxysms of sweating (to say nothing of actual flirtatious comments), so that this latest assault on his person had left his clothing dangerously damp.

From behind his rabbit hedge, Charming pulled out the plethora of clandestine handkerchiefs that had hitched a ride in his sleeves, letting them fall to the ground. He found his own handkerchief and dabbed at his moist face.

The cool night breeze helped dry him off, and he lifted his face to it, enjoying this brief moment of peace. The breeze brought him the sound of voices—women calling his name, playfully searching for him among the hydrangeas that lined the balcony. Charming crouched further down. After a while, he started to hear impatient sighs and grumbles as it became obvious to the princesses that he wasn't there.

For a moment he feared that they might push the search to the gardens, but the voices slowly drifted off, swallowed by the faint music that wafted out of the palace doors, until at last some thoughtful soul closed the doors, and the night was blessedly silent once more.

Charming sighed miserably, wondering how long he would be able to stay hidden in the garden this time before he incurred the Motherly Wrath.

A large part of being a prince meant entertaining a bevy of princesses in an endless procession of balls, some masked, some unmasked, with the expectation that he would eventually select one of said princesses to be his wife.

His mother would not be swayed on that last point, and since she had decided that his father the king agreed with her in this, as he did in all things, Charming was left with no choice but to comply.

But how he was supposed to select a wife from the squawking multitude when he couldn't bear to speak to them, let alone spend time with them, was beyond him.

A cramp began to crawl up his leg, and he stood up to relieve it, stepping out from behind his hedge.

"Ah, there you are!"

Charming started at the interpellation and, turning, found a woman regarding him severely with her hands on her hips. She was wearing a ballgown, as they all did, but she was somewhat older than his usual pursuers. Quite a bit older, in fact. She had grey eyes and a surprisingly hooked nose. That is to say that it protruded more than the button nosed norm he was so accustomed to seeing at every turn.

In fact, there was a distinct lack of prettiness to her features, which was highly unusual. Princesses were always pretty, so much so that they all vaguely resembled each other, and Charming had the hardest time remembering who was who.

Charming steeled himself, stoically awaiting the usual assault of flirting, but to his surprise, nothing came. The woman was still watching him expectantly. It occurred to him that maybe she was awaiting a reply to her previous statement.

"Yes, here I am," he said.

The conversational requirements having apparently been met, the woman sprang to life like a toy whose mechanism had been wound up. She marched towards Charming, who shrank back reflexively.

"I have been waiting and waiting for someone to show me the gardens. I have heard many good things about your gardener, mainly that he isn't Cornish, and I'm very interested to see what he has done to your roses."

While Charming had been bestowed with many qualities at birth, as all princes were, speed of deduction wasn't one of them, and said speed decreased exponentially when in the vicinity of a member of the female sex. He stared at the woman, nonplussed. What was she on about?

"Well, are you going to show me your roses?" she asked, proffering her elbow.

The mist of confusion that had hitherto filled Charming's mind melted like snow on a furnace. She wanted a tour of the garden! Not only was this not flirting, it was a real and legitimate excuse to stay out of the ballroom. He could have kissed the woman, if propriety, nerves, and inclination had permitted.

Instead, he took her arm and replied, "I'd be delighted to."

He led her away from the laughter and the music, towards the cool and silent gloom of the rose garden. Never had a sight been more welcome. That was until he realised that as a host escorting a (female) guest through the garden, he should really be offering some sort of commentary on the flowers. Worse, maybe he was expected to rhapsodise about the woman's beauty in the dark, or some other such nonsense.

Charming began to sweat once more. He knew next to nothing about flowers, and how was one supposed to comment on a woman's beauty when it was too dark to see it? And in any case, she wasn't beautiful.

Thankfully, he didn't have to sweat for long, as the woman began to monologue at him (or at the night—it was unclear who, if anyone, she was addressing) about the state of the roses. Charming did his best to listen and follow the Unusual Female's chatter, but he kept tuning off and wandering off into his own thoughts. Every few minutes he would catch himself adrift in reverie, and he would return to the flow of words that poured from the woman's mouth, much like a man who, despite his best efforts to stay awake, keeps finding himself asleep with his head hanging at an awkward angle.

After a time, it became apparent that no answer was required of him. Not only that, but the Unusual Female didn't even seem to expect him to pay her any attention.

Charming smiled. What a delightful woman. He followed her through the rose garden, letting her drag him by the arm this way and that, while he ambled pleasantly amongst his thoughts. Just as he reached the conclusion that this was the most pleasant evening he had passed in memory, the Unusual Female anchored herself to a point on the ground, causing him to jerk to an abrupt stop as she still held his arm tightly, thus yanking him out of his reverie.

"Ah!" she exclaimed triumphantly, pointing at a rather haphazard cluster of roses among the bush. "There! There! Nature's whimsy at its finest. I cannot wait to tell Lowen of this. Would you believe it, he wants all my roses to be symmetrical and evenly distributed, and he proposes to have them enchanted to achieve that end. Have you ever heard anything more preposterous in your life? An enchantment? On *my* flowers? A little nonsense is to be expected—he is Cornish, after all—but that is just poppycock. Don't worry, my dear, I told him. I said, 'Lowen, you are a gardener of great skill'. He isn't, you know, but I find the best way to deal with the Cornish is to first butter them up with a compliment. Mind you, Lowen is the only Cornishman I know, but he strikes me as particularly representative of his kind—I'm sure you agree. Then I told him, 'It behoves the professional gardener to know when he is out of his depth. This, my dear Lowen,' you'll note how unfailingly polite I remained. 'This, my dear Lowen,' I said, 'is one of those instances. Under no circumstance, whatsoever, are we enchanting my roses!'"

This last exclamation was punctuated by the forceful jabbing of her index finger in the air. The gesture startled Charming into retreating as much of his neck between his shoulders as he could, like a frightened turtle. After a couple of blinks he realised that what had ignited the Unusual Female's passions was either the roses or the gardener, or both, but thankfully not him. By the time he had reached this conclusion, the Unusual Female had departed from the topic of the symmetry of roses, and she unanchored herself, dragging Charming forward by the arm once more.

"The Cornishman was a whim of my late husband's, you see," she continued. "You're wondering why I let him have his way when it is wreaking such havoc with my garden, to say nothing of my nerves. I have to admit, my late husband never interfered with my garden—never. The darling man knew his place was indoors, god rest his soul. So when he told me that his only wish was to have a Cornish gardener, well, I couldn't deny him. He loved their accent, you see. Can't see why myself—it's so full of 'r's, it's a wonder they manage to squeeze in any other consonants. Anyway, I let him have this little whimsy. I thought it would be perfectly harmless. Well, my dear, what a disaster, I cannot even begin to tell you. Putting up with Lowen's botanical heresies has frayed my nerves to such an extent..."

Charming tuned out once more, missing the extensive report on the state of the Unusual Female's nerves, and returning instead to that pleasant state of aloneness with his thoughts. They strolled on from one end of the garden to the other, and two hours passed with what seemed to Charming to be the speed of mere minutes. During this time, he had moved from just thinking this was the most pleasant evening he had ever spent to thinking this was the most amazing woman he had ever met. She brought out the best in him and put him in a state of contentment like no one had ever been able to. That is to say that she left him in peace and neither required him to listen nor respond. He had never felt so happy and at ease. So complete. So understood and appreciated.

Yes, by the time they reached the camellia maze, Charming realised that he was totally, utterly, and unequivocally in love.

Finally, he had found the woman for him.

The clock struck ten to midnight as it always did to allow princesses time to leave before their spells, curses, and other enchantments ran out. Charming turned to gaze adoringly at the newfound love of his life. As he did, the fog of adoration parted long enough for him to realise that the Unusual Female was dragging him back to the palace at brisk speed. No doubt heeding the call of midnight. His blunt powers of deduction told him that he only had a few minutes before they were back at the ballroom, where he would once again be drowning in feminine charms and would therefore lose the opportunity to ascertain his love's name along with his ability to speak or think.

For the first time in his life, Charming felt a wave of assertiveness wash over him. He acted. Decisively.

"I say, we haven't even been introduced," he said. "I—"

"Oh yes, quite right. Petunia, Queen of Viridi."

Queen? Charming would have been startled into stopping if the Unusual—that is Petunia—wasn't still dragging him forward by the arm.

There were very strict rules as to who a prince could marry. Princesses and any kind of pauper were fair game, but the bourgeoisie was wholly off limits (whoever heard of a prince falling in love with the middle classes?).

Charming wasn't sure where a queen featured on the eligibility spectrum. Of course, kings married queens, but that was always after their first wife had died, generally in childbirth, and then they always married evil women, most often witches.

Charming had no dead first wife, he wasn't a king, and Petunia didn't seem like an evil woman or a witch, despite her slightly hooked nose (in fact now that he had had time to get used to it, it wasn't so much hooked as charmingly pronounced.) His brow knotted with concern. This was problematic. But princes were, after all, supposed to conquer insurmountable obstacles to win their fair ladies. He would simply have to find a solution, which would no doubt require a significant number of hours spent in the library researching the matter.

Cheered by the prospect of uninterrupted time with his precious books, Charming turned to inform Petunia of his plans and of their forthcoming engagement. He was shocked to discover that, unbeknownst to him, his arm had been released, and Petunia had climbed the stairs to the balcony, reaching the double doors that led back to the ballroom.

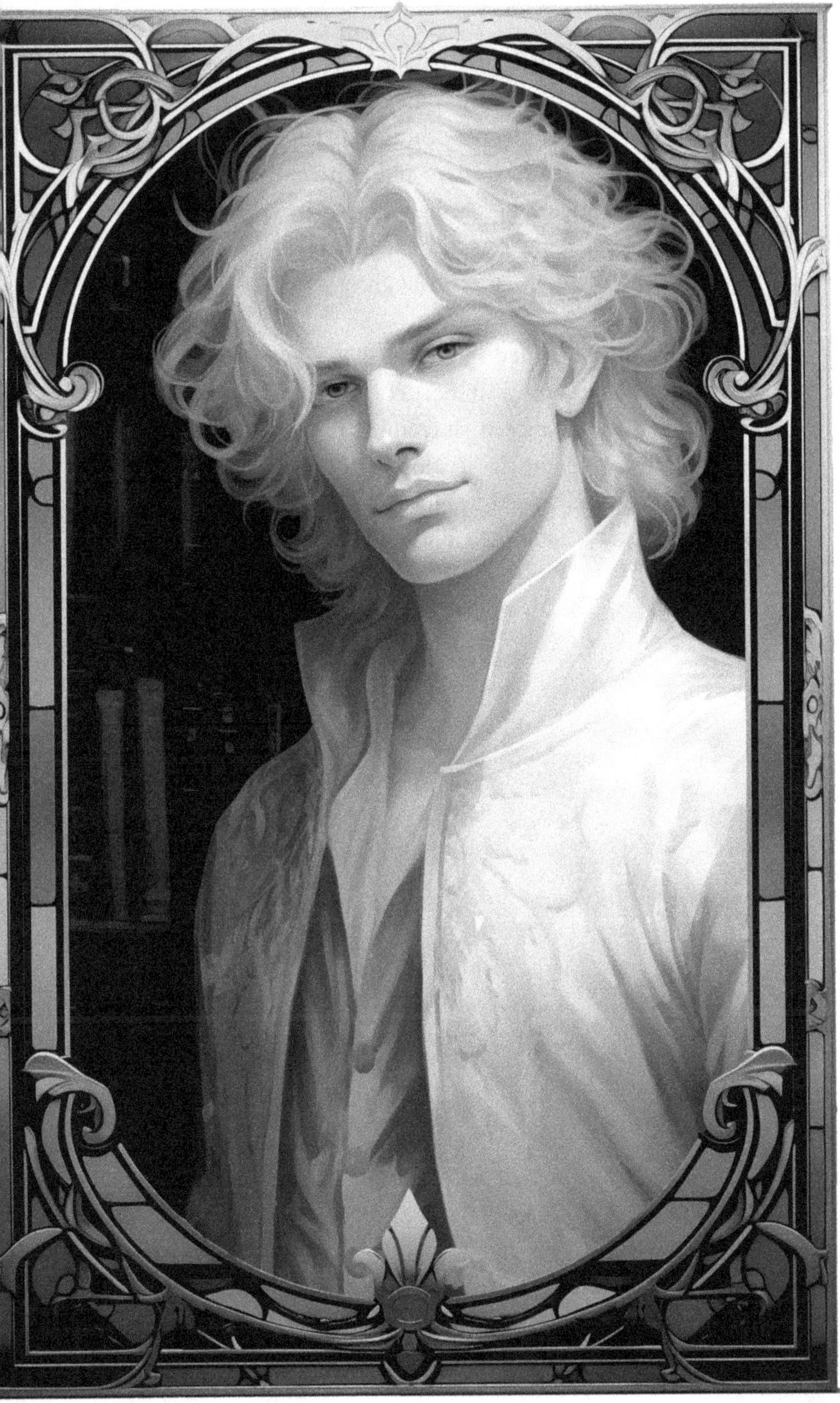

This was so startling a development (no woman save for his mother had ever walked away from Charming before) that he could do nothing but gape as she disappeared into the sea of bustles and petticoats. He only had the time to notice that she had steel-grey hair, a fact the night had kept from him till then, before she was swallowed up by the light and the laughter and the whispers of silk.

Charming remained in the darkness, mulling over the events of the evening. It occurred to him then that he hadn't had the chance to introduce himself. Did Petunia even realise who he was? No matter, he would simply introduce himself when he informed her of their engagement. For now, though, the library awaited.

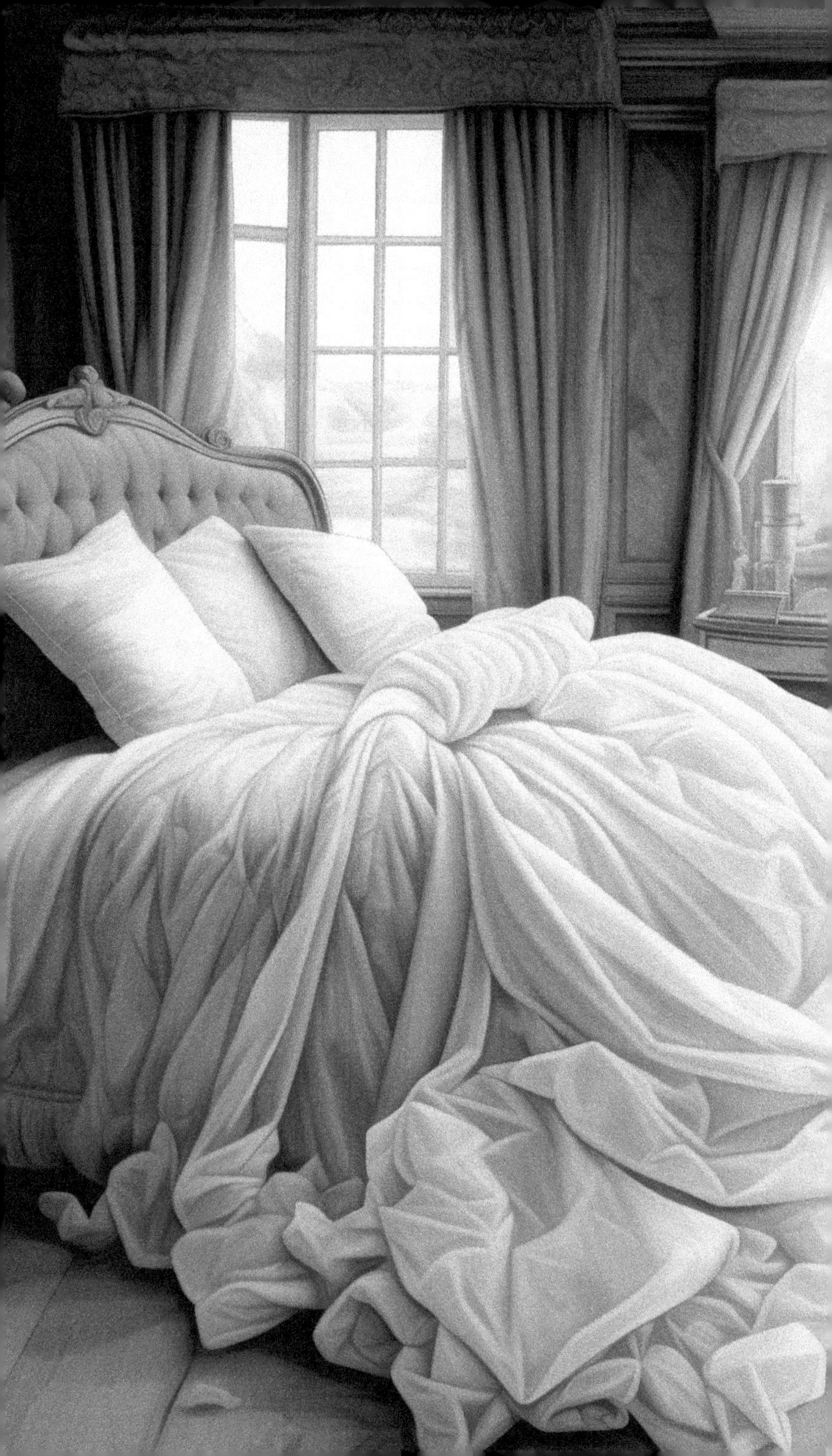

CHAPTER 2

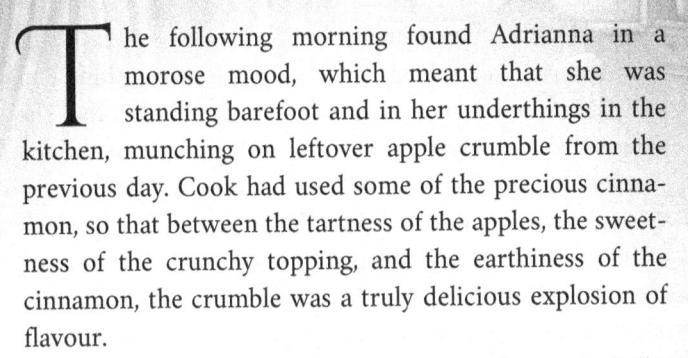

The following morning found Adrianna in a morose mood, which meant that she was standing barefoot and in her underthings in the kitchen, munching on leftover apple crumble from the previous day. Cook had used some of the precious cinnamon, so that between the tartness of the apples, the sweetness of the crunchy topping, and the earthiness of the cinnamon, the crumble was a truly delicious explosion of flavour.

And yet Adrianna munched it absentmindedly, mechanically shovelling one spoonful after the other into her mouth. The kitchen's stone floor was cold beneath her bare feet, with a slippery smoothness brought about by centuries of kitchen staff rushing over its surface. Of course, it had been a long time since there'd been any staff to continue the polishing of the stone floor. Cook only came every other day, so Adrianna, her evil stepmother, and the rest of the household made do with leftovers on the days off.

Today was such a day. The kitchen was clean and silent, its myriads of pots and pans and spatulas and other things

Adrianna knew nothing about put away out of sight. She always felt a sense of expectation from the kitchen, as if all those tools couldn't wait to be brought back out in a bustle of activity to assist in the making of food. The faint smell of warm meat pies that seemed to have gotten encrusted into the stone over the centuries was like a prediction of the food that Cook would prepare tomorrow.

Adrianna finished the last bite of the crumble, scraping her spoon against the earthenware dish to remove the caramelised bits that had stuck to the bottom, both enjoying this ritual and feeling disappointed that there was no more crumble. She really should have paid more attention to it and actually enjoyed the eating of it rather than mindlessly shoving it into her face.

Never mind, next time.

The problem was that if there was no more crumble to eat, then she was back to contemplating the fact that she had failed yet again. She knew, of course, that all she needed was to succeed once. She just needed one prince to choose her one time, and then she would fulfil her role as princess. But it was disheartening to keep failing over and over again.

She put the crumble dish in the sink for the maid to clean and headed out of the kitchen, back upstairs. Veridi Castle was a very far cry from the luxurious and lavish palace she'd been at last night for the ball. It was a higgledy-piggledy pile of bricks, a ramshackle structure that had been built without any planning or thought towards practicalities.

Which was why there were stairs that led up to a blank wall, rooms deep within the castle without windows, while others had so many it was hard to keep them clean, especially the windows that were situated right beneath an overhanging roof that pigeons and doves loved roosting in.

They covered the glass in guano with gay abandon, no matter the efforts to shoo them away.

The decoration wasn't much better. In Adrianna's opinion, what made Veridi castle unique was its wonderfully haphazard collection of parapets, extensions, tiled roofs, and its myriad of Gothic flourishes. All of it scattered about with no apparent plan or thought to creating any sort of cohesive whole. One of the most obvious quirks of the castle, though, was the lack of mirrors. They had all been removed apart from the one in Adrianna's room and another one in Alinor's room—Adrianna's evil stepsister. Otherwise, there wasn't a single reflective surface in the castle.

Adrianna truly loved her home, as fiercely as if it were a family member. She loved the fact that her father had had the foresight and open-mindedness to install running water in a couple of the rooms, but had never succeeded in doing so properly, so that turning on the taps made an awful groaning, rattling sound before letting forth a spray of disturbingly red water. They'd all thought it was blood due to some kind of curse at first, but the late king had assured them that it was simply a matter of the red clay to be found in the soil around the castle.

He'd passed before finding a way to pump clean water to the castle. Adrianna thought of him every time she washed herself in the red water.

She reached the first floor, stepping through the servants' door and into the main part of the castle. From there she took another set of stairs down, before climbing back up two storeys. Corridors and passages twisted throughout the castle, putting the most convoluted ants' nest to shame. Yet more levels sprawled beneath the ground, although those were seldom used anymore, given over to rot and mould and general decay. Adrianna knew every last nook and cranny, from the sun-filled music room to the dank and dark sub levels.

Her bedroom was just after the triangular room, so named because it was a triangle, the corridor making sharp bends around it.

She flung her bedroom door open and let herself collapse backwards onto her bed, the scrunched-up quilt making for a soft landing.

"Been at the crumble?" Mirabelle, her fairy godmother, asked, appearing in the doorway.

Adrianna nodded, not taking her eyes off the large web a spider was diligently spinning between the dust-covered chandelier and the nearest panel of the dark oak coffered ceiling. That part of the ceiling was still in decent shape. It was best not to look at the left corner, though. Damp was seeping in through the wall near there, the wallpaper in that corner marred by ever expanding, ugly, brownish-yellow rings, while above it the wood of the ceiling was slowly rotting, turning black and dotted with patches of white mould. Maybe polka dots would make a comeback and then her ceiling would be fashionable in its decayed state. Adrianna snorted to herself, amused by the thought.

The room above was now condemned in case the rotten floorboards gave way beneath the weight of furniture or people. Not that it was a great hardship to lose the use of the room—there weren't enough servants to fill all the rooms on the top floor, anyway. Not by a long way.

"I don't think last night was too bad in the end," Mirabelle said, entering the room.

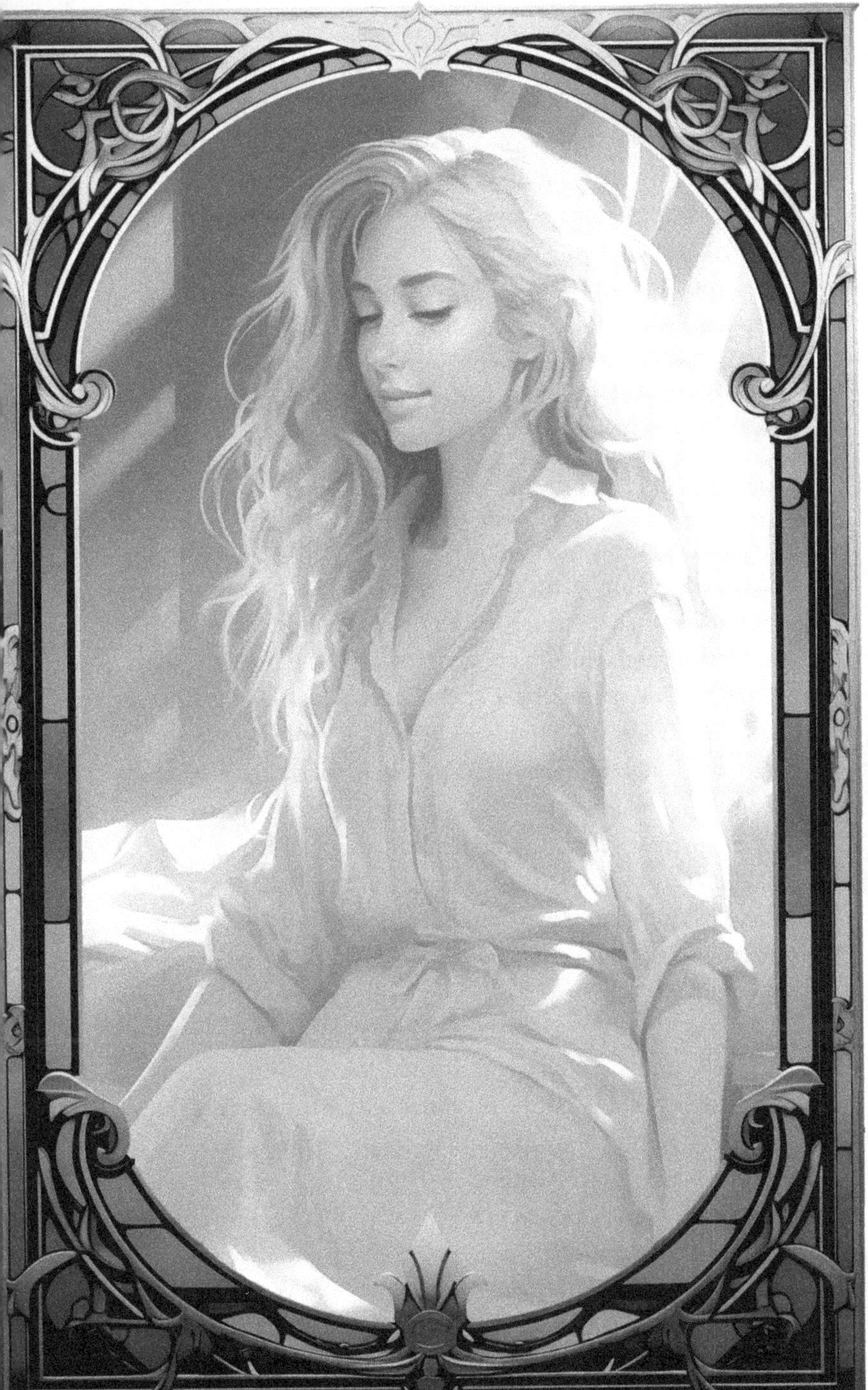

"Total and utter disaster," Adrianna muttered. "I don't think he even noticed that I exist." Which stung all over again. The worst part, of course, was being so completely ignored by a man she found as appealing as a limp handshake. Being a princess required having almost zero self-esteem, which wasn't easy to do.

"Yes, he was a rather peculiar young man, wasn't he?" replied Mirabelle, ringing for Helga, the maid. "Very distracted, I thought. Surprisingly fine hair too. Princes should always have thick, curly hair, in my opinion. And so very blonde... His fairy godmother did a rather poor job of blessing him at birth." She settled herself among the cushions of a divan, stretching back luxuriously like a cat.

Adrianna's fairy godmother was a woman, or rather a fairy, on whom nature had bestowed generous proportions. She had a generous rump, a generous bosom, a generous laugh, and a very generous appetite for the good things in life, particularly chocolate and Cornish gardeners. She always wore the same gown, in cerulean blue with a dramatically low neckline. The corset she favoured was a feat of engineering that defied gravity so impressively, her ample breasts seemed to be floating. She had frizzy russet hair that was always in perpetual danger of escaping from the pins that struggled as mightily to keep it in place as her dress's neckline struggled to keep her breasts from popping out.

Helga, being well accustomed to the habits of the princess and her fairy godmother the day after a ball, arrived bearing a bottle of wine and two glasses, along with a large silver bowl full of chocolate truffles.

Adrianna sat up alertly.

"Really, Adrianna, wine so early in the morning?" reproached Mirabelle.

"Oh leave off it, I know you've already had a brandy—I can smell it on your breath."

Mirabelle chuckled heartily. "Touché."

"Anyway, what else is there to do today other than eat and drink my feelings, since no one is going to come and ask for my hand in marriage?" Adrianna watched despondently as the maid poured out two glasses of wine.

If this were a normal castle, Helga would then have proceeded to tidy Adrianna's room, which looked like an explosion had taken place, flinging her things all over the furniture and the floor. But seeing as they couldn't afford to employ anyone else to help Helga, she had far too many duties to be able to keep up with the tidying of everybody's bedroom. So long as she brought food and drink when summoned, nobody minded too much about the cleanliness of the castle, certainly not Adrianna.

Mirabelle began eating the chocolate truffles, with much smacking of her lips and licking of her fingers. "You know, precious, you're never going to succeed at snagging yourself a prince unless you really, truly want it."

"I do want it," Adrianna protested half-heartedly, reaching out for one of the wineglasses. She had to reach so far to the side of the bed that she almost toppled out as she grabbed the glass, laughing as a little wine sloshed over the rim and onto her fingers. "Oops." She sat back up and swapped the glass from one hand to the other, licking her wine-covered fingers. "I do want it. It's just that I want the *right* one."

"Yes, of course you want to fall in love—"

"Not even that. I just want someone who will let me live in peace in my castle while he goes and lives in his. That would be ideal."

"That's not how our world works, and you know it. Happy Ever After does not involve living in separate castles."

"No, what it does involve is me dying a few years later in childbirth if I give birth to a daughter, so that she might grow up an orphan and repeat the exact same cycle I went through." Adrianna took a hearty gulp of wine. Sometimes life as a princess was truly depressing. In fact, make that often.

"Well then, just be an old maid, like me. There really are many great advantages to being single in one's golden years. Such as being able to pursue certain delicious Cornishmen." Mirabelle gave her a saucy wink.

"You should really stop tormenting the poor man. He lives in fear that you'll either snap him like a twig or gobble him up."

"Ah darling, what can I say? I can't resist the burr of his accent, and the way he throws those skinny little arms of his around."

"He looks like a pigeon if you ask me, always bobbing his head at the flowers and fluttering around Petunia."

"Don't criticise Lowen just because you're bitter about your prince," said Mirabelle curtly.

"He wasn't *my* prince," Adrianna muttered into her glass. "That's exactly the problem." He'd had potential as a candidate, as well, seeming to be utterly devoid of personality, and therefore more likely to be prodded into agreeing to the living arrangement Adrianna wanted.

"I think I feel a headache coming on," Mirabelle announced suddenly, apparently unaware of the dusting of chocolate on her generous bosom. "Maybe I'll ring for a port and brandy. Excellent remedy for a headache, that. In fact, excellent remedy for most ailments."

Before she could summon the maid again, the bedroom door opened, and a head stuck through the gap. Alinor looked like a slightly plainer version of Adrianna, which wasn't in itself a judgement of Alinor's prettiness at all. Instead, it simply reflected the fact that Adrianna had been born of a king and queen, and therefore had been blessed with staggering beauty at birth, whereas Alinor had come ten years later, after Adrianna's father had married Adrianna's evil stepmother.

Technically, Alinor was Adrianna's evil stepsister, to go with the evil stepmother. But then, as with the rest of the castle, nothing quite worked the way it was supposed to, and Adrianna and Alinor got along like a house on fire, in spite of their ten years of age difference and the rivalry that was supposed to exist between them.

Alinor caught sight of the wineglass in Adrianna's hand and wrinkled her nose. "You really need to stop drinking so early in the day—it's not good for you."

She entered the room fully. At fourteen she still had that long-limbed, slightly clumsy bearing, like a doe coming into her long legs. Her wide mouth was perpetually further widened by a smile. Adrianna remembered being like that before she came of age and had to deal with the pressures of being a princess. Now it was all frowns and crumble and wine for breakfast.

Despite her age, Alinor refused to graduate to the longer dresses that she should by rights be starting to wear, preferring the lighter, shorter styles worn by little girls, since it left her legs free to run. Adrianna agreed with the sentiment, but since she no longer had any short dresses that fit her, she most often ran around the castle in her underthings. Nobody ever visited, and the few people who still lived in the castle didn't care how improper she looked.

"I guess last night didn't go well?" Alinor asked, approaching the bed.

"I'm destined to be a fabulous spinster," Adrianna

replied with a flourish of her right hand, sending a little red wine sloshing over the rim of the glass, staining the bedsheet as well as her fingers this time. Not the first red wine stain, and very unlikely to be the last. Every so often she badgered Mirabelle into returning the bedsheet to the pristine white of its origins, which the fairy only did with much grumbling that her magic wasn't supposed to be used to clean out wine and chocolate stains.

"She's taking inspiration from me," Mirabelle added smugly from her chocolate-stained divan.

"I'm sorry." Alinor frowned and sat on the side of the bed.

"It's all right. It's probably for the best. Better to be alone than to be married to an invertebrate." Adrianna did her best not to think about what it meant that she had been rejected by said human invertebrate.

"Can I have a sip?" Alinor gestured at the glass.

Adrianna knew that as a responsible sister she should say no, but she was already a little tipsy, and anyway, a sip would do no harm. She handed the glass over.

Alinor snatched it, jumped to her feet, ran to the window, opened it, and flung the wine out. Then she grabbed the bottle.

"Hey!" Adrianna protested.

"Race you to the library. The first one to arrive gets to keep the bottle."

Alinor didn't wait for an answer, sprinting off. Adrianna cursed, jumping off the bed after her, and almost falling flat on her face, tangled up in the bedsheet. She yelled a rich selection of swearwords as she yanked the bedsheet away, but she found that in spite of her annoyance she was already smiling.

Racing through the castle was one of their long-standing childhood games. There were so many twists and turns, so many corridors and stairways and secret passageways that there were a myriad of ways to cross the castle. Adrianna and Alinor had spent endless days figuring out the best possible route to every room, challenging each other to race after race after race.

Adrianna had won all the recent races to the library, so she ran in the opposite direction to Alinor, confident in her ability to get there first. She slid down a wooden banister, its balusters carved with vines and flowers. The wood was polished to a shine from years of sliding. She jumped off at the end, bursting through a door so low she had to bend in half to fit through it. Beyond it was a narrow, tunnel-like corridor that had once been used to spy on the room next door. Of course, given that anybody could find the door to enter the corridor, everyone knew that the room next-door offered no privacy.

Adrianna sprinted through the corridor, breathing the air that was thick with damp and mildew. The feather-soft, ever so slightly sticky feel of a cobweb against her face didn't so much as slow her down—she had picked hundreds of spiders from her hair over the years and no longer cared if one hitched a ride for a while.

Back up another set of stairs, through two rooms, one of which was entirely shrouded in sheets, down a final set of stairs, and then she stopped abruptly. The library door was already open.

Alinor stood beyond, grinning and waving the bottle of wine, taunting.

"How d'you get here so fast?" Adrianna asked, genuinely impressed, and not at all bothered that she had lost.

"There's a new hole in one of the ceilings. I made it bigger and dragged a mattress underneath it so I can jump down from one floor to the other."

"Nice."

Alinor bit her lip, turning serious. "Do you really need

the wine bottle? If you do, you can have it, you know. I know balls are always hard for you."

Adrianna sighed and shook her head. She wasn't sure exactly when she had started drinking wine as a way to feel better after her endless failures, but she wasn't exactly proud of it. It was probably after she'd heard of her childhood friend consenting to being robbed of speech for the rest of her life just to secure herself a prince. It had worked, leaving Adrianna facing the very bleak prospect that she may one day be also forced to make such a terrible sacrifice, and all in the name of securing something she didn't even really want in the first place. This was hardly unusual. Princesses were forever being locked away in towers, made mute, and tortured in a hundred inventive ways, all in the name of providing the kind of insurmountable odds princes needed in order to work up the courage to make a marriage proposal.

"We could go check on the mouse nest?" Alinor suggested, brightening.

Adrianna smiled indulgently. "Let's do that."

In moments like this, when she was with her sister—Adrianna never thought of Alinor as a stepsister—Adrianna struggled to see what the importance was of securing a prince. She was happy here, in this ramshackle, crazy little castle, with her ramshackle, crazy little family. Living a quiet life with them all out here sometimes seemed far more appealing than chasing the fabled Happy Ever After.

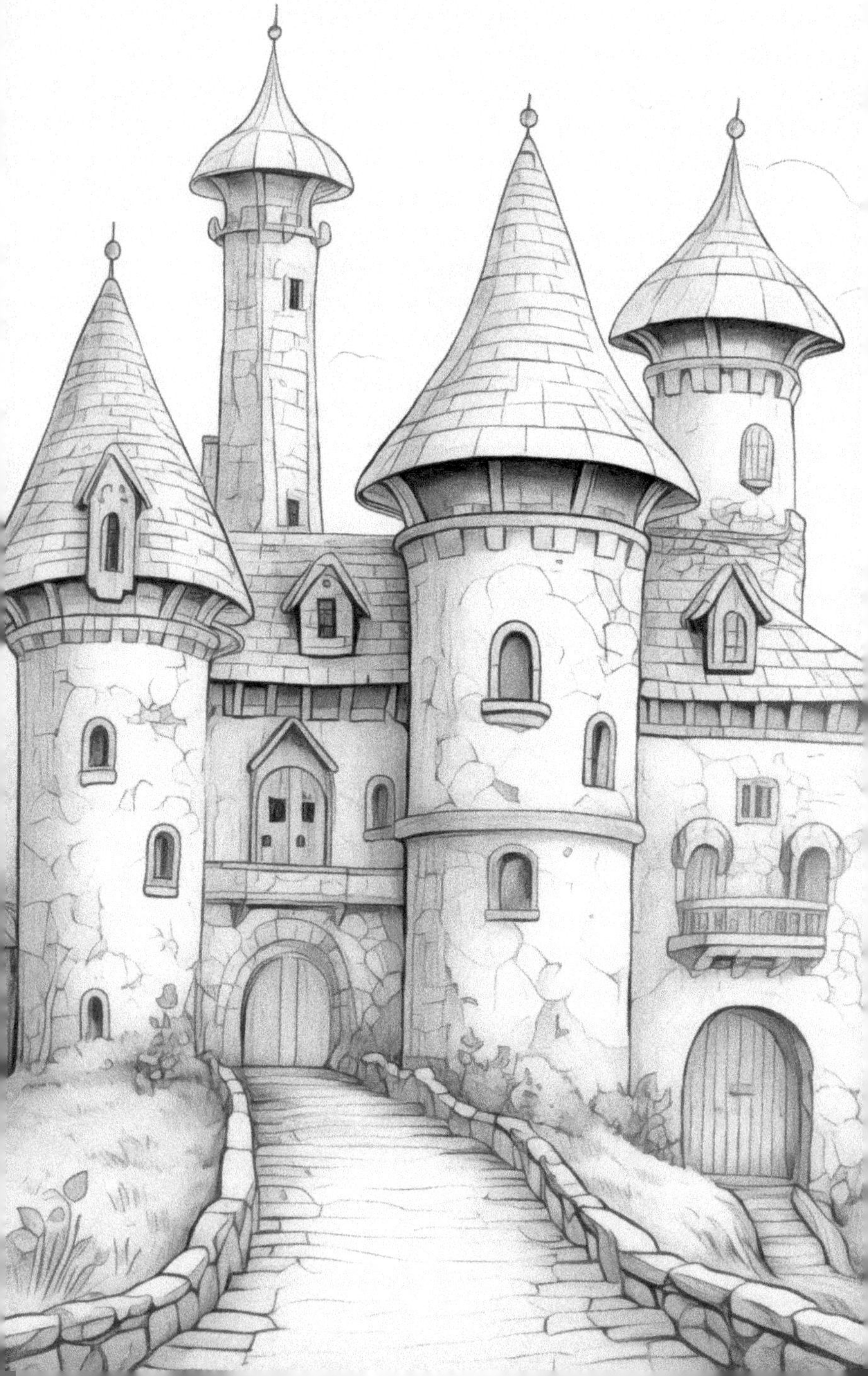

CHAPTER 3

The castle was its very own ecosystem, a whole self-contained universe. Its state of general disrepair meant that a plethora of little creatures and creepy crawlies had taken up residence within its walls. There was always something to look at—a new plant that was making a life for itself with its roots digging into a crack between two stones, or a neat little nest diligently made by a small furry creature.

"Before we go check on the mice, there might be eggs over with the doves," Alinor said hopefully. Sometimes she acted with all the maturity of a young woman, other times she was still very much a kid, and the combination made her all the more endearing.

"All right, let's go check on them first, then," Adrianna said as she had said hundreds of times over the years—in fact, every time Alinor wanted to go check on some animal or another.

They climbed up to the attic, and from there to a ladder that reached all the way up to the high and massive beams that supported the roof. One after the other, they crossed one of the beams, walking with arms carefully stretched out to keep their balance, until they reached a small nook on the other side. There wasn't much space, only just enough for the two of them to crouch next to each other. They called this nook Dove Cove since every year doves made their nests here.

Alinor had been right. Nestled between two woodworm-chewed struts was a small nest and in the nest were four perfectly smooth eggs, the shells a delicate pink, like the inside of a shell.

Alinor beamed, turning to look at Adrianna with shining eyes. Adrianna couldn't help but smile back, her sister's joy contagious. She slung an arm around Alinor's neck, yanking her close, and leaned her cheek against the top of her sister's head. They stayed like this for a moment, silently watching the nest.

Yes, moments like this really made it hard to remember what exactly was so important about bagging a prince.

Adrianna looked up at the rustle of wings followed by anxious cooing. "We should go. That'll be the mother, and she won't be happy to have us so close to her eggs."

Checking on the mice was equally successful. The sisters waited a couple of metres away from the nest, their backs against the eaves, their noses full of the smell of the cedar chests that crowded the attic, housing old clothes and other belongings. The slightly medicinal smell of the chests mixed with that of the flaky, slowly decomposing piles of newspapers—a legacy from a crazy old uncle who had, for some reason, collected them obsessively.

The girls had to wait for a while before their patience was rewarded with a mouse coming to feed her little ones. They watched in silence as the little mouse went about her business, feeding her babies before scampering off, no doubt to go back to the kitchen in search of more treats. She might be able to steal some leftover crumbs in the crumble dish.

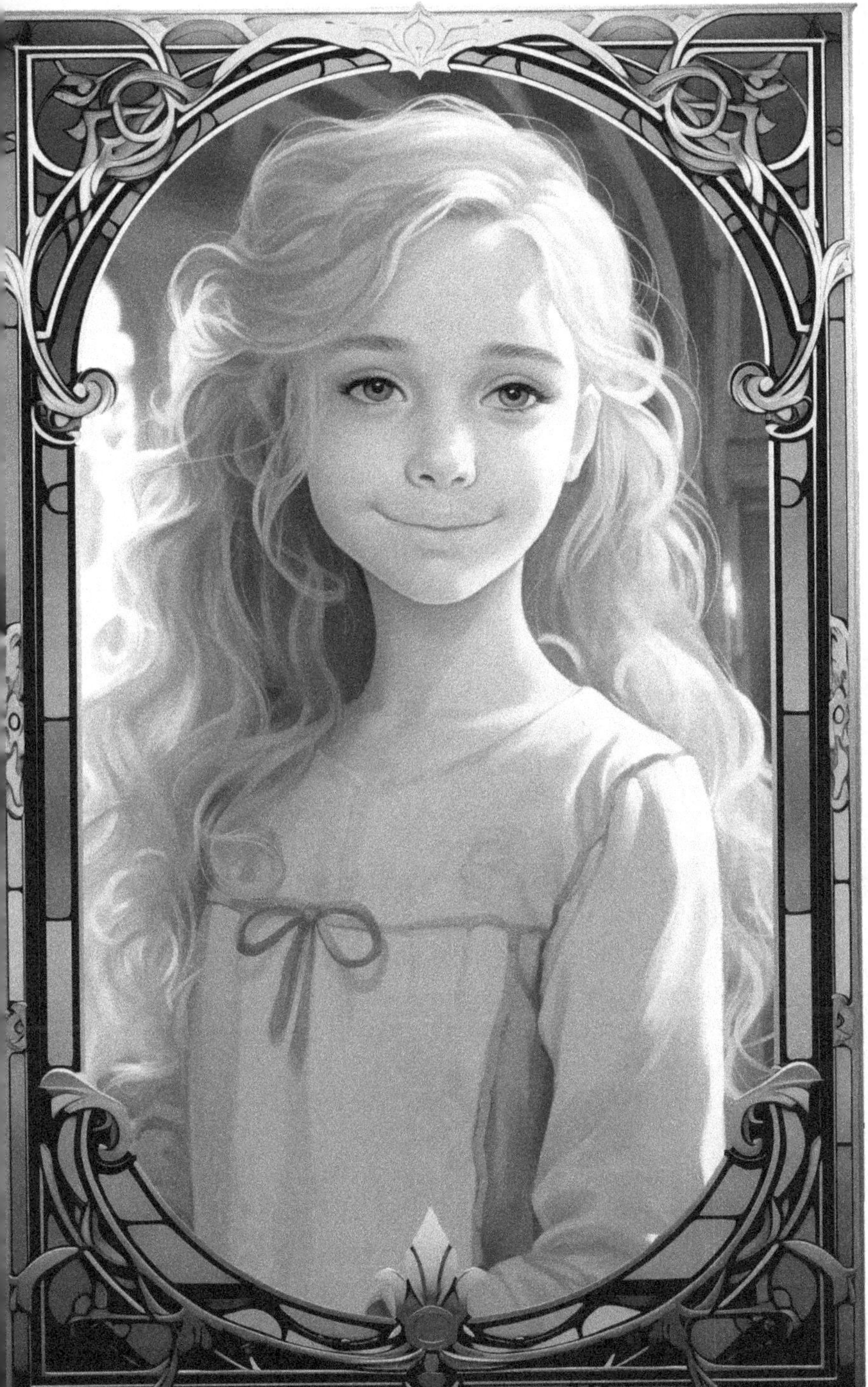

"See, checking on the mice and the doves is much more effective than a bottle of wine," Alinor pointed out smugly as they clambered down from the attic. "You look happy again."

Before Adrianna could formulate a reply, a voice called out to them.

"There you are!" Helga, the maid, looked positively blown as she ran over to their side, red splotches standing out starkly on her cheeks.

"Everything all right?" Adrianna asked.

"This arrived a while ago, but I couldn't find you anywhere." Helga handed over a letter.

Adrianna recognised the ornate seal at once—it had also been stamped at the bottom of the invitation she had received to Charming's ball. Her heart pounded, although she wasn't sure if it was excitement or dread, or something else entirely.

"Charming wrote to me?" she asked aloud, voicing her confusion. He hadn't so much as looked in her direction last night.

She cracked the seal and unfolded the stiff, creamy paper. The note was short, almost terse, the handwriting perfectly neat. It stated that Charming intended to call before midday.

"Shit, shit shit." Adrianna looked around her wildly. "What time is it?"

"Nearly eleven," Helga replied. "I looked for you everywhere, but I couldn't find you, and…"

"Not your fault," Adrianna snapped before the maid overwhelmed herself with misplaced guilt. The last thing she needed was for anyone to panic, given how little time there was to get ready. "Mirabelle!" she yelled. "I need you!"

They waited for a moment, but nothing happened. "Urgently, damnit!" Adrianna shouted again.

Again, nothing happened.

"Mirabelle, I swear, if you don't get your arse over here right *now*—"

"What, what is it?" Mirabelle appeared next to Adrianna looking flustered as she patted her hair and rearranged her clothing.

"The prince is coming to call, and he will be here any minute now." Adrianna thrust the letter at her.

"Prince? What prince?"

Adrianna was having a hard time containing her growing impatience. "Charming, who else?"

"That damp sock? Well, I guess beggars can't be choosers, darling."

Adrianna skewered her with a glare.

"Which storyline are you going to go with?" Mirabelle asked brightly, either oblivious or so used to Adrianna's glares that she wasn't affected.

"Do I have to play the evil stepsister?" Alinor asked morosely.

Adrianna shook her head. One thing she had promised herself was that she would never force Alinor into that role. She would simply have to find a way to bag herself a prince without needing a storyline involving an evil stepsister.

"Well, you have an evil stepmother," Mirabelle pointed out. "So you could simply have her lock you away in your bedroom and let Charming batter the door down."

Adrianna shook her head again, growing increasingly impatient. "That won't work. We didn't even speak last night. That kind of story only works if he has already had time to fall in love with me. I'm amazed he even knows who I am—I very much doubt he'll be battering doors down to get to me at this point. But, you're right, I have to use the evil stepmother angle since it's the only one I have."

She briefly thought back to that other princess, a mermaid called Ariel who had infamously given up her tail and her voice to make herself appealing to a prince, and then, on top of that she'd had a witch trying to sabotage her. All the odds had been stacked against her, which is of course what princesses needed, since princes were driven by some baffling need to prove themselves. It made princess's lives a right misery.

A single, lowly, evil stepmother was poor fare compared to a witch, a curse, and sacrificing a part of her body—especially because Petunia was remarkably useless as an evil stepmother. But then, that was a perfect representation of Adrianna's lot. Her evil stepmother was more interested in the garden than in being evil, her fairy godmother was a jolly drunkard who was more often than not found snoring with her mouth open, and Adrianna loved her evil step sister dearly, completing the trifecta of uselessness.

But now, in spite of all this, a prince had come to call. This was her moment. Her one chance to fulfil her destiny and secure herself a prince, and she wasn't going to fail.

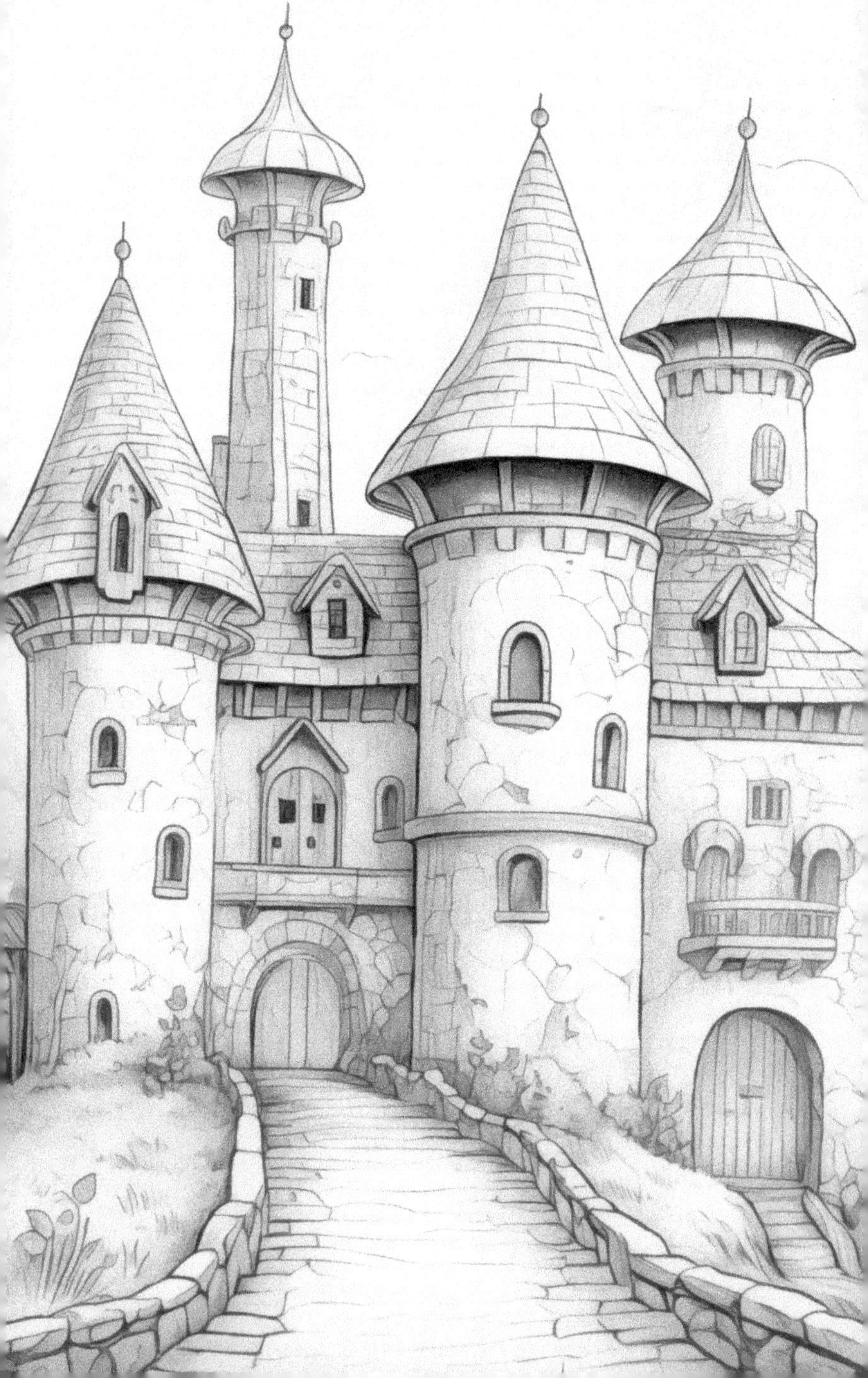

CHAPTER 4

"I will pose as a servant girl in the orchard," she decided. "I don't think it would serve us best to go for a storyline where we assume Charming is already in love with me." After all, he hadn't even noticed her at the ball. "Instead, this might be the moment when he falls in love with me without realising who I am."

"Oh, yes, yes!" Mirabelle replied excitedly. "That's a brilliant idea."

"I need you to rearrange the entrance to the castle grounds to make him go past the orchard," Adrianna told her.

"I might need Lowen's help..." Mirabelle began.

"Don't you dare go and harass the gardener," Adrianna snapped. "I need everyone to be focused, and if you're chasing after Lowen, that's the very opposite of what you'll be. You don't need a gardener, just use your magic."

"I see, and I suppose you will also need my magic to make you look right," Mirabelle said.

"Of course."

"So, as usual, the fairy godmother does all the work," Mirabelle sniffed.

"I wouldn't complain if I were you—I'm the one who's going to have to marry the damp squib. You get to continue enjoying your life after this is done, whereas me..." Adrianna cleared her throat and stopped speaking. There was really no point going down that line of thinking. She needed to get a prince, and that was the thing to focus on. "So come on, make me look like a gorgeous, fresh-faced peasant girl. Make sure you give me freckles."

"Freckles?"

"Freckles. I need a flaw to highlight my perfection once you're done making me look perfect. Perfect perfection is boring. Every girl needs a flaw, and freckles, just a few on the nose and cheekbones, should do the trick. It'll give me a healthy glow too, like I've been in the sun. Get to it, Mirabelle. We have a lot to do, and I can't be late."

The fairy grumbled, patting her generous bosom, and then she stuck two fingers into her corset. She giggled as the first thing she pulled out was a thin cigar she normally kept stashed there for emergencies. Adrianna had the hardest time also keeping a straight face despite the seriousness of the situation. The temptation to throw in the towel and just go back to her bedroom to drink and laugh some more with Mirabelle nearly won out. Nearly.

Mirabelle pulled out her magic wand from between her breasts. Adrianna had never worked out the real reason Mirabelle kept her wand tucked away there. Maybe so that she could pull it out in the vicinity of the gardener, as a way to seduce him. Which of course would do precious little to help, since the man was already terrified that one day she would gobble him whole—seeing her magic at work would likely only increase his fear.

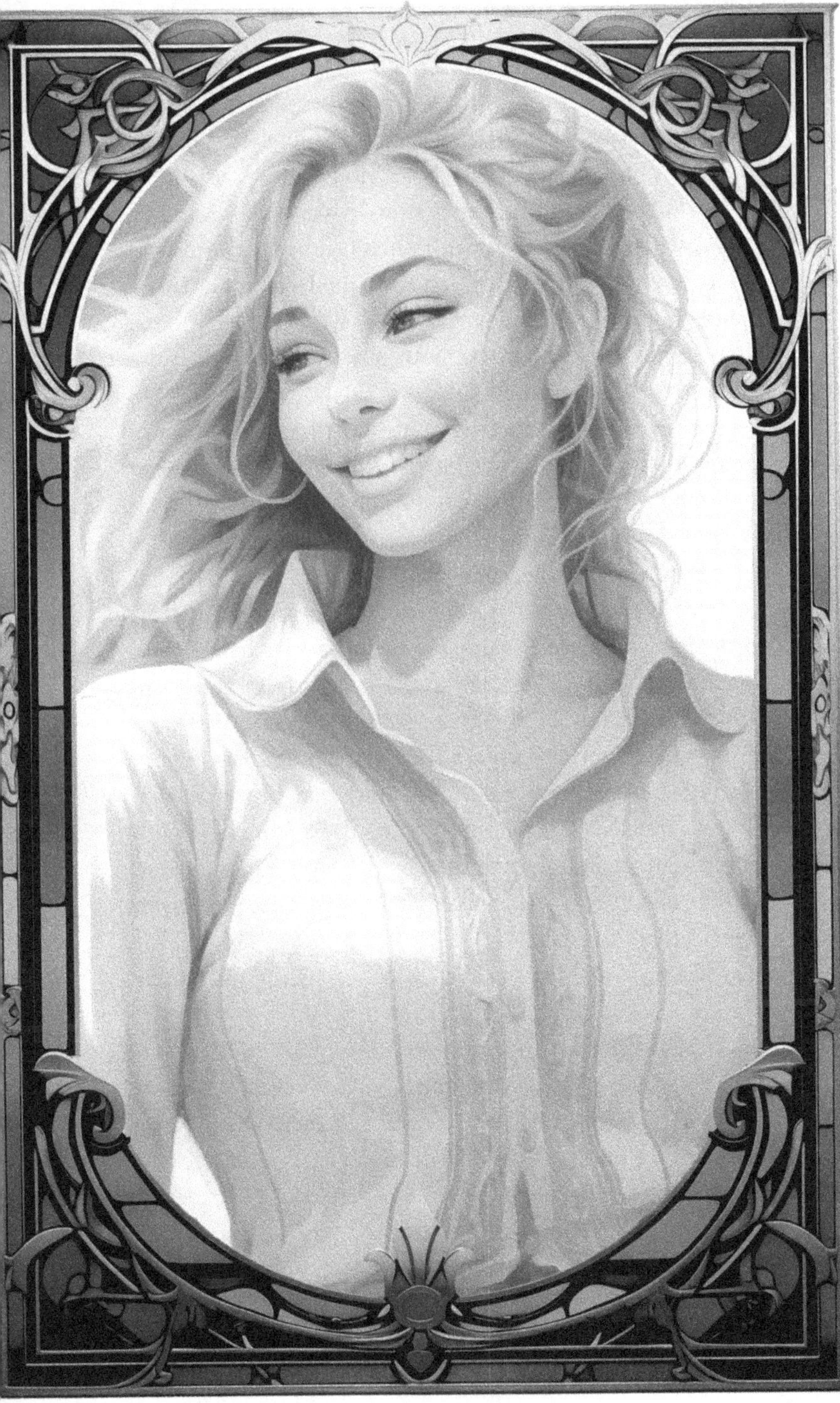

Mirabelle lifted the magic wand but then let out a belch, filling the air with the smell of the port and brandy she'd obviously been drinking just before appearing here.

"Oops." She grinned widely, obviously not sorry at all, before waving the wand and getting to work.

As with every princess, Adrianna had been graced with good looks at birth. Her hair was golden and lustrous, falling in gentle waves down her back when she let it loose. Her skin was pale and smooth, and her features were perfectly symmetrical.

But even then, there were always things that a fairy godmother could improve on. The way a princess looked naturally was never enough, not when it came to a prince.

Her skin went from being smooth to having the texture of fresh cream, further enhanced by the tiniest smattering of freckles across her nose. Her eyelashes grew thicker, providing the perfect frame for her eyes. Her hair looked like beaten gold, cascading down all the way to her waist, which had shrunk by at least an inch, while her breasts and hips had widened to create the perfect hourglass figure. Finally, the undergarments Adrianna had been wearing disappeared, to be replaced by a full dress, complete with corset—and a sinfully tight one as well. Adrianna groaned at the sudden constriction of her insides. The dress itself was pretty but simple.

"There, I do declare that you are ready." Mirabelle stepped back, cocking her head, looking satisfied.

"You really have to question the stupidity of men and their tendency to judge a woman's attractiveness based on the distance between their breasts and their chin," Adrianna said, pointing at the shelf her breasts now created almost at the level of her collarbone, thanks to her corset.

"They can come in handy though," pointed out Mirabelle, as she balanced her cigar on her ample bosom.

Adrianna laughed despite herself. "We don't all have cigars in need of storage."

"I fancy you could sort something out with a cleverly designed wine glass," replied Mirabelle.

Again, Adrianna felt the pull to just throw in the towel and spend the day enjoying herself, but she dismissed the idea with a wave of her hand.

Even though an afternoon spent designing said wine glass had the potential to be a lot of fun. They could file down the stem of a regular wine glass… But no.

"You look really pretty," Alinor said with envy in her tone.

"Not as pretty as you," Adrianna said at once, grabbing her and kissing the top of her head once more. "Remember, none of this is real. And no matter what Mirabelle does to make me prettier, nothing can compete with the way you smile when you see a mouse nest."

Alinor nodded distractedly.

That was something else Adrianna hated about this whole princess business. It was all so fake, and yet it was heralded as the ultimate, the thing every young girl should be wishing for, and it was responsible for making girls like Alinor feel bad about themselves.

"You should go and hide in your room," Adrianna told Alinor. "Read a book or something while I get this stupid business out of the way."

She had no sooner spoken the words than an alarm bell sounded.

"A little magical improvement I made while I rearranged the property," Mirabelle said smugly. "The prince approaches."

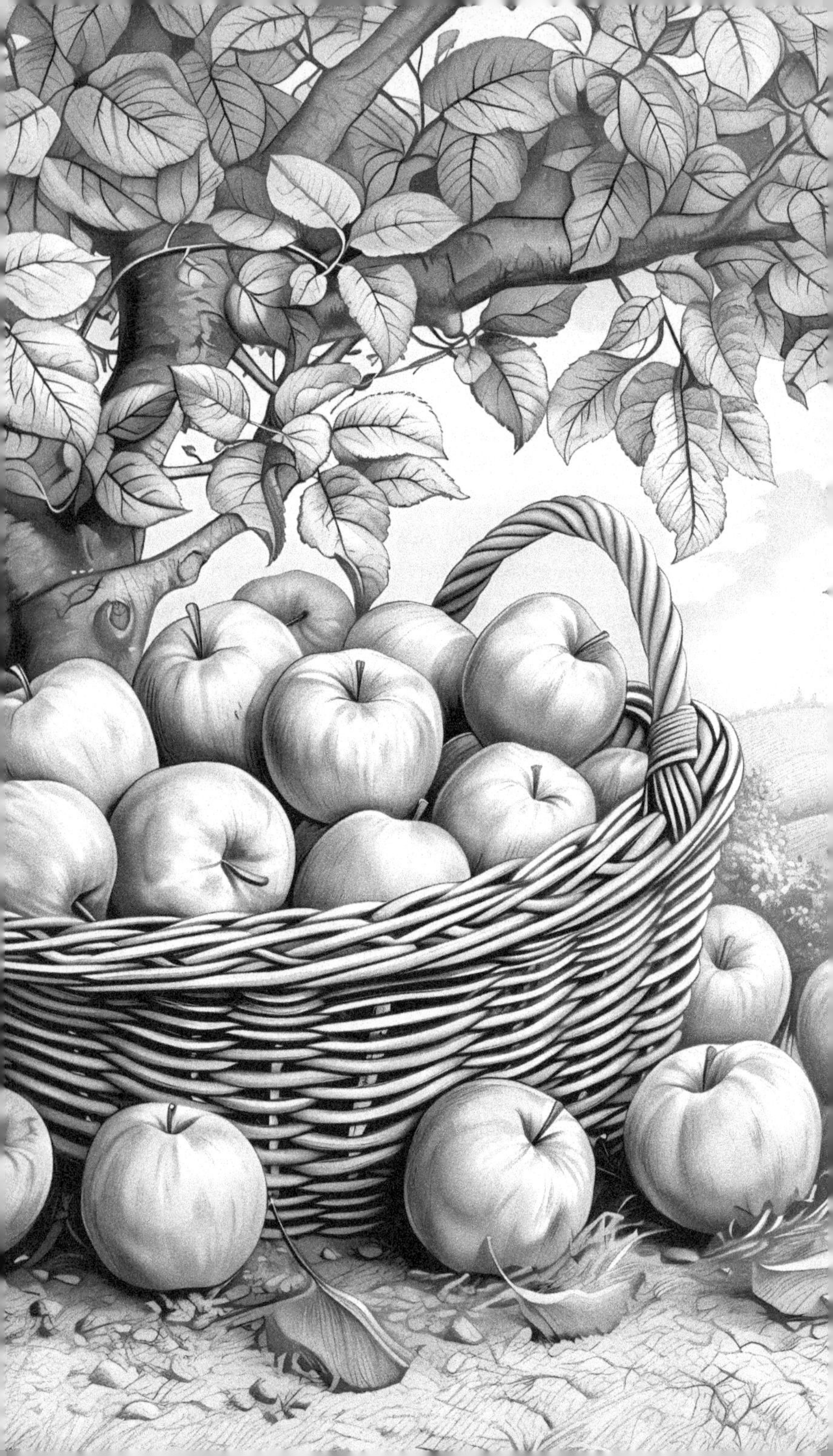

CHAPTER 5

Since she was posing as a servant girl in the orchard, Adrianna needed a basket for the apples she was supposed to be collecting. The problem was that since she wasn't going to pick apples for real, she needed a few already in the basket for veracity's sake, which made it surprisingly heavy.

Adrianna had barely made it out of the castle when her arms and back began to ache, and in no time at all she was panting heavily, unable to breathe properly from the corset. She should have gotten Helga to carry the basket for her, but she couldn't risk someone spotting her—and by someone, that meant the prince. That would ruin the illusion and therefore cause the story to fail.

She trundled on, the basket balanced on one hip, the wicker digging painfully into her flesh, beads of perspiration rapidly appearing on her forehead. If she hurried, she should have enough time in position to cool down and dry off. She distracted herself by wondering what part of her flesh the basket was digging into exactly—was it fat, or was there muscle there? She wasn't sure, although given that she never did any kind of physical exercise, it was unlikely to be muscle.

This was just the kind of rabbit hole she and Mirabelle could waste hours on, having ridiculous, entertaining, and far-ranging conversations while sipping wine. Alinor loved to take part in those conversations as well, giggling at all the silly things they came up with. Adrianna wished she could just drop the basket, forget about the prince, and go back home.

When Adrianna reached the orchard, she selected a spot close enough to the road that she would be easily seen, and positioned herself near an apple tree so that it would look realistic for her to be picking apples. She was careful, however, to remain out of its shade—she needed the sunlight to play with her hair and skin. She wouldn't have much time to make the prince fall in love with her.

A few apples went on the ground around her so she could pick them when in sight of the prince and his retinue. She spotted a few apples that had genuinely fallen on the floor, but they were brown and half rotten, spoiling the tableau. She picked them up and flung them away. One of them was mushy, leaving brown stuff on her fingers.

"Ugh." Adrianna looked guiltily around her as she wiped her hand on her petticoats. Few things lacked glamour as much as the preparation for the romantic, beautiful, and spontaneous scenes required for the storylines to work.

Once ready, she sat on the ground, spread her skirts around her, and then she leaned on one arm languidly, careful to ensure that the light hit her face just right.

Fake, fake, fake. The whole thing was just so fake, but this was the way the world worked, so there was no choice but to work with it.

Then, Adrianna waited.

She tried singing to herself—that would no doubt

charm the prince as he arrived. She quickly abandoned that idea, however, when she realised that she had forgotten to ask Mirabelle to bestow her with a singing voice for the afternoon. Her natural talents in the singing department left a lot to be desired.

Adrianna's arm began to ache, and her bum was growing numb. She shifted a little, trying to get comfortable and still look graceful. After a while, she realised that the apple tree's shadow had grown so she was now out of the sunlight.

Muttering a string of curses, she got up to move back into the sun, and as she did, the corset forced a belch from her lips. She let out a snort of laughter then stopped abruptly, looking about worriedly should someone have overheard.

Thankfully, the orchard was still empty.

She repositioned herself in the sunlight, tossed her hair back and continued waiting, doing her best to ignore the corset as it dug into the tops of her thighs. Goodness, she could do with a glass of cold, crisp white wine.

Finally, she heard the melodious sound of galloping in the distance. She put on a wistful expression and stretched one arm towards an apple, poised in perfect apple picking position. Around her, the grass rippled in the breeze and her hair fluttered prettily about her face.

Adrianna knew that at this very moment, she looked perfect. Utterly stunning. The prince would be powerless to resist.

A company of horses tore down the road at full speed, their hooves kicking up dust that flew into her face and hair, making her cough and stinging her eyes. And just like that, they were gone, thundering on towards the castle.

Not one of them had thrown so much as a glance in her direction.

"Shit, shit, *shit*!" she yelled in frustration, getting up.

All that waiting and posing for nothing. Now the prince was going to arrive, and she wasn't going to be there to greet him. Worse, she was going to have to make it back on her own, and that was going to be uncomfortable with her corset.

"Shitting shit and fuckwits on a stick!" Her frustration was making her revert back to the childish curse she had favoured when she was younger. Why did it all have to be so complicated?

"I do love a woman who isn't afraid of swearing," said a deep voice behind her, startling her.

Adrianna spun around. A man sitting astride a white horse was regarding her with a very amused expression. His hair was dark, curling at his temples. He had the swarthy complexion of a man who worked outside, and the heavily knuckled hands and thick forearms of one who is no stranger to physical labour. And yet his clothing was clean and comparatively neat.

The only thing that Adrianna cared about, though, was the fact that he was on a horse, which meant that she might be able to make a speedy enough return to the castle to avoid the day turning into an unmitigated disaster.

"Take me back to the castle," she ordered.

"Just that?"

"You're going in that direction anyway, aren't you?" she snapped impatiently, thrusting out a hand for him to hoist her up onto the horse.

He laughed. "You're a feisty one, aren't you?"

"I'm about to get a lot more feisty if you don't do as I say and take me back to the castle right now."

She couldn't afford to tell him who she really was—she couldn't have the idiot ruin everything by revealing her identity to someone in the prince's retinue, not given that she was going for the angle of having the prince fall in love with her without knowing who she was.

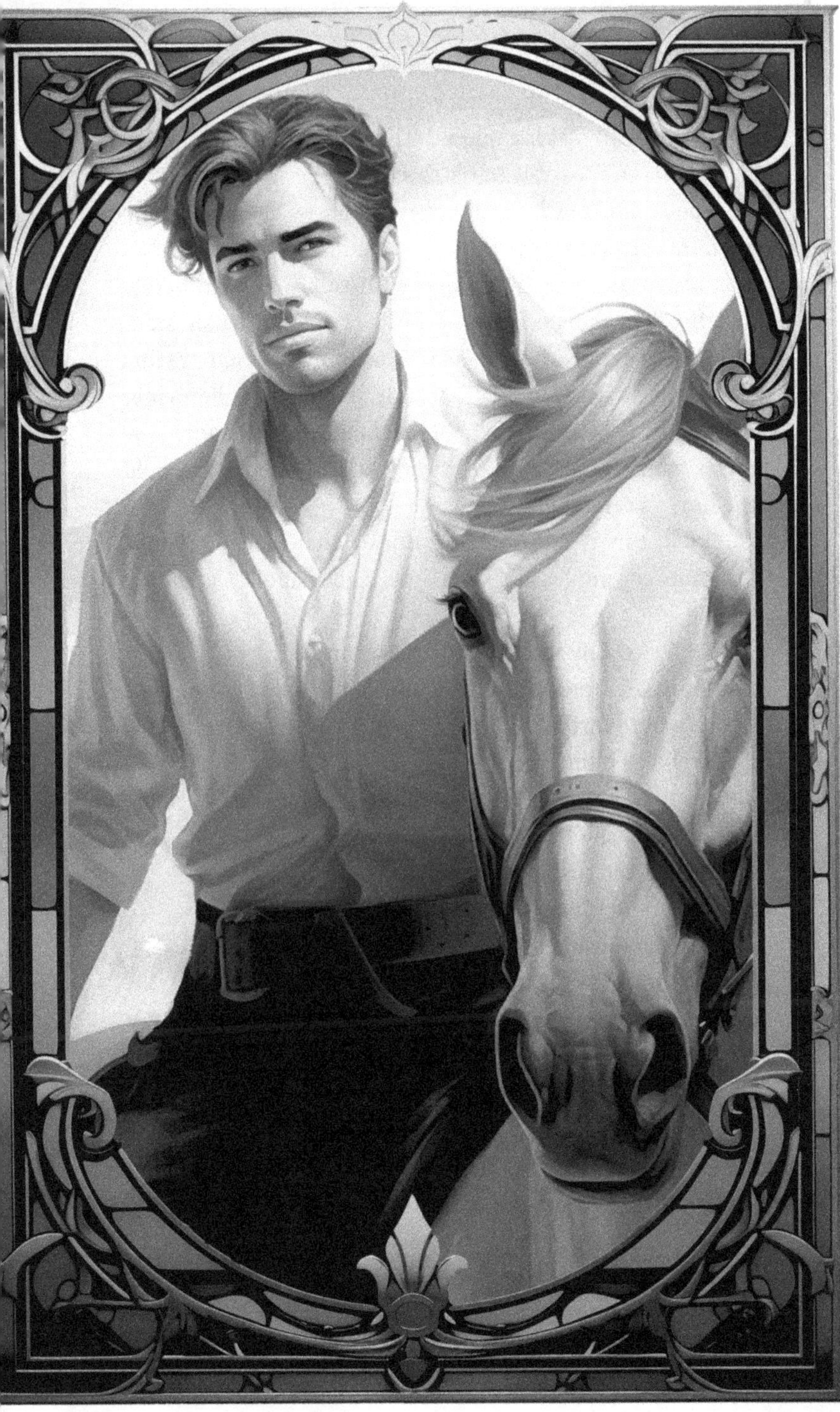

Of course, so far the falling in love wasn't exactly going to plan, given that the prince still hadn't noticed her. Her pride was really taking quite the beating. She needed to get back as fast as possible to try to salvage the situation.

The man reached down, his heavy hand closing around her wrist and forearm, engulfing both. His skin was warm and dry, but rough with calluses. With barely an effort, he hoisted her up onto the horse to sit side-saddled in front of him. Adrianna found herself resting against his chest on her left side, while with her right hand, she held onto the horse's mane for balance. The man's arms framed her to the front and back as he held the horse's reins.

"Well, this is definitely an unexpected turn of events, but not an unpleasant one," he said happily, grinning widely.

"Don't get any ideas," Adrianna grumbled.

"On such a pleasant day as today, a man can't help but have a whole variety of ideas."

"Well, keep them to yourself. And make your horse go a bit faster, we're plodding along as slowly as my grandmother. And she's dead."

"What's the rush, Princess?"

"I'm not a princess," she snapped back immediately.

"Yes, I realise that. It's a figure of speech. Anyway, I have no desire to go any faster, not given how pleasant this moment is. It's sunny, I've got a beautiful girl in my arms…"

"Well, I need to get back to the castle in a hurry."

"Hmmm." The man pretended to mull this over, while the horse plodded on, the movement rocking Adrianna gently. "If you want me to exhaust my horse by making him—"

"Exhaust? We're not that far from the castle. And I'm not asking you to go at a full gallop, just a nice canter."

"As I was saying, if you want me to push my horse, it's going to cost you." He grinned widely. Suggestively.

Adrianna didn't like the suggestive part at all.

"What do you take me for? Just so we're clear, you will never get to lay a finger on me, got it?" Adrianna managed to stop herself just in time before she really turned on her imperiously outraged princess.

"All right, Miss High and Mighty. Then I guess we'll carry on going slowly."

"You're seriously making that kind of demand?"

"I'm not demanding anything. I'm quite happy with the way things are right now." He gave her a smile. An infuriating smile. "Has anyone told you that you're very pretty when you're angry?"

"Stop with that at once."

He shrugged. "I was just paying you a compliment."

"Well, I didn't ask for it, so stop. And you will make your horse trot. Right now."

"I won't."

"You will or—"

"Or what? You know, I'm starting to find your attitude tiring. You may be pretty as you like, but I prefer girls with a nicer temperament than yours."

"You mean you expect girls to be pretty, decorative, agreeable, and silent?"

"Well, that sounds quite nice, if you ask me. A hell of a lot nicer than being harassed by some shrew wrapped in nice packaging. If you'd asked me nicely, I would have helped you, but you've been rude since the first moment you opened your mouth."

Adrianna wanted to slap the man, and especially to slap that smug expression from his face.

"You're an ass," she informed him. "A total and utter ass, and I'd rather walk than spend another moment in your company."

"Your wish is my command."

She'd expected him to be abashed, embarrassed by his oafish behaviour. She'd expected him to apologise. Instead, she barely had the time to let out a squawk of outrage before the man pushed her none too gently off the horse, holding her back with one hand so that she landed softly on her feet.

"You're... You're just going to leave me here?" she spluttered indignantly.

But the man had already pressed his heels into the flanks of his horse, trotting away. "Next time, try being a little more pleasant," he called over his shoulder as his horse broke into a canter. "It might work better!"

Adrianna resisted the urge to stand there cursing him, his entire family, and all his descendants. She didn't have the luxury of wasting time on anything, not even on plotting the annihilation of the world's most irritating man. Not only had the horse ride not sped things up, if anything, it had made her journey back to the castle longer because the road curved away before turning back in.

She'd have to cut through the fields and run, hoping she made it back with enough time to be able to salvage something from this rapidly growing disaster.

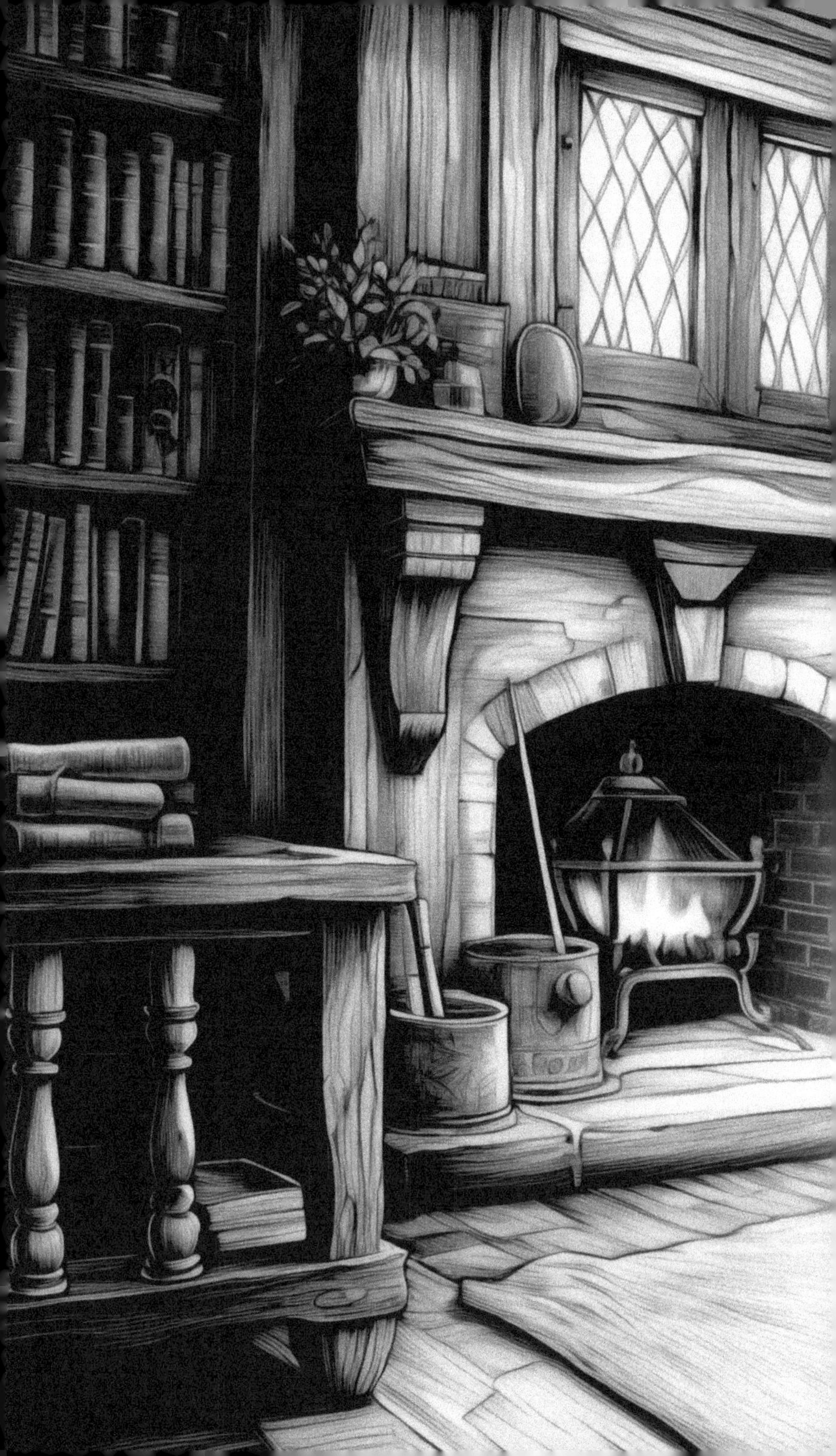

CHAPTER 6

Charming was shocked at how small Veridi castle was. He had always assumed that all castles looked like some version of the sprawling palace he had grown up in, and having never set foot outside his palace, he had never been confronted with anything to contradict this idea. Princes, after all, didn't get invited to the balls of other princes since they would just get in each other's way. Instead, they stayed in their palaces while an endless stream of princesses paraded past them.

Of course, some princes chose to go out into the world and manfully overcome impossible obstacles, but Charming was nothing if not a realist. He was aware and accepting of his shortcomings. Manfully slaying fire-breathing creatures was simply not for him. Passively waiting in his palace for the right princess to come along and drop into his lap was far more his remit—he hated to leave his rooms.

And now the right woman had come his way! Well, not quite dropped into his lap because he was still here, away from his home, in a foreign castle. So he was, in the end, having to perform manly duties, which he would have to try to discharge himself of as manfully as possible.

He shifted his weight awkwardly from one foot to the other as he waited in the—surprisingly dusty—entrance hall. The maid had been highly flustered by his appearance at the front door, in spite of the fact that he had sent word ahead to inform that he would be calling. She'd simply abandoned him, rushing off in search of his beloved. She seemed to have absolutely no idea where Queen Petunia was to be found, which was most bizarre.

After all, this was such a tiny castle, barely more than a big house, really. There couldn't be much more than fifteen bedrooms—not counting the servants' quarters, naturally. How could one lose a person in such a small space? Back home, the small army of servants that kept the palace running seemed to know at all times where all the members of the family were. This wasn't without its inconveniences, of course. If Charming's mother wanted to locate him, she could do so in a matter of mere minutes, for no room in the palace was free from the efficient bustling of servants.

Whereas here, in this tiny castle, he had seen nobody since the maid had run away. Charming's eyes widened in awe, suddenly understanding the wondrousness of what he was beholding. If there were barely any servants, that meant nobody to locate one when one wanted to be alone with one's thoughts. It meant peace, privacy, tranquillity.

That must be why Queen Petunia had so few servants! This ingenious, wonderful woman had created the ideal situation where one was free to do as one pleased without the pressure of being checked on by servants.

The love Charming felt for his beloved swelled, doubling—nay, tripling in size. The woman was simply brilliant. Perfection incarnate.

He was still floating on his little cloud of love and

adoration for the woman he was intending to marry, when the maid return red-faced and out of breath, looking most unbecoming.

"This way, please, sir." She gave a clumsy, awkward curtsy. Then she hurried off again, not waiting to see if he was following.

Which, of course, meant that if he chose to, he could not follow, and she would not realise. The servants at his palace would never allow such a thing. If he failed to follow, they immediately enquired if something was wrong, asking him awkward questions that he never wanted to answer. Especially because his answers were inevitably reported back to his mother.

Charming followed the maid, since she was taking him to his beloved. Normally a princess would move to the prince's castle once they were wed, but of course, this wasn't a princess but a queen, which bent the rules somewhat. Charming hadn't yet found a storyline where a prince and a queen married, but he was confident that he would. And if there was no such storyline, well, he would be the first to create it! And he would create it manfully. He smiled to himself, please with his burst of confidence.

And since he was going to bend the rules anyway, he was now caressing the idea of living here, in this pokey, ramshackle, and servant-free little house rather than bringing his new wife back to his palace. He fancied he could be quite happy here.

The maid opened the door and stepped reverently aside. Charming took a deep breath, preparing himself to ask the most important question of his life. He straightened, thrusting shoulders back, chest forward—which was both awkward and uncomfortable—and thus ready, strode manfully through the door.

Beyond was a library with shelves of books that hadn't felt the touch of a duster in quite some time. But the selection of books was impressive, especially given the smallness of the castle. Charming's gaze was caught by the gold, embossed lettering on a few spines—books he hadn't yet read but that sounded fascinating. He didn't even notice as he stopped thrusting his chest out, his shoulders rounding back to their usual sloping position.

A fireplace, in which was a little log burner, waited to warm the feet of whichever readers sat in the large and comfortable-looking, if a little ratty, leather armchairs. Charming could picture himself in this room, in winter, sitting in one of those chairs, secure in the knowledge that there weren't any servants to disturb him or report on his reading habits to his mother.

Given that the library smelt of dust and old paper, with that slightly stale feel to the air indicating that the windows hadn't been opened in a long time, Charming felt reasonably sure that the servants didn't bother cleaning this room.

Yes, he really could be quite happy here. And all he had to do to secure said happiness was to inform his beloved... Charming blinked as he came crashing back down to reality. He wasn't in the library to peruse the books, to sit and read in one of the armchairs, or to escape his mother, but to inform Queen Petunia of their betrothal.

He looked around, a touch disorientated as he always was when he was found himself abruptly yanked from his thoughts. He discovered that the love of his life was standing to his left, running her fingers along the spines of the books there, obviously in search of a particular tome.

She was taller than he remembered, more statuesque. She had a striking profile, what with that pronounced nose and her steel grey hair, and Charming realised with a jolt that she was a lot older than he'd expected. She wasn't quite his mother's age, but she was closer to his mother than to his age. He should have put two and two together when he'd noticed her grey hair, but speed of deduction wasn't his forte, and he'd had a lot on his mind.

That would be another break with convention as princesses were always younger, normally. And smaller. Not that it should matter, since Charming was already throwing out the rule book in getting engaged to a queen and not a princess.

"Gardening Is An Art... Gardening Is An Art... I know I saw it in here somewhere." Queen Petunia was preoccupied with her search and hadn't yet realised that Charming was in the room.

This was his moment to make himself known. He straightened his spine from its default, droopy sock position. Shoulders back, chest forward. Little pot belly sucked in and out of sight. Manly.

He stepped forward and cleared his throat. He had intended it to be a manly sound, a sound replete with power, a sound that would encapsulate all his wonderful qualities. But instead, it came out strangled and closer to the bleat of a nervous sheep than he would have liked.

"I'm sure that's the title—Gardening Is An Art," his beloved continued to mutter.

"Queen Petunia?" Charming ventured, wishing his voice sounded more confident, more sure of itself.

"Hmm? Yes. Quite. Lowen is an obstinate, stiff-necked son of a—ah-HA! There it is." Petunia plucked the aforementioned tome from the shelf and began flicking through its pages feverishly.

"Queen Petunia, um..." Charming suddenly realised that it was a lot harder to inform one's beloved of one's upcoming nuptials than he had hitherto expected. He had pictured himself striding manfully into the room and informing Petunia that they would be wed as soon as arrangements could be made, and after she was done swooning and falling into some kind of faint, he would ride manfully back to his palace, to share the good news with his mother and enjoy the peace and quiet he would have finally secured for himself by selecting a wife.

It had seemed very simple and straightforward in his head. Not so in real life.

Petunia looked up from her book. "Who are you?"

"Prince Charming."

She frowned at him.

No, things really weren't happening the way he had envisioned. "I came here to say… that is to ask… that is to inform you of…"

But Queen Petunia had returned to her book. "See, the writer of this book, clearly a woman of sense and sensibility, states here *black on white*—oh, I will strangle Lowen when I find him next. Wring out his botanical heresies from him."

"…That is, the fondness that I felt for you upon meeting you last night has blossomed into an ardent love…" Charming found himself sweating, and he fished around his pockets for his handkerchief.

"If I have said it once, I have said it a hundred times. Lowen knows nothing of wisteria. *Nothing*!" Petunia looked up angrily from her book, skewering Charming with a look that made him want to shrink his head back into his shoulders like a frightened turtle. But he could not resort to this well-practiced method of defence since he was here to propose marriage. Men didn't shrink away from their betrothed.

"And said love," he continued haltingly, "Means that I have… I mean that I most ardently wish…" Charming's speech was rapidly disintegrating into a mere mumble. "We will be married as soon as arrangements can be made," Charming said at last, somehow finding the strength to expel the words from his mouth like one might expel a glob of phlegm.

Petunia looked up from her book, her face alive with surprise. "Marriage? Whose marriage?"

"Yes, as soon as arrangements can be made," Charming continued, warming to his newfound confidence. Thank goodness it had arrived when it did—he had very nearly screwed it all up.

"What arrangements? Have you been talking to Lowen? I swear, there is no end to the damage that man is doing to my garden."

"It will take place at my palace," Charming continued, steamrollering forward with the desperation of a man who knows his spell of energetic confidence is not destined to last very long, and who therefore must get everything he needs to say out in the open as quickly as possible. "You will not have to worry about anything. We can discuss our living arrangements after we have been married."

He let out a sigh of relief. There. It was said. And he'd even informed her of his desire to live in her castle, thus breaking with tradition.

Queen Petunia still held her book, but she now stood watching him with a look of glazed shock in her eyes. Charming emerged enough from his fog of stress at having made his proposal to realise that normally she should have said yes by now. And then swooned.

Petunia's frozen demeanour was, however, something he could well understand. He was continuously placed in situations that made him uncomfortable, without being allowed the time to get accustomed, to ease himself gently into it.

"I will come back in a few days so you can tell me yes," he told his betrothed kindly.

Still she didn't move, shock written on her face. Charming was at a bit of a loss, but then again, women had such odd ways of behaving—very few of what they did made any sense to him.

"Yes. Quite." Charming cleared his throat. He felt quite sure that he had now discharged himself of all the requirements for a proposal. He gave Queen Petunia a polite bow, turned, and left, replete with the warm afterglow of satisfaction that came from a task well done.

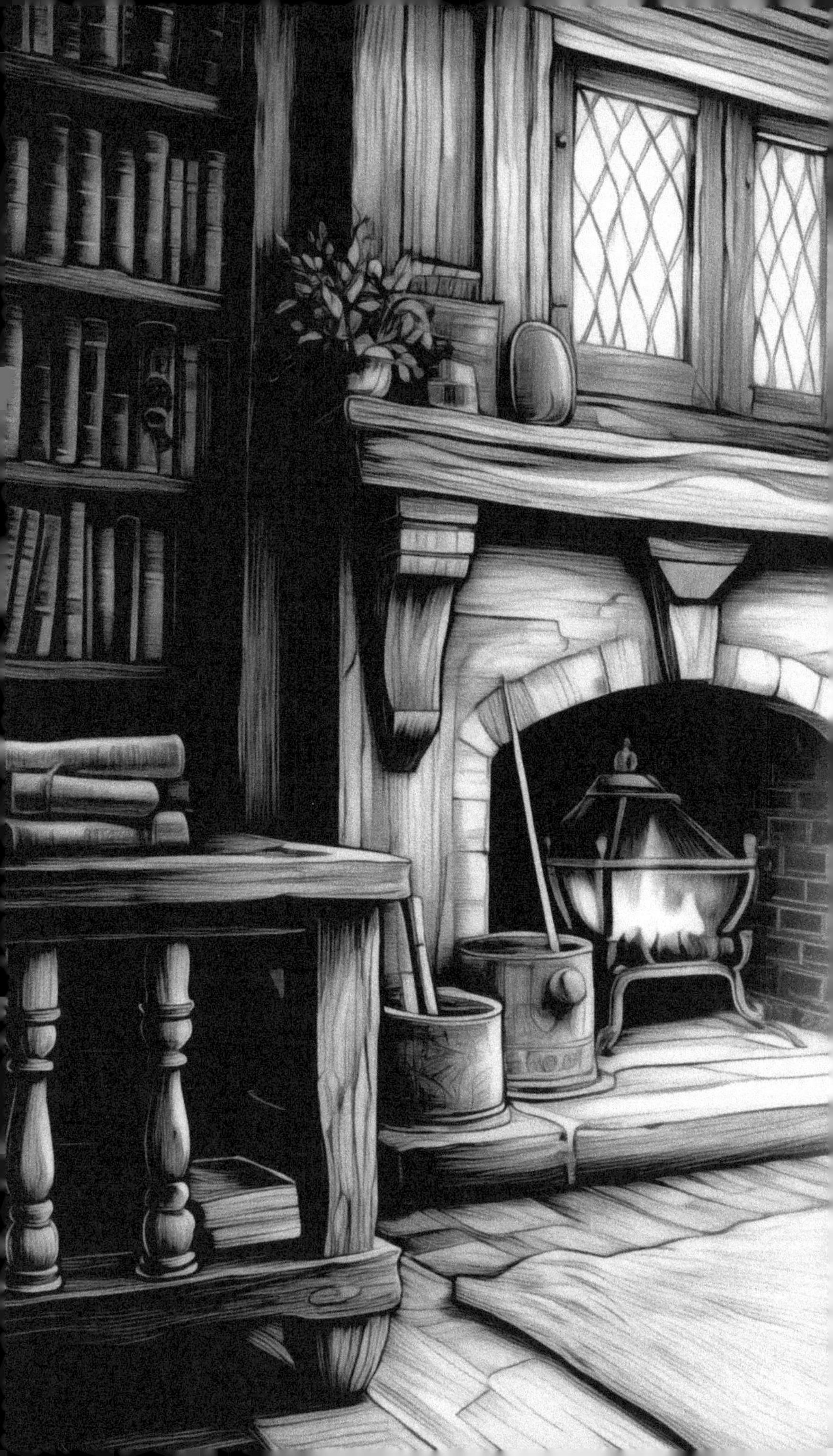

CHAPTER 7

Adrianna began to run across the field, cursing the man and his horse at first, despite her resolution not to. The cursing extended to his family and descendants, and she didn't stop there. She also cursed the entire male species, the whole bloody stupid situation, the ridiculous amount of effort she was having to put in, all in the name of getting a prince's attention, and the fact that princesses had to secure themselves princes in the first place. Then, of course, she cursed the whole, bloody, idiotic population of princes.

She quickly stopped cursing, though, because the magic that kept her figure looking perfectly lovely did nothing for her fitness and she was wheezing and gasping for breath after a few short moments. Sweat was trickling down between her breasts, the corset squashed her lungs, making it hard to breathe, and her dress was making her skin hot and unbelievably itchy.

She couldn't arrive at the castle in this state, and yet if she didn't run, she took the risk of the prince leaving before she actually got there. The whole point of passing herself off as a servant girl was for him to find her lovely and fresh-faced so he could fall in love with her. Arriving red-faced, sweaty, and wheezing was definitely not going to achieve that.

She slowed down, taking a deep gulp of air, finding a little surge of energy, enough to curse the man and his horse once more, before she trotted forward again. She carried on like this, alternating between bursts of running and walking, interspersed with gasping, cursing, and sweating.

In short, it was exactly the unmitigated disaster she had been hoping to avoid.

She reached the castle and let herself in through one of the servant's back entrances.

"Where have you been?" Mirabelle asked, appearing next to her.

"No time for your questions," Adrianna gasped, running into the kitchen and snatching a tea towel to mop her face. "Sort me out. I'm a mess." Thank god the dress was sleeveless or she would have had unsightly sweat rings under her armpits. She patted herself dry with the tea towel, patting her armpits dry as well. The indignity of being a princess truly was never ending.

"That's the thing, darling—"

"Mirabelle, for once in your bloody life just do as you're told and sort me out!" Adrianna exploded, reaching breaking point. She knew she would owe her fairy godmother an apology later, but at this point her nerves were frayed beyond all imagining, and worse was the awful sinking feeling in the pit of her stomach that she had, once again, failed. Always a failure, never chosen, that was Adrianna.

Mirabelle waved her wand, and although Adrianna's hot itchiness and general discomfort didn't abate, a quick glance in the mirror confirmed that she was once again fresh-faced and beautiful, as if she had just gotten out of bed.

"Thanks."

She hitched up her skirt and pelted up the stairs.

Adrianna hadn't truly expected that she would be able to salvage the situation at this point, but she was not prepared for the true extent of the absolute shit show her life had become.

She burst into the library far too forcefully, given that she was supposed to be a shy, sweet, and beautiful serving girl that the prince would soon fall in love with.

Luckily, the limp handshake incarnate was nowhere to be found. Instead, Petunia was standing at the French windows, gazing out at the garden.

"Where is he?" Adrianna asked. "The prince. Charming. Where did he go?"

Her evil stepmother didn't answer for a beat. Adrianna feared that Petunia had been so absorbed by one of her usual gardening obsessions that she hadn't even received the prince, leaving him waiting at the door until he'd had no option but to turn and leave. She really was the most useless evil stepmother.

Then again, she might be a truly evil genius, since the evil stepmother's purpose in life was to prevent the prince from falling in love with the princess.

Petunia turned finally. "He left already."

"Oh."

So all that effort, all that running around, all that plotting—all of it for nothing. Adrianna let herself sag in one of the leather armchairs, suddenly exhausted.

"I know I've not been the best evil stepmother to you, dear," Petunia said.

Adrianna dismissed that thought with a wave of her hand. "You've been great, Petunia. And I'm sure Lowen would testify that you are a true incarnation of evil."

Adrianna could actually see the way the mere mention of the gardener sent Petunia's mind shooting back to her garden like a homing pigeon heading back to roost. The effort it cost her to return to the present moment was visible.

"No, I mean I haven't been a very good stepmother to you in terms of helping you in your search for a prince."

Adrianna lifted a limp shoulder. Right now, she found it hard to care. "There will be more balls, more princes. That's the one thing we have a lot of in this world—princes and princesses. Well, technically, that's two things."

But Petunia would not let the subject alone. She approached the chair opposite Adrianna's, her face grave, almost embarrassed.

"There's more…" She sat, hesitating. "The prince has proposed."

"Oh." Adrianna knew she should be elated, but the prospect of spending the rest of her short life with that wet blanket of a man didn't exactly fill her with joy. Still, at least it would put an end to—

"He proposed to me," Petunia added.

For a few heartbeats, Adrianna sat looking at her stepmother without understanding the meaning of the words. She could understand them independently, but all together they created a sentence that she simply couldn't wrap her head around.

"Proposed? He proposed what to you?"

"He asked that I marry him. Or, rather, I think he informed me that we would be getting married. It wasn't so much a proposal as an order."

For a moment, the burn to Adrianna's pride was such that it left her breathless. Not only had the prince not chosen her, but he had instead chosen a woman nearly old enough to be his mother, who was far less attractive than her, and who wasn't even a princess. It was hard not to feel worthless in the face of that level of rejection.

She tried to rebel against the feeling, but she quickly gave in, having lost all will to fight.

"Well, at least someone has managed to marry a prince, so I guess that's something to be celebrated." She'd go drown her sorrows with Mirabelle in a bucket of wine later. Maybe after Alinor had gone to bed—her little sister hated to see her drunk. And right now she needed to get totally, blindingly, pass-out-spooning-the-wine-bottle-drunk.

Petunia shook her head. "I'm afraid it's more complicated than that."

"What's complicated? The prince proposed to you, so…"

"And if I accept, I will have to go and live with him in his palace. Since a castle cannot simply be left in the hands of a princess and her evil stepsister, you two will have to move as well. We will have to abandon Veridi Castle."

"No way," Adrianna said at once. "He will just have to come live here."

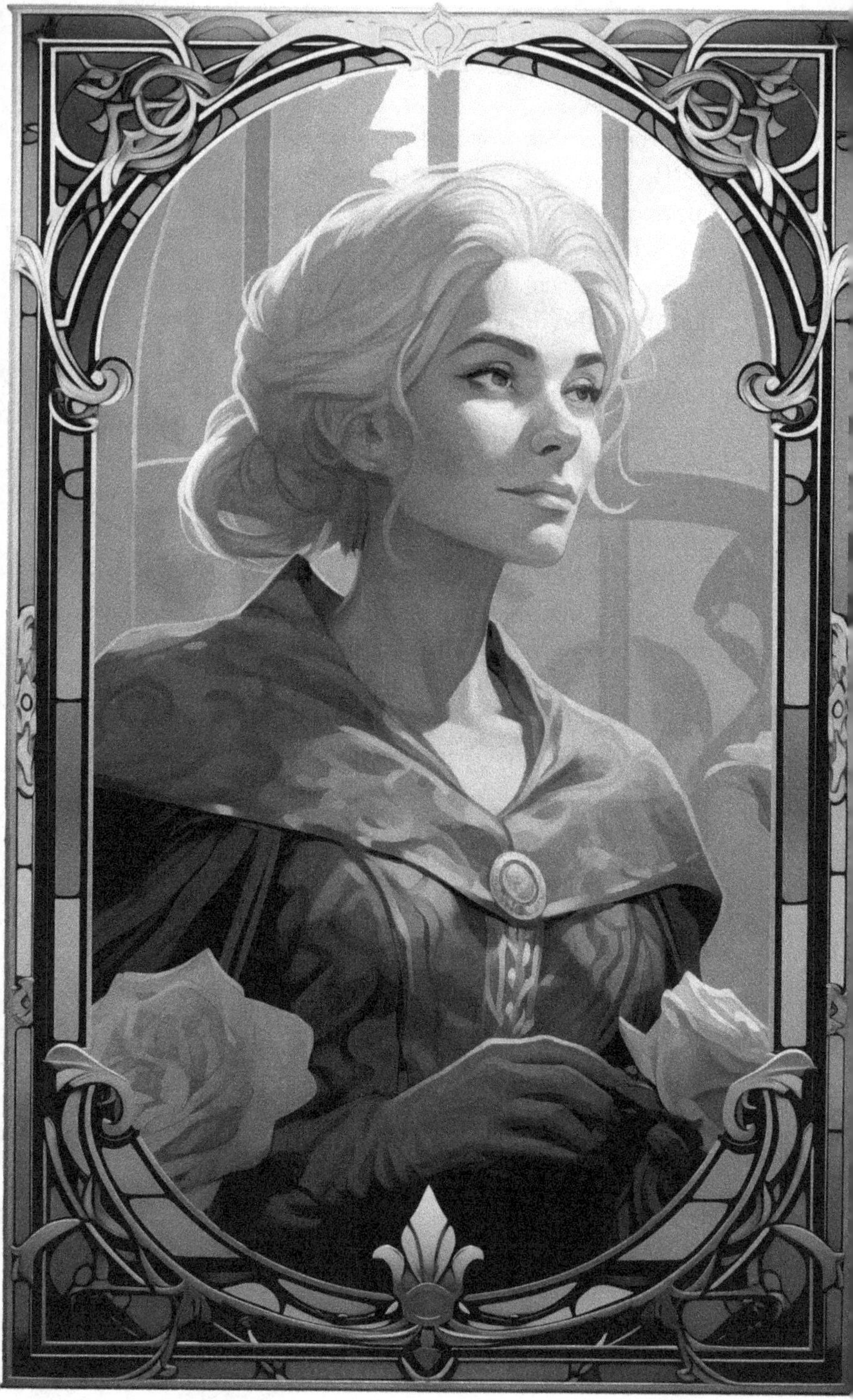

"But even if he does, things will not be allowed to remain as they are. He and I will have to have a child. You would cease to be the princess, and instead you would become the evil stepsister. Alinor wouldn't be allowed to stay either, because she'd have no role." The last she said in a voice barely louder than a whisper, her face ashen.

"What? But why? Why wouldn't she be allowed to stay?"

"Evil stepsisters never originate from the mother of the princess. Always from an external woman. I would become a true queen since Charming hasn't previously been married, so as my daughter, Alinor could no longer be an evil stepsister. But Charming and I would need to have a child, and so Alinor would be a stepsister to her, even though she isn't supposed to be. If I marry Charming, Alinor becomes out of place."

"What if you have a boy?"

"Princes never have evil stepsisters. Haven't you noticed?"

It was true. Adrianna had never paid attention since she didn't care about the princes, but it was true.

"Well, we'll just have to be an exception, won't we?" It was all making Adrianna's head ache.

Petunia sighed. "We're already in such a precarious position. We flout a lot of the rules of our world. I am not really evil, not to you, at least. You and Alinor are very close, which also isn't right. Why do you think it's been so hard for you to secure a proposal? You don't fit within the rules of our world, not well enough for things to flow as they should. The storylines are not working naturally for you."

"But…"

"If it helps, I don't fit either."

"Well, who cares about fitting in? We're happy, we're not causing anyone any harm…"

"But we will not be allowed to remain like this indefinitely," Petunia said sadly.

Adrianna shook her head. Petunia was just being paranoid. It was understandable, really—it must have been quite traumatic to be proposed to by an invertebrate. Adrianna was also surprised by the depth and duration of the conversation they were having. Talks with Petunia normally were more like being monologued at about gardening things, and on the rare occasions Adrianna tried to talk back, her stepmother's eyes would glaze over as her mind returned to her garden. Petunia must care about this deeply to set her garden aside for so long.

"I never told you about how your father and I came to be together, did I?" Petunia asked. She smiled distantly, her face getting that wistful expression it always found anytime she thought of or mentioned the late king.

Not only did Adrianna not know, it had never occurred to her to ask. No one ever cared about how a king met the evil stepmother. Adrianna felt a stab of guilt that she hadn't taken more of an interest. She'd been too young when it happened, and later, she was too preoccupied with her own challenges in trying to be the right kind of princess.

"We actually fell in love a couple of years before we were married. I wasn't royalty, but a merchant's daughter. Part of the forbidden middle classes. Not a milkmaid, no shepherdess, just a woman from a prosperous family. Your father and I were forbidden from seeing each other, but we truly loved each other, so we did our best to find some solution, some way to allow us to be together within the rules of our world. And I found a solution."

Petunia shuddered then. "Your father was resolutely against it, because the sacrifice I needed to make was large, but I didn't care. I loved him, and nothing and no one would stand in my way."

"That sounds quite romantic," Adrianna said, surprised.

"Do you know that I used to be quite pretty?" Petunia asked. "Not as stunning as you are, of course—I didn't have a fairy godmother to bless me at birth—but as far as normal women go, I was considered to be quite beautiful."

Adrianna tactfully refrained from asking what had happened, because no one would describe Petunia as anything other than quite plain now.

"Since the only way we could be together was for me to become an evil stepmother, I had two options. Either I could become more beautiful, but I would have to be cruel, or I could become ugly and be stupid and petty. You were a little girl back then, and I'd met you a couple of times, but we had hidden who I was from you. I simply didn't have the heart to be cruel to such a lovely little girl, so I chose the option of being ugly, stupid, and petty."

Adrianna frowned as she took in all of this.

"They rearranged my face," Petunia said simply, "And then placed a spell over it so the scars wouldn't be obvious. You can still see them in mirrors, though."

"That's why you've had the mirrors removed from the house," Adrianna murmured.

"Yes. To you, my face looks plain, but it is not painful to look at. What I see in the mirror is the true mess that is beneath the enchantments. The scars where they broke my nose, where they widened my chin. Look."

She pulled out a small hand mirror from her pocket, gesturing for Adrianna to come next to her. "I always keep this on me, but I almost never use it."

Adrianna came to Petunia's side, and she looked into the mirror. Petunia hadn't lied. Her nose had been broken and badly reshaped into a grotesque approximation of the hook nose she had, the skin nastily scarred. More scars on her cheeks highlighted where her mouth had been widened, and same for her chin, the skin pink and puckered. She smiled sadly, and it twisted horribly.

Petunia lowered the mirror. "I needed to be on the plain side of ugly, not horrific and grotesque, hence the enchantment. But for an enchantment to last this long without slipping, it needs to be close to the face underneath—hence the physical rearrangement that was first required."

Adrianna found herself mute with shock.

"This is the price I paid for flouting the rules of our world. I paid it willingly, because it bought me many happy years with your father, and it brought me Alinor. But I'm also keenly aware of how heavy a price would fall on both your heads if we are not able to create some kind of normal outcome." Petunia lowered her head. "Unfortunately, the enchantments to make me stupid and petty were efficient enough that I haven't been able to properly set things up to make sure you secured yourself a prince in a timely manner. I should have done more, I should have done better…"

"Don't feel bad," Adrianna said at once. "Truth be told, I don't actually want to marry a prince. The whole business is so ghastly, so depressing, so—"

"But that's it, Adrianna. That's what you don't understand. If you are not able to marry a prince within a reasonable timeframe, both you and Alinor will end up subjected to some treatment or another that approximates what I went through."

"But why? Why can't we just stay as we are, and live out our lives without anybody getting married?"

"Because you're a princess. You can't just disappear off the face of the map and live out your life quietly, as you want. You are part of the stories that make our world go round. As are Alinor and I. Alinor has been safe all this time because she's less pretty than you, and because as your evil stepsister she can act as a foil to a prince trying to get to you, so she has a role. But if you are no longer eligible for a prince to choose, Alinor loses her place in this world, and she may have to be turned into an ugly evil stepsister, since just being an evil stepsister on its own wasn't enough. Or worse, maybe she will have to become a witch."

"She will not have her face rearranged," Adrianna said at once.

"We may not have a choice in the matter," Petunia said miserably.

"Alright, so say you accept the prince…"

"Then you become the evil stepsister, so you will have to be made ugly—there is no option for beautiful stepsisters. An evil stepsister is always more ugly or more plain than the princess. Beauty is only for evil queens. And Alinor will have no role, so she has to leave."

"Fine, then you turn the prince down."

"I'm not sure that's even possible. But even if I do, and even if it is allowed, what then? The problem still remains that you need to be married to a prince. And you are very close to turning twenty-five, at which point you will be considered an old maid, and no longer eligible. So you will have to become a witch, or you will have to marry a king and become an evil stepmother to someone. Both outcomes require your face to change, and both outcomes cause Alinor to lose her place in the world."

"Then what?" Adrianna asked miserably.

"I will stall the prince as long as I possibly can, but you have to find a prince to marry, and very soon. I'm so sorry, Adrianna, I really should have done more to help you with this. But most of the time, my mind is in such a fog from all the enchantments… Gardening is the only thing that feels normal anymore. It's what keeps me sane…"

"Why did you never say?"

Petunia gave her a sad smile. "I didn't want to burden you. I'd hoped you'd be able to secure a prince by yourself so you could have remained in blissful ignorance. I'm sure it's quite nice to truly be part of a fairytale. To fall in love and marry and have a Happy Ever After." Petunia's voice was turning distracted, her eyes distant. Adrianna realised she was losing her, her stepmother slipping back to her normal manners.

Petunia frowned. "I think I'd better go check on Lowen. He's been without supervision for a while now, and who knows what gardening atrocities he has committed?"

She wafted out of the library, muttering about Cornish gardeners and roses in the way she always did.

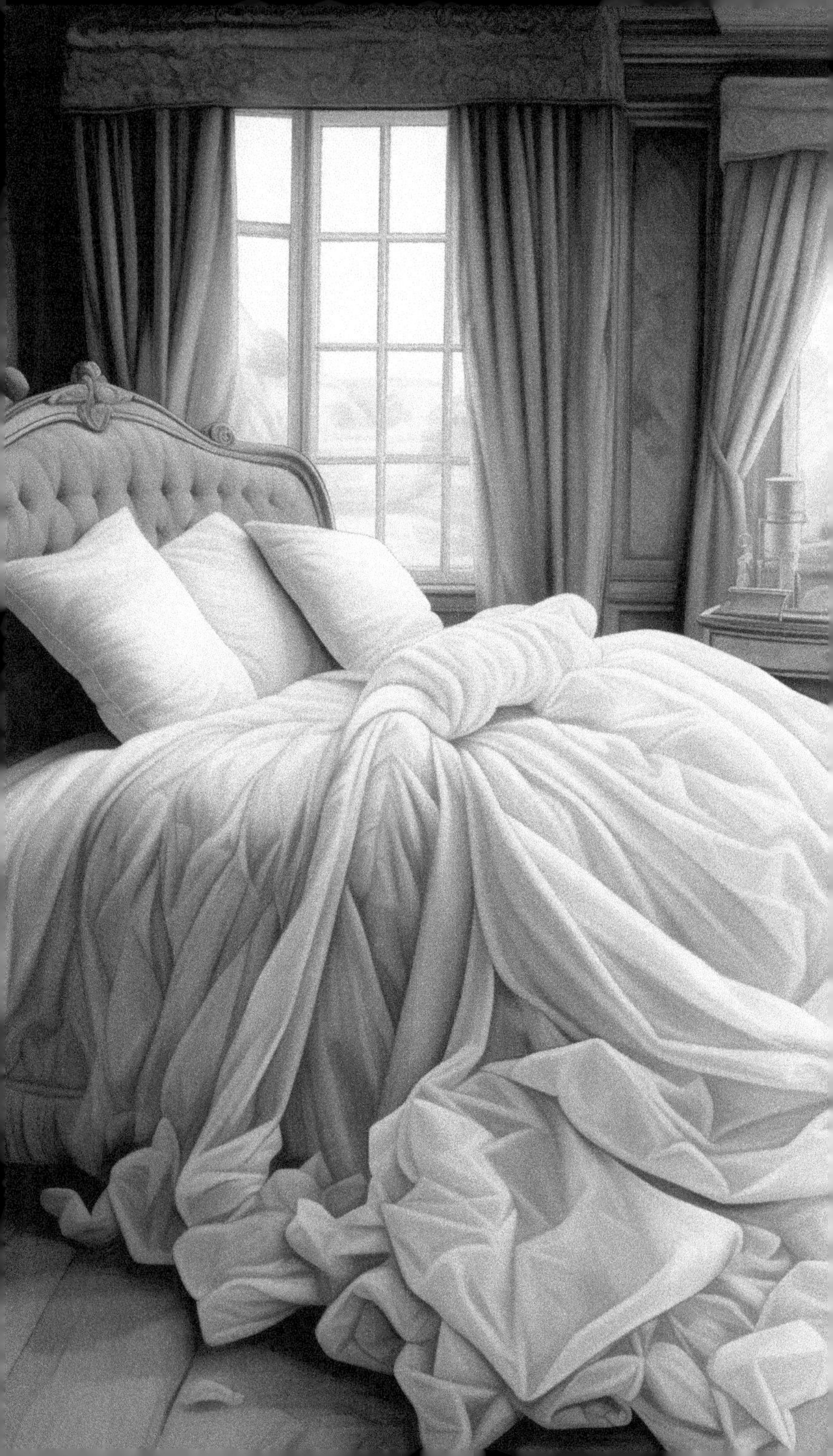

CHAPTER 8

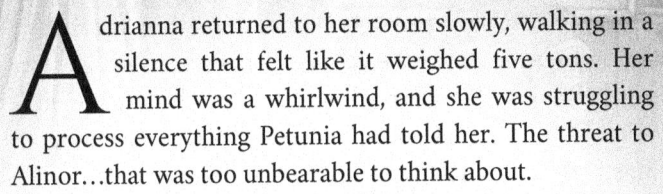

Adrianna returned to her room slowly, walking in a silence that felt like it weighed five tons. Her mind was a whirlwind, and she was struggling to process everything Petunia had told her. The threat to Alinor…that was too unbearable to think about.

She ran her hands along the walls. The thought of one day being separated from the castle made her chest tight. She loved this ramshackle place as if it were a member of her family. And maybe she was making it up, maybe it was just fanciful thinking, but she felt like the castle felt the same gloom. The air was dense, denser than usual, as if it too carried the same weight. And as she neared her bedroom, the whole castle gave a groan and a faint, creaking shudder, like a sigh.

This wasn't the first time the building had done this—it was, after all, old and higgledy-piggledy, so it was forever creaking and groaning, the beams, the stones adjusting and shifting with the passing of time. But still, Adrianna couldn't shake the feeling that the castle was somehow sighing along with her.

She entered her bedroom to find her fairy godmother on her usual divan.

"So you spoke to Petunia?" For once, Mirabelle wasn't sporting her usual cheeky, smiley expression, nor was she scoffing truffles or quaffing brandy. Her features were sober, her eyes sad and sympathetic.

"Did you know? About what was done to her?"

Mirabelle nodded.

"Why didn't you tell me?"

"It wasn't my story to tell. And if Petunia and your late father wanted you to remain ignorant, the only thing I could do was to respect that."

"Yeah, I guess that makes sense." Adrianna collapsed backwards on her bed, staring up at the ceiling where the spider had finished her web. "I have to fix this, Mirabelle. I am not letting Alinor be cast out, or worse, have her face rearranged and be forced to be a witch." Gentle little Alinor—how could anyone even consider touching so much as a hair on her head?

She propped herself up on her elbows to look her fairy godmother in the eyes. "You do realise the irony of it all, right? Alinor makes a far better princess than me. She's kind, she's sweet, she's incapable of harming an animal. I mean, she's the reason we stopped killing all the damned spiders in the castle…" The thought of Alinor having her face rearranged, Alinor who beamed every time she found eggs in the dove nests, made Adrianna nauseous.

"You'll fix it," Mirabelle said reassuringly. "You'll find a prince."

"But I can't just keep on doing what I've been doing until now—half-heartedly attending balls and hoping that something comes of it. That's a one-way ticket to failure. I need to be proactive." Adrianna pushed herself up to be fully seated, staring into the distance. "What I need are Impossible Odds. Given that I don't even have a proper evil stepmother, things as they are aren't sufficient to appeal to a prince—I get that now. I need to create something else." She snapped her fingers. "I need to get a dragon."

"Oh, great idea, darling. Why don't you go ask your friend, Aurora, for tips on how she managed to get her dragon?"

Adrianna grimaced. It wasn't that she disliked Aurora, per se. The woman was perfectly pleasant. It was just that she was so damn perfect. Like the way she got her prince. It wasn't enough for her to just have a dragon guarding her. No, she'd had a sleeping curse and a witch for the prince to defeat on top of the dragon. Not only that, but she'd also managed to pull off the 'prince falls in love with a simple country girl without realising that she's a princess' storyline as well as line up all those Impossible Odds. It really boggled the mind how she had managed to set all this up.

But Mirabelle was right. Aurora probably would be able to dispense advice on how to go about getting yourself guarded by a dragon. A single dragon would have to do—Adrianna didn't think she was capable of lining up all the other stuff—the witch and the curse and the simple country girl story line.

And Aurora would enjoy dispensing the advice too—she was a bit of an insufferable know-it-all. At least she had been before getting married, and Adrianna wasn't sure winning a prince was likely to have improved that. It would simply be just one more blow to Adrianna's pride that she'd have to swallow. By this point, she'd already swallowed so many, one more shouldn't make much of a difference…

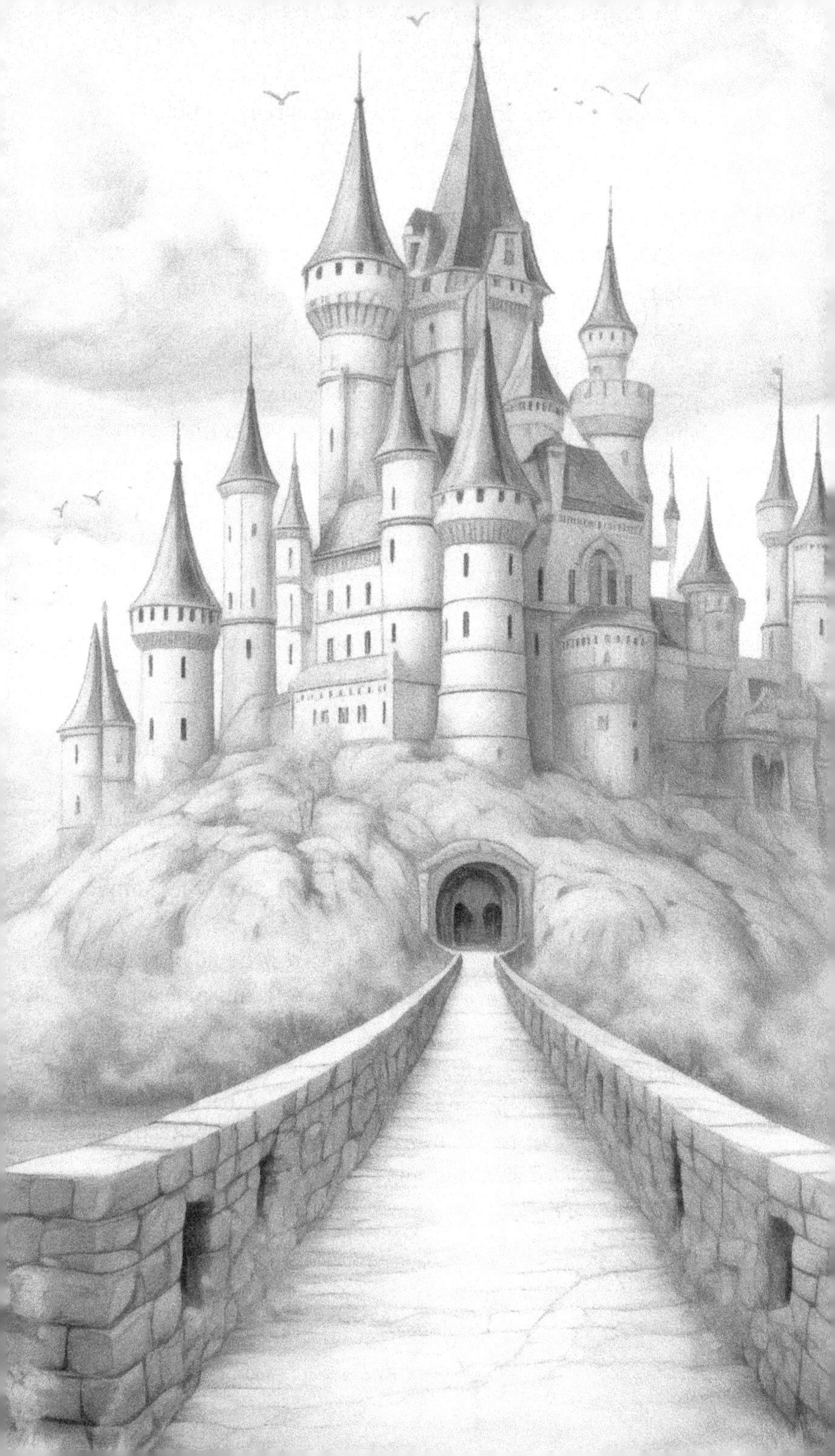

CHAPTER 9

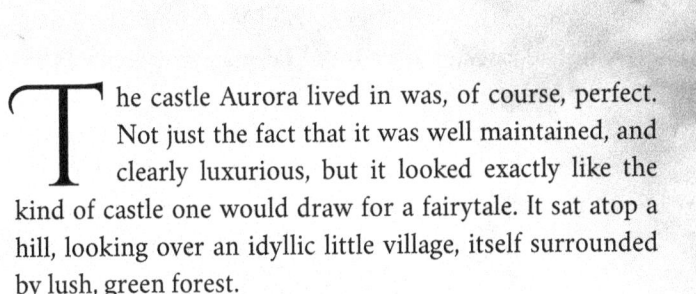

The castle Aurora lived in was, of course, perfect. Not just the fact that it was well maintained, and clearly luxurious, but it looked exactly like the kind of castle one would draw for a fairytale. It sat atop a hill, looking over an idyllic little village, itself surrounded by lush, green forest.

The castle had those little round turrets with pointy roofs, its various wings laid symmetrically around the centre. The stones of its walls were a flawless, creamy white, somehow immune to the vagaries of time and weather.

Adrianna thought back to her own castle walls, so heavily covered with moss, lichen, and other small plants that they looked more like pieces of vegetation than actual walls. And the comparison between the two castles became even less flattering as Adrianna entered the pristine, luxurious, sunlight-flooded interior.

The servants were both discreet and invisible while performing their duties with impressive efficiency. Adrianna could feel their presence but didn't really see any of them as she was swiftly shepherded through to a gorgeous, dusky-rose and silver sitting room.

It wasn't so much pink or so much silver as to look tasteless or ridiculous. Instead, it looked charming and feminine and shimmery.

Sitting amongst the beautiful furniture was a blonde woman of luminous beauty—Aurora. She wore a turquoise dress which contrasted with the colours of the room, making her stand out without clashing. Her waist was tiny, her generous skirts spread around her on the divan.

Her hair was as fine and as shiny as spun gold, the comparison apt since her fingers were moving swiftly, deftly manipulating a spinning wheel. In short, she looked like she had just stepped out of a fairytale story—which she literally had.

This was a stark reminder to Adrianna that princesses weren't supposed to drink wine in their underwear with their alcoholic fairy godmothers while laughing at crude jokes. They were supposed to be beautiful, ethereal, modest, and to do things like spinning.

Aurora stopped her work as Adrianna entered, her face lighting up with a big, genuine smile. "Adrianna!"

"Aurora. How are you?"

The princess stood up, and the two women kissed each other's cheeks.

"Sit, sit. I'll ring for some tea." Once that was taken care of, she turned back to Adrianna, her eyes shining. "So, to what do I owe the pleasure of this visit?"

Adrianna gestured to the spinning wheel with her chin. "I'm surprised you can still bear to see one of those. Wasn't your curse set off by you pricking your finger on a spinning wheel?"

Aurora gave a shrug. "Philip has developed a bit of a fetish for them. He likes me to be working with one."

Adrianna reached out to touch the smooth wood of the spinning wheel, and Aurora chuckled. "He even likes us to make use of one in the bedroom."

Adrianna snatched her hand away with a grimace. "Ew, you mean...."

Aurora burst out laughing. "Don't worry, I have a separate set of spinning wheels that are kept for that very purpose. This one is only ever used here, in the sitting room, for genuine spinning."

Adrianna struggled to hide the disgust from her face. A spinning wheel in bed? How did that even work? She didn't want to know. "Still... Doesn't it bother you?"

Aurora shrugged. "It's a small price to pay. Life is otherwise pretty good. If the worst thing I have to contend with is having to spin for a couple of hours every day, it's no great hardship."

"I guess..." Adrianna's eyes took in the beautifully, tastefully decorated room. It did look like a good life. And yet, she would choose her own sitting room, with its mismatched furniture, dusty shelves, and watermarks on the table any day of the week. Even though she knew she wasn't supposed to. Even though she was supposed to yearn for a ballgown of shimmering silk and for a diamond tiara and for a handsome man on whose elbow she could hang.

But then again, she was a princess whose worth was so low, a prince would rather marry an older, uglier evil stepmother than her.

The maid entered silently, gliding across the room in a whisper of fabric as she deposited a tray full of things to make tea with. Aurora busied herself with the tea preparing ritual for a while, asking all the questions about milk and sugar.

"So listen, I came here because I need to ask you for

some advice," Adrianna said, once she was furnished with a delicate china teacup and saucer—matching, of course, and in a pattern of dusky rose and silver that complemented the room. She wouldn't be surprised if Aurora had a separate tea set for each room.

"I'm…" Adrianna paused, hating that she had to admit she couldn't land herself a prince.

"You're creeping up towards old maid age and you need to do something drastic," Aurora guessed.

It didn't sting any less to hear someone else speak the words. Adrianna took a deep gulp of tea to settle herself, forgetting the water was too hot and burning her tongue. She gasped and grimaced. "You got it in one. I need a dragon, and I was hoping you had some advice as to how to go about getting one, since that's how you got your prince."

Aurora leaned back in her divan. "Darling, absolutely. I'll tell you exactly how to secure yourself a dragon—and I'm so glad you came to me. It really is time that you nabbed yourself someone, and your evil stepmother just doesn't cut it."

Adrianna bit down on the curt reply that wanted to bubble up to her lips in defence of Petunia. Before today she would have defended her evil stepmother to anyone criticising her, but now that Adrianna knew the truth of Petunia's story, it seemed even more unfair for anyone to speak badly of her. "I'd really appreciate your advice," she said instead, not wanting to antagonise Aurora.

"The problem with dragons is that there aren't that many left. Princes have been killing them for so long now, their numbers are down quite a bit."

"Oh… Then maybe it isn't right for me to try to secure one?"

"Why on earth not?"

"Well, because if I secure one, the whole point is for a

prince to come along and kill it." Adrianna found that she felt quite uncomfortable with the idea.

Aurora laughed blithely, the sound like the tinkling of delicate silver bells. "Oh, darling, don't worry. They're basically just overgrown, fire-breathing lizards. Who cares if there's less of them in the world? Anyway, they can lay a few eggs and make more. It's not a real problem."

"Yeah, I guess you're right." But the mention of lizards brought back to mind the way Alinor liked to monitor the lizards who sunned themselves on the castle walls in the summer. How they made her laugh, how she liked to mimic what she called Superior Lizard Face.

Adrianna's feeling of wrongness and guilt briefly increased until she also remembered that if she didn't secure this dragon, Alinor might be left to face the same fate as Petunia. At that, cold resolved settled on Adrianna's shoulders. She'd slaughter the whole population of dragons herself if it meant keeping her little sister from harm.

"So, how did you find yourself a dragon?" she asked.

"The key is actually to get a dragon's egg. Take the egg and the mother will follow you wherever you go. Then all you need to do is lock away the egg in your castle, and you'll keep the mother hovering nearby. It used to be a lot easier to get dragon eggs, but since there aren't many dragons left, it's a lot trickier these days to find them if you don't know where to look. There's an organisation that dedicates itself to tracking the location of dragon eggs, so the easiest thing to do is to go to them, find out where the nearest dragon egg is, and then just go get it."

"Why on earth are they tracking the location of dragon eggs?"

"I'm not sure. They explained it to me, but I didn't pay attention. To be honest, if they won't give you the location, you can just get your fairy godmother to get it from them using magic. Keep it to yourself, though. If everyone hears about it, it will stop being a useful source of information."

"Right, yeah. Of course."

"Then bring the egg back to your castle, and there you are. The moment word gets out that your castle is under siege by a dragon, you'll have all manner of princes flocking to you. Dragons are like catnip to princes."

"Great." Adrianna couldn't bring herself to muster up any fake enthusiasm. The whole thing was just so bleak, so depressing. A bunch of pompous idiots blustering about her castle, competing to prove themselves by slaughtering a mother dragon who just wanted to get to her egg. And Adrianna would wind up marrying one of them—a dismal prospect. But what other option did she have?

A pretty clock on the mantelpiece rang the hour. "Oh, that'll be my cue," Aurora said brightly, putting down her cup and saucer. "Philip will be coming back from his hunt, so I'd better go and get the spinning wheel upstairs ready. He likes it when we play 'cursed princess', and I prick my finger on the spindle and then pretend to be unconscious while he—"

"That's fantastic, thank you so much for your help," Adrianna said quickly, standing up in such a rush that she almost knocked over a side table. "I'll leave you to your, er, preparations." She would rather stick hot forks in her ear than hear of Prince Philip's proclivities. That man was clearly a bit of a sick puppy if he liked his wife to pretend she was unconscious.

She barely waited for her friend to reply before she hurried out of the sitting room. When the stories told of the Happy Ever After, they never mentioned princes who had fetishes for women who were unconscious.

Nor did they mention making use of spinning wheels in bed. Adrianna had often had the sneaky suspicion that life after the Happy Ever After might not be quite as rosy as the Happy Ever After implied. Now it was more than a suspicion.

But that no longer mattered. She wasn't chasing down a prince for the Happy Ever After. She was keeping her family and her castle safe.

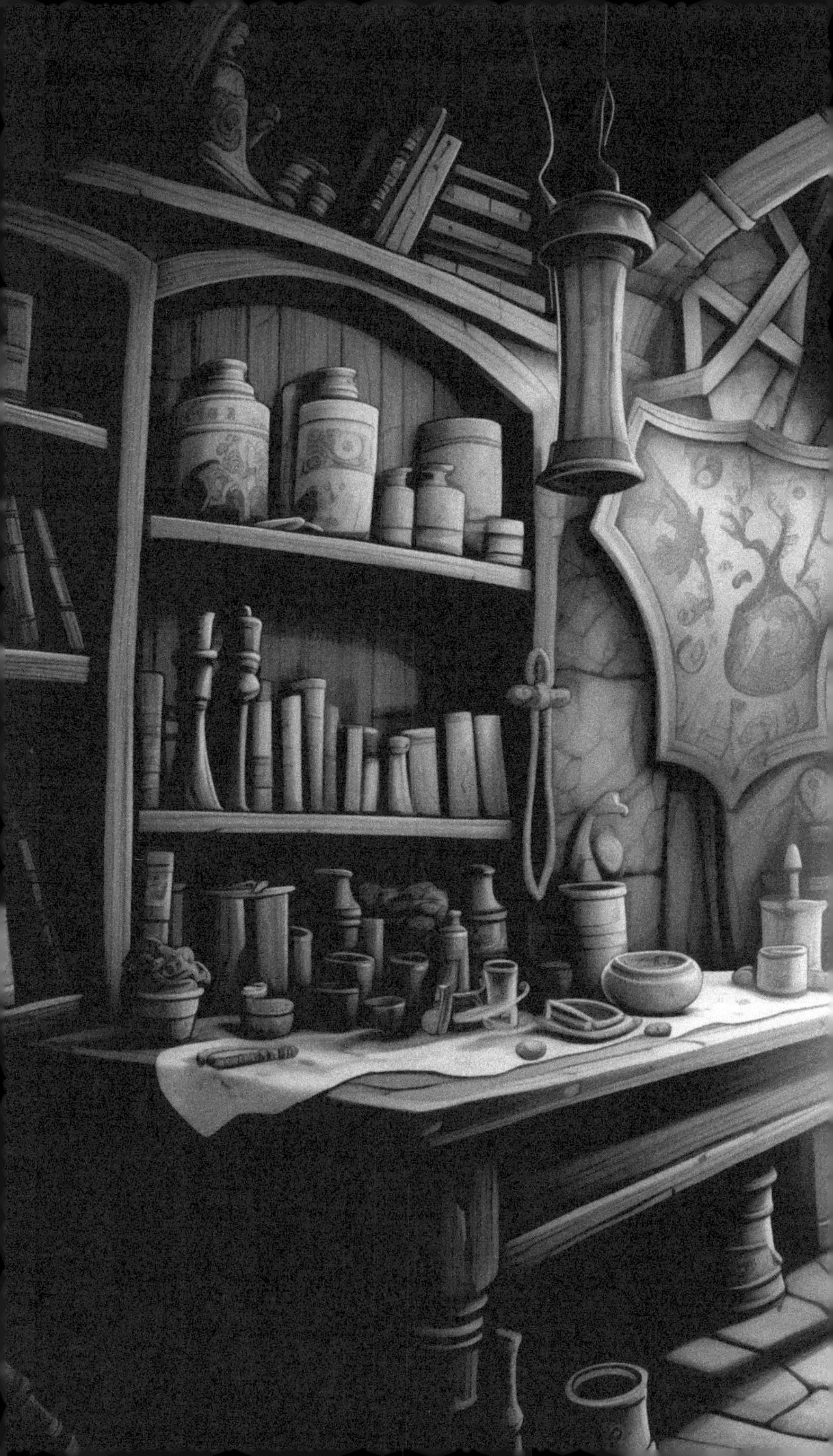

CHAPTER 10

Adrianna rode off at a fast gallop. She had to be grateful that there was a storyline that allowed princesses to ride properly, astride the horse rather than side-saddle. That was a tough storyline to pull off, though. The whole tomboy, tough cookie exterior, creating an antagonistic relationship with the prince at first, but then with the help of the Impossible Odds, things worked out in the end. The prince would overcome the odds, at which point the princess would stop being a tomboy and fall back into rank and into a dress, just in time for the Happy Ever After.

There weren't many success stories with that storyline, but at least it meant that Adrianna could legitimately go out dressed in trousers and a shirt and ride horses properly, something which was forbidden to all other women.

At the same time, though, it really grated on Adrianna that no matter what she was doing or where she was going, she constantly had to be keeping in mind the storylines. Even doing something as stupid as riding a horse had to be in keeping with a storyline. At no point could she just relax and just forget about the whole prince thing and just live her life.

Just thinking about that made her want a glass of wine. No wonder Mirabelle was an alcoholic. This fairytale business was exhausting, and Mirabelle had been around for a long, long time. She didn't speak of the other princesses she had been fairy godmother to before—in fact she refused to say so much as a word about it. But on very rare occasions, Adrianna could detect a certain melancholy in her usually cheerful fairy godmother. A weariness. Probably why she liked spending her time eating chocolate, chasing after the gardener, and drinking wine or port (or brandy).

Adrianna wondered what would happen to Mirabelle once the prince business was taken care of. That was something the Happy Ever After never described—what happened to the hard-working fairy godmothers? Were they retired? Redistributed, most likely. Maybe Adrianna could find a way to settle Mirabelle so she wouldn't have to be redistributed to another princess once Adrianna was married.

Married. A shudder ran down her spine. Adrianna wilfully pushed the thought away. She couldn't afford to think about the marriage and the life that awaited on the other side of it—and the weird fetishes she might have to cater to, if Aurora's situation was anything to go by. A few years of weird fetishes followed by an early death in childbirth. Bleak, bleak, bleak.

No, she wouldn't think of that now. She'd think of it later. For now, the wind was streaming in her hair and her mare was galloping fast, hooves pounding rhythmically against the hard-packed soil of the path, the fields around a green blur.

A small thrill ran down her spine at the thought of

going away on a mission to find the dragon egg. She'd never done anything remotely close to that before. It would be an adventure. Something princesses weren't allowed to have since they always had to wait passively for someone to rescue them.

She pushed her mare faster. Galloping across open fields had always felt like flying to her. She tilted her face up to feel the sun on it. For now, she was free, her family was happy, and the castle remained hers. Everything else was a problem for tomorrow.

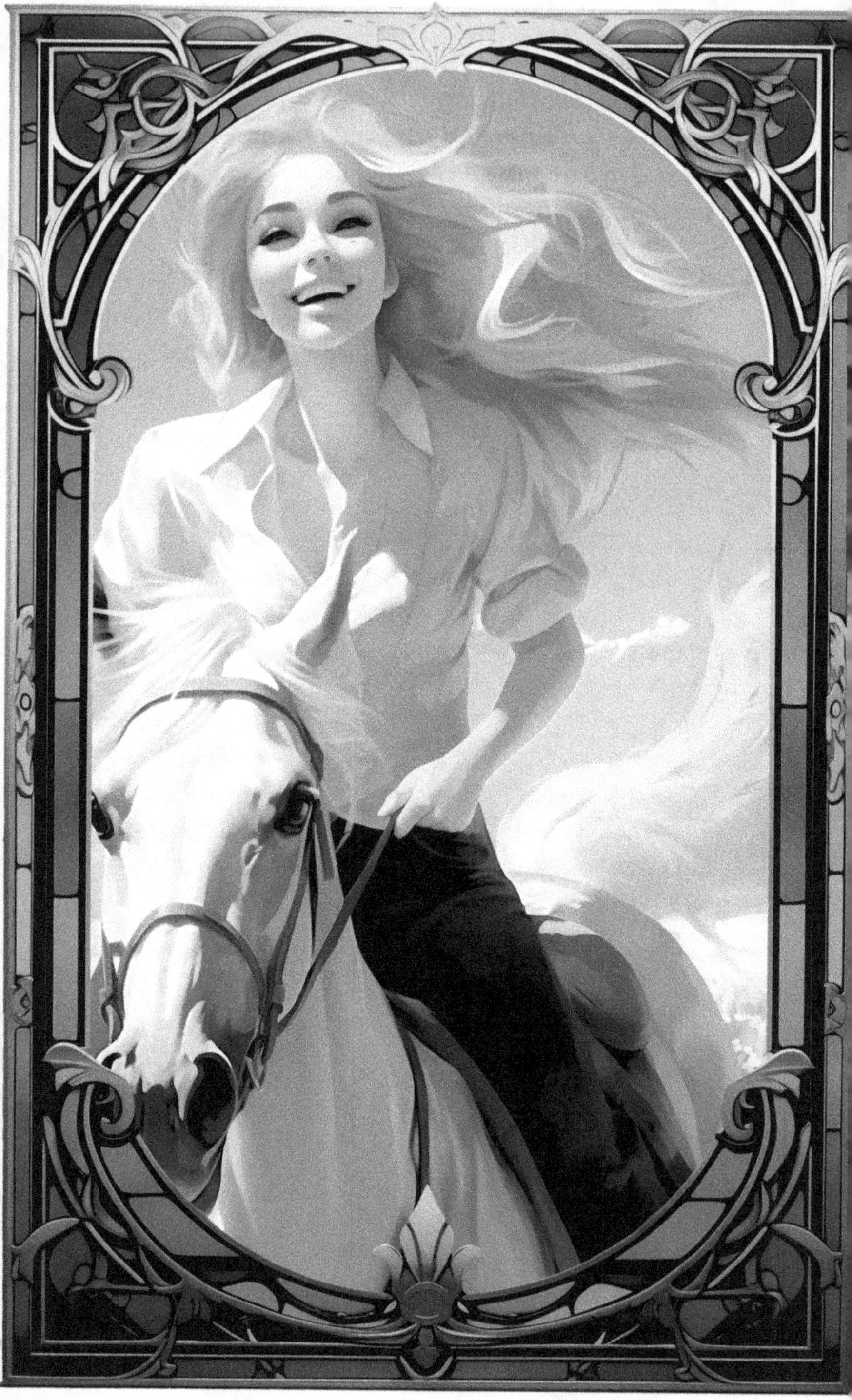

Adrianna arrived at the address Aurora had given her. It was a small, dingy looking shop on the edge of town. The town itself was as pretty as all the towns and villages in Once-Upon-Thyme, with streets of pale cobblestones, neat houses with chimneys that puffed smoke from red-tiled rooftops.

An average, normal building was always neat, smelling of clean herbs. Places of interest, of mystery, were always dingy—this was part of why Adrianna loved her home so fiercely. It had character, intrigue, mystery—it was dingy and dirty and ramshackle, meaning it was most definitely a place of interest.

For now, though, the state of the shop was a good omen, and she felt cheered by the thought that something might finally go right in her life.

She dismounted her mare and grabbed the reins, leading the horse down a side alley where she found a narrow courtyard for tying up horses. She tied her mare with enough space to spare that the horse would be able to dip her head to reach the trough of water.

Adrianna patted the silky shoulder twice, an automatic and almost absent-minded gesture of farewell, and then she walked back to the main street.

The shop had a sign above the door that read 'Zephiera's Store'. Adrianna opened the door to the shop, its glass cloudy with grime. A little bell chimed as she stepped in, announcing her arrival.

It seemed tracking the location of dragon eggs was not the only service the shop provided, its shelves crammed with all manner of goods. Jars of ointments, numerous dried herbs, and a quantity of books cluttered the space. Scientific sketches were pinned to the walls, depicting various animals, including dragons. Complicated, scientific words in cursive script hovered at the edges of thin arrows pointing at different parts of the animals.

One particularly large poster was titled 'How Dragons Benefit the Ecosystem', and beneath it were a myriad of illustrations of plants and animals with a river running through it all and little boxes of text dotted throughout.

The smell that pervaded the place was thick but not unpleasant, and not quite as stale as the outside appearance might suggest. Adrianna couldn't identify what it was, probably because it was a mix of many things, the strongest undercurrent being the pungent scent of some sort of dried herb.

"No," a female voice called out from the back of the shop, where light from the grimy windows failed to penetrate.

"I'm sorry?" Adrianna asked, peering into the gloom. She took a couple more steps into the shop.

"No," the voice repeated.

A woman, probably Zephiera, stepped out from behind the counter at the back. She had to be a little older than Adrianna, but not much more than thirty. Messy auburn hair in a bun that struggled as mightily to contain it as Mirabelle's corset struggled to contain her. A green dress with a filthy hem that spoke of time outdoors, the white sleeves rolled up and heavily stained.

"No what? I haven't asked anything yet," Adrianna said.

"You're a princess, aren't you? No other women wear trousers." Zephiera's tone was far from friendly. In fact, it was downright hostile.

"Um, yes, I am. But..."

"Then the answer is no."

"I haven't asked anything."

"You don't need to ask. I already know what you're here for. I will not give you the location of dragon eggs."

Adrianna's stomach sank. So much for things going well. "But..."

"My aim is to *protect* dragons. What on earth makes you think that I'd give away any of their locations to someone who means to have one killed?" Now Zephiera's tone was downright withering, her eyes flashing angrily.

Which was understandable. Adrianna wished Aurora had explained that this was a dragon protection association, not just a place that tracked dragons. Aurora probably didn't even realise, though—she'd been extremely unconcerned by the fate of dragons in general.

"I didn't realise... I needed to find a dragon, and a friend mentioned—"

"Are you aware of the ravages caused to the dragon population by princes and princesses and the games you lot play?"

"Yes, I've heard that the numbers are down," Adrianna mumbled.

"Down? Dragons are getting close to becoming endangered, thanks to your ridiculous games. *Endangered.* We're working tirelessly to try to help the dragon population recover from the blight that is the royalty, and still the numbers are going down. And all so you can feel good about yourselves, prove to yourselves that you are somehow worthy, because none of you are able to achieve that for yourselves, internally."

Adrianna found herself unable to do much beyond swallowing awkwardly in response to that accusation. Which she couldn't really deny. "I don't... I didn't realise it was so bad."

"Didn't realise, or didn't care?"

"It's not that, it's just… They're dragons. They breathe fire and they're huge—I thought it was incredibly hard to kill one. I had no idea…"

"Of course you didn't. Because you lot don't care about anything beyond your precious storylines and your damn Happy Ever Afters."

At that, Adrianna's own anger flared up. She didn't even want the Happy Ever After, and she was so fed up with the storylines. But her anger dissipated as fast as it came up. She couldn't argue back, given that she *was* trying to follow the storylines and aim for the Happy Ever After. She couldn't pretend to be doing otherwise, and she had no interest in sharing Petunia's sob story and getting any sympathy from Zephiera. That would be a little unbearable, in fact.

Because at the end of the day, she knew that she was in the wrong—she had already felt uncomfortable earlier when Aurora told her about the dragons. Maybe it was for the best. Maybe she should just walk away.

"Please just leave," Zephiera said curtly.

"Fine. Sorry to have bothered you," Adrianna mumbled.

There wasn't much point in doing anything else, anyway. As she turned back to the door, her eyes caught on a sketch of a field mouse, and Alinor came to her mind. As did Aurora's suggestion that she could simply get Mirabelle to obtain the necessary information about the location of the dragon eggs.

Adrianna wasn't sure she had it in her to be this mercenary, this cowardly—to send her fairy godmother to snoop in Zephiera's affairs and steal the information.

If she couldn't get a dragon, her only other option would be to go find some witch and strike a bargain. Get a curse put on her, trade her voice for some advantage, and hope a prince chose her within the witch's deadline. But what if the prince failed to overcome the Impossible Odds? What if she still wasn't enough to spark that level of determination? What if she lost her voice forever, or her legs forever? What if she was turned into a swan, a bird, a doe, and no one chose her, and she was forced to live out her life in that form?

Adrianna's face felt warm and prickly with shame as she walked out of the shop. It wasn't just shame from having to confront her own cowardice—that she didn't have it in her to take those kinds of risks. It was also the shame at the reminder that at the end of the day, she wasn't good enough as she was for a prince to just choose her.

Even Petunia, who was older, not as pretty, was gardening obsessed and had many, many quirks, had been chosen, not once but twice. By Adrianna's father, and now by Charming. Petunia hadn't had to resort to such desperate scheming as to get a witch's curse or a dragon to get a prince's attention. Charming had just noticed her and proposed marriage.

Easy, simple.

Not so for Adrianna. No one wanted her. No, for her, it was securing a dragon or asking a witch to curse her. But the thought of going to a witch, the level of sacrifice and risk it implied, made her feel downright panicked. Getting a dragon was the easiest option, and it would ensure Alinor's safety. Cowardly as it was.

At the end of the day, Adrianna wasn't the hero of the story. She wasn't the one who was expected to do great deeds. That was for princes.

No one expected a princess to do anything other than be pretty and wait passively for someone to rescue her. Courage and bravery were foreign, superfluous, even. The word 'cowardly' wasn't normally used to describe princesses, and yet that was the reality of what was expected of them. To shy away from challenges so someone else could step in and do the hard work.

So if she got Mirabelle to find out the location of the nearest dragon egg, Adrianna would simply be acting in accordance with her nature. Doing what she was designed to be and do. Following the expectations of the world she lived in.

But still, the shame of it failed to abate. She was a princess in a rundown castle who drank wine for breakfast and ate crumble straight from the dish. She wasn't dainty or particularly feminine, other than in her magic-enhanced appearance. She wasn't gentle, she didn't sing to the birds, she didn't spread sweetness and light around her.

Instead, she set up cockroach races in the damp basement and made crude jokes with her fairy godmother and got drunk at inappropriate times of the day as a way to deal with her feelings. She was cowardly and selfish, trying to get what she wanted with minimal risk and discomfort.

In short, she was a terrible princess who was failing to meet the only expectation the world had of her—for a prince to fall in love with her. That was why Charming had looked her over in favour of her stepmother. And now, because of Adrianna's failings as a princess, Alinor's safety hung in the balance, which surely was the greatest shame of all.

So Adrianna would have to get that dragon, consequences be damned. If she had to be even more of a coward to get there, so be it. If she had to plumb the depths of shame, so be it.

One way or another, she would finally redeem herself, and most importantly, she'd keep Alinor safe. And if a dragon had to die for it, well, that was just too damn bad. Life wasn't fair, at the end of the day. She hadn't asked to be a princess any more than the dragon had asked to be a killed by a prince.

But as she slunk out of the shop, knowing she'd get Mirabelle to come back later, Adrianna felt like she needed to wash herself. She had truly reached a new low, and it was an awful feeling.

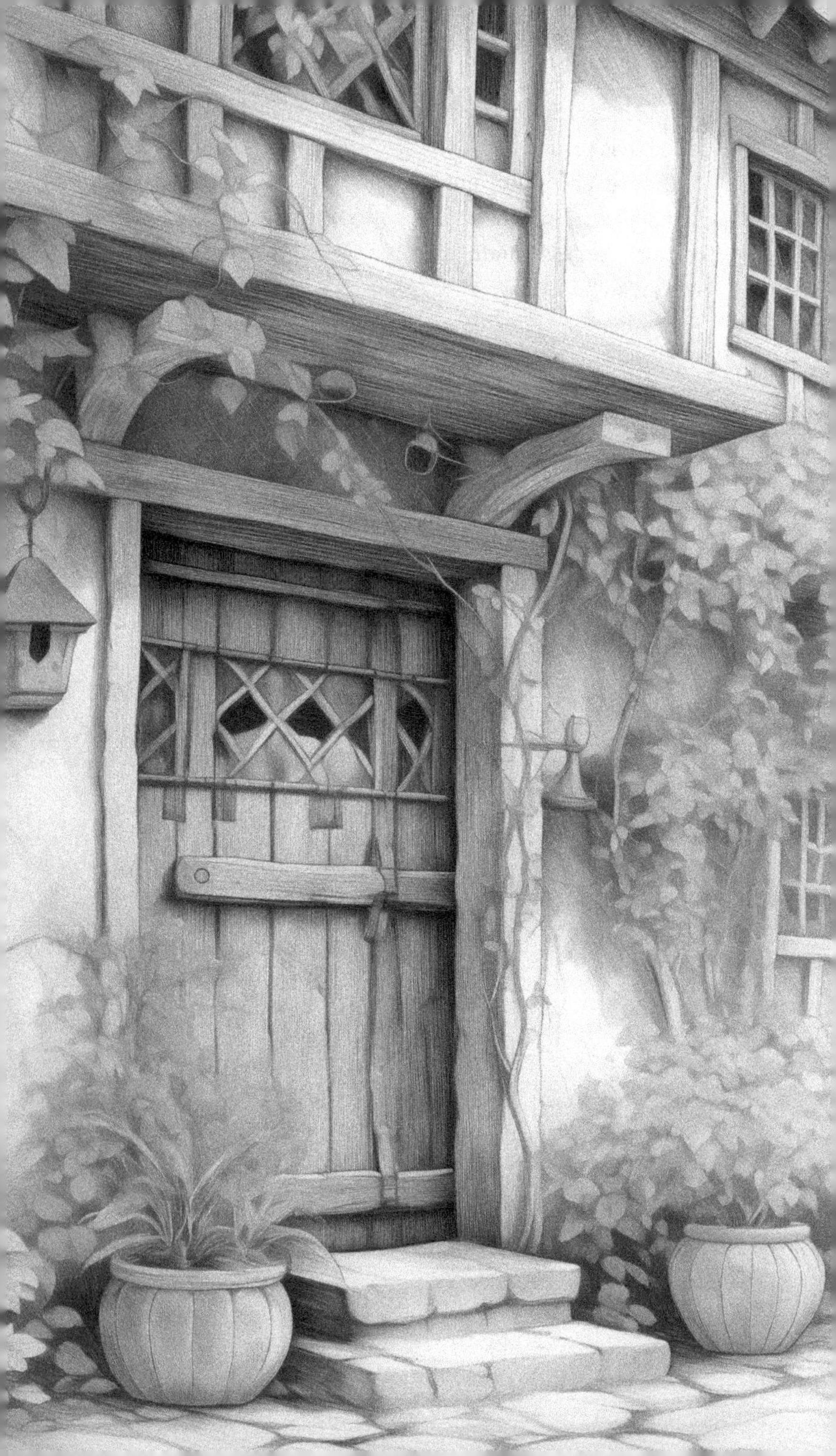

CHAPTER 11

Adrianna returned to the courtyard where she had left her mare, only to find a man thoughtfully attending her, brushing down her shiny coat with a handful of straw while whispering gently.

"Thank you," she said, grateful for something finally going well today.

The man turned, opening his mouth to reply. Adrianna recognised him at once, the dark, curling hair, the tanned complexion, the strong arms and, mostly, the irritating smile.

"You!" they both blurted at each other.

"Do you know how much trouble you caused me yesterday?" Adrianna asked.

The man looked her up and down. "So you *are* a princess. Playing a game yesterday, were you? Is that why you were so annoyed when I called you Princess?"

"None of your damn business," she snapped back.

"And I guess if you're here, you went to see Zephiera. You're after a dragon, aren't you?"

"Like I said, none of your damn business."

He considered her thoughtfully, tossing the straw on

the floor and crossing his arms. "Let me guess. You're going to get your fairy godmother to obtain the information about the location of the egg. But have you really thought things all the way through?"

"Things, what things?" Adrianna replied in spite of herself, not wanting to miss out on any useful information but hating that she had to ask him.

"Once you've found the location of the egg, do you have someone who can help you secure it?"

Adrianna hadn't thought about this at all. "Obviously."

"You hesitated. You don't have anyone, do you? Well, in spite of my better judgement, because I'm so good-natured, I'm prepared to help you."

"I don't need your help."

"No? So you know how to handle a dragon egg without getting burned by it? You know how to move the dragon egg so that the mother follows you and doesn't kill you? How do you think it will happen? You think that you'll just pick up the egg, stick it in your bag, and peacefully return home while the mother gently follows you?"

Flustered, Adrianna attempted and failed to come back with some sort of curt reply. Because he was right. She hadn't given any of this any thought, and more worryingly, she had no idea how to go about any of it.

Why did it all have to be so hard?

"It's as I said—you need my help," the man said with that irritatingly smug smile. It was just like the one Adrianna had so badly wanted to slap off his face the other day.

"And why on earth would you help me?" Adrianna caught herself. That was the wrong line of thinking. "Anyway, I don't need your help. I have a fairy godmother. She can bring the egg back for me."

"Are you quite sure about that?"

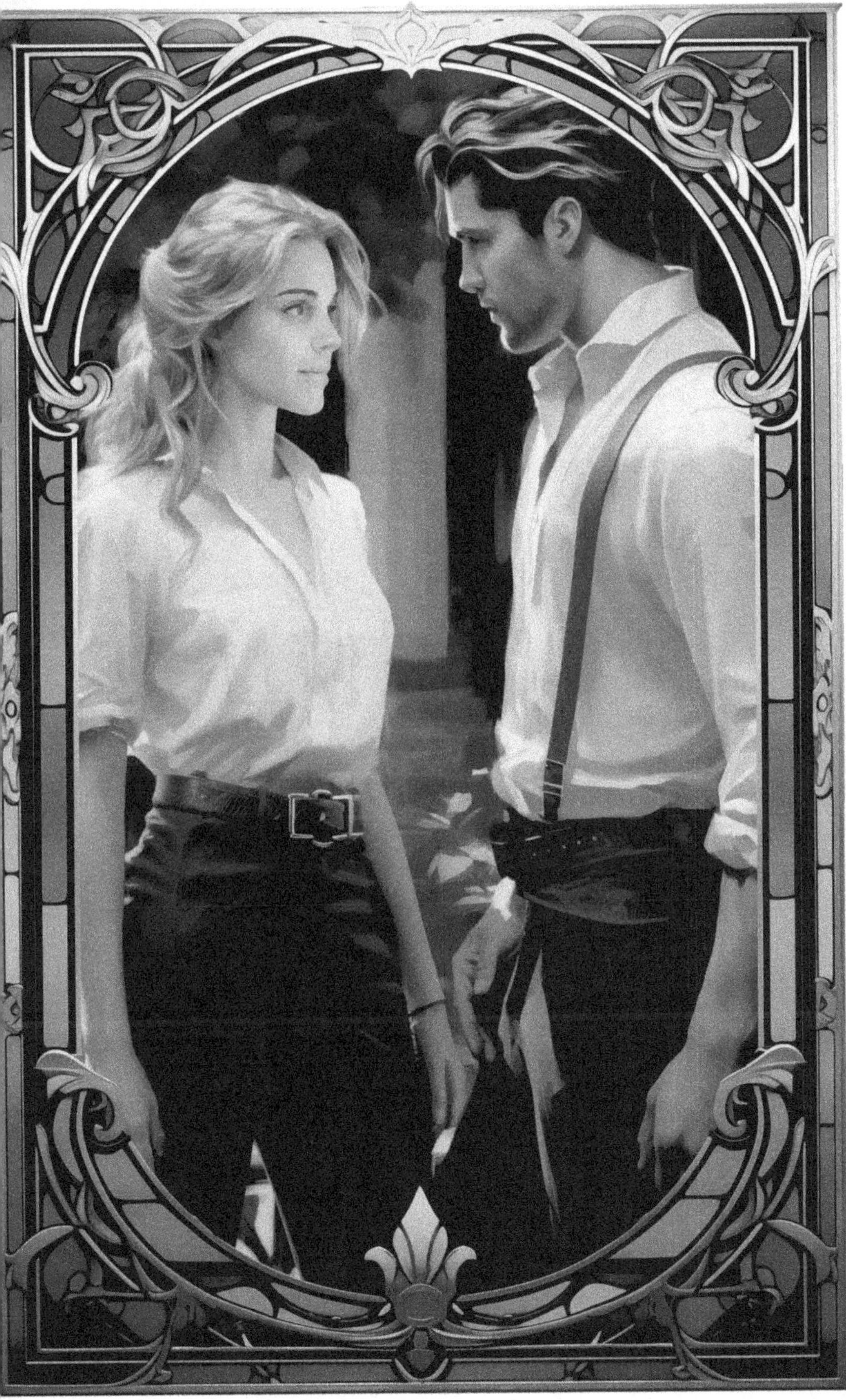

"Of course I'm sure." Adrianna really didn't like the amused expression that now gleamed in the man's eyes. She pushed past him to get to her mare. "You're not used to fairy godmothers, but they can pretty much do anything that a princess needs."

"Lucky you." Except he didn't sound like he meant it in the slightest. "Well, if you find that you need a bit more help than what your fairy godmother can provide, I'll be at the Prince's Arms tonight. Just ask for Sam."

Adrianna scowled at him as she mounted her mare. "There's no need for that. I won't be coming to the Prince's Arms."

"Suit yourself. And will you want to untie your horse before you try leaving?"

Adrianna felt herself go red with embarrassment. She had completely forgotten that her mare was tied up.

Sam moved to her horse's head, gently untying the reins and passing them back to Adrianna. She noticed the way he touched the mare's cheek and whispered something to her, too low for Adrianna to hear. The mare's ears twitched, pointing towards him.

"You're good with horses," she said grudgingly, taking the reins.

"I'm good with all animals. Including dragons."

He turned and walked away before she could reply. Since the opening of the courtyard was narrow, too narrow for two, Adrianna had to wait and watch him leave. Going with him would mean following him out, and her pride wouldn't take that final sting. She had swallowed way too many toads of late. She'd go out by herself, head held high.

Still, she was annoyed that it wasn't her leaving first, forcing him to watch her ride away.

She shook her head. It really didn't matter. She needed to keep her focus and energy for the important thing—securing a dragon first, and then securing herself a prince.

Next stop, talking to Mirabelle.

Unfortunately, Adrianna's day did not improve as she returned to the castle. Her brilliant plan of asking Mirabelle to take care of the dragon egg rapidly proved to not be so brilliant that all.

The first hurdle was to locate her fairy godmother. Since she wasn't in her room, nor in Adrianna's room, and she wasn't in the kitchen sneaking a drink from the brandy bottle, there was only one place she could be.

Adrianna headed out to the garden just in time to cross paths with a harried-looking Lowen. Petunia's voice was ringing out shrilly somewhere behind the rhododendrons, quoting a passage from some book, but she didn't seem to be aware that Lowen was rapidly moving out of hearing range.

He wasn't looking back at her direction though, but was wildly scanning the garden to his left, with the look of a hunted animal fearing being pounced on by a predator.

Adrianna would never understand what Mirabelle saw in the man. He was tall and lanky, all elbows and knees, and surprisingly pale, considering he worked outdoors. Sure, there was a wiry strength to him, his forearms corded with sinew and muscle, but it lacked grace, causing Lowen to move with jerky, birdlike movements. His hair was a salt and pepper halo, his eyes wide, and he perpetually looked like he was strangling himself on his own saliva.

"Yoo hoo, Lowen?" a voice called softly.

Lowen quickly retreated behind a rosebush.

"Mirabelle, there you are," Adrianna said loudly, to capture her fairy godmother's attention and distract her from the gardener, since it would take a heart of stone not to take pity on such a terrified man.

Mirabelle stepped out from beneath a wisteria covered pergola.

"Have you seen—"

"I have made progress with our dragon situation," Adrianna interrupted.

"Hmm?"

"Mirabelle." Adrianna snapped her fingers a couple of times in front of the plump fairy to pull her away from thoughts of the gardener. "I needed you to attend me. We have a dragon to secure, remember?"

"Hmm? Yes, yes." Mirabelle sighed, obviously disappointed to have to tear her attention away from Lowen and onto the situation at hand. "You spoke to Aurora?"

Adrianna told Mirabelle of her errand with Aurora, moving as she did and forcing her fairy godmother to move as well to follow the conversation. She stopped when the fairy had her back to the rosebush behind which Lowen was cowering. Adrianna had expected him to make a hasty exit, maybe to even crawl away, but he seemed content to remain behind his rosebush. In fact, he even seemed to be spying on Mirabelle from between the leaves.

Adrianna might have wondered what exactly he was playing at if she didn't already have so much on her mind. Petunia's voice droned on in the background, still quoting from her book, apparently unaware that Lowen was no longer at her side but was instead gawking at Mirabelle from behind a bush.

It wasn't until Adrianna explained her plan of getting

Mirabelle to magically transport the dragon egg back to the castle that Mirabelle's attention finally snapped to her.

"Are you quite mad, dear?" Mirabelle looked flabbergasted.

"What?"

"You want me to move a dragon egg?"

"Yes."

"A dragon egg, Adrianna. A *dragon* egg."

"Yes. That's what we've been talking about this whole time. What's the big deal? You can move things around—you rearranged the entire orchard so that the prince would ride past it when he arrived on our grounds."

"Yes, because it was an orchard."

"If you're going to quote the obvious at me, I'm not magically going to understand what you mean, not unless you give me the ability to read your mind."

Mirabelle gave an impatient huff, and Adrianna felt a twinge of regret for having spoken sharply. None of this was Mirabelle's fault, after all, and the fairy was nothing if not a great help. Adrianna was being short with everyone at the moment—the stress of her situation was clearly getting to her.

"An orchard has no more magic than a stone," Mirabelle explained. "No more than the soil beneath our feet. That is to say that it has some magic, same as every living thing—although some living things have more magic than others..." Mirabelle briefly cast a glance around her, searching for Lowen. Not seeing him, she pouted, disappointed, and continued. "So something like an orchard, I can completely control with my magic. But dragons have their own magic. I am no more capable of moving a dragon egg than you are. In fact, I am less capable—our magics cannot interact. I'm sorry, dear, I thought Aurora would have told you. In this, I am utterly useless to you. Locating the dragon I can do, but that's as far as my magic will go."

Adrianna let forth a torrent of curses, all the more heated for the memory of how smug Sam had looked. He must have known—he must have known that Mirabelle wouldn't be able to move the dragon egg.

"Bastard," Adrianna said through gritted teeth.

Because now she was left with only one course of action. Go to the Prince's Arms, where she had no doubt that he would be expecting her.

Smugly.

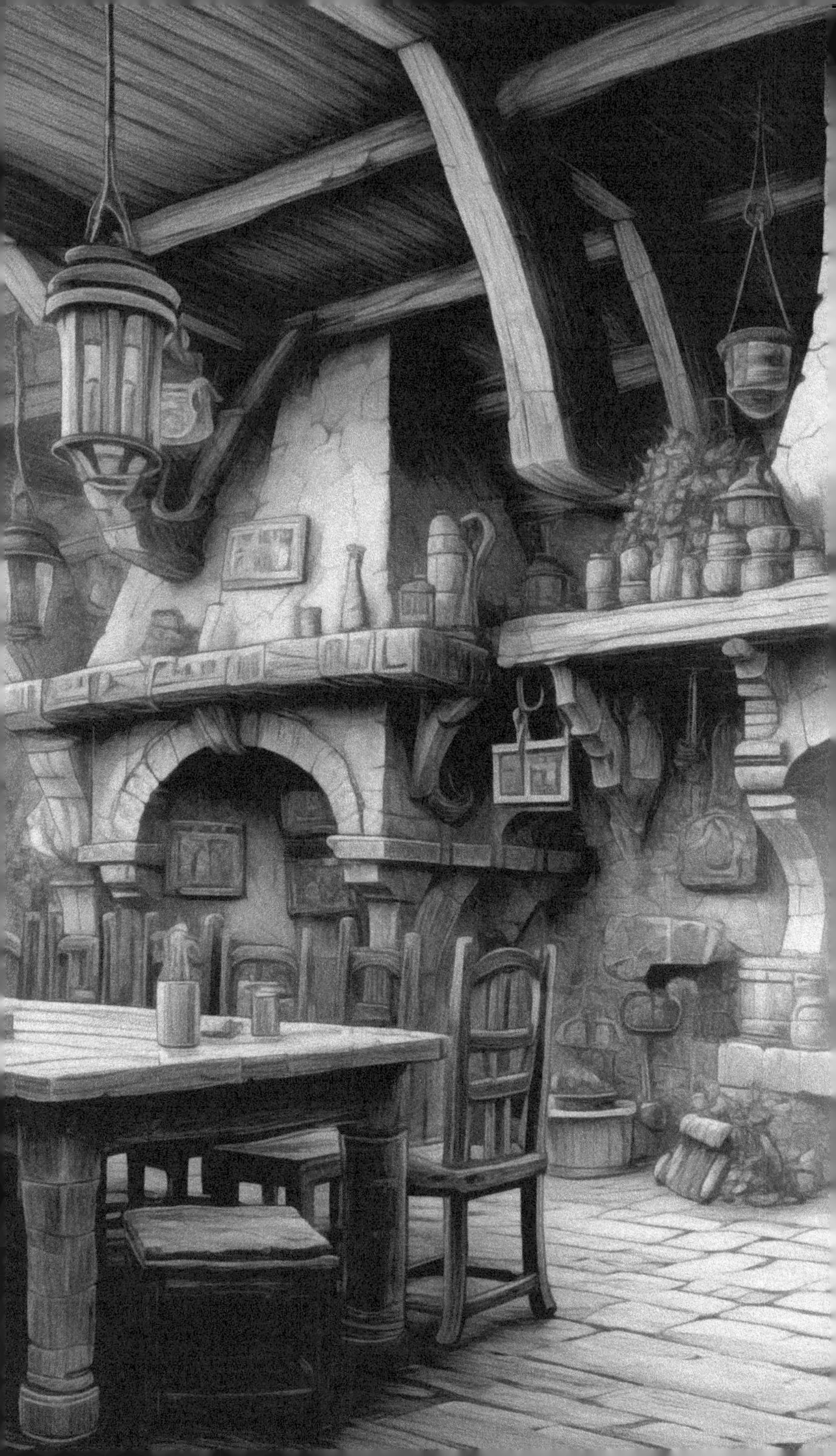

CHAPTER 12

The Prince's Arms turned out to be a surprisingly rowdy place. Adrianna had expected Sam to suggest meeting somewhere quiet with a few patrons hunched over pewter tankards of beer. Instead, the main room was filled with people—men and women—talking and laughing loudly.

In a corner, a man played an energetic tune on a fiddle, while another beat out a frenetic rhythm on a bunch of wooden cowbells. Three waitresses slid between the many tables carrying either heaving trays of beer tankards, or armfuls of empties. They all looked like each other and like the man behind the counter—clearly the barkeep and their father.

The room was warm, almost stuffy from so many bodies in an enclosed space, but it wasn't unpleasant, far from it. If anything, Adrianna could feel the warmth drawing her in, making her want to be a part of the cheerful crowd. Her belly rumbled as one of the waitresses, having gotten rid of her empty tankards, passed in front of her, carrying a tray laden with four large meat pies. The smell of the buttery pastry and spiced meat filled Adrianna's nose, mixing with the yeasty smell of the beer.

Adrianna scanned the room to find Sam. She could ask after him, as he'd suggested, but she preferred to find him herself and keep her business private. She hadn't prepared an excuse in case someone asked why she was looking for him, something she should have thought of in advance. Standing at the pub's threshold, she felt too nervous, too scattered to come up with a convincing lie on the spot.

As her gaze reached by far the loudest, most raucous table, she spotted him. He was throwing his head back and roaring with laughter. It was such a genuine laugh, such a full belly laugh, that Adrianna realised she was smiling in response without meaning to.

She straightened her face, mildly annoyed. She wasn't here to socialise. And yet, for the first time in a very long time, Adrianna found herself hesitating because she felt shy. She couldn't remember the last time she'd felt this way. Awkward, sure—that pretty much described every single ball she went to, largely because she was having to play someone other than who she was, someone she didn't even want or aspire to be.

But this was something else. There was no expectation for her to fulfil right now, no role for her to play, because this wasn't part of any storyline. She didn't need to perform, to convince. She didn't need to try to be dainty or feminine. No one expected her to be gentle, kind, graceful, or anything of the sort.

Instead, she would be approaching as herself—a rather daunting prospect, made all the more daunting by the fact that she would be approaching quite a large, rowdy group. She didn't have the ballgown, the complex ball etiquette, the other princesses, or even Mirabelle to hide behind.

She suddenly wished she could turn around and go back to the castle. She'd pour herself and Mirabelle a glass of wine, and they could talk about how ridiculous the whole situation was. That was, after all, how she dealt with most situations. But of course, if she did that, she would eventually run out of time and options and find herself unable to drink wine with Mirabelle ever again. And then there was the matter of Alinor and of the castle.

Still, she hesitated, hovering at the entrance of the pub, her awkwardness growing such that it was nearly unbearable. Sam caught sight of her and raised a hand up, waving her over.

She should have turned tail earlier. Left right away and found some other way to proceed. Because now that he had seen her, she really couldn't leave, not without adding public embarrassment to her cowardice. It turned out there was a limit to how many blows her pride was willing to take.

Feeling her face grow steadily warmer and praying she wasn't blushing, she headed over to the table. She realised she'd have to find a discreet way to tell Sam why she had come—she didn't want the whole table to know her business. But her mind was growing more and more blank as she approached, until she had no idea what on earth she would say.

Thankfully, she didn't have to join the group and speak to Sam in front of them all. He stood up, said something to his companions, and came towards her. Adrianna found herself incredibly grateful for his consideration in doing this. He was still smiling as he reached her side, and she was forced to admit that although he wasn't a particularly handsome man—at least not compared to princes who were blessed with sickening good looks at birth—he had a nice, warm smile that was framed by two dimples and that lit up his face.

"Come this way." He took hold of her elbow and guided her towards a nearby empty table. Adrianna found herself grateful again that he was taking the lead. It gave her a bit of time to compose herself.

Sam got them both settled and ordered them two mulled ciders.

"I know it's still early in the year for mulled cider, but Bethany's cider is second to none—trust me." He winked at Adrianna.

"I've never tried mulled cider," she admitted.

"Well then, even better that I ordered you one. It will help relax you as well. You looked very lost just now, at the entrance. Like a little lost lamb."

Adrianna wasn't sure if he was mocking her. The waitress brought the mulled ciders over, saving her from having to figure out an answer. Adrianna had to recognise that it was delicious. The spices were an explosion of flavour, and the warmth of the drink was comforting.

Sam took a sip of his own cider and leaned back in his chair. "So, what will it be, Princess?"

This time, there was no mistaking it—he was mocking her. Far more comfortable territory than the earlier ambiguity. "Is that really sarcasm over the word 'princess'?" she sniffed.

"It is whatever you want it to be."

Adrianna rolled her eyes at the cheap line. "Is this really what passes for humour among the common folk these days?"

"I can't speak for all common folk any more than you can speak for all princesses." Sam frowned. "Why did you take such great offence at me using the word 'princess' before, by the way, when you clearly are one?"

He was talking loudly, far too loudly for Adrianna's liking. "Shhh," she hissed, glancing around to see whether anybody was listening to the conversation. "I don't want people here to know who I am."

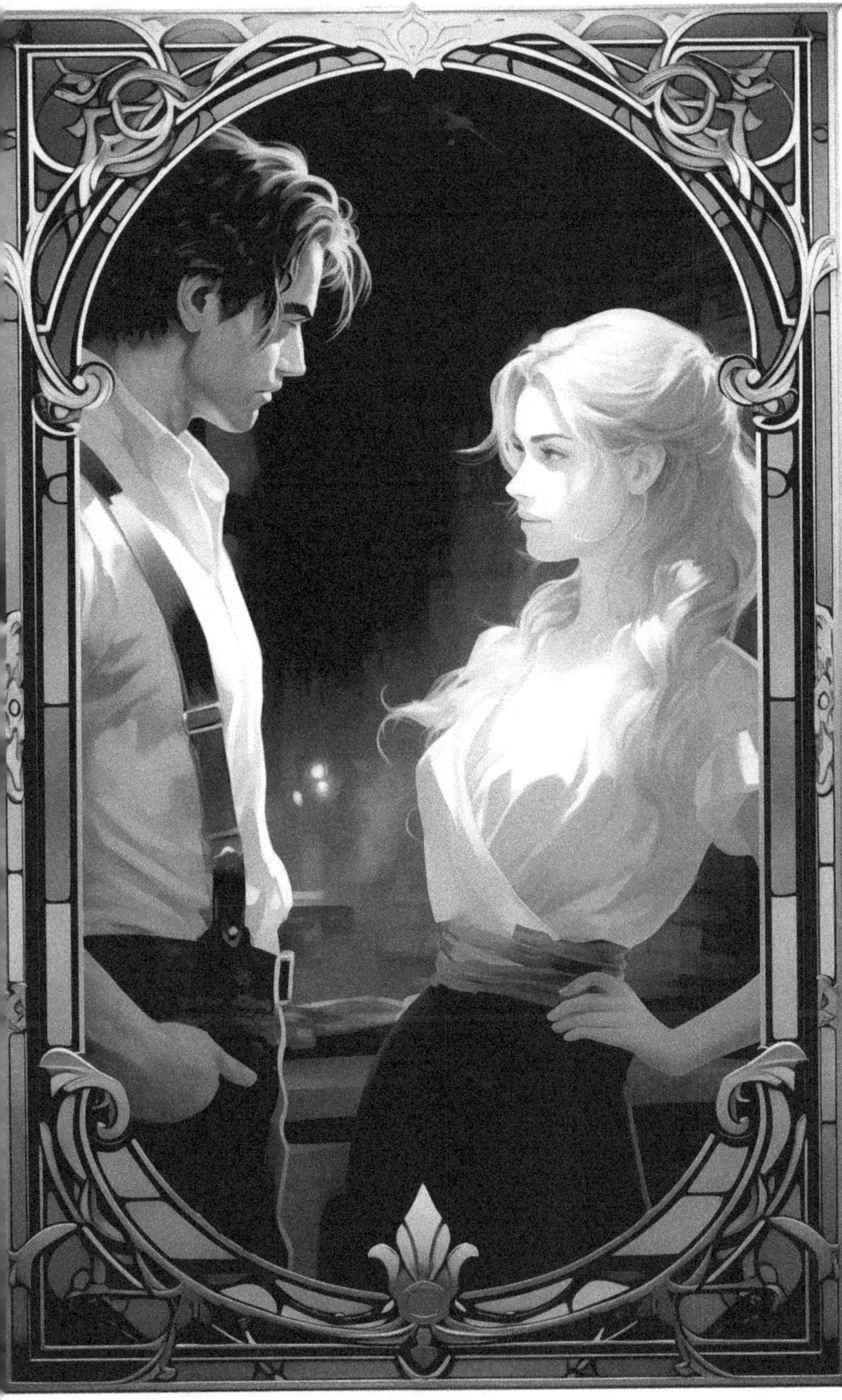

The curiosity left his face, his expression closing off. "Why? Because you're embarrassed to be seen with me?"

"This may come as a shock to you, but not everything is about you. I want my business to be private, that's all."

"Ah. You're embarrassed that you need me to get you a dragon in order for your precious storyline to work."

That was, of course, exactly the problem. It was embarrassing enough that she wasn't sufficiently attractive for a prince to fall in love with, that she had to go to such lengths to get someone interested in her. But it grated on her, oh, did it grate on her, that Sam was aware of it.

"I'm not going to repeat myself over and over—my business is private, and I want it to stay that way. How I feel has nothing to do with you."

"Seems I touched a nerve," Sam said smugly. "So, did you speak to your fairy godmother?"

"You know, I've never slapped someone before, not properly. But seeing the smug expression on your face right now, I don't know why, but my right hand is tingling."

"That's no way to start going into business with someone."

"Neither is being an insufferable ass."

Sam threw back his head and laughed. "I like you," he told her. "You're a lot more interesting than the last couple of princesses I met—simpering and bland, they were."

Adrianna was once again at a loss for what to reply, so she brought the conversation back to the thing she was here to talk about. "You may have been right about my fairy godmother," she said grudgingly. "So, go on, let's hear it. What's your fee to help me bring back the dragon egg?"

"What if I told you it was a kiss?"

She rolled her eyes again. "We both know that's not true. I wouldn't dream of hiring you if all you required was a kiss—that would mean your skills are of no value."

"You really don't value your kisses very highly, then."

Adrianna was flustered, yet again. He had an uncanny ability when it came to doing that. She steamrolled on rather than allowing the truth of that statement to land. "Anyway, you can go climb up a poison ivy covered tree if you think there's any possible situation in which I would be prepared to kiss you."

His smile widened. "I hope you're not expecting that I'll take that as a challenge." Adrianna opened her mouth to reply, but he continued before she could speak. "You had the right of it before, of course. I wouldn't just charge you a kiss for something as dangerous as helping you secure a dragon. That level of stupidity is reserved for princes, who seem to think it's worth going into combat against such a powerful creature, just to win the approval of a woman they don't even know."

Adrianna bit her lip. Part of her wanted to respond to this, to agree, because she felt the same way. To ask if all the common folk thought this way. To ask Sam if he thought a world would be possible without the storylines that ruled and ruined the lives of princes and princesses.

But she didn't have the luxury of considering such ideas. She wasn't going to change the world all by herself, and she needed to keep Alinor in mind. Nothing was more important. So she had to work with the stories. She had to work within the rules of her world. At the end of the day, she was only a princess, not a hero.

"You have no idea what you're talking about," she told Sam curtly to end that line of conversation.

"Don't I? You're luring a dragon to your castle just so that a prince will be able to come along and slaughter it, and all for what? So you get the validation of being chosen by him? I mean, do you realise how ridiculous the whole thing is? The amount of destruction that is brought on the world just so that a bunch of insecure people can feel good about themselves? And what about that dragon? It hasn't done anything to you. It's just living its life far from here, minding its own business, minding its egg—minding her egg, since it will be a female—and you're going to get her killed."

"If I had another choice, I would take it, but this is the way the world works, and I don't get a say in the matter."

"There's always another choice."

Adrianna looked down at her cider tankard. "Not for someone like me." Her voice came out more low and with more pain in it than she had intended.

She looked up sharply to find Sam regarding her with a slightly puzzled look edged with something that may have been approaching concern. Adrianna tossed her head to dismiss the moment.

"Keep your judgements to yourself—I'm not hiring you for your thoughts," she told him. "I have no interest in your opinions on the matter. And anyway," she added, having just found a point she could score against him, "If you truly think that and yet you're still prepared to help me with the dragon, what does that make you?"

"A realist."

"Great. Then don't reproach me for being the same. You're going to bring the dragon to the slaughter every bit as much as me. Now, are we going to keep dancing around the matter all night, or are you actually going to tell me what your fee is?"

Sam took a gulp of his mulled cider, regarding Adrianna, his eyes shrewd. Then he gave a small smile, as if he were enjoying this.

And named a number that had Adrianna spluttering into her drink.

"Are you mad?"

"No, I assure you, I'm quite sane."

"Do you really think I'm going to pay that much just to…"

"Tell me, how many other people have come forward to help you secure your dragon? And beyond that, do you know anybody else who can help? Can you even afford to advertise, to let it be known that you're having to get a dragon yourself? Isn't that going to mess with your precious storylines?"

"So you think you have me over a barrel, is that it?"

He cocked his head and gave her a suggestive look. "Well, that's not the most unpleasant of thoughts."

Adrianna felt her face grow hot. "Pull your mind out of the gutter. I don't go for paupers."

"Well, lucky for me, apparently a small fortune will be making its way to me in the very near future."

Adrianna shook her head. "Your price is too high."

"It's reasonable given what you want me to do. And before you think that you can negotiate, I'm not budging from this number. I have something in mind—a project, if you will—that I need the money for. So it's not worth it for me to do this job for anything less than what I need. If I'm going to help bring a dragon to the slaughter, it will have to truly be worth my while."

Something in his expression convinced Adrianna that he was speaking the truth. The problem was that she didn't have that kind of money. Not even close.

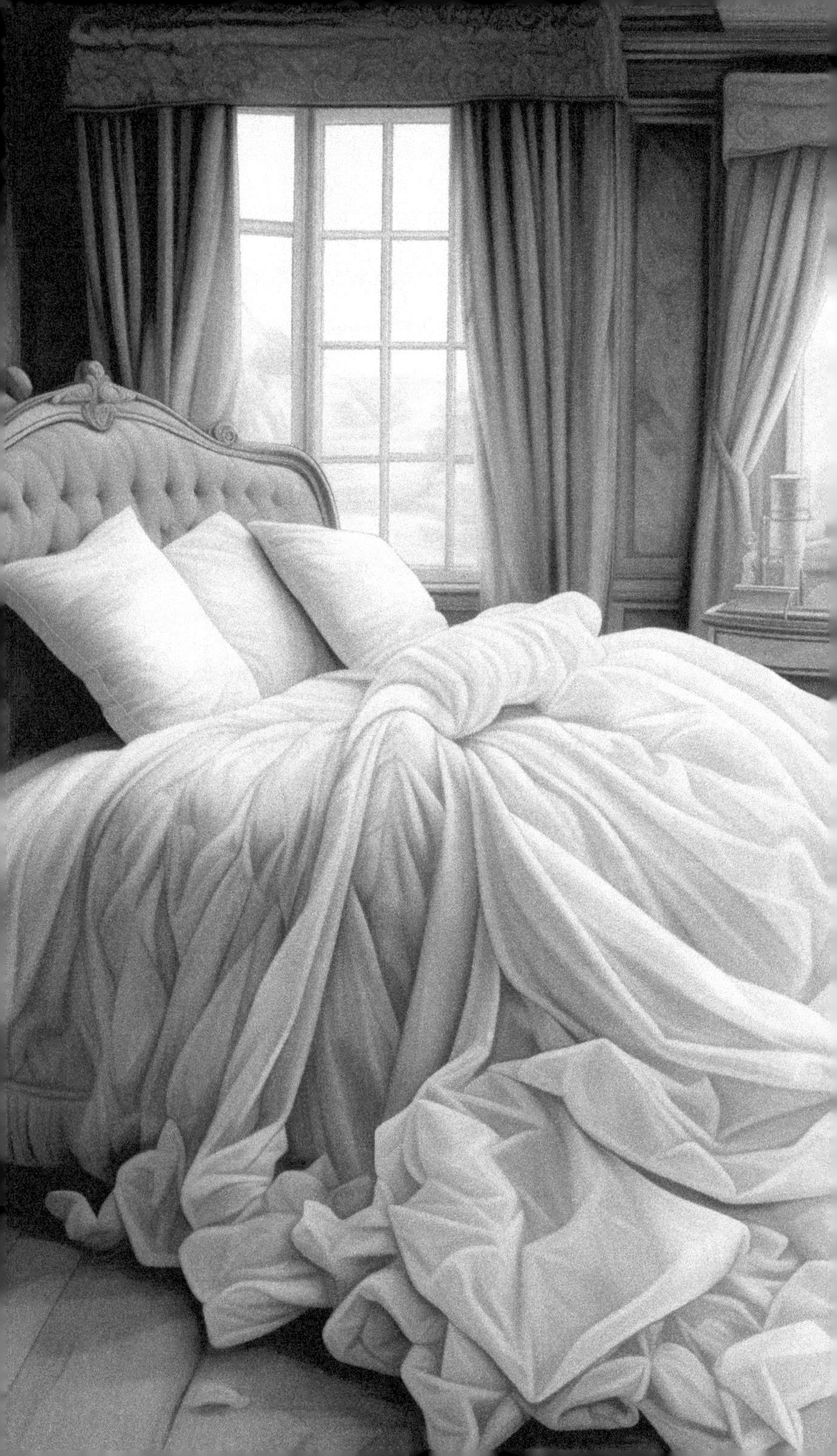

CHAPTER 13

Adrianna wasn't surprised to find Mirabelle awake when she returned to the castle, in spite of the lateness of the hour. Which was good, given that Adrianna needed to ask for her help. Her fairy godmother was waiting for Adrianna in her bedroom, sipping brandy, reclining in her usual spot on the divan. The usual chocolates were also in evidence, although there weren't many truffles left in the bowl. That there were any left at all was a testament to Mirabelle's restraint—normally the truffles were as likely to survive as Lowen was likely to be left alone.

"How did it go?" she asked, sitting up, her face alight with interest. "By the way, I didn't ask you before, but is he handsome?"

Adrianna frowned and kicked off her boots. "Why does that matter?"

Mirabelle took a hearty gulp of brandy. "It always matters, darling. The point is to have a good life, is it not? To do that, you must enjoy the journey now, not wait until the Happy Ever After to be happy." She grinned, raising her glass. "And the fact that you didn't reply to my question means that he *is* handsome, otherwise you would simply have said no, and probably said something funny about how he looks. Wonderful, darling, wonderful. So much the better. Always better to have something nice to look at while going about your business."

Adrianna snorted. "He's not. Handsome. I mean, he has a nice smile—all right, he has a very nice smile, but—"

"That's plenty to work with. Lowen doesn't even have that, and I find him *irresistible*. Your eyes have just been burnt from too much time spent looking at princes, so you have to adjust, that's all. Now, stop gushing over the new man in your life and tell me how it went."

"I'm not gushing," Adrianna said crossly, padding barefoot over to the sideboard where Helga had thoughtfully left a bottle of wine and a glass. "And he's not the new man in my life. In fact, he's not in my life. I mean, he is, but…" She threw Mirabelle an annoyed look over her shoulder. The fairy looked very happy with herself. "Stop looking so pleased with yourself," Adrianna grumbled.

She poured out the wine and sank into a large, comfortable armchair, tucking her feet under herself. The burgundy velvet upholstery was so worn it looked like the chair had mange, but the stuffing had moulded itself perfectly to her body over the years, so that she always felt perfectly cocooned when she sat in it.

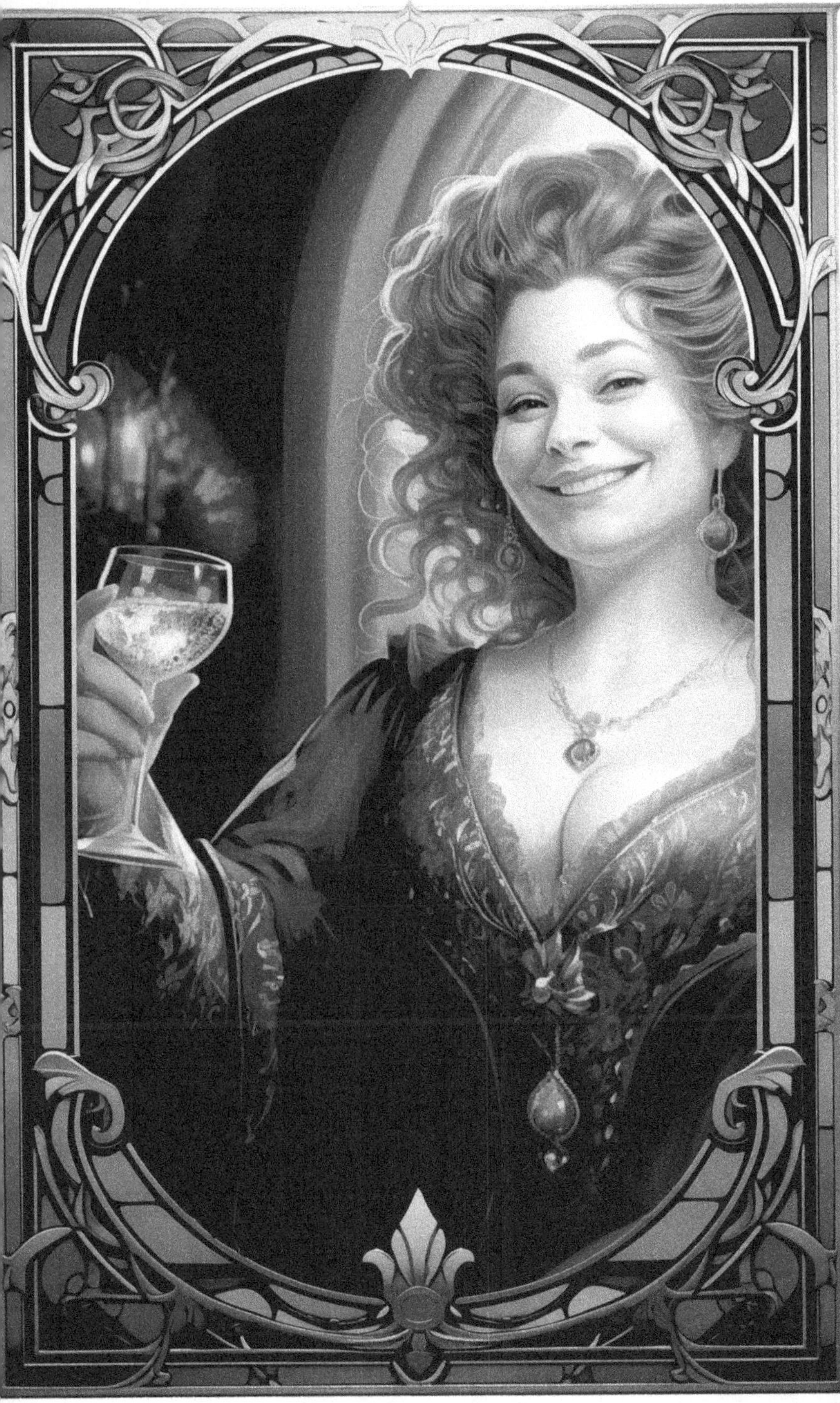

"The meeting went as well as can be expected, I suppose. His price is... really steep." Adrianna took a sip—well, a gulp—of her wine. "Is there any way you can help with that?"

Adrianna couldn't quite keep the hopefulness from her tone. She knew the rules, of course. Fairy godmothers were able to produce coins using their magic, however, since everybody and their dog had a fairy godmother, these coins weren't accepted as any kind of valuable currency. In fact, they weren't accepted as any kind of currency at all.

The only coins accepted by common folk were of a kind that could not be produced by fairy godmothers. These coins had a magic all of their own, which meant they couldn't be tampered with or reproduced or duplicated by fairy godmothers.

It was why Adrianna and her family were so poor. If it was as simple as a fairy godmother creating coins, every single princess would live in a lavish palace. But wealth was one of the few things princes and princesses could not fake.

"You know I can't do that," Mirabelle said regretfully.

"I know you can't create coins I can use to pay him with, but isn't there something else you could do? Hypnotise him to make him think we've paid him?"

Adrianna took another large gulp of wine, and then another. She'd made the decision to do whatever was necessary to secure that dragon and keep Alinor safe, consequences be damned. If she had to screw Sam over in the process, well... His warm, open smile came back to her. He was annoying, no doubt about it, but whether he deserved to be screwed over... Adrianna wasn't sure anyone actually deserved that.

Another low. Another new level of cowardice for her to mine to its full potential. Funny how being a morally bankrupt coward wouldn't stop her from getting a prince, so long as she was pretty, passive, and in trouble.

"I can't do that either. I can't affect him to make him think he's been paid." Mirabelle shook her head. "This is another area in which I am as powerless as you, darling. In this you will have to secure the money the way any pauper would. Borrow it."

Adrianna nodded and knocked back her wine. She'd been afraid of that. Well, since she had already decided she'd be as morally reprehensible as she needed to be to reach her ends, she might as well make the same commitment to no longer care about her pride. She'd go and humiliate herself one more time in the morning and hope that would be enough to get things on the way.

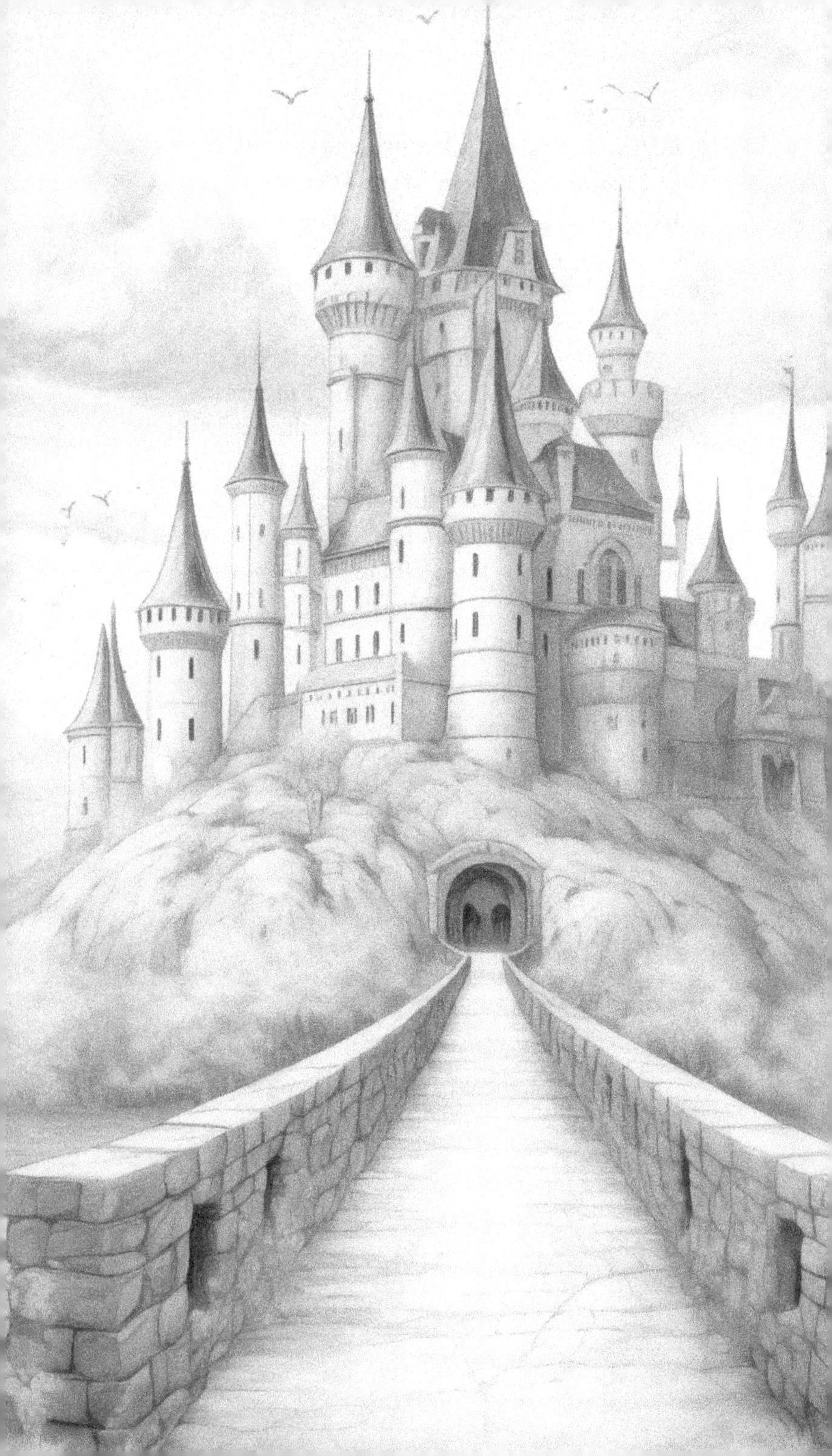

CHAPTER 14

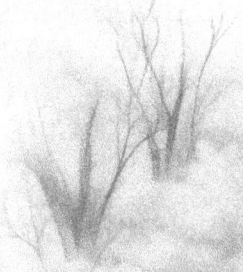

"Two visits in two days. Well, well."

At least that was what Adrianna thought Aurora said. It was hard to understand her speech right now. She was dressed every bit as beautifully as last time, in an emerald-green dress trimmed with gold. But this time there was no spinning wheel in evidence. Instead, she was reclining on the cushions of a sofa, but she was leaning so far back that she was almost lying down. Her arms rested stiffly on either side of her, and her eyes were half-lidded. If not for the gleam of her gaze visible in the slit of her eyelids, she'd have looked unconscious. What distorted her speech was that she seemed to be attempting to speak without moving her lips, which, naturally, was a tricky thing to achieve.

Adrianna took all of this in with some alarm. "Um, are you... Aurora, is something wrong?"

They were in a different sitting room this time, larger and a little less feminine if every bit as luxurious as the last one. The room was decorated in duck-egg blue and light-grey, simple and light. A number of plush armchairs and sofas were dotted about the room in clusters, inviting conversation.

Adrianna glanced over at the other side of the room where Prince Philip—or was it King Philip?—was sitting in a chair, one leg crossed over the other, reading a book.

Shouldn't he be concerned by the state of his wife?

He looked every bit the same as every other prince Adrianna had met. Handsome—that went without saying—with wavy brown hair and blue eyes, and of course a very straight nose. In fact, it was hard to differentiate him from the myriad of other princes Adrianna had met in her time. Generically handsome, was how Adrianna now thought of it. Yes, they had nice, symmetrical features, but there was something truly dull about all those perfect faces. They lacked character, they lacked flaws to make them interesting.

No, Adrianna was not going to compare them to another face she'd gotten to know recently, one who wasn't as handsome but had dimples, and a wide smile... No, she just wasn't going there.

"Philip likes me to be as close to unconscious as possible when I'm not spinning," Aurora whispered through her stiff, barely moving lips. "He has a thing for unconscious women."

Adrianna looked over at Philip, who turned a page in his book, as if this was completely normal. The paper rustled loudly in the silence.

"I suppose that makes sense, given that he came for you when you were asleep from your curse," Adrianna whispered back, doing her best to hide her distaste.

Philip turned another page, but he paused midway and looked up, considering Adrianna with a frown. She bit down the urge to ask if her talking to his wife ruined the illusion for him.

Philip continued looking at her, obviously displeased.

He stood up suddenly, snapping his book shut. "I believe I shall go for a walk," he announced to the room.

Nobody cares what you do, Adrianna replied silently, wishing she could voice the thought and knowing that would be a terrible idea. How did princesses believe that Happy Ever Afters were worth all the hassle and effort it took to get there? Spinning wheels in bed and pretending to be unconscious—that seemed like an utterly depressing way to live.

The moment Philip walked out of the room, Aurora returned to normal, her face once again animated.

"Thank goodness, I was starting to get a cramp. Be a dear and help me sit up?" She stretched out both hands. "These cushions are impossible to get out of when I'm wearing a corset."

Adrianna yanked her up to sitting.

"That's better." Aurora smiled.

"How can you stand it?" Adrianna asked, genuinely curious. "Isn't it awful to pretend to be unconscious?"

"Not really, it just means not moving for a while, that's all. Sometimes it's a bit boring, but I'm used to it by now."

"But that means you're little more than an object to him if you're never talking. No?"

Aurora shrugged delicately. "We talked a lot more back when he thought I was a pretty peasant girl he'd met in the woods, that's true. These days, he's less interested in conversation. Who knows, maybe princes only like to talk to paupers."

Adrianna found herself scrambling for something to reply that wasn't pitying or awkward.

"Anyway," Aurora said brightly, "How did you get on finding out about the dragon eggs?"

Adrianna couldn't tell if the brightness was genuine or fake, but she had enough to contend with not to have the energy to dig into someone else's prince-related problems.

She explained about the little man's anger at her presence in the shop—Aurora seemed both unsurprised and unconcerned.

When Adrianna relayed Sam's offer, Aurora looked interested.

"What price did he quote you?"

"An eye watering one."

Aurora rolled her eyes to the heavens. "They're so expensive, those men who handle dragons."

"You had to hire one too?"

"Of course! I wasn't about to do it myself." Aurora scoffed as if this was the most ridiculous concept, and Adrianna quickly agreed. And yet she couldn't forget that little tremor of excitement she'd felt at the thought of going after the dragon egg herself. But there was no storyline where a princess did something like that. Not one.

"The thing is, it's more money than I can afford," she said carefully.

"Ah." Aurora shook her head. "I'm sorry, darling, but I can't loan you the money."

Adrianna didn't know if she was relieved at not having had to actually speak the request, or mortified at being turned down before she had even asked.

"You have to understand, the chances of success of such excursions are rather low," Aurora explained. "I have no doubt you will achieve all of your goals, but if you don't, what then? You will be unable to pay me back, and where will that leave us?" She darted a glance at the door. "The thing is, Philip is very close to his purse strings. Very. I lack for nothing, of course. Imagine the shame for him if I wasn't dressed beautifully or lavished with luxuries every day. But for anything else…"

"He's tighter than a duck's arse?" Adrianna asked.

Aurora hiccuped with shock and gave her a wide-eyed look. "You did not just say that."

"I... No, I meant..." There were no storylines for a princess who used expressions like that, either. Not that it had stopped Adrianna until now, but she had always been careful to keep it for the castle and Mirabelle. "I'm not sure what came over me. Maybe some little curse or something."

"Hmm. I hope so." Aurora gave her a look as if Adrianna suddenly didn't smell so good. "Anyway, Philip would be quite furious with me if I loaned you money and didn't get it back in a timely fashion. Furious." She darted another glance at the door.

She didn't look scared, exactly. But there was a definite edge to her at the thought of her husband's anger.

Adrianna couldn't ask about it, of course. She already knew what answer she'd get. A princess was always happy in the Happy Ever After—the clue was, after all, in the name. And of course, princes never yelled at their wives. Nor kings. In fact, kings were always kind and fair or kind and distracted. At the very worst they were allowed to be overly strict with their daughters, but they never treated their wives poorly. At least not in public. No one cared about what went on in private.

Aurora leaned forward and put her hand on Adrianna's. "Whatever you do, though, don't borrow the money. Moneylenders are awful, as I hear. Worse than witches, except that no prince is going to want to rescue a princess being threatened by bad debts." She made a small, delicate grimace. "That's just in poor taste."

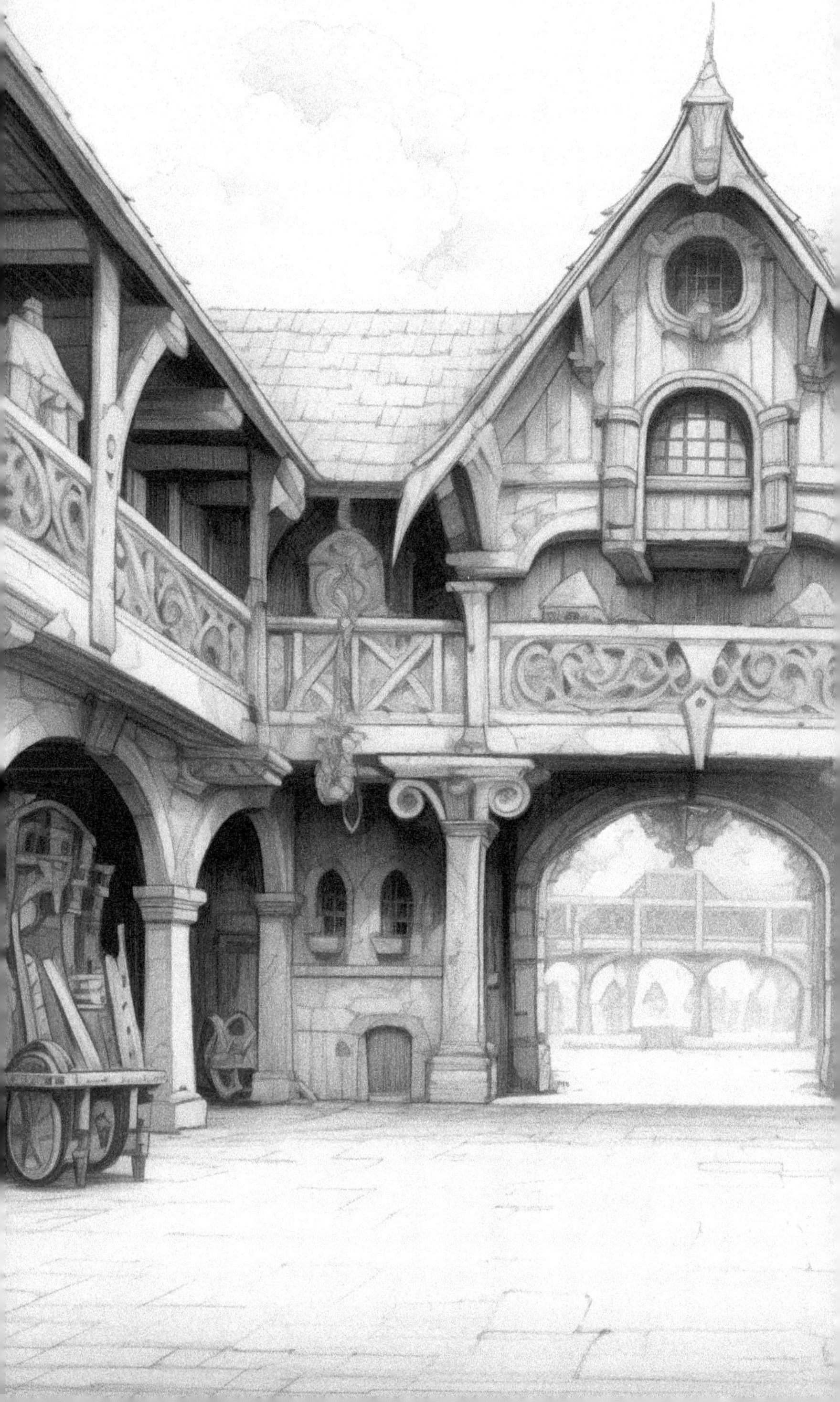

CHAPTER 15

Adrianna was running scarily fast out of options. She had no way to obtain the funds she needed to secure the dragon, and the only asset of value she possessed was the castle. It went without saying that she would never in a million years of curses consider selling her home to generate the funds she needed. She wouldn't let it pass on to someone who wouldn't appreciate it or worse, tear parts of it down and rebuild it.

But what if it came to a decision between selling the castle or risking Alinor's safety? If there truly wasn't another way, then Adrianna would be forced to sell.

But if she sold the castle, would she still be a princess? Would selling the castle create some impossible storyline or have some consequences she didn't yet understand? And if she did that, what would happen then? To her, to Alinor, to Petunia and Mirabelle? Where would they live? And what would the dragon guard if Adrianna eventually secured it? Would a prince still come if there wasn't a castle?

Thinking about all this was making her head ache, and yet again she yearned for the simpler days when all she did was attend balls and then laugh about the ridiculousness of it all the next day. Even when it had started to get depressing enough that she needed a glass of wine the day after, it was still better than her current situation. When finding a prince was just a chore, not something on which the safety of her family depended.

However, yearning wouldn't achieve anything. She needed to do something to get herself out of this predicament, and there was one obvious option that she hadn't yet explored.

Sam had quoted an extremely high price, but what if she could negotiate with him so that he was paid on completion of the mission? After all, she would need some sort of guarantee that her money was truly buying her a dragon, not a failed attempt. So she couldn't just pay it all upfront. That would be naïve—stupid, even.

Adrianna warmed to that line of thinking. It seemed like a smart way to go about it. Maybe she would be able to convince Sam to wait until the prince had come along, slaughtered the dragon, married her, and then as his wife she should have access to his funds—enough to pay Sam.

She hoped. Unless she managed to attract one of the few broke princes out there – there weren't too many of them floating about, thankfully. Most of the 'poor man, wealthy princess' storylines were reserved for poor but valiant shepherds.

Adrianna decided to go try her luck with Sam. It was her best hope for now.

It didn't take long to establish where Sam was. A quick visit to the Prince's Arms and the barkeep happily gave her directions to the manor house where Sam tended horses during the day. If the barkeep realised that her outfit of trousers and a loose white shirt made her a princess, he didn't comment on it, for which Adrianna was grateful. She really needed to remember to have excuses ready for these types of situations, a story to explain what she was doing, and why she needed to talk to Sam.

She reached the manor house and headed straight for the stables. Her horse's hooves clipped neatly against the grey stones that paved the courtyard around which the stables stretched out on either side.

Adrianna tied up her mare to a nearby post, as always leaving her ample room to be able to reach the water. She was about to go over to the stable to her right to see if she could find Sam within, when she recognised his voice, drifting out from the building on the left. She walked over quickly but froze when she heard a second female voice speak up.

"Sam, you can't be serious. You're not really considering going after a dragon egg, of all things? The dragon population is already critical—"

"Of course I'm not actually going to go after it." Sam sounded irritated.

Adrianna crouched down, flattening herself against the outside wall next to the doorway so she could hear the conversation as clearly as possible without being seen.

"Well, that's what you just told me you're planning to do," the woman said. "That you're getting paid to help a princess secure herself a dragon."

"That's what I told her. I've quoted her a handsome price as well. But I'll make sure somewhere along the way that the whole thing fails."

"And then you'll lose the money."

"Well, of course, I can't expect to get paid in full for a job I have no intention of fulfilling."

"That means that the farm…"

"You're having a go at me for going after a dragon and getting paid, and then having a go at me for not going after a dragon and losing the money?" Sam said impatiently.

"I'm only trying to make sense of what you're doing," the woman sniffed. "Because it makes precious little sense that I can see."

"Well, money I can make more of. I've made my peace with that. This is more important. If I can stop a dragon from being slaughtered, I have to do it. I'm not going to stand by and let her find someone else who will actually deliver her a dragon egg and get the mother killed."

Adrianna suddenly realised that the voices were growing louder—Sam and his interlocutor were obviously heading in her direction. She could hear their footsteps coming her way.

Feeling a jolt of panic, she scrambled to her feet. As she did, she found herself face to face with Sam, and she felt a wave of heat crawl up her face at having been caught eavesdropping. He did not look amused to find her in this position. In fact, he looked downright angry.

"What is the meaning of this? You're eavesdropping on me?"

Adrianna jutted her chin defiantly, refusing to be embarrassed. "I came to talk to you about our deal and also to check on the safety of my investment. Seems it's a good thing I did. Since you obviously have no interest in dealing with me fairly."

The words helped blow away the last remnants of embarrassment. She kept her tone calm and so cold that it bordered on icy. It was no real effort, since she was truly angry.

In a way, it was a relief to find out Sam wanted to screw her over, given that she'd considered doing the same to him. Then they were both as bad as each other.

Sam seemed about to respond, but instead he turned to the woman next to him. She was pretty, genuinely pretty, not orchestrated by a fairy godmother pretty. Or rather she would have been pretty if not for the ugly expression that marred her face as she looked Adrianna up and down. There was no misunderstanding her opinion of princesses, or at least of Adrianna.

"Look, why don't you go home and let me deal with this," Sam told her.

She opened her mouth to reply, but he cut her off with a short, sharp shake of his head. "This is my business to deal with. I will see you at home." His tone brooked no arguments.

The woman hesitated then shrugged. "Fine."

She pushed past Adrianna and left.

"Charming," Adrianna remarked dryly. "Who was that —your wife?"

Neither Sam nor the woman were wearing rings, but then again, rings were often too great an expense for the average couple to afford.

"She is none of your business."

Definitely his wife, given how they spoke. The way he referred to 'home', meaning their joint home. And married for a while at that—there was nothing left of the initial romance Adrianna had heard characterised the early years of a marriage. She was surprised to notice a small stab of disappointment in her stomach.

"You're right," she said aloud. "Let's stick to the actual business at hand—my business. My business, which you were clearly planning to screw up."

Sam's face grew more closed and more dark, if possible. "Look—"

"No, *you* look." Adrianna found herself growing angry again. Angry and reckless, as an idea came to her. An idea to help push Sam to accept her suggestion. "I wanted to treat you fairly because I have been approached by another mercenary who can help me with my dragon situation."

"Another? I'm not a mercenary."

"Muscle for hire who seeks to screw over his employer?" Adrianna asked, raising an eyebrow. "What's your definition of mercenary, exactly?"

"I mean, I'm not a soldier. Or an ex-soldier," Sam grumbled.

It felt good that mentioning his attempt to screw her over left him without a leg to stand on.

"Anyway," she continued, "Since we had made a deal, I wanted to come to you first, to give you the opportunity to match his offer. And given that you apparently seem to care about dragons so much, this may suit you better, anyway. The new deal is that I won't pay you for your services, but when this is all said and done, you get to keep the dragon egg. That way you get to save it, which will make you happy, and I get the guarantee that I don't end up just paying for—what was it your wife said, your farm?"

"She's not my wife," Sam said through gritted teeth.

Adrianna refused to feel glad at the admission. She was focused on the business at hand. "Well, whoever she is. It doesn't matter. You get to keep the dragon egg, that way you save the baby dragon."

"No deal, I'm not going into this much danger free of charge."

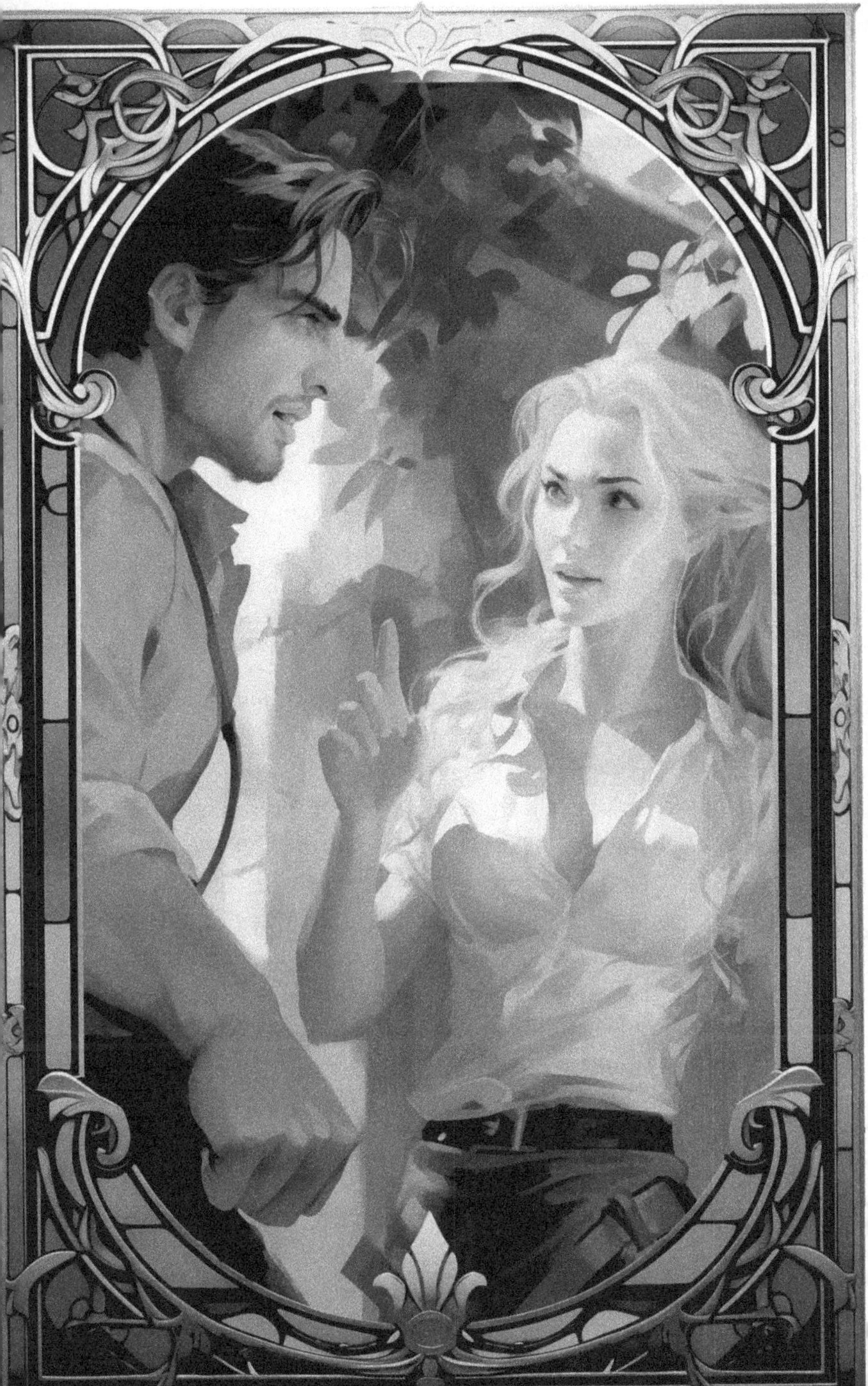

"Did you hear anything I said? I didn't say free of charge, I said your payment will be in the form of the dragon egg. A dragon egg must surely be highly valuable."

"No, I need to be paid upfront. At least in part."

Adrianna shrugged. "You lost that opportunity when you decided to try to screw me over."

Sam ran a hand through his hair and grimaced. "That wasn't fairly done of me, I'll admit it."

"How generous of you," Adrianna replied sarcastically. And then she played her trump card—a card that was entirely fabricated, of course, since there was no other mercenary. She had no idea what she was doing, and yet it felt wild and good. Completely breaking with the script. She was so far from the delicate, gentle princess she was supposed to be, but who cared. There was no prince present, no one to try to impress. The storylines be damned, for once.

"Anyway, if you're not interested, I'm going to this other mercenary, and he'll keep the dragon egg. Whatever you decide, a dragon is getting slaughtered. I'm sorry about that, but it can't be helped. If you at least want to save the dragon egg, this is your opportunity. If I go with the other mercenary, I'm pretty sure he doesn't have your altruistic values…"

Sam threw her a dirty look. Adrianna knew she was being every bit as mercenary as the person she was inventing. That she was being just as bad as Sam when he had decided to double cross her—probably worse. Much worse because the dragon whose life hung in the balance had nothing to do with any of it.

Once she was married, she'd try to make amends for her actions. She'd find a way to save some dragons, protect them from princes. Maybe donate money to Zephiera. Do what she could in the few years she'd have after the Happy death claimed her in childbirth...She pushed the thought away.

"You would truly do that?" Sam asked. "You'd go to that mercenary?"

"Yes." Adrianna jutted her chin out. Wild and free. She was wild and free. Nothing and no one would stop her. She almost believed her own lie about there being a mercenary, and it gave her the confidence she needed to be believable.

Sam looked down at the ground. He scuffed his boots against the flagstones a couple of times before looking up again. "That's a dirty, dirty move."

"What can I say? We're as dirty as each other, I guess."

This time, Sam gave a snort of laughter. "You're not what I expected."

"What do you mean?"

"As a princess. You're not what I expected. I expected vain and shallow, or boringly pure and innocent—you know, the type to talk to the birds and get dressed by mice."

"Hey, my sister's like that and there's nothing wrong with it. With her. And she's not boring."

"I guess there isn't anything wrong with that, per se, no. Just not my cup of tea." Sam looked Adrianna over, considering. "Fine. I'll take your deal. But you have to cover the upfront costs to the expedition. I'll need—"

"We will need," Adrianna corrected. "I'm coming with you. To keep an eye on things." Just saying the words made that thrill shiver down her spine again. "And yes, if you tell me what will be required, those costs I can cover."

"No, I go alone."

"No deal. I don't trust you."

"You'll just get in the way. You're a princess."

"You just said I'm not what you expected of a princess."

"That may be, but you still know nothing of these things. You know nothing about anything."

"Well then, you'll have to show me."

"That will make things more complicated and difficult. Why don't you just wait in your castle for the dragon and prince to show up? Isn't that what princesses are supposed to do?"

"Ah, but as you pointed out, I'm not a normal princess."

"No, you're not. You're annoying is what you are."

"Why, thank you. I try."

Sam shook his head and blew out a huff of air, like an annoyed horse. "Why do you need to keep an eye on things, anyway? Paying me with the dragon egg is your guarantee. It's the best way to make sure I actually do what you tell me and complete my mission. Once I take the egg, I will need someone to deal with the mother or she will kill me. I won't be able to run from her forever. Which is where your precious prince will come in. So there's no need for you to come along."

That was true, but now that Adrianna found herself in front of a potential adventure, in front of something exciting, now that she had an opportunity to finally do more than wait for a prince to choose her, she couldn't let it pass her without grabbing it.

To finally do something with herself, with her life. To be finally worth something. When she was married and in the Happy Ever After, she wanted to be able to remember that she had ridden out into the wild and found a dragon herself. When she died in childbirth, she wanted to know that she had done something with her life, at least one time.

For a brief moment, she considered telling Sam this, but she quickly stopped herself. There was reckless and then there was stupid. She wasn't about to reveal how she felt to Sam. She'd never told anyone of how worthless this whole being a princess thing made her feel, and she wasn't about to start telling him, of all people.

Instead, she raised an eyebrow at him. "What's to stop you from taking the egg and running away with it?"

"The mother," Sam replied dryly. "The mother will follow me to the ends of the earth. Once you take a dragon egg, you don't have that much time. You either have to find a way to kill the mother or you have to return the egg to her. So I will need to bring the egg to you as quick as I can so a prince can kill the mother."

At that Adrianna's previous excitement about her adventure deflated like an old balloon, leaving a bad taste in her mouth. It hardly seemed fair for the dragon to die for doing exactly what Adrianna was doing—protecting her family.

"I'm coming. That's not up for negotiation," she told Sam curtly. "If I'm to be responsible for the dragon dying, the least I can do is face the reality of what I'm doing in person. Now tell me what supplies you'll need so we can get that sorted."

A muscle feathered in Sam's jaw, but he sighed and nodded. They had a deal.

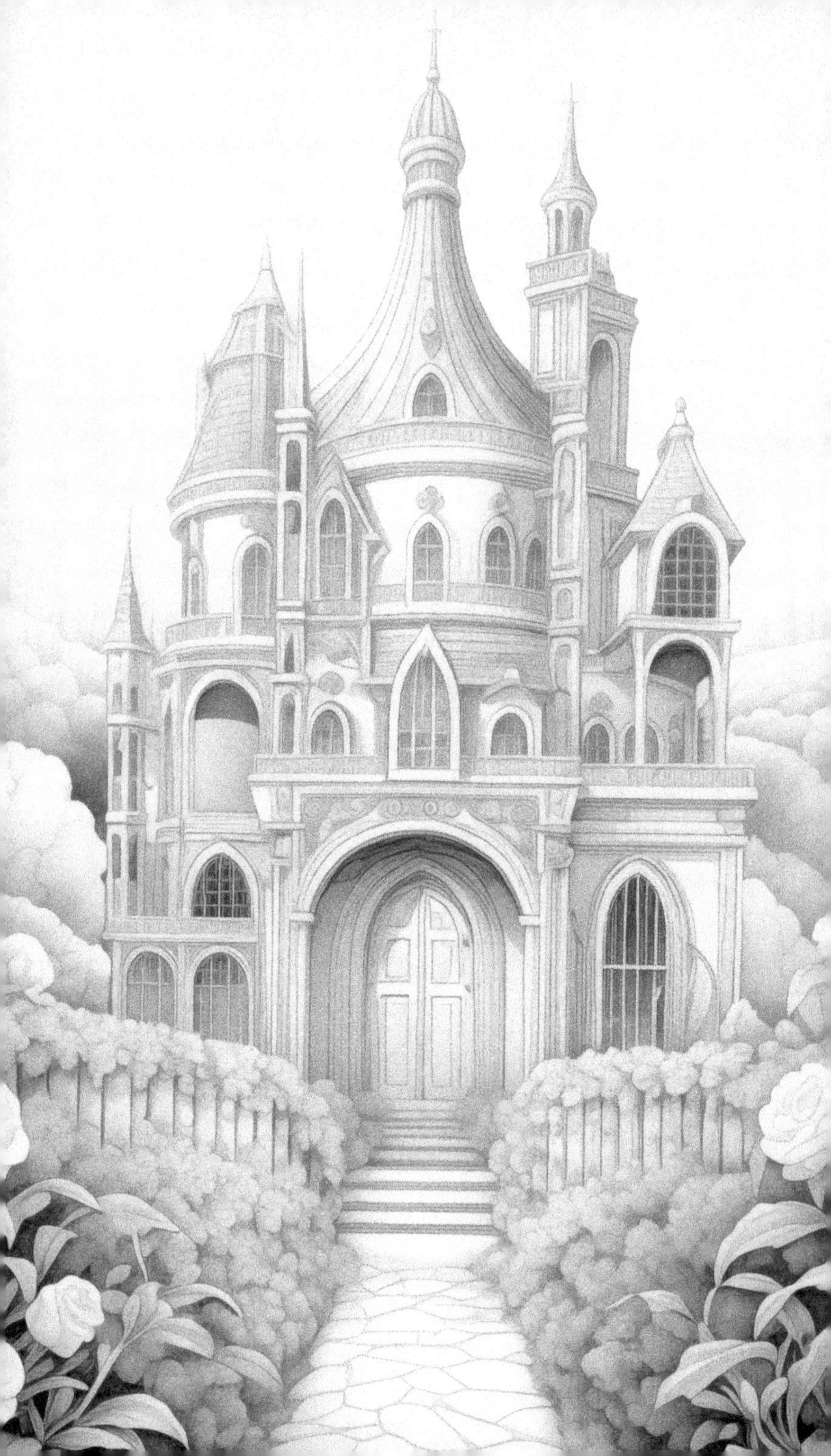

CHAPTER 16

Charming wasn't sure it was normal to be afraid of your own mother. Princes, after all, were supposed to be fearless. Courageous. To boldly go into the unknown and rescue distressed maidens. They were not supposed to live in fear of the Motherly Wrath, and yet said fear had ruled Charming's life for as long as he could remember.

However, today things would be different. Charming was no longer a boy. He was a man, a betrothed man, a man who had gone forth into the world and chosen his wife.

Charming reminded himself of this as he climbed the interminable staircase that led up to his mother's private quarters. As he climbed the steps, he rehearsed how the conversation would go. He had, sadly, been unable to find a precedent, a storyline where a prince married an evil stepmother with a daughter of her own.

Which was why Charming would need to exhibit the full strength and courage of a prince to face down the Motherly Wrath. In fact, he would not give her the opportunity to express her disapproval. He would simply stride into his mother's personal sitting room, and firmly—in a tone that would allow no arguments—inform her of his decision to marry Petunia. Then he would walk back out. There would be no discussion. He wouldn't apologise for his choice, either.

Charming's decision was final.

Charming could have sworn that the staircase was somehow longer today than all the previous times he had climbed it. His legs were starting to ache, and there was a hint of dampness to his forehead as he reached the final step. His heart was also pounding as hard and fast as if he'd been running.

As he reached the huge double doors that led into his mother's private quarters—doors flanked by a pair of footmen in matching midnight blue and silver livery—he found he had trouble holding onto the confidence he had felt just a moment ago. Something about the doors, maybe the size of them, always made him feel like he was regressing back to boyhood, being summoned to be scolded.

But not this time. He had seen his potential happiness before him, laid out like a beautiful mirage, so tantalisingly close. Now that he had seen it, Charming could not turn away from it. This must be what it meant to be truly in love. This must be why princes were prepared to face such overwhelming odds.

"Shall I announce you, sire?" one of the footmen asked, looking at him curiously, and Charming realised he had been standing in front of the doors for probably longer than was considered normal.

"Yes," he replied, or at least tried to, but all that came out was a thin, reedy sound.

The footmen looked back at him impassively, but he could have sworn he detected judgement in their eyes.

Another reminder of why he had to marry Petunia—a castle free of servants. What a thrilling concept.

Charming cleared his throat. "Yes," he said, more decisively this time.

He was a man. He was an engaged man. He was a man on whom his beloved now depended, on whom both his and Petunia's happiness depended.

The footman knocked, announced Charming, and opened the door.

The queen's private sitting room was like a shrine to King Charles Spaniels. It wasn't just the gaggle of small dogs that were laid about the room. It was the small porcelain figurines carefully displayed on the shelves. It was the paintings of the queen with the various King Charles Spaniels she'd owned over the years. The vast tapestry covering the right wall featured King Charles Spaniels. As did the embroidered cushions.

The queen herself was at this moment sat in her favourite chair, working on a piece of embroidery. Charming didn't need to look to know the pattern she was embroidering.

"Hello, Mother." His voice came out as a squeak.

"Charming." She didn't look up from her work. "Come and give me a kiss."

The queen was a beautiful woman, as befitted all queens, although not so beautiful that she could be mistaken for a witch or an evil queen. But it wasn't a soft beauty. In fact, there was nothing soft about the queen. Her features were fine but cold. She sat with a spine that was poker straight, and she went about her embroidery so forcefully, she looked like she was stabbing the fabric with the needle.

The sight of that needle made Charming falter in the doorway, that feeling of regressing to boyhood returning with a vengeance.

"Well?" his mother asked, still not looking up.

Charming crossed the room, putting one foot before the other in an impressive display of coordination and dexterity. His head was feeling increasingly distant from his body, like it might detach itself if he wasn't careful and float up to the ceiling.

He reached his mother's side and bent down to kiss her cheek. Her skin was smooth and cool.

"Sit," she commanded, as if he were one of her dogs.

Charming did as he was told automatically. The queen controlled everything in the castle and that included Charming and his father, the king. Charming secretly suspected that the reason the queen's private quarters were always the most immaculate in the palace was because the dust didn't dare settle in this room, any more than the dogs' hair dared fall on the floor.

The clock on the marble mantelpiece—both polished to a shine—ticked away the seconds as the queen continued to stab her embroidery. Charming realised that he was sweating.

"You'll have tea," the queen said. It wasn't a question.

She didn't even have to ring a bell. A maid materialised carrying a tray with tea and cakes, as if she'd been waiting with the fully loaded tray just outside the servants' door. The maid poured out the tea—milk and sugar for Charming, black and unsweetened for his mother. The queen never ate the biscuits or cakes that came with the tea, either. She was a remarkably thin woman, as if fat didn't dare settle on her body any more than the dust dared settle in her rooms. Charming had actually never seen her eat. Sometimes he wondered if she maybe just survived on air —on the air that she sucked out of every room she entered.

He chastised himself at the thought. Princes were not supposed to think such things of their mothers. Princes were supposed to dote on their mothers.

He took a sip of his tea and then returned the cup and saucer to the little table before him. Then he took a deep, steadying breath.

"Mother, I have news. I have chosen a wife." There. It was out in the open.

The queen paused halfway through stabbing the embroidery and looked up at him. Her face broke into a smile, a sight so rare, so outside of Charming's experience, that he started at the sight of it.

"My dear boy, that's wonderful."

Charming knew this was the moment he had to push forward. While his mother was well disposed towards him.

"Who is it?" The queen asked.

"Petunia, Queen of Veridi," Charming's voice was once again a squeak, but he managed to get the words out.

The queen's eyes widened for a moment. And then the temperature in the room began to drop. Precipitously.

"*Queen* of Veridi?" Icicles clung to each of the words. The spaniels, sensing their mistress's displeasure, raised their heads to look at Charming, adding their judgement to his mother's.

Charming was very cold. His feet felt very far away. He wished he had kept his cup of tea to warm his hands on, but they'd probably be shaking enough to spill the tea.

"We're..."

"Don't tell me you're already engaged."

"Yes." The word came out so quietly, Charming wasn't sure he had actually spoken it.

"Hmm." No magic in the world would be able to cram as much disapproval as the queen could communicate with that one syllable. Not even a syllable, a sound. Thick with disapproval. Dripping with it. That Charming managed to keep from collapsing like a failed soufflé was an impressive display of strength and fortitude.

This was the worst of it, Charming reminded himself.

This was ripping off the plaster. Lancing the boil. Everything would feel better afterwards. Afterwards... Charming remembered that wonderful library, with its thick layer of dust and absence of servants. With its lack of mother to hover over him. The thought gave Charming the last little fragment of courage he needed to see this through.

"There is nothing to be done, Mother. I have proposed and been accepted."

Charming stood up slowly, like a man in a dream. Like a man drunk. He sidestepped away from the tea table, feeling as awkward as a walrus attempting to dance the waltz.

The queen made another sound, this time like a kettle suppressing the urge to boil. Charming gave full rein to his cowardice then, slinking out of the room as fast as his awkward legs would allow him for fear that the Wrath would catch him before he could get to safety.

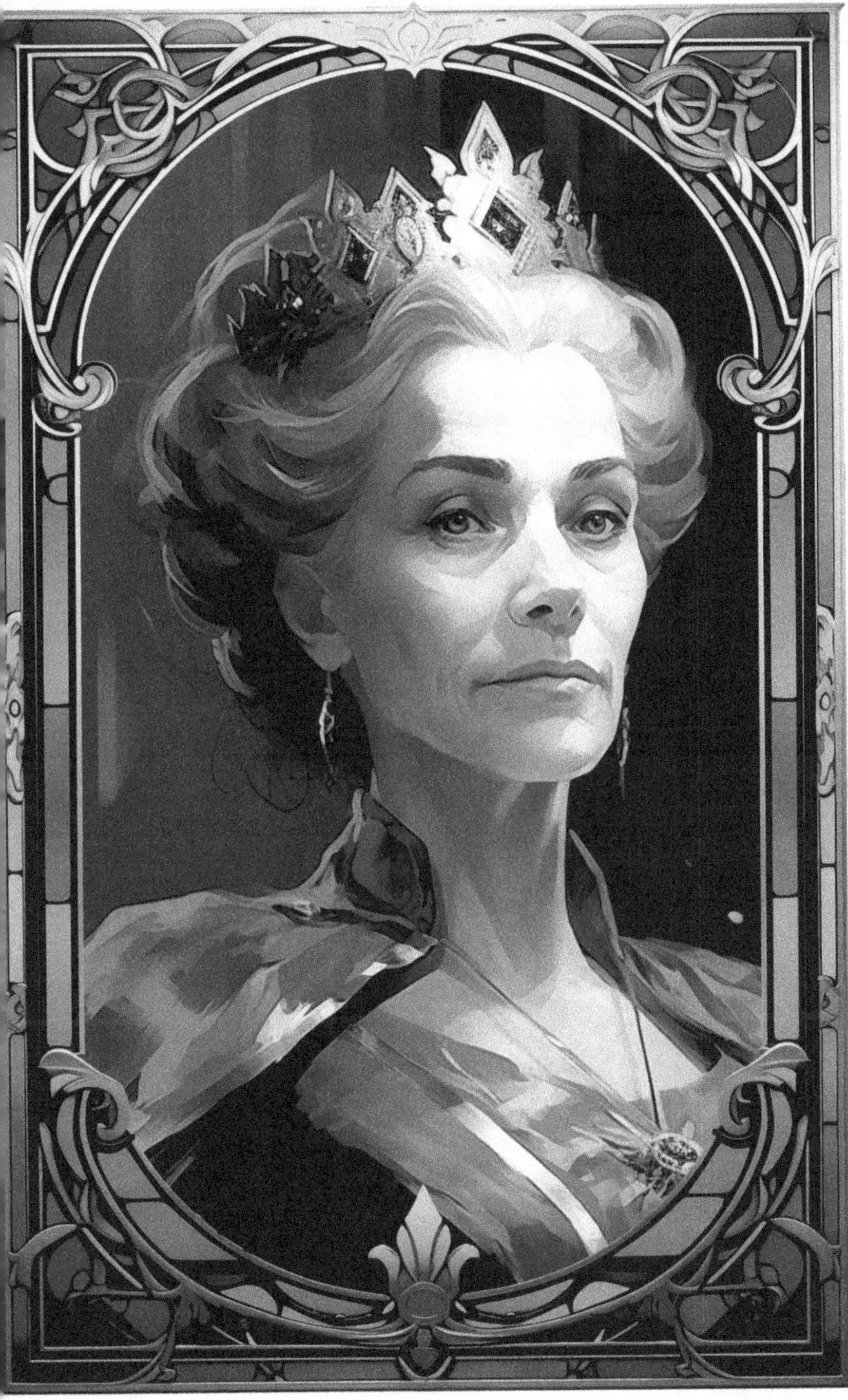

The queen didn't move after Charming had left the room. She kept perfectly still, a petrified statue of disapproval, her beautiful features stuck in a haughty, angry expression. The only thing that moved, the only sound in the room, was the clock's pendulum. Even the dogs held their breath, pausing their usual snuffing sounds. The temperature also remained frozen in place, not daring to return to its normal levels.

The queen finally put down her embroidery and reached into a hidden pocket in the skirts of her dress. She pulled out a tiny silver bell. She rang it, the sound barely audible even in the pristine silence. It didn't ring like a normal bell. The sound was liquid, seeming to coil about the air before disappearing off as if rushing away.

For a while, nothing happened. The queen remained as she was, a living tableau, the slight rise and fall of her chest the only clue that she hadn't spontaneously petrified. The dogs exchanged looks, but they knew better than to move.

Finally, a cold draft—colder than even the current temperature—shivered into the room, indicating that the secret doorway had been opened. The tapestry, featuring a King Charles Spaniel, that hid the door from sight didn't move, the visitor staying hidden behind it.

"I need to report a breach in the storylines," the queen said, her voice clipped. "A correction needs to be made."

A sigh from behind the tapestry. "I'm listening."

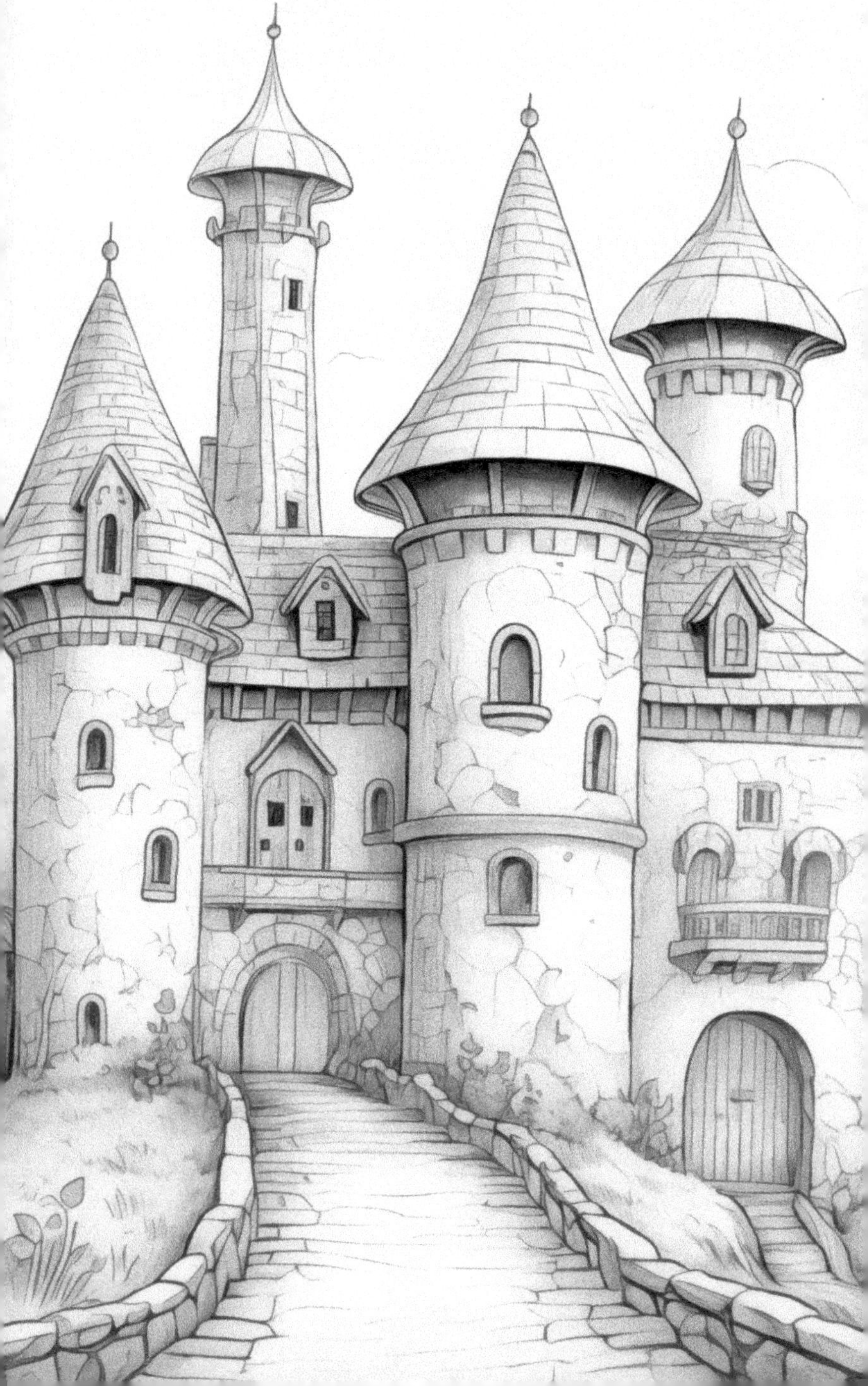

CHAPTER 17

Adrianna was feeling so many emotions as she mounted her mare, she was in a complete whirl. Shudders of excitement shivered up her spine every so often at the thought that she was finally doing something. She was finally going on an adventure, but more importantly, she was finally taking an active role in her life, rather than passively waiting for things to happen.

The thought inevitably brought nerves and no small amount of fear. It wasn't just going to a new place; it was the fact that if everything went according to plan, her life would soon change completely. A prince would ask for her hand in marriage, and then she would reach the Happy Ever After. And even though this was what Adrianna was seeking to achieve, she was also mildly terrified of it. Make that totally terrified. It wasn't as disturbing as the idea of failing and the possible consequences, but it was close enough.

And then she felt large stabs of guilt at the reminder of what she was going to do – she was going to bring a dragon to the slaughter. A mother dragon, who would be trying to protect her egg, in exactly the way that Adrianna was trying to protect her sister.

There was something else fluttering in her stomach, something she couldn't quite identify, but it was at the idea of spending time with Sam. Annoyance, for sure, but something else, as well.

Sam didn't seem to share that something as he sat on his horse with a face like thunder. He had assembled the supplies they would need for the journey, and Adrianna had paid for it all. It was a surprisingly small amount of things. They weren't going away for very long. It turned out that Sam knew the location of a dragon not too far from the castle, so the supplies for the trip fitted in saddlebags distributed across all the horses.

Mirabelle had insisted on coming so she could keep an eye on things and provide magical assistance as and when needed. Even though her magic was useless against the dragon, there may be other situations where she could help. Adrianna was grateful for the comfort of having her fairy godmother there. It helped with the nerves and with the fear of what would happen if they succeeded.

The conditions of the day seemed to be ideal for the start of a journey—the weather bright and sunny. A small breeze agitated the leaves on the trees, ruffling Adrianna's hair.

"Are you ready?" Adrianna asked Sam.

He didn't even bother looking at her. "As ready as I'll ever be."

"Oh, Lowen, you came to see me off," Mirabelle said, delighted.

Adrianna turned in her saddle, surprised. True enough, the gardener—looking every bit as terrified as always—had appeared and was standing on the front steps, hovering not far from Petunia.

"Don't forget about me, Lowen, dear," Mirabelle said.

"We're only going for a couple of days," Adrianna pointed out.

"If you pine for me," Mirabelle continued, ignoring Adrianna, "You only have to look East and think of me."

Lowen bobbed a single nod. Adrianna frowned. Was Lowen really going to miss Mirabelle? How was that even possible? The man was terrified of her.

Mirabelle floated up until she was level with her horse, and then she landed heavily on her saddle. She gathered the reins and turned to Lowen once more.

"Farewell, my love," she said dramatically.

Lowen took a careful sidestep, half hiding behind Petunia.

Alinor came to stand by the head of Adrianna's mare, stroking her neck.

"You don't have to do this, you know," Alinor muttered to Adrianna, not looking at her. She and Adrianna had argued all the previous evening. Alinor was soundly against the idea of a dragon being slaughtered, prince or no prince. Neither Petunia nor Adrianna had explained about the dangers to her if Adrianna failed to secure a prince, not wanting to frighten her.

Adrianna sighed. "I explained enough times last night why I don't have a choice. I have to secure a prince, and this is what I need to do to achieve that."

Alinor muttered something intelligible and turned away. Adrianna bit her lip. She didn't like her sister being annoyed with her, but there wasn't much she could do about it. Alinor would get over it, in time. In fact, if Adrianna's greatest problem was her sister sulking, she would call that a resounding success.

"Good luck," Petunia said soberly. She didn't seem quite as focused as that day in the library, when she had revealed the truth about her face, but she also didn't have that distracted, almost hazy look that indicated she was obsessing over her garden.

"Thank you." They exchanged a long look, and a nice, warm feeling spread through Adrianna's chest. This was probably the most connected she and Petunia had ever been. Adrianna had always liked her evil stepmother, but it was hard to build a deep connection with someone who was rarely aware of your presence.

Alinor scampered off back into the castle, not waiting for them to leave. Adrianna didn't blame her.

She turned and looked from Sam to Mirabelle. "I think we're ready to go."

Sam didn't bother to reply, clicking his tongue. His horse began to walk. Adrianna and Mirabelle fell into step with each other behind him, Mirabelle waving enthusiastically back at the castle.

"How did you get Lowen to come and bid you goodbye?" Adrianna asked, genuinely curious. "Did you enchant him? Brainwash him?"

Mirabelle sniffed. "I know you don't believe me, but Lowen and I share a special connection. Even though most of the time he's too terrified to acknowledge it."

"How can you share a connection if he's terrified of you?"

"Love is complicated," Mirabelle replied.

"Apparently so."

"And you? Won't it complicate matters to try to secure your prince with Sam around?"

Luckily, he was far ahead enough and up wind so their voices wouldn't have carried to him. Adrianna rolled her eyes. "It will complicate nothing. He's good looking, I'll give you that. But that's it."

"Ah-ha, so you *do* think he's handsome," Mirabelle said triumphantly.

"I'm in serious danger of straining my eye muscles."

"And *I* think you protest too much," Mirabelle replied primly.

"I protest the right amount for someone who is being badgered over something stupid. And anyway, it doesn't matter if he's handsome or not. Firstly, because, as you can clearly tell, I don't like him and he certainly doesn't like me. And anyway, I don't get a choice. I have to have a Happy Ever After so Alinor will stay safe. And that's all there is to that. So what I think of Sam is irrelevant."

Mirabelle gave her a sympathetic look. "For what it's worth, I'm sorry, pet… I really wanted you to have a happy life."

"I know. And it's been pretty perfect until now. At least I had that."

They rode on in silence.

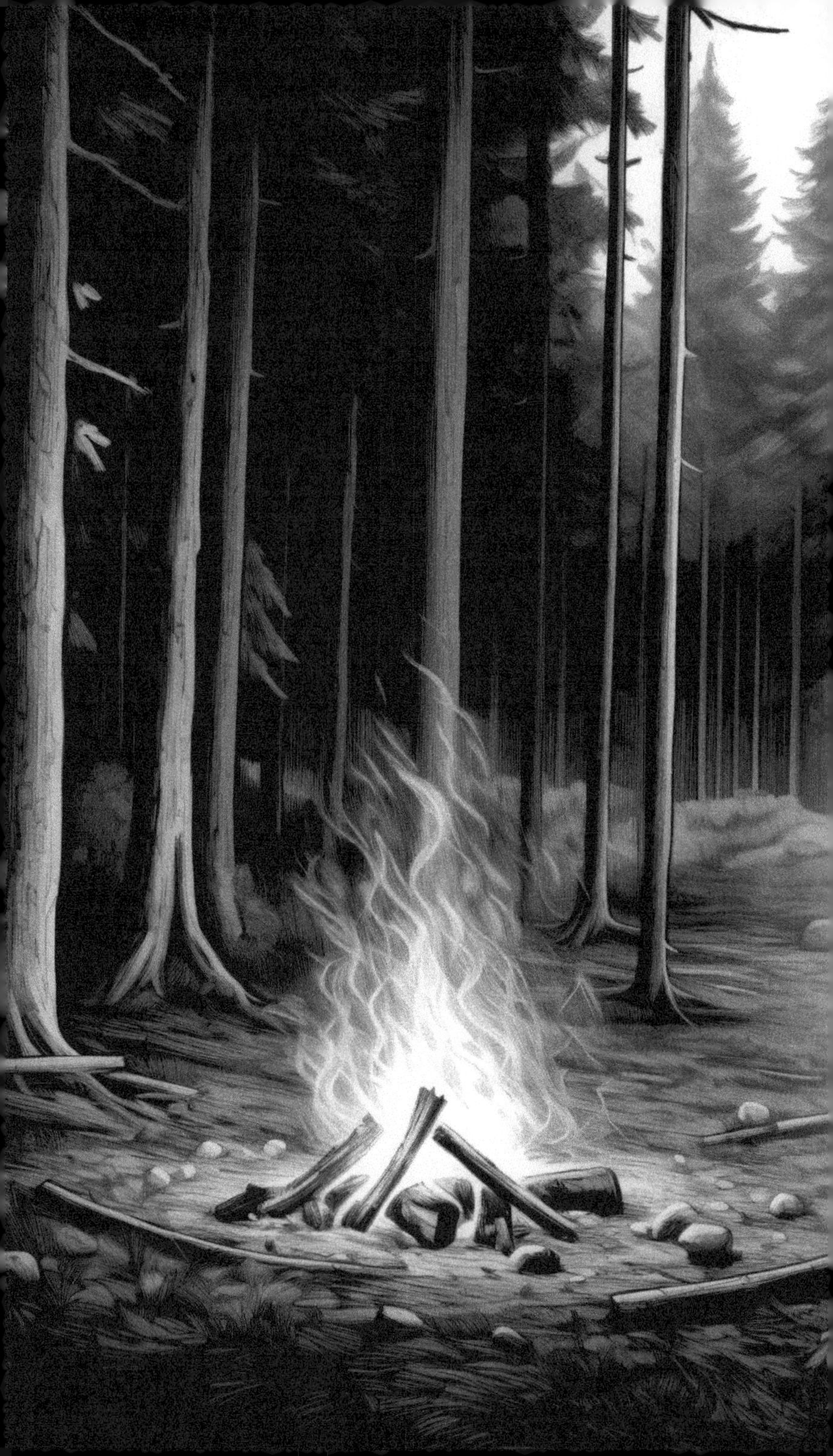

CHAPTER 18

For the whole day, Sam rode ahead in silence. He didn't speak a word to them, not one. Adrianna tried not to let it get to her, but knowing that someone had such a bad opinion of her wasn't the most comfortable thing to carry. And it was even more uncomfortable to know that said opinion was justified, because she was doing a bad thing.

But there was nothing she could do about it. She had no other option. She'd been over this again and again, so there was no point continuing to torture herself over it. She'd made her bed and now she had to lie in it, and no, it wasn't the most comfortable of beds.

Then again, this might be the only adventure she would ever have in her short life, so she didn't want to miss or ruin the experience by worrying about what someone thought of her. If this was going to be the one highlight of her life, she was going to enjoy every moment of it. One day she'd be stuck in a castle with a husband and a swollen belly, knowing that if it was a girl, she'd die in childbirth.

She wanted to have these memories to look back on. At

least she'd know that even just for a brief time, her life had been exciting.

So she chatted away with Mirabelle and admired the scenery as it went past. She'd never been this far from her home before, and she let go of the worries, just enjoying the feeling of freedom and easy happiness that came from riding her horse out into the unknown.

Sam remained sullen when they stopped to eat. He continued being sullen into the afternoon. As they set up camp for the night, he seemed to grow even more taciturn, if that were possible.

In fact, it was impressive just how closed his face could be—talking to him was like addressing a prison door. One with all the deadbolts pulled tight and a stout oak bar across the middle of it. Nevertheless, he set up the fire and prepared the food with care, although he ate in silence.

"I've brought some supplies myself," Mirabelle announced when they'd finished eating. She produced a small, cloudy glass bottle from the depths of her bosom. "Brandy is essential for the health of the traveller."

She pulled out the cork with a small 'pop', grinning, and took several large swigs. "Here." She handed the flask to Sam.

He shook his head. "There probably isn't much left in there by now, and I don't want to rob you of your health tonic." The latter was said with a trace of irony, a rather impressive departure from the brick wall he had been presenting all day.

Mirabelle smiled widely. "My dear, I'm a fairy godmother—emphasis on 'fairy'. This little bottle refills itself for every sip you take. You could drink from it all night and still it would be full."

Sam hesitated, then took the flask with a nod of thanks. He took a couple of gulps and returned it to Mirabelle.

"And what about me?" Adrianna asked him.

Sam looked surprised. "Oh, I didn't think princesses—"

"Princesses don't, but *I* do." She took the bottle from Mirabelle and drank.

She didn't like brandy much, but she'd grown used to drinking anything and everything when she'd needed to numb the feeling of hopelessness her life brought her. Although right now she didn't feel hopeless, she was just making a point. She hated the expectation that she was supposed to be dainty and delicate and feminine and not have bodily functions or vices.

Mirabelle also drank some more before passing it back to Sam. He tried to refuse.

"I probably shouldn't…"

"Nonsense. You're travelling with a fairy godmother. I make short work of hangovers." She grinned and snapped her fingers. "We'll all be fresh as daisies tomorrow."

Sam didn't seem to be able to help the ghost of a smile that crept across his face. "I didn't realise this is what fairy godmothers did."

"My dear, we do everything." Mirabelle gave him an evaluating look. She raised an eyebrow. "Well…not quite everything. Some things we like to get help with."

Adrianna knew Mirabelle's modus operandi well. If Sam protested at the innuendo, she'd put him back in his place primly, saying she was referring to the dragon. Which was true, but she was also hinting at a whole wealth of things Adrianna didn't want to think about right now.

"Keep your mind out of the gutter," Adrianna told her godmother as Sam handed her the flask.

"My mind is only on the purest of topics," Mirabelle sniffed. She sighed dramatically. "I was thinking about Lowen, actually. I miss the dear man so."

"We just left this morning." Adrianna rolled her eyes and took a swig.

"But this is the longest that I've gone without seeing him. What if he forgets me?"

"Unlikely given how terrified he is of you. I think the word traumatised would be apt. He probably couldn't forget you if he tried—his nightmares must be keeping him up at night." Adrianna grinned.

"You understand nothing of love," Mirabelle replied.

"Is it love, though? I thought you wanted to gobble him up."

"Well, that too. He *is* rather delicious."

"I will never understand what you see in him. He looks like an overgrown pigeon with a giant Adam's apple."

"He does *not*. You're just too young and have poor taste. I didn't bless you at birth for your taste in men and look at what a disaster things are now."

"No one ever gets blessed with good taste in men. Anyway, no one cares about what I want, so long as I marry a prince," Adrianna replied moodily, staring down at the bottle in her hands. For a moment, the hopelessness and pointlessness of her life caught up with her.

"Well, given how dull some of those princes are, I'm amazed you have to nerve to consider Lowen anything other than the most charming of men," Mirabelle said.

Arianna laughed at that, letting Mirabelle pull her out of her funk. It was true—some of the princes whose balls she'd attended were downright dismal. Handsome, of course, in that generic, magic-enhanced way, but so dead inside as to be as appealing as a damp sock. Like Charming. Adrianna had found him quite representative of his species. He was more shy and awkward than the norm by far, but he was every bit as unappealing as the rest.

"Do you remember the one with the spring collection?" Adrianna asked Mirabelle. "I thought he was talking of some magical objects linked to the season of spring, but no, he actually collected metal springs."

"Do I just? I believe I'm still finding damp spots from where he sprayed me with spittle as he gave us the tour of his private collection." Mirabelle pretended to mop her brow. "I was so wet by the end of that tour, I believe I was in danger of catching some kind of wasting sickness from too much humidity."

"Can you imagine if I'd actually managed to charm him, and he'd proposed?"

"Possibly a better prospect than the one who picked his nose."

Adrianna grimaced. "The nose picking I probably could have stomached, but he had the most awful breath." Like all the others, though, he had been devastatingly handsome.

They carried on like this for a time—the comfortable, well-worn usual conversations. Sam stayed quiet. Given that he already had a poor opinion of Adrianna, she didn't try to censure herself or to say things to portray herself in a particularly positive light—what was the point? She wasn't likely to sink any lower in his esteem, and if she did, it wouldn't change much.

After a while, Mirabelle yawned and announced that she was tired. She got up and toddled off to lie down on her blankets, which immediately transformed into a cosy little bed, complete with eiderdown and wrought-iron frame. She was already snoring softly by the time the transformation finished.

"A bed?" Sam asked with a raised eyebrow.

"Mirabelle is always comfortable wherever she is," Adrianna said, eyeing her fairy godmother affectionately.

"You both seem close," Sam said.

"We are. Very."

They both stared at the fire in silence for a while.

"Those princes you were talking about," Sam said. "They sound..."

"Depressing? Bleak? Head-shakingly dull?"

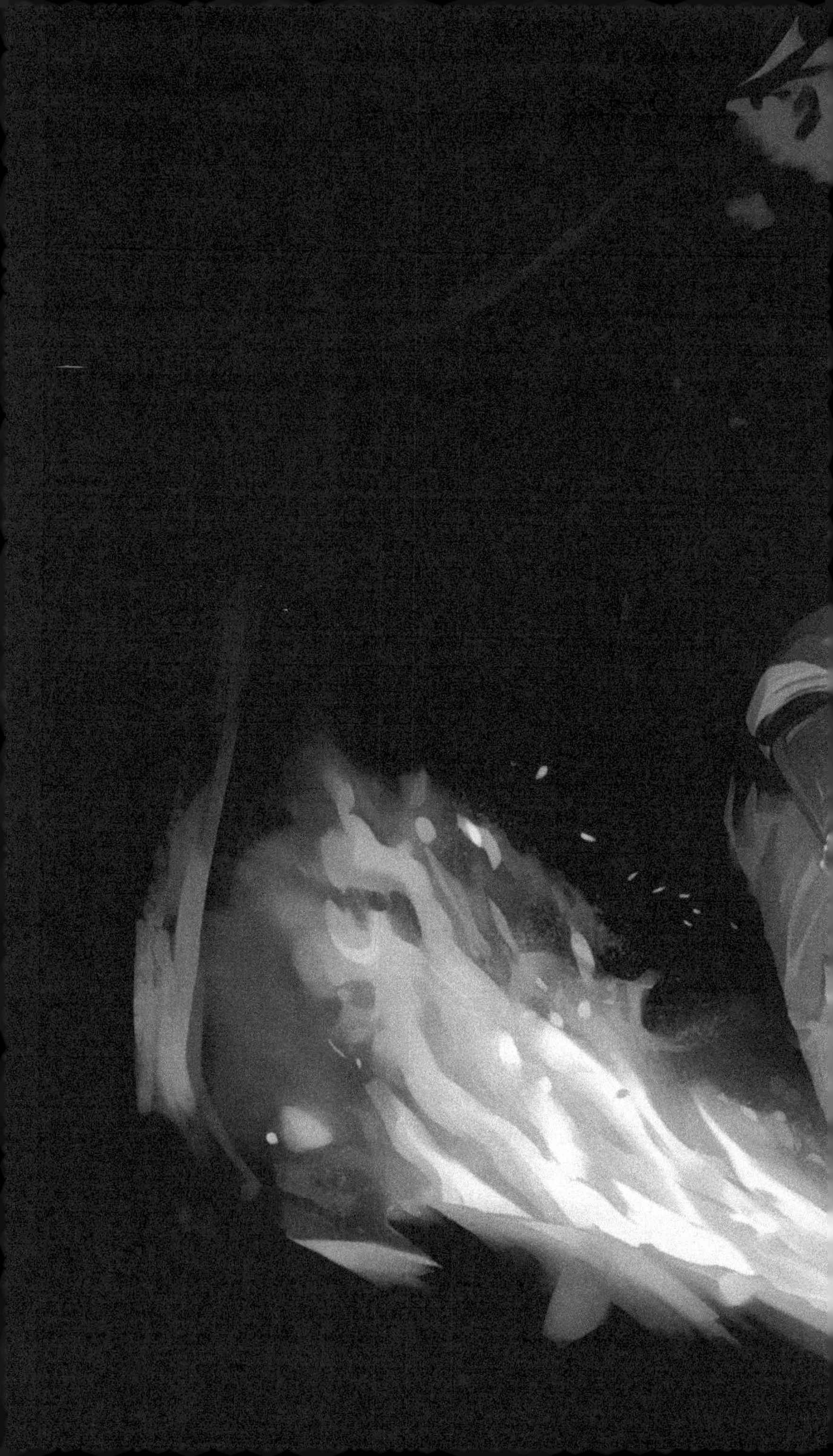

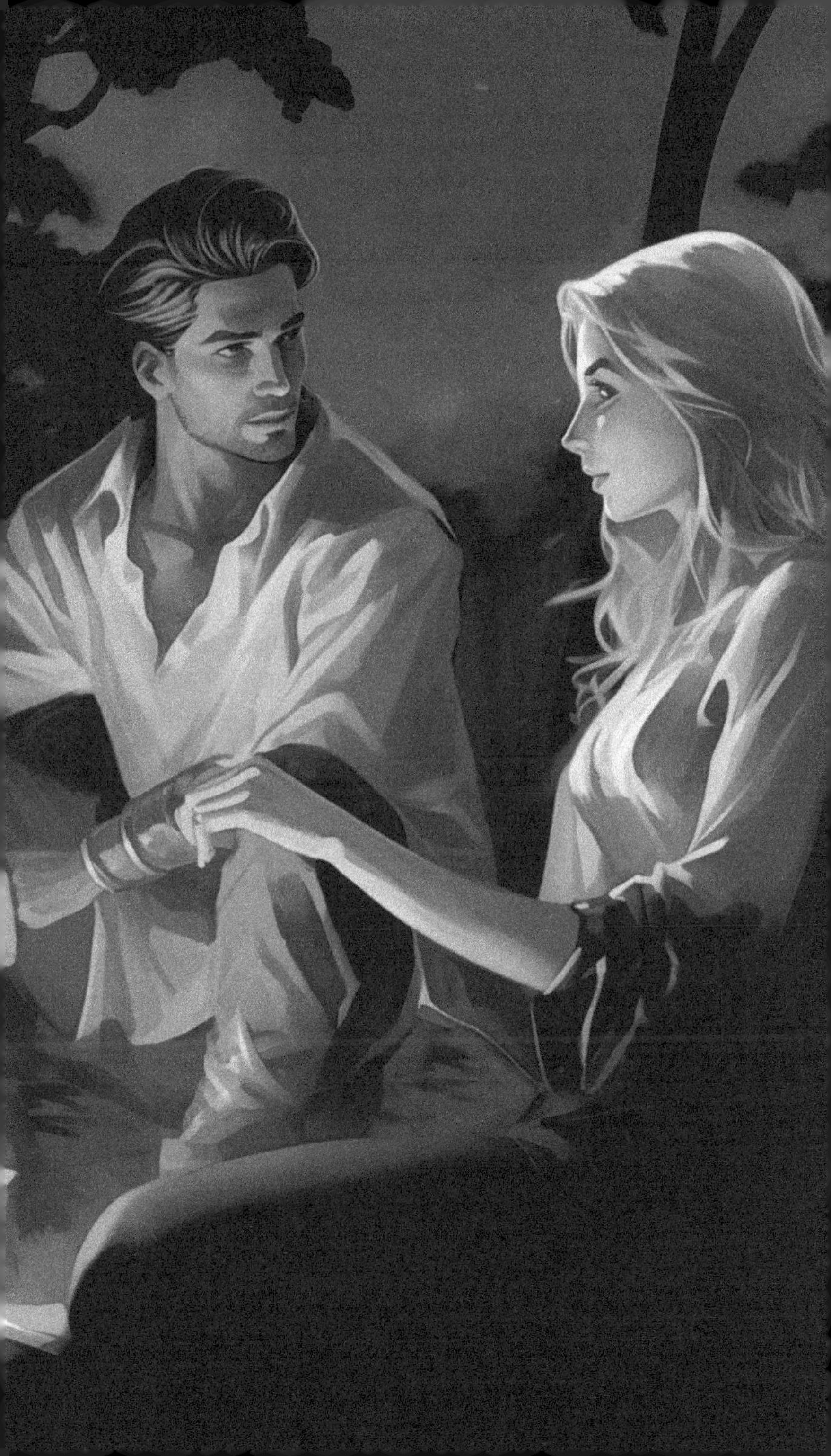

"And you're going to marry one of them?"

Adrianna shrugged, swigging more brandy.

"Are all princes like this?" Sam asked.

"Not all, of course. But the good ones get nabbed immediately, and then the rest of us get left with the dregs."

Another pause.

"You don't have to do this, you know," Sam blurted suddenly.

Adrianna looked up at him.

He shrugged. "The dragon. You don't have to do this. You're... smart and funny and pretty enough for someone to be interested in you without a dragon." That last part seemed to cost him. A great deal.

Adrianna gave a bark of joyless laughter. "Then you clearly have zero understanding of what life is like as a princess. I could be the smartest, the most charming princess in the world, and it wouldn't matter. They need the Impossible Odds to fight against. If I'm just available, then I'm both invisible and worthless. No, I'm not saying that to go fishing for compliments. It's true. I've spent my adult life attending balls and fighting for the attention of men who barely notice my existence because I don't have the right...'accessories'. A curse, a truly evil stepmother, a dragon, being locked in a tower. And the worst part is that I've been fighting for the attention of men who, in my opinion, can at best be described as wet blankets, knowing that the best outcome I can hope for is to be married to someone I don't love and to then die in childbirth, so that my daughter can be forced to go through the same ridiculous charade I did. Happy Ever After, indeed."

"Then to hell with it all—why even take part? Dammit woman, if you talk about wet blankets, then show *you* have a spine. Have the courage of your convictions and walk away from it all."

Adrianna made a pretend shocked face. "You're right. The thought had *never* occurred to me. Thank goodness you're here, Sam, to tell me about how my life works. Do you want to explain how walking works as well? Maybe you want to tell me how to breathe?"

"Okay, then why don't you just do it?"

She reached across to take back the flask from him. "Did you know that a castle can't be left in the hands of a spinster princess, her evil stepmother and evil stepsister? In fact, have you ever heard a story about a spinster princess?"

Adrianna shook her head before he could reply. "Me neither. That's because it doesn't exist. A princess who doesn't marry and cross the Happy Ever After is an aberration. So if I don't marry, we'd all have to leave the castle, which would then pass to someone else. That's already a huge problem—I love my home, and I'm not just surrendering it to some stranger. But suppose I decided my freedom was worth the price and walked away from the castle. Then what would happen to us? Well, the first thing is that my evil stepsister would cease to have a place in this world—if I'm not trying to get married, she has no function, no value, because she has nothing to get in the way of. She's quite pretty—actually pretty, not blessed-by-a-fairy-godmother-pretty, like me. So she'd most likely have to have her face rearranged, and they'd make her become a witch or something of the sort. That's where most witches come from, did you know? I'd have to go through something similar as well and become a witch. I've seen how it looks when they rearrange a face, too. They did it to my evil stepmother. They messed with her mind, because evil stepmothers are either beautiful and cruel, or plain and stupid. So they made her plain and stupid and scarred her face before enchanting it so she could be plain."

Adrianna shuddered, eyes distant as she remembered

Petunia's true reflection in that little mirror. "What they did to her is horrific." She looked back at Sam, her gaze growing cold. "My sister is fourteen. She likes birds and mice. She's gentle and sweet. I won't let anyone, and I mean *anyone*, hurt her. So I don't care about the dragon. I don't care about any of it. If some prince killing a dragon keeps her safe, so be it. I've run out of options. I should have been a better princess, I know. If I'd been less of a failure, I would have been able to attract a prince on my own. Then I'd be safe, and so would Alinor. It's my failing, and I have to live with it. It's a heavy enough burden to carry, on top of the guilt about the dragon I'll be bringing to the slaughter, so I *really* don't need to add your judgement to it. And quite frankly I don't care what you think—about me, about my mission, about any of it. I care about keeping my family safe. If I have to do it with you sulking all the way, then that's how I'll do it. But make no mistake, Sam. I *will* do it."

Sam was staring at her oddly. "I had no idea."

"Of course you didn't. No one sees beyond the shiny exteriors. Everyone thinks a princess's life is all rainbows and unicorns and getting dressed by bluebirds while we fart glitter."

Sam snorted, although Adrianna wasn't sure if it was in shock or laughter. Bodily functions were most definitely not supposed to be on the list of conversation topics for a princess.

"The life of a princess sucks, Sam. It sucks. But no one cares, so long as we smile and look beautiful in a ballgown and tiara. And after all that, after getting the dragon, securing the prince and all the rigmarole, I'll have to be married to some weirdo with bizarre fetishes, who I don't love, and as I said before, I'll have to die in childbirth just so my daughter can continue the cycle. I don't get a choice in the matter. It's the life I was born to, and that's that."

Suddenly, Adrianna felt exhausted, probably from her rant. "I'm going to sleep," she announced, eyeing Mirabelle and trying to decide if it would be truly mean to wake up the fairy to ask her to magic a second bed from the blankets.

Tiredness won out, along with the desire to not be mean. Adrianna knew she could sometimes be a bit selfish, the unhappiness of her situation providing her with a justification, same as with drinking the morning after a ball. But she wanted all that to change. When this dragon business was done Adrianna wanted to behave better. Be better.

She curled up in her blanket right on the floor. She found she didn't mind the discomfort. It was a nice reminder that she was doing something, for once in her life.

Sam stayed as he was the whole time, staring pensively at the fire.

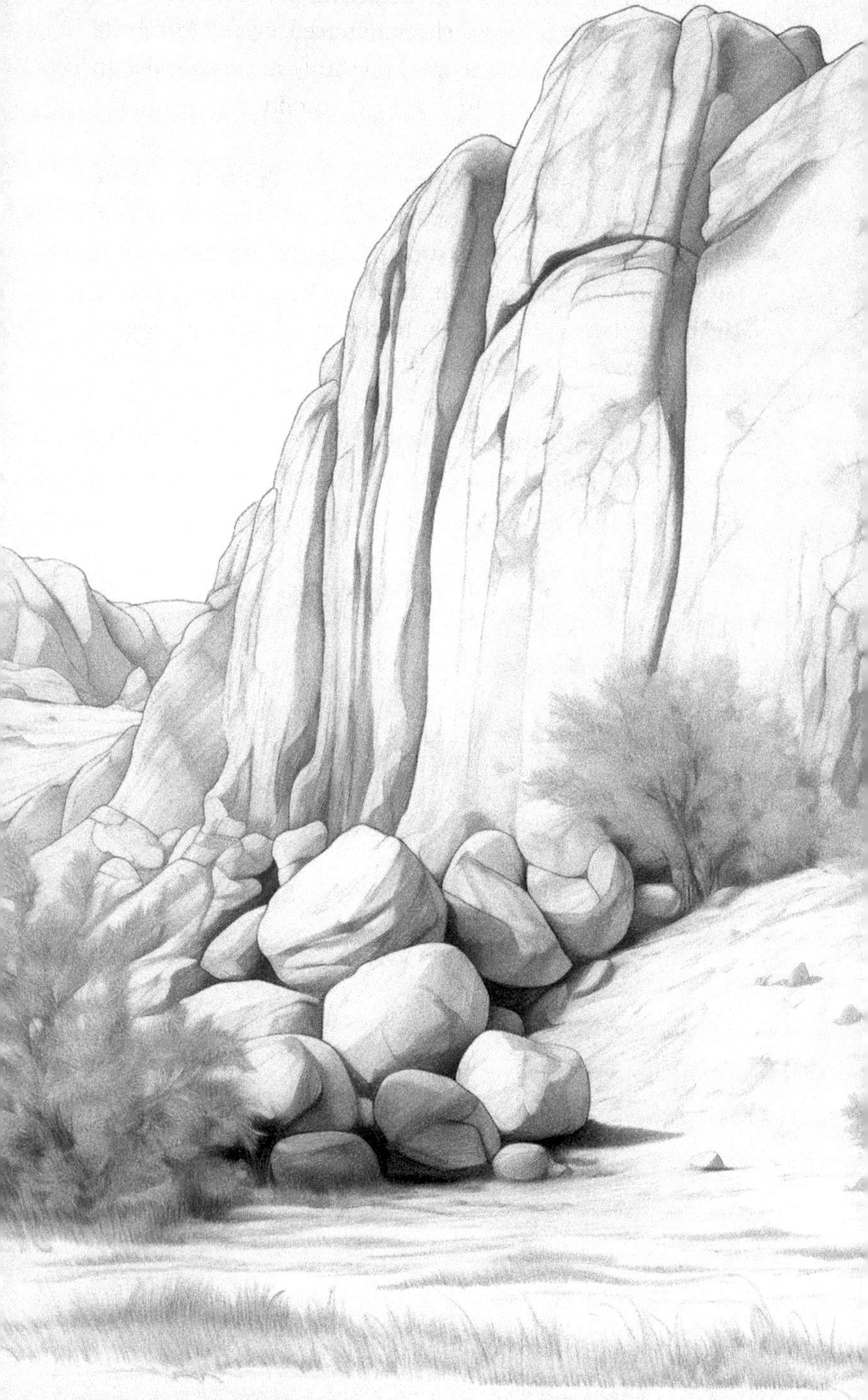

CHAPTER 19

The next day, Sam was a lot less sullen. In fact, the generously-minded might have even gone as far as to call him friendly. As promised, Mirabelle took care of any potential hangovers, tiredness, and soreness, so they all set off as fresh as the proverbial daisies.

Once again the sun was shining, and once again Adrianna found herself trying to suck every last morsel of enjoyment out of the situation, as if she were sucking the marrow from a bone.

This time, Sam joined in when Mirabelle indulged in some of her more crude jokes, laughing along and sending back jokes of his own.

It was, in fact, so pleasant that Adrianna could almost forget the purpose of the trip.

"And what about this wife of yours, then?" Mirabelle suddenly asked Sam.

"Wife?" He looked confused.

"The woman who looked like she was sucking on lemons when she spoke to me," Adrianna replied carelessly, looking aside as if she had other more important things to consider. As if her heart wasn't pounding just a little harder.

"Not my wife," Sam replied. "I told you. She's my brother's wife. He passed a couple of years ago, and I promised I'd look after her, and she promised she'd stay with me. He was a good soul, my brother, a gentle one. But his wife and I can't stand each other, and now because of our promises, we're stuck living together. I have my eye on a farm not far from my house. Small enough that she'd be able to manage it with some help, and derive an income, but independent of me. That's what the money from this endeavour was supposed to go towards. Of course that won't happen now, and that's why she was annoyed." He shrugged. "It's one of those things."

"Ah," Mirabelle said smugly. "So you don't have a wife."

Sam gave her a look, marvelling that this was the only thing she'd retained from all he'd said.

Their horses carried on walking in the sunshine for a time. Adrianna again felt this warm, happy feeling in her stomach, and Sam seemed to be feeling something similar. He was also smiling, relaxed. They chatted away about this and that, laughing easily.

The warm, happy feeling evaporated all of a sudden, leaving Adrianna feeling almost cold. Sam looked as startled as Adrianna felt about the abruptness of the change. He looked about him, and his eyes widened.

"We're nearly there," he said. "I wasn't paying attention, but we're close. I'm going to go on ahead—from memory the dragon's hideout is beyond that knoll."

He trotted off. Adrianna watched him going with a frown. It was odd how suddenly the atmosphere had changed. As if the presence of the dragon had suddenly driven the earlier ease away, even though neither of she nor Sam had been aware of the dragon.

The dragon's magic, perhaps? And then Adrianna understood. She gave her fairy godmother a look.

"What?" Mirabelle asked innocently.

If Adrianna had been suspicious that the fairy might have been meddling—creating that warm, easy feeling—now she knew.

"You're meddling," Adrianna said accusingly.

"I am not."

"You created that nice feeling earlier, and it stopped suddenly because we're close enough for the dragon's magic to interfere with yours."

Mirabelle sniffed and huffed and made some vague gesture with her hand. "I wasn't meddling, just making sure everything happened smoothly."

"Oh yeah, then why the earlier interest in his wife, or lack thereof?"

"For your information, I was just making conversation."

"Conversation? About him not having a wife?"

"Yes," Mirabelle answered primly. "Conversation. I can talk to a man about his wife, real or imaginary, without having a hidden agenda, I'll have you know."

Adrianna felt tired all of a sudden. "Mirabelle, stop whatever you're doing. Now's not the time for meddling—there's too much on the line. I need this dragon thing to go well, and then I need to marry a prince." She looked down at her hands. "It will be a lot worse for me to do that if I have someone else I actually want," she added in a whisper.

Mirabelle looked abashed. "Oh. I hadn't thought… You're right, darling. Of course. I'll stop."

Adrianna gave her a small smile and reached across to squeeze her arm. "But thank you for trying to make me happy."

"You know I want nothing more than that for you."

"I know. But I'm not sure it's possible for me." Adrianna shrugged a shoulder.

Sam came trotting back, then. "Yes, it's just beyond. There's a stone crater, and the dragon is inside with her egg."

And just like that, the reality of what they were about to do crashed down on Adrianna with the weight of fifty ox-drawn carts. She drew a single, struggling breath.

They pushed their horses forward, climbing up the knoll. The silence was leaden. As they crested the hill, the stone crater came into view. It wasn't far, not far at all.

"I need to stop here," Mirabelle said, looking alarmed. "The dragon's magic will soon be too strong for me."

Adrianna's heart began to pound, and her throat tightened. This no longer felt like an adventure or something exciting. She would steal a dragon egg and race back to the castle. It would be terrifying and awful. And then as soon as that was done, it would set wheels in motion. Things would start to happen, and it would probably be impossible to stop them. This brief moment of having agency over her own life would come to an end, things moving inexorably forward until she reached the Happy Ever After.

Adrianna's chest felt tight.

"I guess it's time," she said, although her voice sounded faint and strangled to her ears.

She and Sam dismounted, leaving the horses in Mirabelle's care. They couldn't hobble them, because once Sam came out with a dragon egg, they would need to move quickly. Sam grabbed a rolled-up blanket from behind his horse's saddle.

The crater looked like something huge had fallen from the sky and rammed into the earth before disappearing and leaving behind a natural, rocky bowl. The rocks were grey and sharp as they rose up towards the sky. It almost looked incongruous against the lush, green grass that surrounded it, all springy and speckled with splotches of colour from little wild flowers.

There was nothing in the air to indicate that a dragon was nearby. No smell of brimstone and fire, no heavy breathing, no sense of impending doom.

Adrianna squared her shoulders and lifted her chin defiantly. This was it, the moment of truth.

"We better get going," she said. She steeled herself. She couldn't let anything interfere with her goal now. She had to be cold, ruthless. She would do whatever it took.

Sam glanced at her then looked away, nodding. All his earlier cheer had evaporated, his features now grim.

"You don't need to come for this part," he muttered.

"If I'm leading a dragon to the slaughter, I will get my hands dirty," Adrianna said. "It's the absolute least I can do. I'm not going to hide myself away like a coward, so I don't have to see the reality of what I'm doing." She would do that much for the dragon. At the very least, she would respect it. Respect *her*.

Sam gave her another one of his odd looks—he had a lot of those, it seemed, a whole array of them—and nodded. "Then you can help me create the distraction."

"What do I need to do?"

"It's actually not that complicated. You just have to make a noise to distract the dragon while I grab the egg in a blanket so I don't burn myself, and then we run like hell."

"That's it?" Adrianna asked, so aghast that she stopped walking. "That stupidly steep price you named was just to get in, make some noise, grab the egg, and leave?"

Sam shrugged, looking a little awkward. "I wanted the money for the farm, and I figured neither you nor your fairy godmother were likely to know anything about dragons. The reality is that anyone who charges money to get a dragon egg is operating a scam. It's dangerous because you're dealing with a dragon, but it's frighteningly easy to do. Why do you think the dragon population is so critically low these days?"

"But they're *dragons*. It can't be that easy to take their eggs."

"That's why taking dragon eggs is such a vile thing to do. Female dragons don't move away from their egg once they have laid it. They don't eat, they don't drink, they don't move, not until the egg hatches. So if you catch a female dragon towards the end of her brooding period, she's weak from the lack of food and water, and her abilities are greatly reduced. Still not to be underestimated, of course, but much more vulnerable than a normal dragon."

"So you can really take a dragon egg, just like that?

"Dragons don't have very good abilities to register touch. They lie next to their egg, but if they're distracted and you're careful, you can get the egg away without them realising right away, yes."

Adrianna shook her head in amazement. "If it's that easy, how are there any dragons left at all?"

"Well, they hide. Also, it doesn't always work well—sometimes things go wrong. It's not without risk. You're still dealing with a massive beast, and a fire breathing one at that."

"Right. On that—how do we stop the mother from just roasting us?"

"You'll have to stay close to me. The mother won't breathe fire on us if we have the egg for fear of harming the youngling. And as far as attacks from her talons, we have to all remain close to this." He pulled a talisman from inside his shirt. It was simple, just a dark-red stone carved in the shape of a dragon, hanging on a leather thong. Adrianna recognised it. It was part of the supplies Sam had said he required.

"The dragon's bane you asked for," Adrianna said.

"Yes. It's a very simple and rudimentary kind of magic, but it keeps dragons at a distance. For a time. The dragon's own magic will gradually erode it, and once it does, we have no defences. At which point the mother will be able to swoop down, grab us with her talons, snap us in half like dry twigs, and get her egg back. Now do you see? It's possible to get the egg. But what happens after you get the egg? A mother dragon might be weakened, but she still has the stamina and strength to go on far longer than a human or a horse. Which means you either have to abandon the egg and flee, hoping to get away…"

"Or have her killed," Adrianna finished.

"Exactly." Sam's expression shifted, as if he were eating something foul. "Which is where your precious prince comes in."

"He's not my precious prince. I don't…" The whole thing made Adrianna angry all of a sudden. She wanted to wipe the world of the plague that were princes. And princesses. And the whole stupid, sorry concept of the Happy Ever After.

"One more thing," Sam said. "Well, one more question. Was there really another mercenary? Now that you know the full truth of how I was scamming you, you can admit your lies as well."

Adrianna hesitated. She still needed him to help her with the egg now, and if she admitted she'd made the whole mercenary thing up, he might turn tail and leave her high and dry.

A muscle feathered at Sam's jaw, but a grudging smile tweaked his lips. "I knew it. I just knew it."

"I didn't say anything."

"Your lack of response is a response."

"It's not. Now let's go. I don't want to waste time." For a moment, Adrianna feared Sam would walk away, but he fell into step with her.

"For what it's worth, now that I know about what's at stake for you, I... I kind of understand."

Adrianna looked up at him, surprised. "Oh. I... Oh." She didn't know what to say to that.

They reached the foot of the crater, and Sam placed a finger against his mouth to indicate they should be silent as they clambered up. The rock was rough and jagged, making it easy to find foot and handholds, and the crater lip wasn't too high.

Still, Adrianna couldn't see or hear anything to indicate a dragon was nearby. Nor could she smell anything, and she had assumed that a dragon would have quite a distinctive smell.

She whispered as much to Sam.

"Female dragons have a special kind of cloaking magic to keep themselves and their eggs hidden away," he whispered back. "That makes them harder to find."

As they reached the lip, Sam gestured for Adrianna to move carefully, keeping himself flat against the rock. He nodded as he reached the lip.

Adrianna stifled a gasp as she reached his side and looked down at the inside of the crater. The dragon's cloaking magic obviously didn't work at such close range —the moment Adrianna stuck her head above the crater lip, the smell and the sounds of the great beast hit her in the face with all the subtlety of a brick.

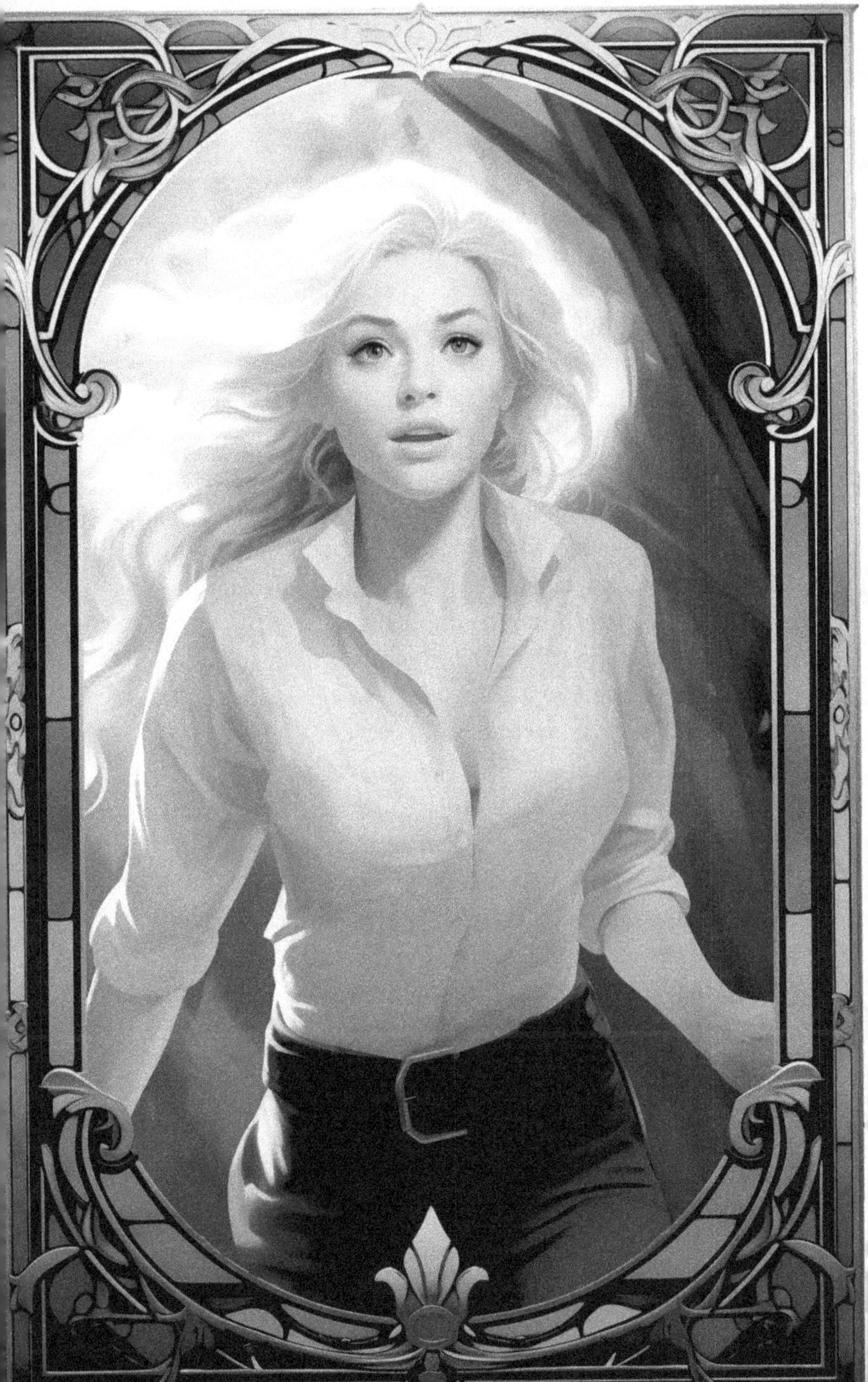

The dragon did indeed smell like brimstone and sulphur, but also like something that reminded her of horses—a kind of clean, hay-like smell. She was curled up, wrapped around an egg, which was surprisingly small given how huge the adult dragon was. About the height of two wine bottles stacked end to end. The egg was iridescent blue and green and covered with fine golden veins that pulsed gently.

The mother was all of dark teal, save for a crest of gold spikes along the back of her head and all along her spine, right to the tip of her tail. Her scales were dull and even cracked in places. Adrianna remembered what Sam had said about mother dragons never leaving the side of their egg—and she wondered whether the dull scales were a sign that this dragon had been here for a long time. Her huge, leathery wings were tucked around her.

She was resting the tip of her nose against the egg, making a soft and regular *'rhoooooo'* sound against it. The sound had been impossible to detect until Adrianna had crested the lip, because of the cloaking magic.

"She's breathing on the egg to keep it at the right temperature," Sam whispered. "Her body isn't enough to keep the egg warm, so she has to breathe on it."

The dragon had a reptilian face, with heavily lidded eyes but even from a distance, even though it was a great, terrifying beast, the gentle care and love the mother had for her egg was as obvious as the nose in the middle of a person's face.

And that would be the thing that killed her. She would chase down after them, desperate to get her egg back, all the way to the castle, just so that some pompous idiot could slaughter her. Some idiot who liked unconscious women and spinning wheels in bed, or who collected springs, or who had bad breath, or…

Rhooooooo. The dragon took a deep, patient breath, continuing to warm her egg.

The side of the crater had a kind of overhang to it, and the dragon was lying beneath it. She wasn't fully covered, but it did give her additional protection. She had chosen well, she just hadn't accounted for being within reach of a princess's castle.

The more Adrianna looked, the more she could see the signs of neglect on the mother. Places where the leathery, scaly skin looked overly loose, as if it were a size too big or hanging from too small a frame. Great strips of dry skin hanging from the great, leathery wings.

"She's been here a long time, right?" Adrianna whispered.

Sam nodded. "Yes. She's the best chance we have of making it out alive with the egg."

Rhoooo. Each dragon breath smelt like a million matches had been struck at once.

The dragon mother was oblivious to Adrianna and Sam. She was entirely focused on her egg. Her eyes were soft, and even though she had a reptilian face, Adrianna could have sworn there was contentment in her expression.

"You promise you'll let me keep the egg so I can save the baby, yes?" Sam asked urgently.

"Of course," Adrianna murmured, unable to tear her eyes away from the dragon.

Sam whispered something, but Adrianna didn't hear him. Wasn't listening.

"I..." Adrianna tried to focus on Alinor. On the memory of the horrific scars on Petunia's face. On the castle she loved like a person. All the reasons she had to get in there, steal the egg, and get the mother killed.

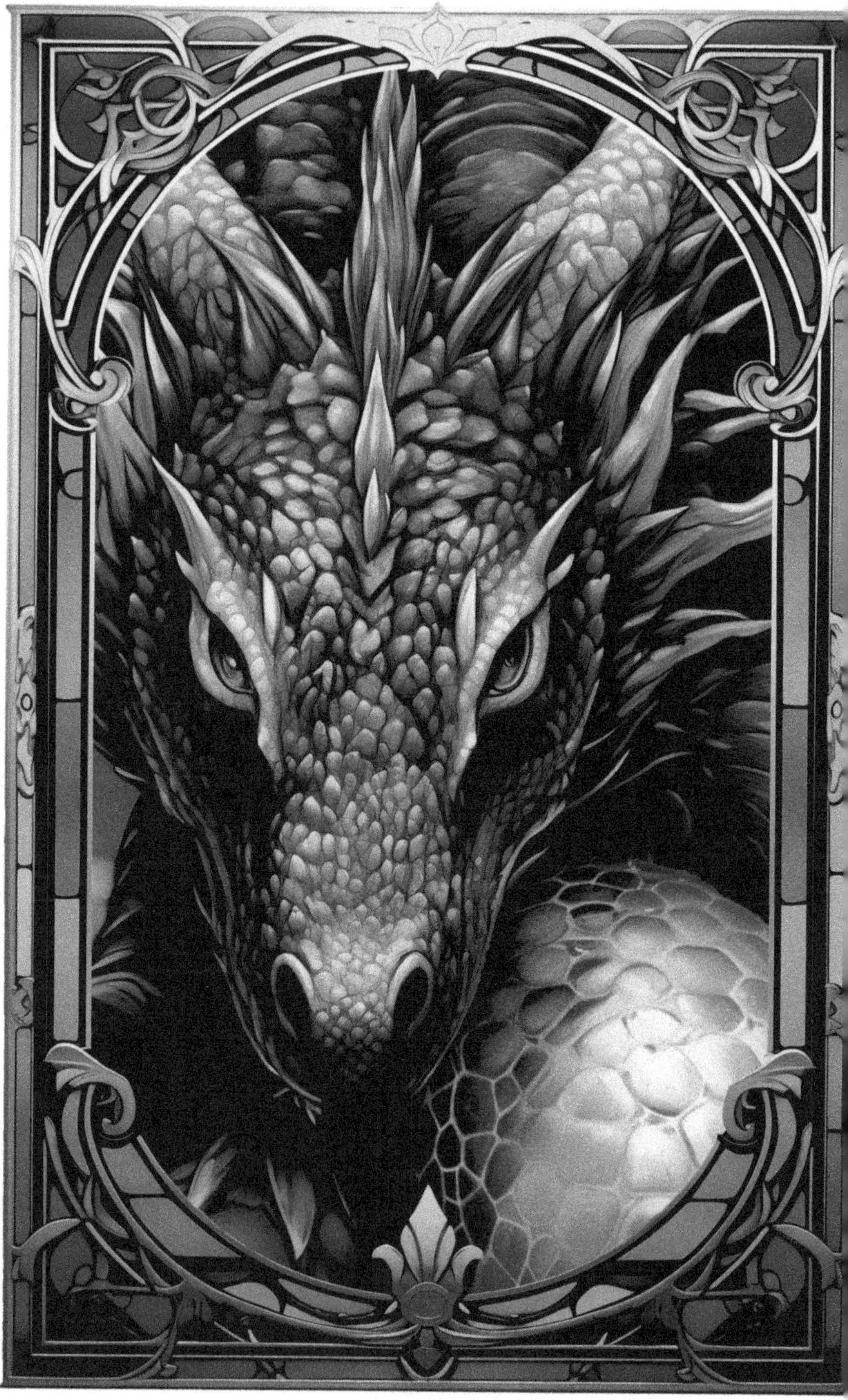

Sam touched her arm, looking worried. "You all right?" he whispered.

"I..." Adrianna stared down at the mother dragon. At the egg, so pretty and so small and so iridescent. Could Sam truly raise the youngling once it hatched? Would it even hatch without the mother's breath to warm it? What an awful, sad thing for the baby dragon to be born without a mother.

Adrianna had had her father after her mother died in childbirth. The baby dragon, if it could hatch alone, wouldn't even have that.

"I..." Adrianna lowered herself and turned so she had her back to the rock, her head below the crater rim. All at once, the breathing sounds and sounds of the dragon disappeared. She took a great, shuddering breath at the relief of it.

And that was when the truth hit her. Her eyes teared up.

"I can't do this," she whispered, wrapping her arms around herself. "I can't do this. I can't." Adrianna shook her head, burying her face in her hands. "Damned if I do, damned if I don't. But I can't do this. I can't *do* it."

And she had no idea what that meant for her, for Alinor, for the future.

Sam came to crouch down next to her. "It's fine. We can find another way. To get you a prince, I mean. We'll get you the prince you need, all right? I'll help you. I promise we'll find a way."

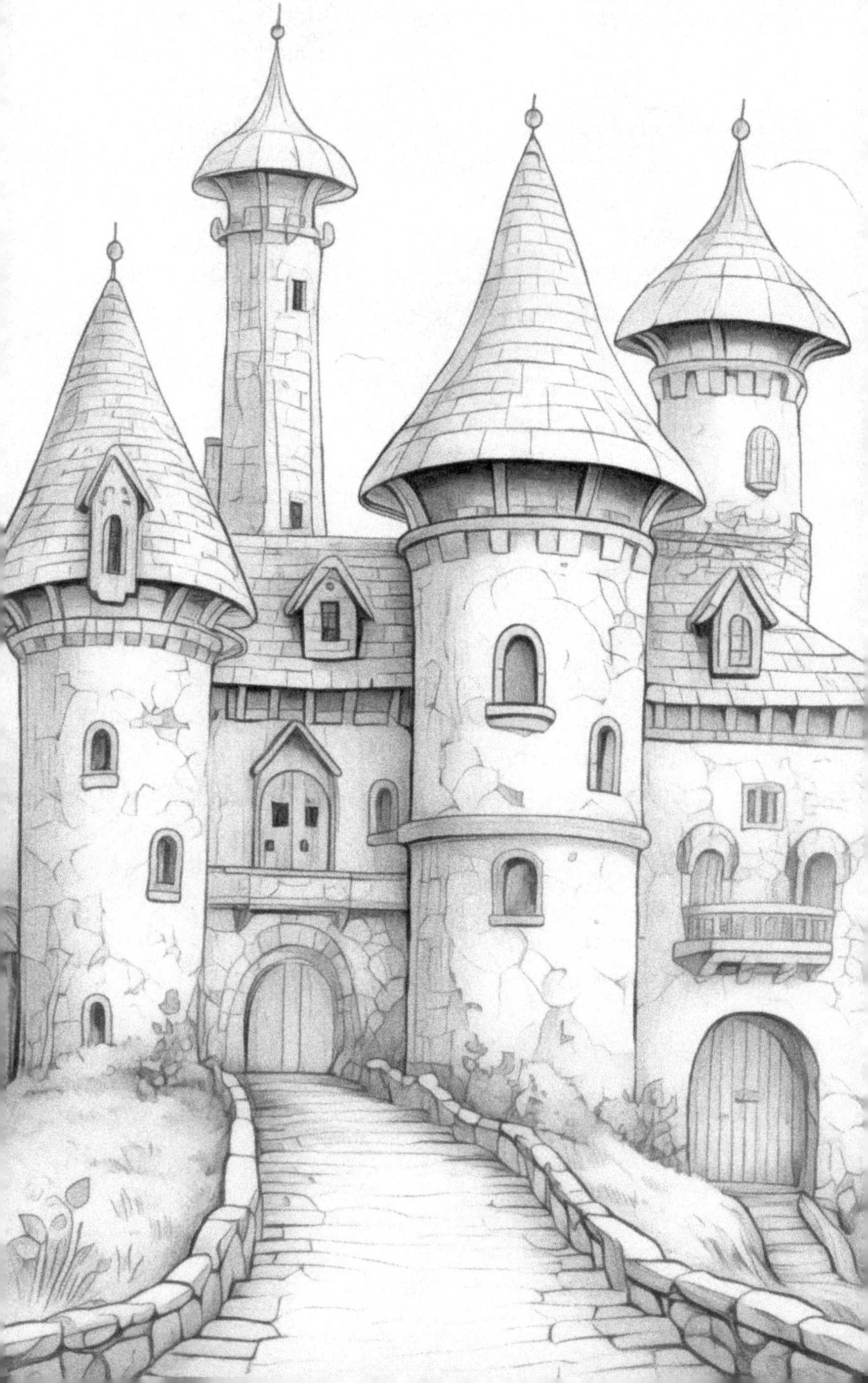

CHAPTER 20

The journey back to the castle took place in complete silence. This time, there was none of the lightness from before. None of the sense of adventure, no attempt to enjoy the moment. At night, Adrianna slept alone, pushing away both Sam and Mirabelle's attempts to talk to her. She couldn't focus enough to listen to them, anyway.

The weight of her failure was crushing. Like it was slowly going to obliterate her.

In fact, the more she thought about it, the more she had to surrender to the evidence: her entire life was a failure. She had failed as a princess, now she had failed to get a dragon—in fact, what had she ever done that was worthwhile in her life? Nothing, that was the answer. She was a coward for going after the dragon in the first place, and a coward for failing to see it through. A coward and a failure.

And now... Now what? What would happen? She had no idea, and she just didn't have it in her to face the enormity of the unknown before her, and worse, the potential consequences of her failure. Of her selfishness at letting her discomfort over killing the dragon win. She should have ignored her feelings and stolen the egg. She should have been so focused on her sister's safety that her own emotions didn't even register.

So she slept alone and refused to be drawn in by Sam and Mirabelle.

By the time they reached the castle, Adrianna felt as exhausted as she felt hopeless. How would she tell Alinor? How could she look into her sister's eyes and admit that she hadn't been able to secure Alinor's safety?

Her mare seemed to sense the darkness of the hour, trudging slowly down the path towards the castle.

Adrianna stopped in front of the main entrance. Normally she would have gone straight to the back to take care of her horse herself, but right now, she was too exhausted. Lowen would have to do it.

The door burst open, and Petunia streamed out. Her hair was dishevelled, only a small part still up in something that might once have been a bun, while the rest was in a mad tizzy around her face. One of her sleeves was torn, and there was a trickle of dry blood from the corner of her mouth. Her eyes were wide, crazed with panic, and tears streamed down her face.

"Adrianna," she wailed. "They took her. Adrianna, they took her!"

As if the words had cost Petunia all the energy she had left, she collapsed slowly to her knees, her skirts puddling round her.

Adrianna didn't need to ask who 'they' were or who had been taken. "Where? *Where??* Petunia, *where?*"

Petunia gasped a breath. "The same place they rearranged my face."

"Mirabelle," Adrianna said at once, turning to her fairy godmother.

Mirabelle's face was white. "I can't go there. I can't get anywhere near that place. They have magic there to keep fairy godmothers away. I'm... I'm as powerless as you."

"I'm not powerless," Adrianna replied. "Tell me where. Right. Goddam. *Now.*"

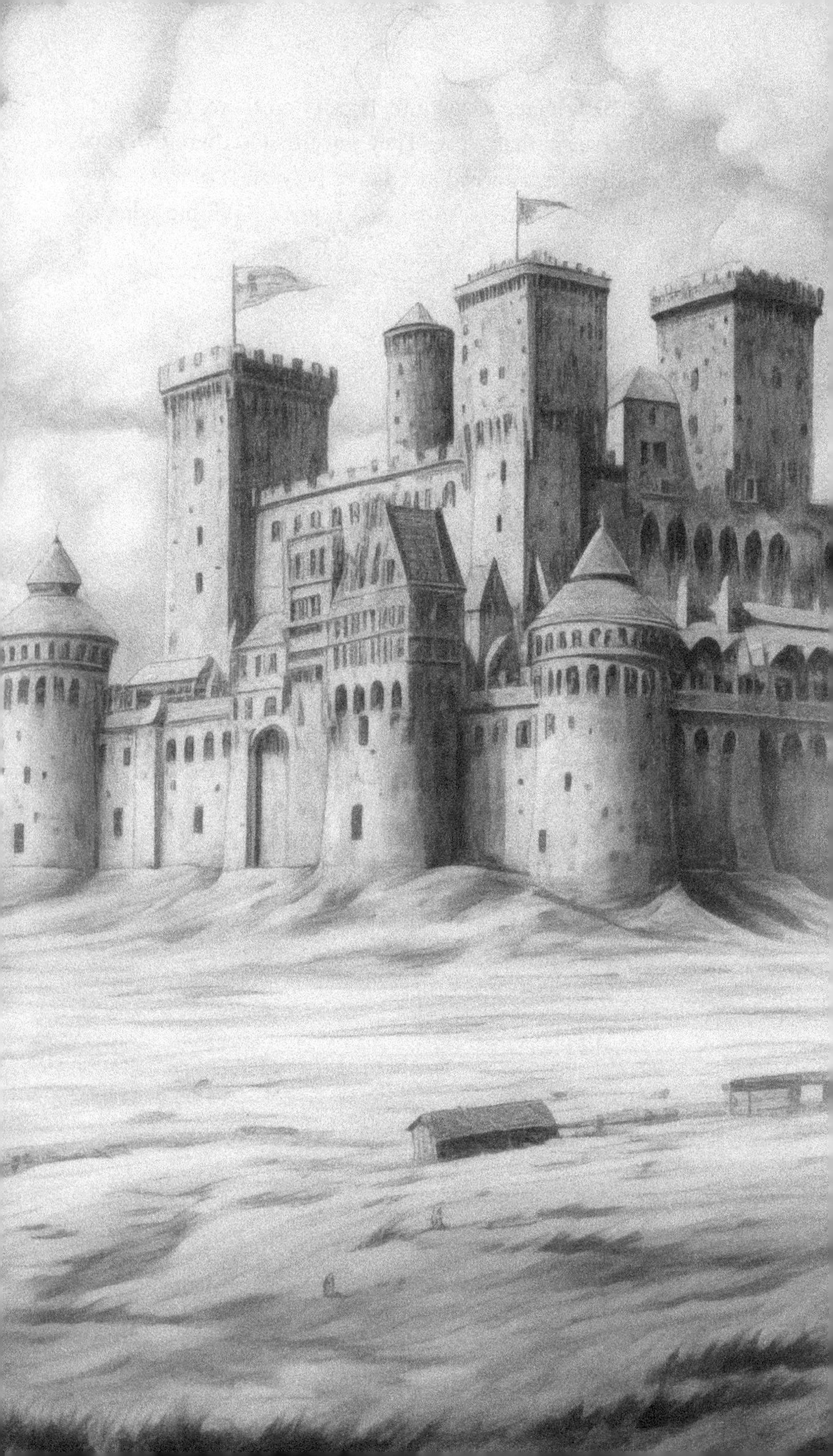

CHAPTER 21

Adrianna and her mare flew forward, the horse's hooves digging into the soft ground and throwing up clods of dirt. The road was like a knife through the lush green forest, each tree another milestone on their race to reach the fortified keep where Alinor had been taken. Adrianna's vision had narrowed to nothing beyond the road ahead of her. Her chest was so constricted, she would have been incapable of swallowing a single thing. Her mind was focused with a cold intensity on reaching Alinor, but beneath the surface of her determined exterior were terror and anguish that could break free at any moment.

"What are you going to do when you get there?" Sam yelled, trying to be heard above the thunder of the horses' hooves and the whistle of the wind. His horse was level with Adrianna's.

"Adrianna!" he yelled louder, and this time, she glanced over at him. "They won't just let you in! What are you going to do?"

Adrianna turned her attention back to the road. Her mind was both blank and racing—blankly staring at the road ahead, while at the same time racing around the thought that Alinor had been taken, Alinor had been taken, Alinor had been taken.

"Adrianna!"

"I don't know!" she screamed in response. "I'll figure it out when I get there. I'll do something. I'll get her back."

They burst out of the forest, and there it was, just at the top of a hill. A heavy, ugly pile of grey stone. Impassable, impregnable. The fortified keep.

It looked like a grey, featureless block, marked only by the scars of old battles. The shock of it caused Adrianna to stop abruptly. Sam cursed as he yanked his own horse to a stop.

"We need some kind of plan," Sam said. "You can't just enter the keep. They have sentries."

He was right—Adrianna could make them out. Two of them, standing one on either side of the entrance. No massive oak doors, no lowered portcullis. Just an open stone archway and two men with a black uniform and matching spears.

Adrianna stared at the keep. The clean, pine resin smell of the forest seemed to disappear, then, and Adrianna fancied she could smell old blood and rusty metal and stagnant water that dripped along old walls. The memory of the horrific scars on her stepmother's face rose back up, and something snapped inside her.

She spurred her mare on, charging towards the keep. "Mirabelle, get me a sword!" she yelled into the air. "Right now. I mean it, right bloody now!" The fairy didn't need to be present in person to work miracles.

Sam cursed again, chasing after Adrianna. "Stop! Don't be stupid. Stop—Adrianna!"

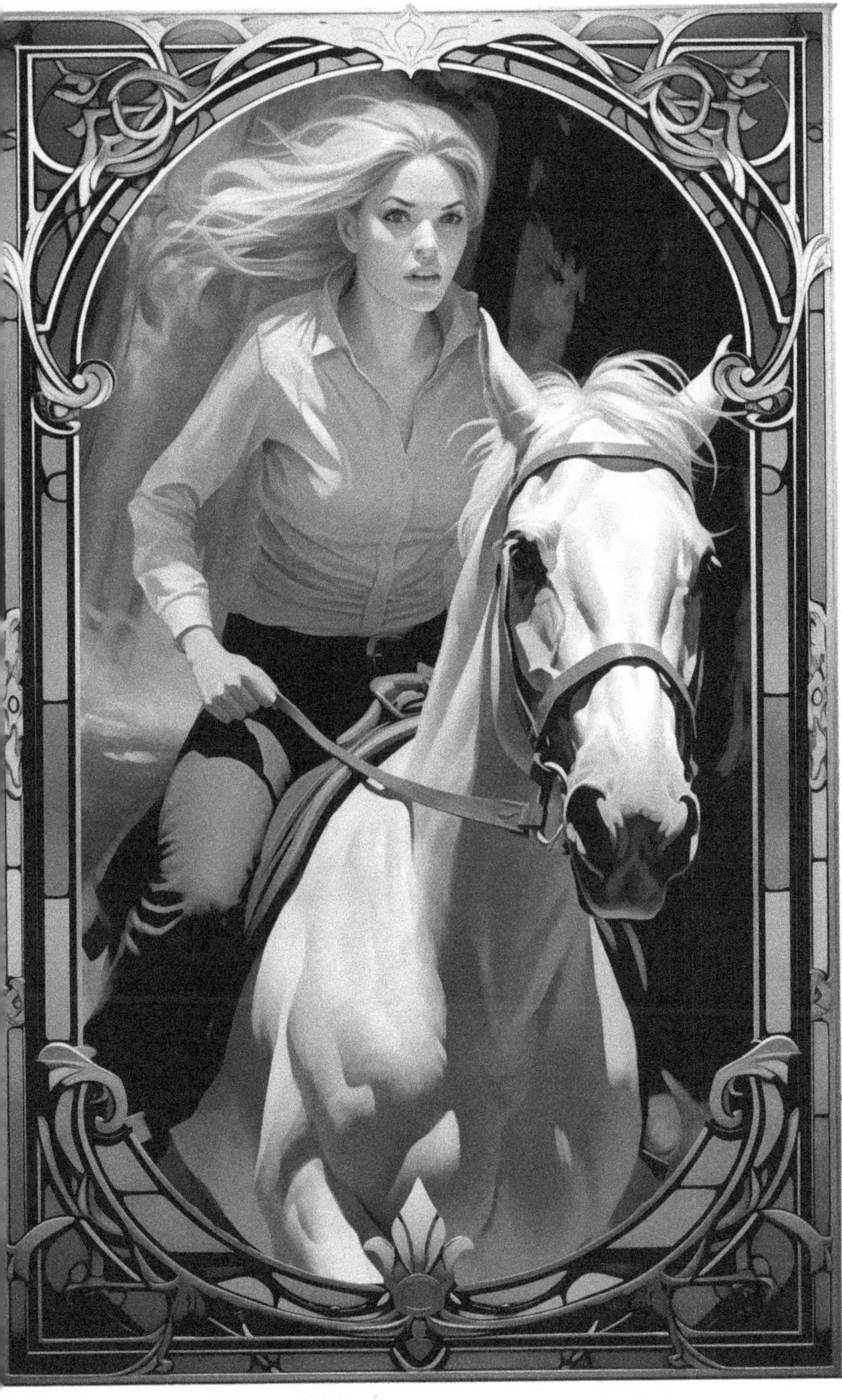

A sword appeared in Adrianna's right hand. She could see the entrance to the fortified keep, as if aiming for it between her horse's ears. They flew like the wind, her and her mare. She would charge into the keep, and once in there, she would just keep on going, and going, until she found Alinor. She didn't need a plan—couldn't formulate a plan, anyhow. She just needed to find her sister, that was all.

The keep seemed to thunder closer to her with every beat of her horse's hoofs. She could see the sentries, the gold emblem on their black uniforms, their metal helmets. Between them was the entrance to the keep, and beyond she could see people, horses, carts.

"Release Alinor," Adrianna cried, pointing her sword forward. She knew she was acting crazy—she felt crazy too, but she couldn't stop.

She could hear Sam shouting at her, but she ignored him.

Her mare thundered forward, aiming right for the middle of the entrance. The guards didn't seem frightened or panicked. They also didn't seem to be doing anything to try to block her. Adrianna could now hear the pounding of something heavy and made of metal from beyond the archway. The ringing out of voices. She was going to charge through the entrance, she was going to—

She didn't actually see the spear move, but she felt it. The spear's handle caught the side of her face and across the chest, knocking her clean off her horse. The sentry had barely moved, just swung his spear cleanly, precisely.

She crashed, landing heavily on her back. All the air left her lungs in one sickly sound. She made a faint, pained noise, arms slowly coming to cradle her stomach, unable to breathe. Her sword had been knocked from her hand in the fall.

Somewhere a horse neighed. Hooves rang out on the flagstones. She heard Sam's voice, but it felt distant.

"Adrianna." Boots close to her. He lifted her head. "Are you alright?"

"Can't… breathe…"

She felt his strong hands checking her head, her neck, her ribs.

"She'll be fine," another male voice said. "She just took a heavy fall."

Sam carefully picked her up and helped her to sit. Her breathing was starting to return, but she still couldn't speak, and her head was spinning.

"She was coming for her sister," Sam said. "A young girl called Alinor. She got brought here today, apparently. Anything you can tell us about her?"

"Ah, you got my sympathies, there. Never pleasant when rearrangements have to be made, worse when it's a young 'un. Still, if you don't follow the rules…"

"Is there any way Adrianna could at least see her? Speak to her?" Sam asked.

Adrianna managed to get enough of a hold of herself to look up at the sentry who was speaking. He looked like an ordinary man, neither ugly nor handsome. Stubble on his cheeks and the brawn that came from having a physically demanding job. He looked calm, not at all affected by the situation.

"Afraid not," the sentry said. "And her attempt to charge in was worse than stupid. Prisoners are kept in the lower levels, underground. There's no getting past all the many, many sentries guarding all the various doors, stairways, and corridors. No one has ever forced their way into the lower levels," he added proudly. "It has to be this way. The Master needs time to lay out the plans for the work he does, so he can't be rushed or be worrying that someone will burst in at an inopportune moment. It takes time to plan such precise work. It's a complicated matter to fix broken storylines."

"And what about—" Sam began.

"No, you can't see her before the work begins."

"Has the work already begun?"

"Not yet, no. It takes a few days of preparation before he can begin."

"Then could we…"

"No. No one goes down there unless they're being re-arranged. And before you get any ideas in your head, once the preparations begin, there's no stopping the process. The Master will do his work, and nothing and no one will stop him."

"But there must be something," Adrianna croaked. "Why did they come? Why did your master take Alinor? She's done nothing wrong. And it's too early. I'm still young enough to marry a prince. I was going to get a dragon. Tell him—your master. Tell him I'm going to get a dragon so a prince can come rescue me. Can come marry me. It will still all work out. The storylines will be respected, and there will be a Happy Ever After."

"Sorry, princess." The sentry shrugged. "Once the Master has made a decision, there's no going back. If he decided on a rearrangement, it means that a rearrangement was needed, and there's nothing any of us can do about that."

"But…"

"Look," the sentry said more kindly. "I know it's hard for a young 'un to get re-arranged. But I heard about this one. A prince proposing to an evil stepmother is so irregular, arrangements have to be made right away for this storyline to work."

Adrianna understood what he meant. For Petunia and Charming's story to be a fairytale, Alinor couldn't exist. Adrianna neither, for that matter, and the only reason she hadn't been taken was because she'd gone seeking the dragon.

"Why can't they cancel that storyline?" Adrianna said. "Re-arrange that storyline by cancelling the engagement and keep my storyline going, with my evil stepsister. I'm just about to get engaged—there's a Happy Ever After on the way already."

"The engagement has already happened, so it's already too late. Engagements don't get cancelled in Once-Upon-Thyme, you know this. I know it's hard, but you have to let it go. The storylines must be respected."

Adrianna gripped Sam's shirt. "Attack them. My sword..." She moved her head to find her sword, and the movement made everything worse. The pounding head, the struggle to breathe. "There—my sword." She pointed weakly at the fallen weapon.

He shook his head while the sentries shifted behind him.

"Attack them," she said through gritted teeth.

Sam looked up at the sentries who were both lowering their spears. "Woah, wait. No need to be hasty. Just ignore her. She's had a bump to the head, and she's still traumatised over the loss of her sister. She doesn't know what she's saying. You fellas stay right where you are. I'm just going to take her away..."

Adrianna was too weak to be able to do more than squawk in outrage as he picked her up and slung her over his shoulder like a sack of potatoes. He grabbed her sword as well.

"You gents have a good day, now," he said to the sentries as he walked away.

Sam's shoulder dug in Adrianna's already painful stomach, making it even harder to breathe, and the way he jostled her as he walked away quickly made the nausea almost overwhelming.

"You... coward," she tried to yell, although it came out far more quiet and pained than she wanted.

"Adrianna, I've never held a sword in my life," Sam said curtly. "What exactly would it achieve for me to attack them with your sword, other than for me to wind up beaten and bloody like you are right now? Or maybe both of us get arrested and taken away, and then we won't be able to do anything."

He stopped marching and lowered her to the ground. The horses were a few paces away, grazing the grass.

"Give me my sword," Adrianna ordered in a wheeze, intending to grab it from him and walk back towards the keep. She wasn't giving up.

But Sam held her back easily with one strong arm, and he didn't let her take her sword.

"Out of my way, peasant," she shouted, her voice finally coming out sounding normal.

"Oh, now I'm a peasant, am I?"

"You are when you stop me from getting to my sister." Adrianna's voice cracked on the last word.

"I'm not the one stopping you from getting to your sister," Sam said gently. "I'm stopping you from getting yourself hurt or killed."

She swung for him, but she was still too shaky from the fall, and she missed. Not that she really had much experience in the art of punching someone in the face.

She swung again, this time slamming her fists into his chest, but it was like punching a wall, and she only succeeded in hurting her knuckles. Sam apparently didn't feel a thing.

"Adrianna..."

"Coward! You total and utter coward. You *are* a peasant. A prince would never fall back before Impossible Odds. A prince would storm the keep, even if he was on his own, and rescue my sister."

Yes, a prince would do that. A prince would storm the keep, would storm the tower, would get Alinor, fighting and killing all the bad guys on the way, and bring her back out, unhurt.

A princess, however, charging a keep with a sword and a horse to rescue her sister, got unhorsed and beaten before she even managed to enter the keep. Princesses were not supposed to charge keeps. They were supposed to be locked away in the keep and find a prince to do the storming for them, something Adrianna had failed to do.

Her eyes blurred with tears.

She wouldn't give up. She tried to get past Sam again, but he held her back easily. She struggled against him. Uselessly.

"Adrianna, stop this! Stop being stupid. What will you achieve if you get arrested or hurt or killed? You can do nothing for Alinor in any of those states. Think! Be smart."

"You coward," she wailed, pounding Sam's chest again, without managing to put any strength behind it. "Coward..." Her tears were falling freely now. She swayed, still as weak and clumsy from her fall as a drunkard at the end of a night.

Sam steadied her with a hand. "Adrianna..."

There was nothing she could do. Nothing. The depth of her failure was more than she could bear. She had allowed Alinor to be taken, to have her face rearranged.

She slowly sank to the floor, sobbing so hard she was once again struggling to breathe.

"Adrianna..."

Through the veil of her tears, she could see that Sam had crouched down with her. He tried to wipe her tears with his hands, his big, rough fingers rubbing against her cheekbones, but it was about as useful as trying to hold back the tide.

Her chest felt like it was being squeezed by a vise. The

thought of her sister in the keep made her want to come out of her skin, and she cried harder, snot and tears mixing.

"I'm sorry I'm not a prince," Sam whispered. "I'm really sorry."

Eventually, Adrianna ran out of tears. Her eyes were puffy and painful. She felt like she had literally emptied herself, and now she was exhausted. At least she had recovered the ability to breathe, which had allowed her to wail quite impressively.

She sat in the grass, Sam in front of her, gazing at her with concern while she looked at the keep dully. He was saying something about maybe appealing to another more influential king and queen, or maybe finding a prince who would be willing to help, but she paid no attention. There was nobody to appeal to. No one would care about the fate of an evil step sister.

Adrianna stared numbly at the keep, as if with enough time, her gaze could pierce the stone walls.

The keep. Ugly pile of grey stones and huge oak beams. Probably full of thick, heavy doors that a princess would never be able to force her way past.

Something about what she had just thought snagged in her mind, as if it were important. She stared at the keep some more, blinking through her swollen eyelids. Something about this was important—what was it?

And then she got it. She got slowly up to her feet, never taking her eyes off the keep.

"Adrianna?" Sam asked, getting up with him.

"Let's go," she said abruptly, turning towards her mare.

"Are we going to appeal—"

"We're not appealing to anyone. No one cares about evil stepsisters. They are not the ones that stories are about, so no one will lift a finger to help Alinor."

"But..."

"The world we live in is completely crazy. So the only way is to go with an equally crazy idea."

"Tell me?"

Adrianna reached for her mare, grabbing the reins with one hand and the saddle with another, but her legs were still too shaky.

"Help me back on my horse."

"Not until you tell me what you have in mind."

She turned and glared at him. "Sam…"

"Adrianna," he replied in the same tone. "I want to help, all right? We're in this together."

Her glare turned into surprise. "We are?"

Now it was his turn to look annoyed. "What exactly do you take me for? Just because I'm not a prince doesn't mean I'm just going to leave Alinor here. For crying out loud, Adrianna, princes aren't the only ones who do things in this world. "

"Oh."

"So, what have you got in mind?"

"There are wooden beams in the keep. And wooden doors."

Sam nodded but looked confused. "A great many of both, I would have thought. What about it?"

"Wood burns."

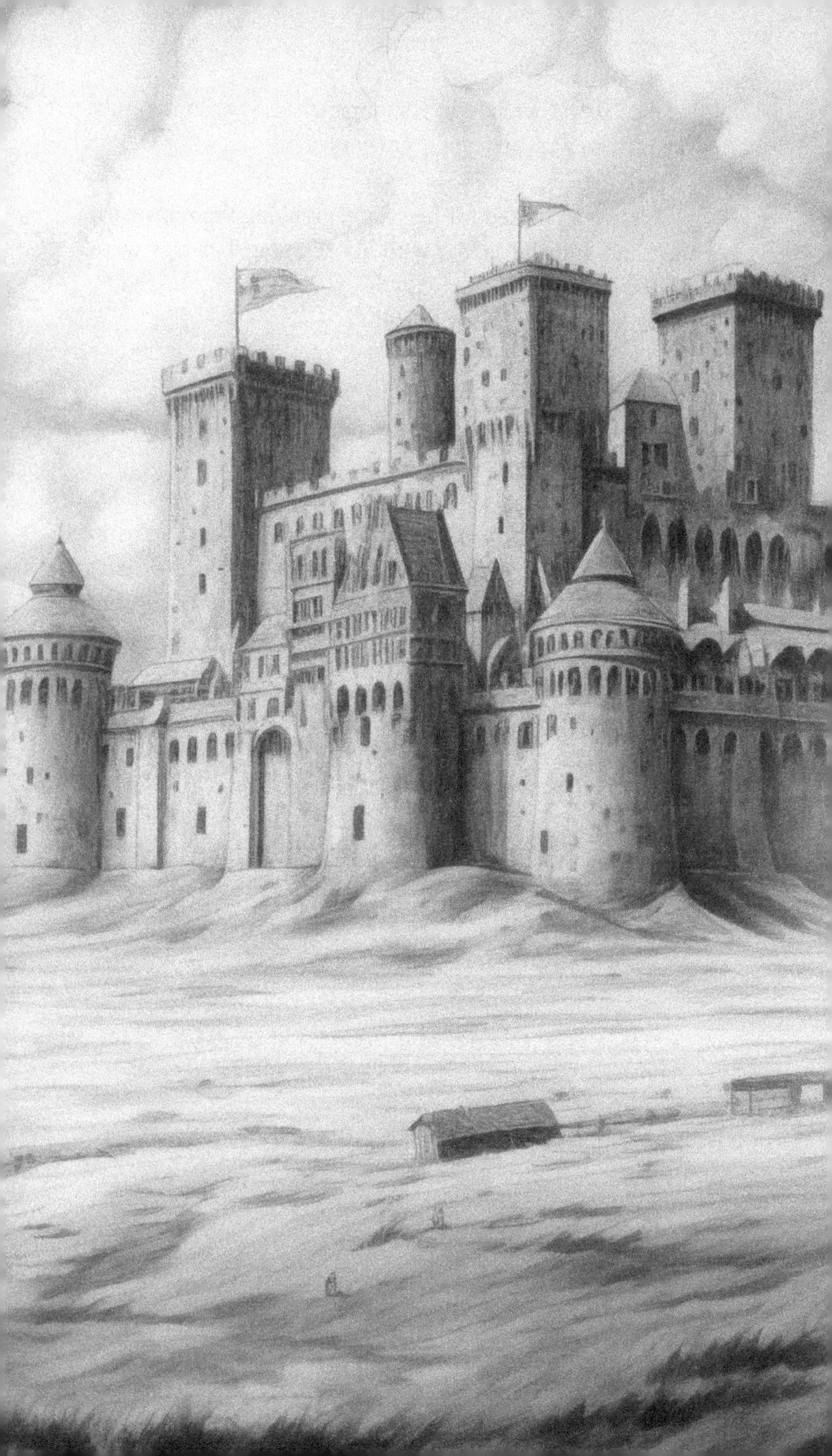

CHAPTER 22

The sentry's words kept echoing in Adrianna's head. It took a few days to prepare the rearrangement work. A few days before they began to touch Alinor's face.

She and Sam raced across the countryside, their horses eating the miles.

"We'll need fresh horses!" Sam shouted to be heard. "For the way back. They'll be exhausted otherwise and won't be able to go fast enough."

"Mirabelle!" Adrianna called into the empty air. "You heard that?"

"You will be blessed with fresh horses," a voice that sounded like the tinkling of silver bells and nothing like Mirabelle said in her head.

"It's taken care of," Adrianna told Sam.

They raced on.

When night fell, Sam forced them to stop and rest. The horses weren't the only ones who were exhausted by the pace, and they would all need some sleep.

It was only the fear of failing yet again that convinced

Adrianna to do as Sam said, although she only snatched four hours of sleep before demanding they continue on.

They thundered past the camp where she and Sam and Mirabelle had stayed, what now felt like a lifetime ago.

That time, when Adrianna had blithely been enjoying the adventure, seemed like it had happened to someone else. She'd been such an idiot to enjoy herself as if all was well, when Alinor was in grave danger.

How had she not known? How had she not felt a shift in the energy, some kind of sign to let her know that Alinor had been taken? Or had Adrianna been given the sign but simply not noticed it, because she'd been too busy focusing on herself and this stupid idea of having at least one adventure in her life?

They found the fresh horses as close to the crater as Mirabelle could manage without her magic clashing with the dragon's. Adrianna and Sam left their own horses, making sure they had access to grass and water. They hobbled them so they wouldn't be able to stray too far, that way someone would be able to come and get them.

Then they set off again on the fresh horses.

Finally, they reached the crater. They manoeuvred so they would be approaching from the back of the dragon. They left the horses grazing near the rocks, tying the reins to a nearby tree to stop them wandering off. They moved in silence, not wanting anything to tip the dragon off to their presence.

Adrianna snatched the rolled blanket that was still stored at the back of her saddle.

Sam shook his head. "I'm—"

"I'm getting the egg. I'm doing this," Adrianna whispered in a harsh tone. She was done having others do her business for her. She was done being small, being scared—she was done being a failure. Maybe her whole life had been a failure until now, but right now was where the failing ended.

Sam looked like he wanted to argue, but the look in Adrianna's eye convinced him. "Better that I be the one to distract the dragon and keep her attention on me, anyway," he said. "I wouldn't want you doing that, either. I'll need to go around and approach her from the other side to keep her attention on me. Wait until I've started to make noise to enter the crater."

Adrianna nodded, tucking the rolled blanket under one arm so she'd be able to clamber up the boulders. "Is there anything else I need to know about grabbing the egg?"

Sam shook his head. "No. Just don't get burnt. And this."

He came to stand right before her, close enough that her heart beat a little faster. Was he going to kiss her or something? Was that how it went in stories? But there was no storyline for this, for a princess trying to save her evil stepsister who wasn't evil, with the help of a stablehand.

She realised her thoughts were whirling completely irrationally.

Sam lifted the talisman, the dragon's bane, from around his neck and hung it around hers.

"Oh, right." Adrianna felt like a prize idiot. She was in the middle of the crisis of her life, about to go steal a dragon egg while Alinor's life hung in the balance, and there she was wondering if a stablehand was going to kiss her. Sometimes her own stupidity astounded her.

"Thanks." Adrianna turned and began to clamber up the rocks.

"Adrianna?" he called in a low voice.

She paused and looked back.

"You're quite something, you know that? I never in a million years expected a princess could be like this."

"I'm a failure, Sam. A total failure. The reason I'm even

in this predicament is because I have failed so spectacularly as a princess."

"Not the way I look at it."

Adrianna had absolutely no idea what to reply that. She blinked a couple of times, but he stalked off to the other side of the crater, saving her from having to reply.

This was even more discombobulating than the thought that he might kiss her. Because this might have been the first time somebody had a high opinion of her. Ever. Yes, of course Alinor had a high opinion of her, as did her fairy godmother, but that was different. They were wired to think highly of her. It was like counting your own mother or father as having a high opinion of you—that didn't count.

Sam had no link to her, no familial bond, and yet he had expressed something akin to respect—the first time anyone had done that in her life. It was an unsettling feeling—both nice and slightly terrifying. Far more terrifying than the possibility of a kiss, for sure.

Adrianna blinked again and went back to climbing the rocks. Now really wasn't the time for this. For any of it.

But Sam's words stayed with her, echoing in her mind.

She was something. Quite something.

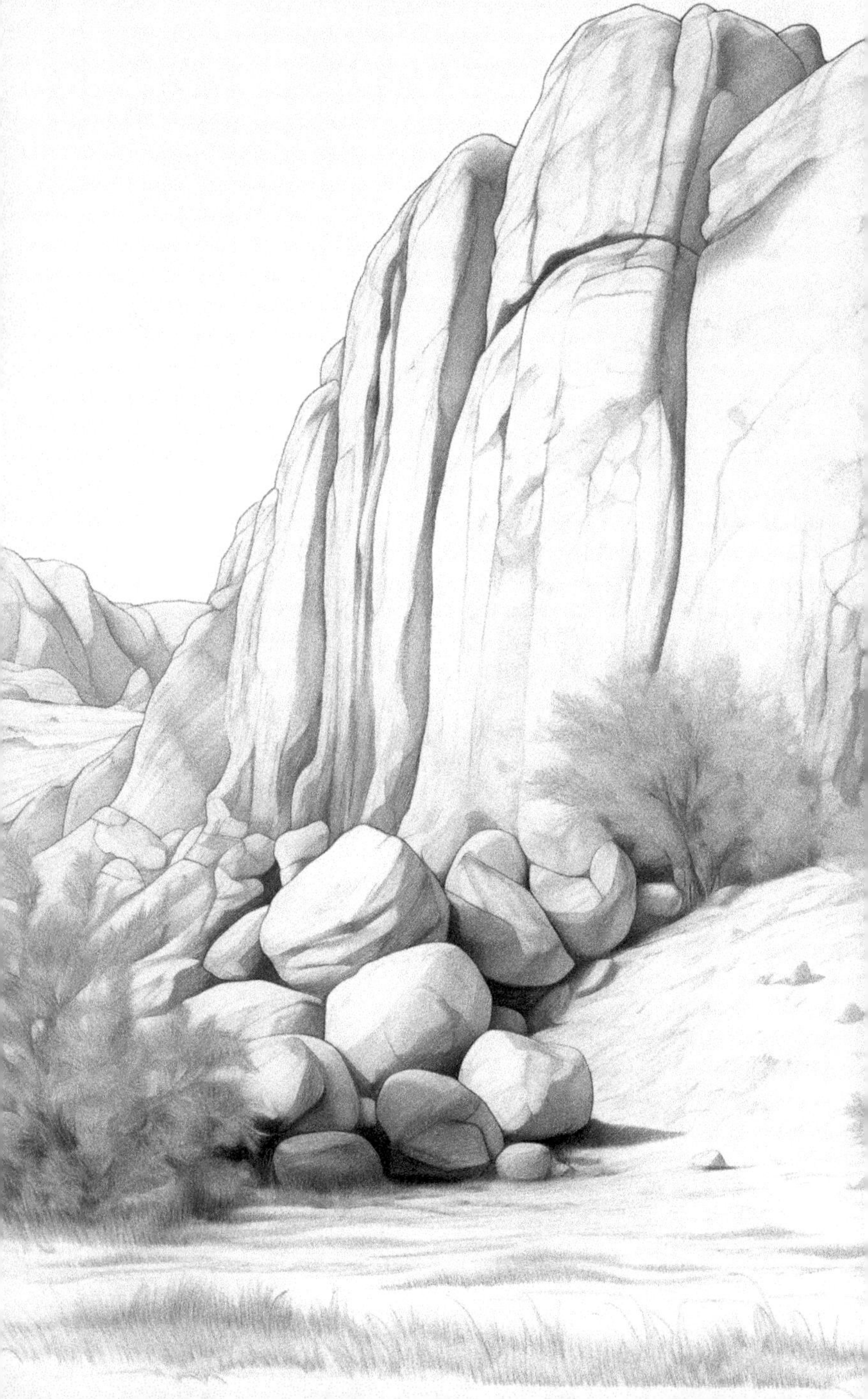

CHAPTER 23

Adrianna peered over the edge of the crater at the dragon. She could see the massive ridge of the dark teal spine with its gold spikes, and all the places where the scales were dull and worn, where the dragon was showing signs of the neglect she was going through in the name of caring for her egg. She hadn't moved so much as an inch, still curled around the egg like a praying mantis.

The smell of the dragon was every bit as powerful as it had been the first time—sulphur and brimstone and something that reminded Adrianna of horses.

Rhooooo—the dragon breathed on her egg.

A thunk rang out, echoing against the walls of the crater as a small stone was thrown against a rock. The dragon lifted her head at once, looking for the source of the disturbance.

Feeling like a thief in the night—a cowardly thief, in fact—Adrianna started to carefully climb down into the crater. She was approaching from the back of the dragon, who was looking away and towards the disturbance.

Although Adrianna had zero doubts about doing this to

save her sister, she was still very aware of the wrongness of what she was doing to the dragon, and the guilt of it was sour in her mouth.

Her heart pounded with fear and anticipation. She placed each foot carefully, not wanting to make a sound. Sam threw more rocks, creating more noise, keeping the dragon's attention focused in his direction.

Adrianna felt like all the world was holding its breath. Every tiny, cautious step she took might as well have been a loud thunder crash in her ears.

"Wooooo!" Sam shouted, his voice bouncing and echoing against the stone. The dragon open her massive jaws and belched out a stream of fire into the air, but it was clear she was confused as to where the sound was truly coming from. The fire seemed more like a warning than an attack.

Adrianna continued her careful descent, half-nauseous with fear. At any moment, she expected to feel a burning blast of fire on her skin.

But nothing happened.

Finally, she reached the bottom of the crater. She was standing only feet away from the dragon.

The dragon still seemed unsure, her head turning from side to side, looking for the source of the sound, but still away from Adrianna. Adrianna took a deep breath and stepped forward. She felt like even the beats of her heart were too loud, that the dragon was bound to hear its thumping and turn around, and realise what Adrianna had come to do.

But still nothing happened.

Sam began crashing around the crater rim, and the dragon sprayed fire. This time it wasn't just a belch of warning, it was a targeted attack. She had seen Sam.

Sam ducked out of the way behind the lip of the crater, the fire passing—hopefully—harmlessly above his head.

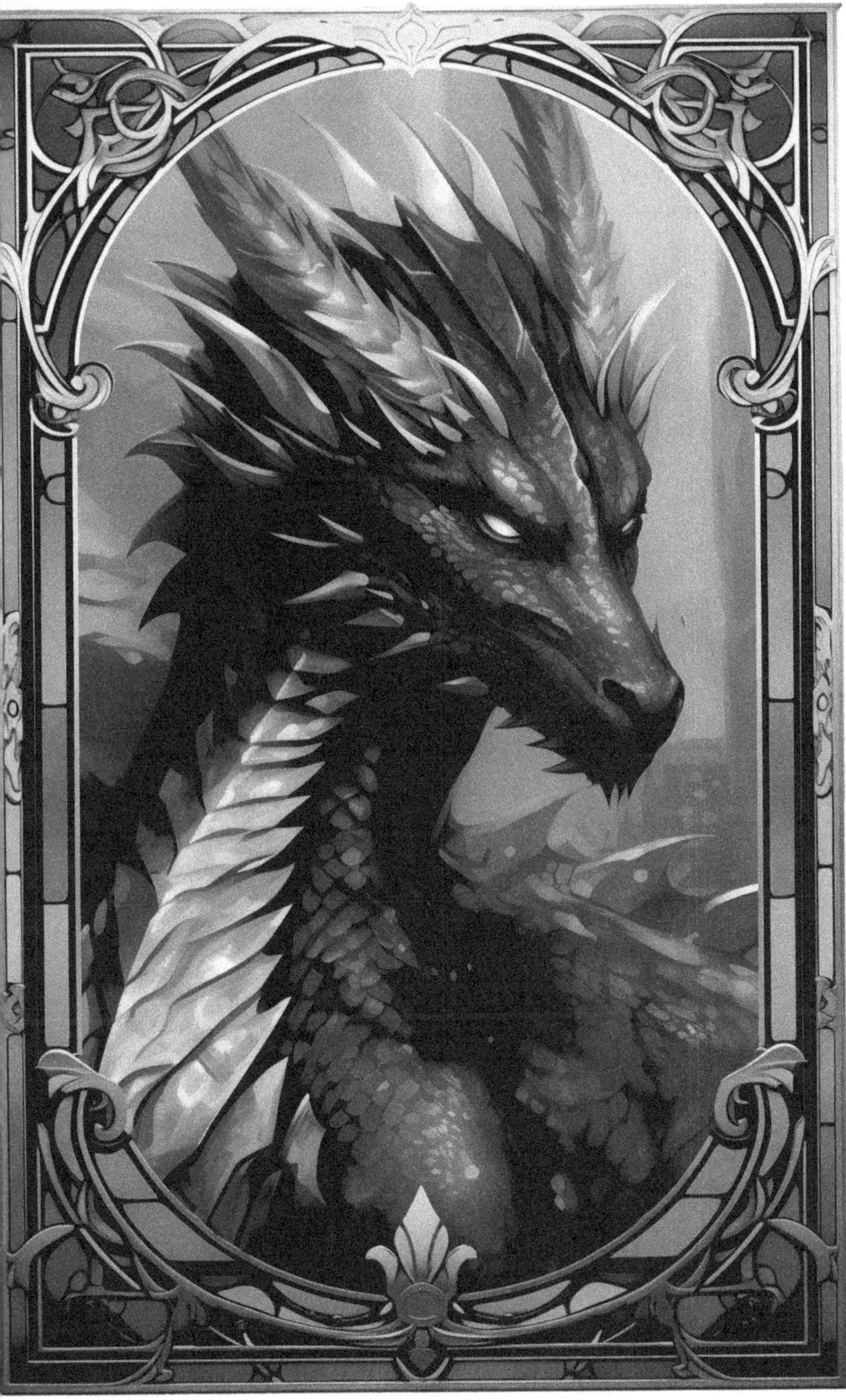

Adrianna forced herself to look away from Sam's location. She had to focus on her own situation—she was in far more danger than him. If the dragon so much as looked in her direction... No point thinking about that, either.

Adrianna continued forward carefully and slowly unrolled the blanket.

The dragon's body was curled around the egg, her front legs and talons close to it. Before, her neck and head had been curled to complete the protective circle around the egg, but now that she was distracted, the egg was exposed.

Adrianna was level with the dragon, walking along the massive hind legs. She could see the huge muscles beneath the thick carapace of scales. The talons were huge and black, and they easily looked sharp enough to gore a person from navel to nose.

The dragon roared, as if she had just heard the thought. Adrianna glanced up. Sam was popping up above the crater rim, shouting and waving, before disappearing and running to another part of the rim, to pop up there. The dragon was blasting fire when she could, but so far had—mercifully—failed to catch him. Her attention, however, was completely riveted on Sam, and her roar was full of anger. Adrianna fancied she could also hear fear.

She reached the egg. Its iridescent blue-green shell was covered with fine golden veins.

No time to doubt now. No time for a guilty conscience, either. She slowly reached out her hands towards the egg, holding the blanket for protection.

She could feel the heat emanating from the egg. She kept her eyes focused on it—she didn't dare look up at the dragon, as if by looking, that would be enough to alert her to Adrianna's presence.

And then she picked up the egg. She held her breath, her whole body tense as she half expected the mother's head to snap back, look at her with her golden eyes, and snap Adrianna with her powerful jaws.

But it was as Sam had said. The dragon didn't seem to notice the disappearance of her egg. Adrianna backed away slowly.

The egg was hot, even through the thick blanket. In fact, without the blanket, Adrianna would have burnt herself. And the shell felt hard, solid—like a thin covering of marble rather than a shell. And she could feel the pulsing that was visible in the golden veins—she could feel the life inside the egg.

She really wasn't just stealing an egg, she was stealing a mother's baby. She hadn't had much choice before, and she had no choice now. She wanted to whisper an apology, but she couldn't risk it, even though she felt the need to beg forgiveness all the way down to her bones.

She crept away with the egg cradled against her, like a thief. Such a cowardly thief. The mother was still blasting fire at Sam, oblivious.

Climbing back up the crater with the egg in her arms was awkward but doable. As soon as she was out of the crater, the cloaking magic resumed. All sound and smells disappeared.

Adrianna felt safer at once, without the stench of the dragon in her nose and the sound of the dragon's fire in her ears. But reams of fire were still bursting out of the other side of the crater, visible in spite of the magic, and reminding her she was far from safe.

She clambered clumsily back on her horse, cradling the egg against herself with one arm. The blanket slipped, the egg temporarily touching her skin through her shirt just below her collarbone, and she hissed in pain. That would leave a mark.

She readjusted the blanket, grabbed the reins of Sam's

horse, and quickly brought the horses around to Sam's location.

"Get ready to gallop like hell!" he yelled as he ran down, only just managing not to fall.

An earsplitting screech rang out, thick with anguish. The dragon had realised her egg had gone missing.

Sam leapt on his horse, and he and Adrianna galloped off in a cloud of dust.

Adrianna felt the dragon rise from the crater in the powerful gust of air created by the beating of her massive wings.

"I need to stay real close to you," Sam shouted. "She won't blast fire at you, but she'll get as close as she can."

Adrianna looked back. The dragon was in the air, and in a moment was above them, creating such a massive shadow that it engulfed them, blotting out the sun. In the air, her scales looked worse than they had in the crater, the skin from her belly dry and flaking off in large patches that dangled in the air.

The dragon shrieked again. Fire erupted just to Adrianna's right. Her horse whinnied with fear, raring up. Adrianna only just barely held on. The egg touched her face in the confusion, but luckily the blanket was between them. She held the egg tighter, holding the reins in her other hand.

But just as Sam had promised, the dragon didn't swoop down to grab them with her talons, kept at bay by the dragon's bane. Adrianna and Sam carried on galloping.

The dragon spouted more fire, this time to the left, barely missing Sam. His horse also whinnied in fear, but he kept an impressive control of it.

They galloped on in their mad race to reach the keep. There would be no rest this time, nothing but a blur of speed all the way to the keep. Sam's jaw was clenched tight as he rode as close to her as he could manage.

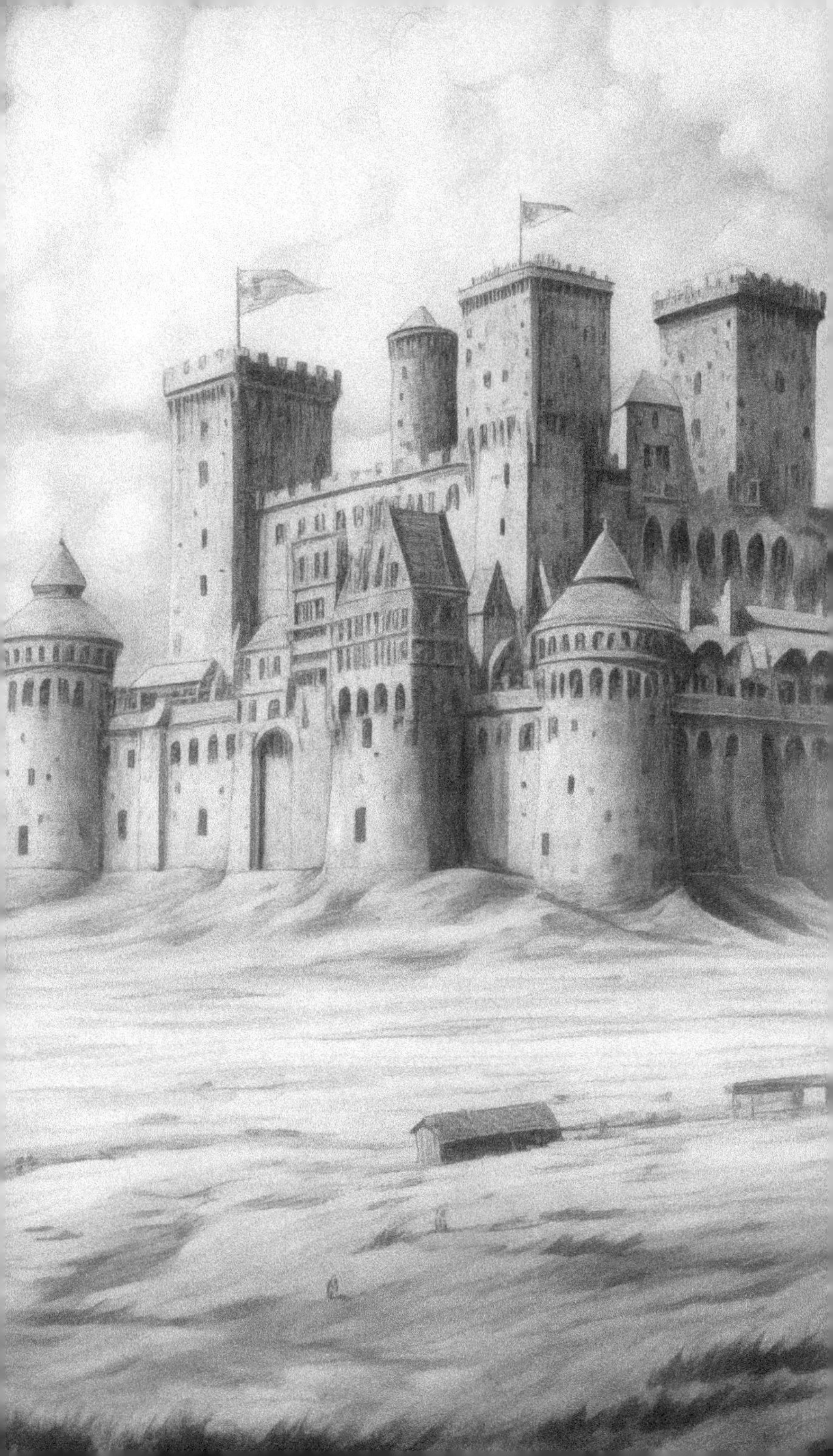

CHAPTER 24

They galloped all day, Adrianna calling to Mirabelle for strength for the horses when they were flagging. Everything was reduced to the aching tiredness in her back, legs, and arms, to the need to hold on to the egg, and keep going, faster and faster.

When they reached the forest close to the keep, things got worse. The canopy made it hard for the dragon to spot them, but flaming trees were infinitely more dangerous than burnt grass.

They pushed their horses even harder, thundering through the narrow path, while trees burst into flames on either side of them. The horses screamed in fear—Adrianna was barely keeping control of hers. Her legs were exhausted, and her arms were an aching agony from cradling the egg tightly so as not to drop it while holding the reins. If not for all the adrenaline pumping through her body, she'd have collapsed long ago.

"Let me go first," Sam shouted. "Your horse will follow mine." In spite of everything that was happening, he seemed to be able to manoeuvre and control his horse with unnerving skill, and he didn't seem as exhausted as Adrianna felt.

The forest erupted into flames right in front of them, and Sam turned sharply left, Adrianna following close behind. The dragon screeched overhead.

Sam had been right. With another horse to follow, hers now knew what to do, releasing some of Adrianna's strain.

The smoke was thick in the air, making her lungs burn. The fire was gaining, spreading from tree to tree, on top of the dragon's efforts.

Sam navigated the burning forest, somehow able to keep a sense of where they were going, whereas Adrianna was completely lost, confused by the smoke and flames that licked even the tallest branches. Her eyes stung in the acrid air, filling with water.

The whole forest seemed to be crackling, like a huge pile of tinder set alight, and the roar of the flames matched that of the dragon overhead who continued to shriek in her pain.

Adrianna cradled the egg tighter and closed her eyes against the heat of the fire. "Alinor," she whispered. "I'm coming. I'm coming Alinor." And then, "I'm sorry. I'm so sorry." That was for the dragon. She understood the dragon's anguish. Had felt it the moment she'd discovered Alinor had been taken. And now she'd gone and done exactly the same as the people who had taken Alinor.

They burst out of the forest, and never had a sight been more welcome than the open space before them, devoid of trees that could burn and potentially fall on them. And there, in the distance—the keep.

The sight of it instantly revived Adrianna. She yelled and kicked her horse, pushing it to go even faster, overtaking Sam.

For the second time, she was charging the keep, but this time, she wasn't powerless. Fire erupted to her right, but she barely noticed, her gaze riveted on the keep. The massive shadow of the dragon that engulfed her was reassuring now, a reminder that this time she wouldn't fail. She wasn't a passive, defenceless princess. She was charging to rescue Alinor, and she had a dragon.

Her horse thundered closer and closer.

Over at the keep, bells were being rung in alarm while people ran along the battlements as they saw the dragon headed for them. The sentries hurried back inside, massive wooden doors closing behind them.

Adrianna rode all the way to the keep, before turning sharply left, galloping along the wall.

"Release my sister!" she shouted. "Release Alinor, or I burn the place to the ground."

Given that her sister was being kept prisoner underground, she'd be safe from the dragon's fire. Still, Adrianna's stomach knotted with fear at the thought that something might go wrong. It was too late to back down, though. Far too late. And it was her best hope of rescuing Alinor.

The dragon, in her rage and powerlessness, gouted fire over the keep. She seemed to recognise what the keep was, and obviously took it to be some kind of enemy, because her attacks became more targeted than they had been before. She still didn't burn Adrianna directly, but maybe she mistook the keep for Adrianna's castle. Dragons and castles had, after all, a long history.

People screamed with fear, and maybe pain, within the keep walls.

"Release Alinor!" Adrianna shouted over and over. "Release my sister, and I leave and take the dragon with me. Release Alinor!" She galloped to the edge of the keep wall and turned right to follow the corner—she was going to circle the keep. She would ride in a circle until they released Alinor or until the dragon's bane ran out.

That was the extent of her plan. Circle the keep with the egg in her arms and the dragon burning everything until they released her sister, and hope they did so in time, before the dragon could swoop down and grab them.

"Release Alinor!" she screamed, her voice cracking a little, her throat still burning from the smoke back in the forest.

Hooves rang out just behind her.

"Release Alinor!" Sam boomed from behind her, coming to ride alongside her. His voice was much louder than hers. "Release Alinor, and we take the dragon away."

They reached the next corner and turned, still galloping along the keep wall. Adrianna shot him a grateful look. His white shirt was covered in soot and dirt, plastered against his muscled chest by the wind. The wind streamed in his hair, and his face was filthy. But his eyes burned bright, and he looked every bit as determined as Adrianna felt.

"Release Alinor!" Adrianna shouted again.

The dragon screeched and landed heavily on top of the keep's tallest tower, smashing its roof. Swaying her neck, she gouted fire inside the keep, burning it all. The air was ringing with voices and bells and screams, with the sounds of human panic.

Alinor would be safe, deep in the bowels. She would be safe. Adrianna told herself this over and over again, like a mantra. And she did her best not to think about all the people in the courtyard who would be getting burnt. They were in the keep, that meant that they worked for a man who rearranged people's faces. It meant that they were making it possible for someone to try and rearrange Alinor's face.

The dragon tore at the roof with her massive talons, sending huge blocks of stone tumbling down. She screeched and roared, flapping her massive wings, which only fanned the flames.

Alinor would be safe below ground. She'd be safe. Adrianna repeated the words to herself, clinging to them.

"Release the girl, Alinor!" Sam roared. "Release her!"

The dragon screeched as if in echo.

"Get the dragon away, and we'll release her," someone shouted from the top of the wall.

Adrianna nearly fell off her horse with relief, nearly let go of the egg.

"But you must get it away now!"

"Go," Sam told Adrianna. "I'll ride to the door and get Alinor. Go!"

Adrianna hesitated only for a moment. She wanted to be at the door when Alinor came out, but she couldn't afford to keep the dragon hovering around. She nodded at Sam and turned sharply, galloping away from the keep.

The dragon took off at once, smashing more of the keep with her massive weight, and she followed Adrianna.

Adrianna looked back over her shoulder to see Sam heading to the massive entrance. The plains around the keep were open, providing an uninterrupted view, so Adrianna could keep an eye on the proceedings, which she did, craning her head painfully to look over her shoulder.

She rode as far as she dared, not wanting to lose sight of the keep's entrance. She traced a wide circle, then, keeping the dragon on her tail, but not wanting to go any further away.

And then she saw it. Sam's horse racing towards her with a second rider in front of him. She recognised Alinor's dress at once.

In that moment, everything else went flying out of her mind. She jumped off her horse and rolled the dragon egg like a ball, so that it sped away from her on the thick grass. She leapt back onto her horse and raced back towards her sister. Behind her, the dragon screeched and beat her powerful wings, but Adrianna paid no attention.

"Alinor!" she cried. "Alinor!" Tears filled her eyes, blurring her vision.

As her horse reached Sam's, she jumped off before she had time to come to a complete stop, reaching for her sister's hand. Alinor tumbled off Sam's horse in a mess of elbows and knees. She clung to Adrianna, crying and babbling about how scared she'd been, how terrifying it had been down in the dungeon, not knowing whether help was coming. Adrianna was crying and babbling incoherently too, her breath coming in half sobs.

She held her sister tight enough to break her, and Alinor did the same. They stood unmoving for a time, clinging to each other, Adrianna letting the dizziness of relief wash over her. Everything was once again all right. So long as they were together, it was all right. The rest she'd figure out later. The storylines, the Happy Ever After, that could wait. For now, she had Alinor back, and that was all that mattered.

"I'll never let anything happen to you ever again," she swore, once she'd calmed down enough to speak coherently. "Doesn't matter what I have to do. Nothing will happen to you ever again, I promise." She kissed the top of Alinor's head.

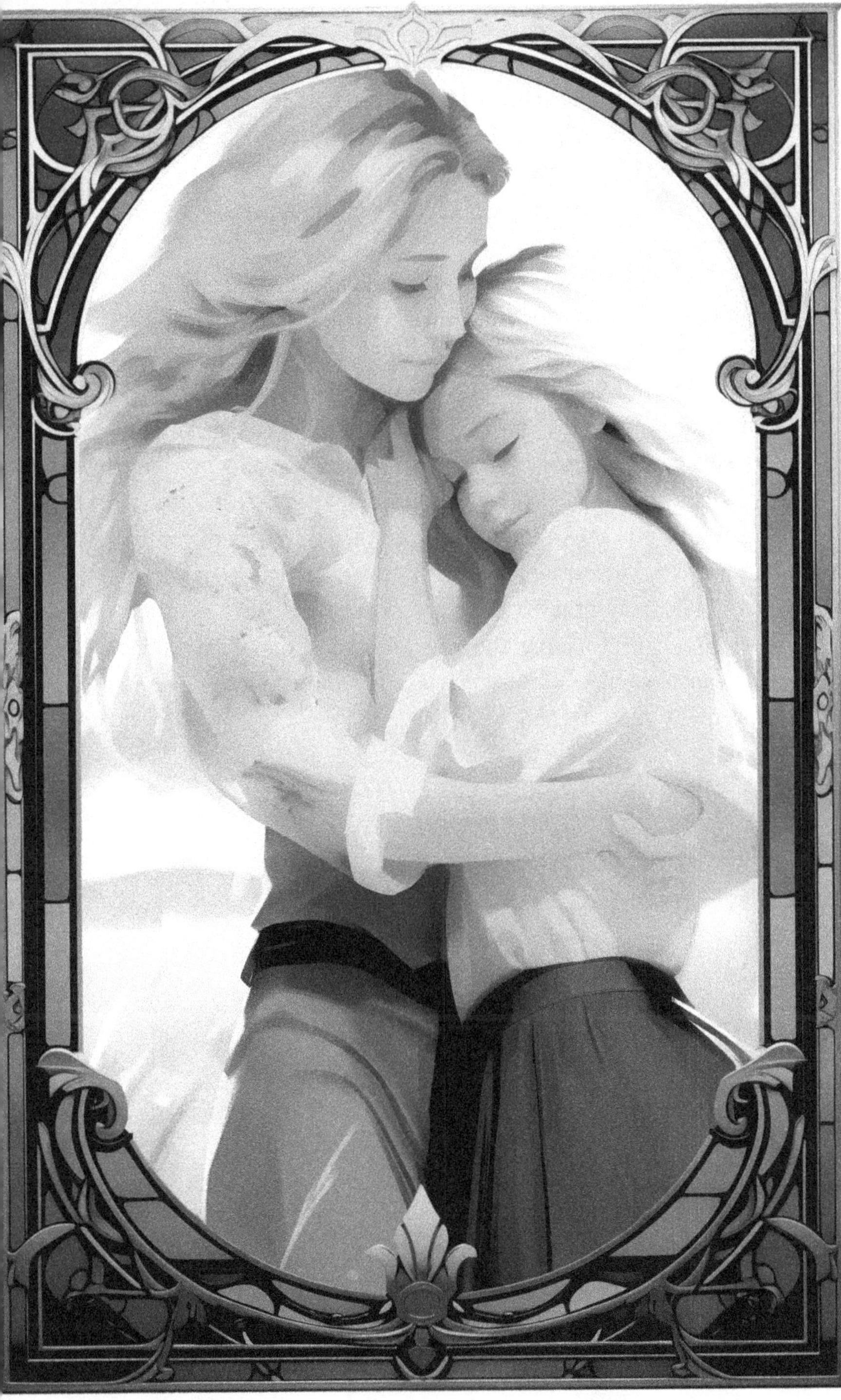

She took another deep and ragged sigh, looking up at Sam gratefully. "Thank you. For helping. Thank you."

He nodded, but he wasn't looking at them, rather at something behind Adrianna.

"What?" She looked behind her without letting go of Alinor.

The dragon was settled around her egg, carefully blowing on it, but this time, there was no crater to protect her, nothing to keep her out of sight. She was completely exposed. And this time there was no way to access the egg. She was keeping it well protected beneath her wings, obviously having learned from her previous mistake.

She was also far from calm, keeping a very close eye on Adrianna and the others. They were, for now, out of reach of her fire, but Adrianna was under no illusions as to what would happen if they tried to get anywhere close.

"We have to hope the egg hatches soon," Sam said. "Because we have no way to make her move now, and she has no protection at all."

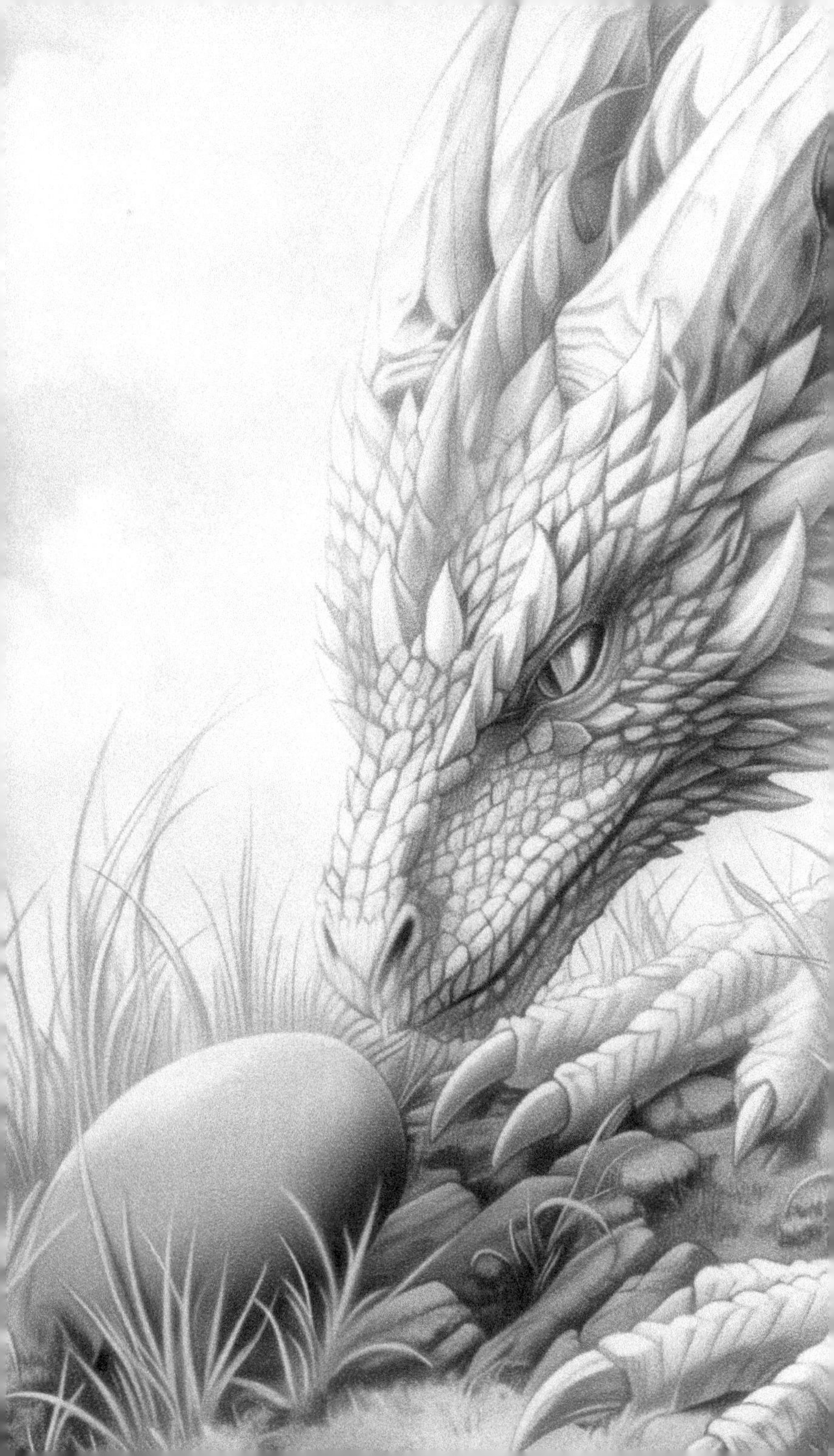

CHAPTER 25

They were still standing there, contemplating the problem of the dragon, when he arrived.

"Step aside, people, for I have come to slay this foul beast."

Adrianna, Sam, and Alinor, turned as one, Adrianna still holding on tightly to her sister.

The prince was handsome, as they all were. Slightly curling, chestnut hair, gorgeous brown eyes, a square jaw —the usual, in short. He was wearing all his finery of green and gold, sitting proud on his white horse, chest slightly puffed out.

Adrianna waved at him. "There is no need to slay the dragon. I am not in any danger from it."

The prince frowned and looked down at her. "Who the hell cares about you, peasant? This dragon is threatening the land, and I have come here to save the good people of this land."

"I am Princess Adrianna of Veridi castle," she replied hotly, standing up straighter and tossing her head.

The prince looked her over dubiously. "Are you really?"

Adrianna probably looked like hell, with dust and

smoke from the fire on her face and hands, and her hair was most likely a knotted mess. To say nothing of the state of her clothes.

"Yes, I am, and I do not appreciate being questioned. This dragon is mine, and it is not yours to slay."

"Don't be ridiculous, you cannot own a dragon. Dragons are here to be slayed," the prince said in a tone normally reserved for halfwits. "This foul beast is threatening the land, and I will not turn my back and ignore the suffering of these people."

"What threat? What suffering? Use your eyes, you fool! She's just breathing on her egg, nothing more. She's not bothering anyone."

The prince coloured at being called a fool. "Step aside, woman, and stop pestering me. This is no place for a princess. This dragon has burnt this castle to the ground—"

"The castle is still standing—and anyway, it's not a castle but a keep. And the only reason she attacked the castle is because I made her do it to rescue my sister. And in this keep they torture people and re-arrange their faces. You should be attacking the keep, not the dragon, if you truly care about justice and about people's suffering."

The prince looked at her like she had just grown a second head, the glazed confusion in his eyes making it clear that he was struggling to compute what she had just told him. Probably because she had just referred to taking part in a rescue herself, which princesses were not supposed to do. Or maybe it was the referring to the keep and the re-arranging of people's faces—he probably had no idea what that meant.

The prince cleared his throat and tossed his head, dismissing what she had just told him. "I shall slay this fiend, this foul—" He let out a shout of alarm as Sam grabbed him and yanked him down from his saddle. His horse neighed and shied a few steps away in fear. Alinor let go of Adrianna and hurried over to it, catching the bridle and murmuring reassurances to it.

The prince got to his feet and drew his sword, face dark with anger. "You will regret this."

"You heard the princess," Sam said calmly, arms crossed. "Leave the dragon alone."

"I heard nothing. All I know is a peasant put his hands on me, the penalty for which is death. And then I will kill the dragon." His features were twisted in a leer, whatever handsomeness he had been blessed with melting away beneath the vile expression.

"Now hold on," Sam said. He opened both hands in a pacifying gesture. "I'm unarmed. And this dragon is not harming anyone. There is no need to do anything here."

"There is every need," the prince replied.

He lifted his sword, but Adrianna had had enough. She swung, whacking him with the hilt of her own sword right in the back of the head. He let out a garbled sound and collapsed, unconscious.

"You cannot even imagine how many times I have wanted to do that," Adrianna said with a smile. "Not to him specifically, but to princes in general."

But before Sam could reply, the sound of trumpets rang out. In the distance, another party was arriving.

The prince was easily identifiable from the gold crown that winked in the sun. Behind him, a squire held a banner of red and gold that streamed in the wind. A small company of four guards followed them.

Sam cursed. "They'll be coming for the dragon." He leapt onto his horse and galloped over in their direction, waving his arms.

"What do we do?" Alinor asked, eyes wide. "We have to protect the dragon."

"Mirabelle?" Adrianna called.

"I can't help, precious," came the tinkling voice and her mind. "I am not allowed to harm princes or obstruct them in any way."

Adrianna turned to her sister. "Looks like we're on our own."

Alinor nodded seriously and bent over to pick up the prince's fallen sword. Adrianna still had the sword Mirabelle had given her before. "Then we'll have to make sure nobody gets to the dragon."

"Wait, I don't want you to put yourself in any danger. I don't—"

"I am not letting anyone hurt this dragon," Alinor said mutinously. She still held the prince's horse by the bridle, and she climbed into the saddle.

"Wait, hold up." Adrianna quickly got back on her own horse, hurrying to overtake her sister. "Stay behind me. Anyway, we might not need to have any kind of confrontation. Maybe Sam will be able to convince them, or maybe I will."

"Yeah, because that went so well with the last one." Alinor gestured at the unconscious prince behind them.

"Glad to see your time in the keep didn't dent your sarcasm," Adrianna replied with a grin and quite a lot of relief.

Alinor grinned back. "The Veridi sarcasm is far too strong to be dented by some cowards."

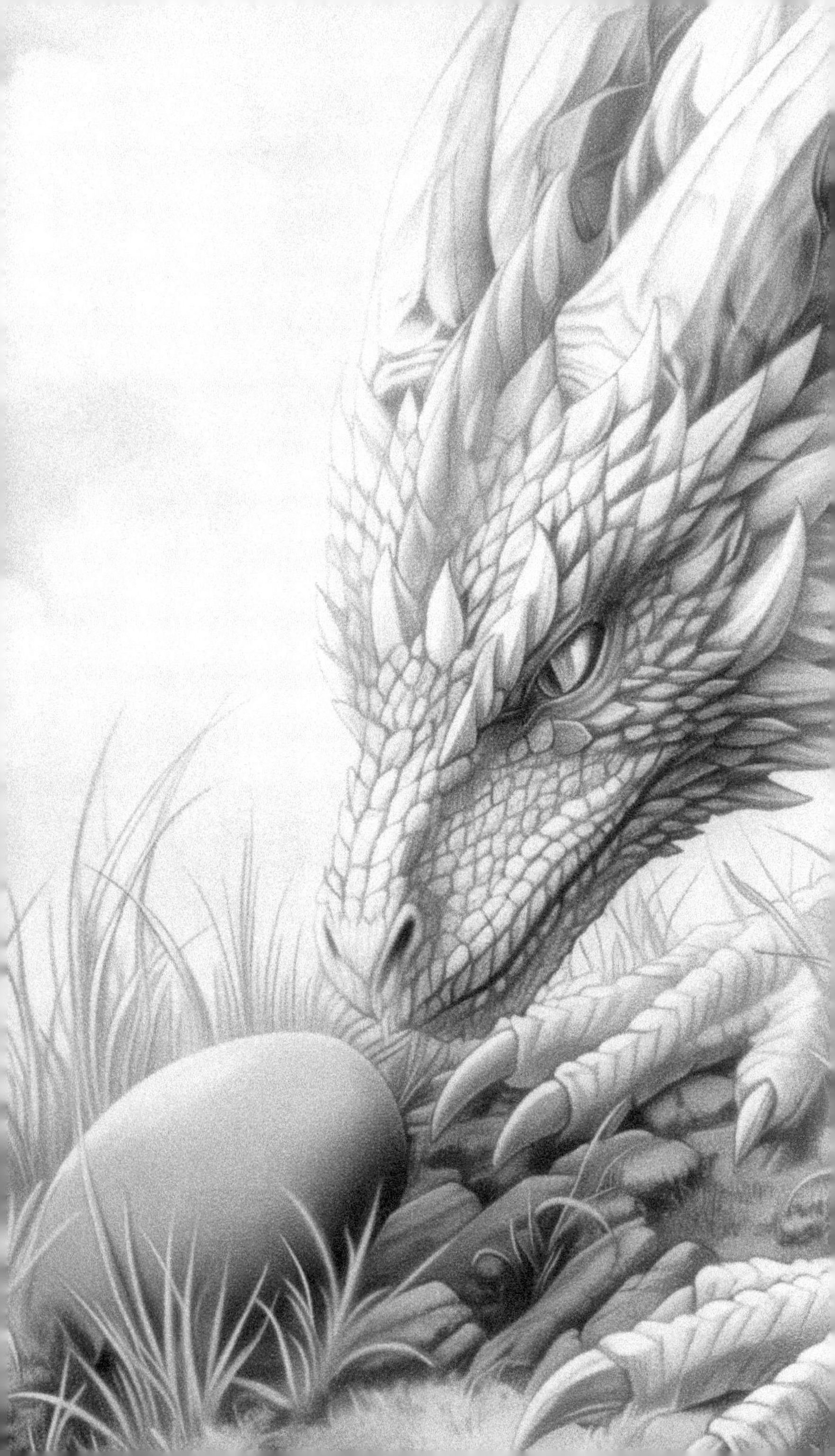

CHAPTER 26

Sam's effort at diplomacy didn't seem to be any more successful than Adrianna's had been. Voices were raised, the prince's stance was aggressive on his white horse. He pushed it forward, getting as close to Sam as possible, so as to invade his space.

"Wait," Adrianna called, as she and Alinor drew near to the prince and his escort. "I am the Princess of Veridi. I am responsible for this dragon."

"You are the princess?" the prince asked, giving her a dubious look that very much matched the one the last prince had given her. He also looked remarkably similar to the last prince, with the brown hair, the square jaw, the generic but handsome features... Someone should tell fairy godmothers that beauty could be quite boring. Maybe one day they would make princes that actually were charming, genuinely charming, rather than just boringly handsome.

Adrianna nodded. "I am perfectly safe, so there is no need to slay the dragon. In fact, because this dragon belongs to me, I will not allow any harm to come to it."

"But... dragons are made to be slain."

"Yes, well, not this one. This one is my private property."

"But it burnt the castle to the ground."

"What is wrong with you all?" Adrianna demanded impatiently. "The castle is still standing, therefore it hasn't been burnt to the ground."

"The dragon has done nothing wrong," Alinor said. "To kill her would be to commit a grave injustice. She was only brought here to rescue me."

"This is a rescue storyline?" The prince asked at once, obviously relieved to return to a territory that was more familiar to him. "I'm sorry, I didn't mean to interfere in another's storyline… Who did the rescuing?"

"Me," Adrianna said.

"Well, and me," Sam added.

The prince looked at them both, the frown returning to his features. "This is most irregular. A princess cannot be rescuing her…"

"Evil stepsister," Alinor piped up helpfully.

The prince shook his head, looking more confused than ever. Adrianna wanted to shake him. It really wasn't that complicated.

The fascinating conversation was interrupted by a shout, followed by an awful screech of pain from the dragon.

Adrianna spun around in her saddle. Another prince had arrived, alone, and he had plunged a spear in the dragon's rump. The dragon had obviously been distracted by the argument happening and not seen the new arrival. She reared her head and sprayed fire in the direction of the new prince, but he galloped off on his horse, dodging the fire.

He seemed to be yet another carbon copy of the other two, but wearing blue.

"This is my dragon!" the red prince protested. "Attack!" he yelled at his guards.

"No!" Alinor pushed her horse forward, into the prince's path.

"Out of my way," he yelled, but Alinor raised her sword clumsily. He batted her sword away with his own, and it went flying out of her hands, unbalancing her so that she almost fell off her horse. She cried out, catching herself on the saddle horn.

Adrianna saw red, spurring her own horse forward, but before she could reach the prince, his escort intercepted her, their own weapons raised.

She parried a sword blow with her own sword, but the force of it also caused her to drop her weapon. The guard pointed his sword at her chest.

Behind her, the dragon screamed again.

"You are not allowed to harm princesses," a prim voice said to Adrianna's right. And all four guards were turned into fluffy white bunnies, balanced on their horse's saddles.

"Mirabelle," Adrianna said, relieved. "You came!"

The plump fairy hovered in the air next to Adrianna, face pinched with displeasure, her wand in hand. "No attempts can be made on the life of my princess." She glowered at the prince.

"Out of my way, all of you," the red prince shouted, charging towards the dragon's rump.

The blue prince now had a massive crossbow which he was reloading as his horse galloped away, drawing a large circle to get away from the dragon's fire and give him an opportunity to fire again. A thick crossbow bolt was already embedded in the dragon's left flank.

"No, stop!" Sam rushed after the red prince.

The dragon screeched and sprayed more fire, twisting her neck so she could see behind her, but she didn't move an inch, nor did she flap her powerful wings. Moving would have left her egg exposed again.

"Stop them," Adrianna begged Mirabelle.

"I can't precious, I can't do a thing against princes."

"We have to do something," Alinor said.

"Don't you dare get close to the dragon," Adrianna told her. "Mirabelle, get Sam a sword."

Sam shouted in surprise as a sword appeared in his hand, but he redoubled in speed, charging after the red prince. The dragon was distracted by the blue prince, giving the red prince the opening he needed.

He charged in but had to sweep away at the last minute as the dragon spotted him and swung her neck around, spraying fire in his direction. The fire narrowly missed Sam.

"Stand back, fair ladies, I have come to rescue you all. I will slay this—"

Adrianna didn't even let the new prince finish. She swung her horse around and flung herself from her saddle to his, catching hold of him.

He yelled in shock. His own horse reared up in fear, knocking them both off. Adrianna fell heavily, half winded as the prince landed on top of her, but she had the presence of mind to wrap both of her legs around his body, still clinging to him with both arms.

Alinor jumped down from her horse and threw herself into the fray.

"What... What is the meaning of this?" The prince struggled, trying to throw them both off. "Get off me, you crazy fools!"

"Mirabelle!!" Adrianna yelled. The prince was stronger, and she was struggling to hold on to him. Alinor weighed as much as a soaking wet bird—the two of them wouldn't manage to keep the prince down for long.

The plump fairy stood aside, looking panicked. "I

can't… I can't…I can't attack a prince. Oh, wait!" She swayed over in their direction and made an odd noise. And then she collapsed in a faint, straight on top of the prince's chest. He made a strangled noise as the weight of her winded him.

The dragon screamed. What little victory Adrianna felt at having temporarily disabled this prince—whose finery was purple—was immediately dashed. The red prince had stuck his sword in the dragon's left back leg.

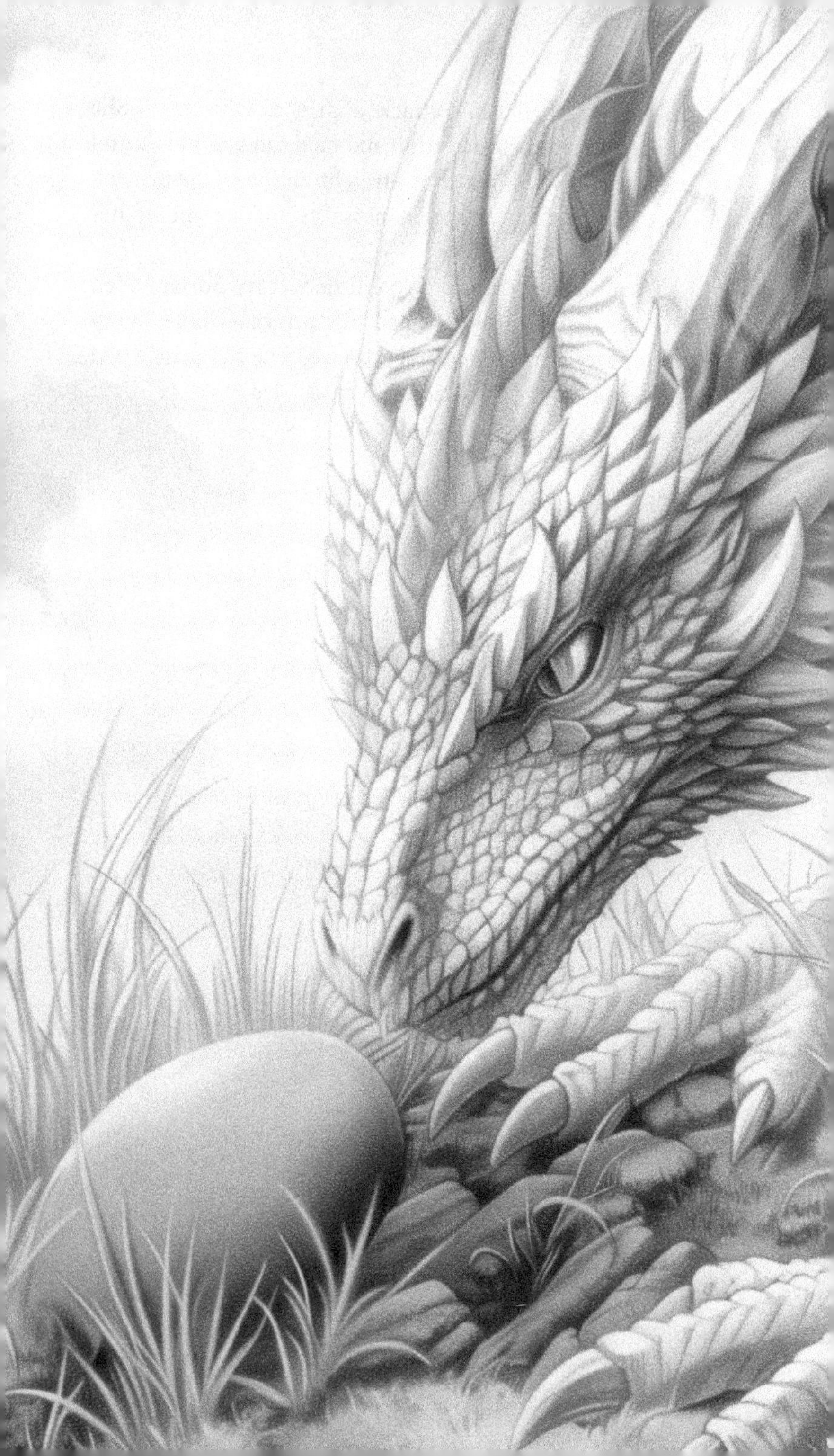

CHAPTER 27

Sam had intercepted the red prince and was attempting to fight him, but it was obvious he was completely out-matched. His movements were clumsy, the sword awkward in his hands. However, although he wasn't winning the battle, he was succeeding in preventing the red prince from attacking the dragon again.

The purple prince threw Alinor off him and then Mirabelle, who continued to pretend to be unconscious. Adrianna clung to him like a baby monkey. There was no dignity, no skill, nothing elegant or feminine or delicate. The prince cursed and removed one of her arms, and then the other, but she clung on with her legs.

"Get off me, woman!"

When the stories spoke of daring rescues, battles to save the life of someone, it was always with great swashing and buckling, fancy sword play, dashing displays of courage. The stories never spoke of a woman clinging to a man with all her limbs because she was so unskilled, it was the only thing she was capable of doing.

"I said get off!" the prince yelled in anger.

Adrianna held on. He let go one of her arms to grip her leg, and she immediately clung back with her arms again. When he tried to grab her arm again, she was hit by a flash of inspiration and dipped her head to bite his hand.

The prince roared in pain and anger, releasing her. And then Alinor was on him again, shouting and clawing with all the grace of a cat attempting to escape a bath.

It wasn't enough, though. They needed a weapon, something to incapacitate him, but the swords were out of reach, and they had nothing else to hand.

The dragon screeched again, and then again, followed by a roar of fire. But even without looking, Adrianna could hear the weakness in both the roar of fire and in the screech. Sam shouted, his voice breaking in a cry of pain.

The purple prince swiped an arm, catching Alinor, who cried out and went flying. There was no way they would win.

"Mirabelle," Adrianna wailed.

The fairy had come to her senses, or at least had stopped pretending to faint, and she was looking around her in panic.

The dragon screeched again, and this time there was no mistaking the sound—it sounded like an animal badly wounded.

Maybe sensing Adrianna's distraction, the purple prince suddenly grabbed Adrianna by the waist and tore her off him, flinging her aside with a grunt. Adrianna rolled and scrambled back up to her feet.

The dragon had three of the massive crossbow bolts embedded in her abdomen, as well as the sword and spear in her rump and leg. She was swinging her neck around, trying to see what was happening behind her, but her movements were unfocused, and again she screeched. But when she opened her mouth, only a small amount of fire came out, not even enough to reach the end of her long body.

Sam was behind her, on his knees, clutching his right side. Even from a distance, Adrianna could see blood seeping out from beneath his hands.

The purple prince jumped on his horse and galloped over, sword raised high.

"Step aside, this foul beast is mine!"

The dragon seemed to rally at the sight of this new foe, and she let out a powerful plume of fire. The prince tried to dodge but didn't quite manage it, and both he and his horse screamed in pain as the fire grazed them both.

But then a figure appeared on the dragon's back, having climbed up from its rump. A small figure in blue. He held a sword that winked in the sun.

"No!" Adrianna screamed, running towards him without thinking. She waved her arms. "No, stop! Stop!"

The prince plunged his sword down, through the scales and into the base of the dragon's neck.

The dragon let out a final, earsplitting shriek, throwing her head back, her whole body tensing and arching from the pain.

And then her neck folded gracefully as her head slowly fell to the ground. Her eyes blinked in quick succession. She turned her head and lifted her wing, revealing her egg.

She let out a slow, final breath—*rhooooo*. A final attempt to keep her egg warm, and then her eyes fluttered shut.

"No," Adrianna whispered. Her eyes filled with tears. "No…" Her legs suddenly didn't seem to have the strength to run forward, and she staggered slowly to a stop.

The prince stood on the dragon, hands on his waist, his blue and gold velvet clothing rippling in the wind, golden crown gleaming in the sun.

"I have slain this fiend, this foul beast. I have defeated this monster," he announced.

Adrianna let out a sob. The prince jumped down from the dragon and came towards her.

"You must be the princess who was being held captive by the beast." He came towards her and made to take her in his arms. "I guess your capture explains the...state you are in." He smiled widely, looking proud of himself. "But we will fix that in no time." He reached for her hand. "But for now, fair lady, I wish to ask for your hand—"

Adrianna didn't even have time to think. Her body reacted before he could touch her. She slapped him so hard that her hand hurt. The prince squawked with outrage, staggering a few steps back, looking at her, eyes wide with shock, holding his reddening cheek with one hand.

"Come near me again and you'll get to experience the joys of blunt testicular trauma," Adrianna hissed.

"But, I..."

"You *killed* her!"

"Her?"

"The dragon, you blathering idiot!"

"Well, yes. That is my purpose. And now we will be married..."

"Are you a halfwit? Did your mother drop you on your head as a baby? I just told you that if you come near me, you'll experience blunt testicular trauma. What on this green earth makes you think I would *ever* consider marrying you?" Adrianna spat the final words.

"Well, I never..." the prince stammered with shock. Then he seemed to recover, drawing himself up. "You're obviously crazy. Or subject to a curse from a witch." He hesitated, obviously debating whether he should be trying to find a way to lift the curse. For an awful moment, Adrianna wondered if he might try to kiss her. If he did she would knee him in the groin.

"There is no curse, you cretin! The dragon was mine,

and you killed her. Get out of here. I never want to see your stupid face again."

"But.. But..."

A filthy, bloodied hand clasped his shoulder. "The lady told you to go away, and if I were you, I'd do as she says." Sam was every bit as filthy and bloody as his hand, and he was obviously in a lot of pain, but at least he was standing.

The prince jerked his shoulder away. "Don't touch me, peasant."

"And you shouldn't talk to your betters in that tone," Adrianna snapped.

"Betters? *Betters?*" the prince spluttered.

"Yes. Sam has a brain, and he, at least, is capable of using it. An ability you clearly lack. Now, how many times must I tell you to go away?"

The prince's face darkened. "Curse the lot of you and your ingratitude. I have never heard of such...such... madness." He turned and stalked off.

The red prince and the purple prince were both also making their departure, although more discreetly, obviously realising there was no point staying now that the dragon had been slain. The green prince was nowhere to be seen, probably having slinked off earlier. Being knocked unconscious by a princess was probably an embarrassment for him.

That was when what Adrianna had just done hit her. She had turned down the only marriage proposal she had ever received, and was likely to ever receive. The one thing she needed, and she'd turned it away without thinking. Because marrying the man who had killed the dragon had felt simply unbearable.

Which meant that it had all been for nothing. All of it. The dragon had died for nothing. Alinor still wasn't safe. Nothing had changed.

Adrianna had failed. Again.

She felt exhausted at the realisation, but there were more important things to take care of for now.

"Sam, are you all right?" Adrianna turned to him. He still held his injured side with one hand. "What happened?"

"What happened is that we are now seeing the consequences of me trying to use a sword when I have no idea what I'm doing." He tried to give a grin but only succeeded in looking pained. "Imagine if I'd tried to fight those sentries before."

He swayed, and Adrianna hurried to catch him, putting an arm around him.

"Dear, oh dear," Mirabelle said, appearing at their side.

"Will he be all right?" Alinor asked anxiously. "Mirabelle, can you heal him?"

"Well, it would be a tremendous waste to have something so beautiful all torn up. Here, take your shirt off, Sam, and I will see to your wound."

Arianna did her best to help him take his shirt off with Alinor's help, given that he couldn't move his right arm much. She also did her best to focus on the task at hand and not pay too much attention when her fingers brushed against the muscles of his chest or his stomach. She certainly wasn't noticing how smooth and warm his skin felt. Now really wasn't the time.

Alinor worked with a focused expression, her eyes on the bloody patch to his side, and Adrianna forced herself to work with the same conscientiousness.

Finally, they had peeled his shirt off him. Adrianna tried not to stare at the planes of his shoulders, of his chest. It wasn't her first time seeing a man shirtless, but definitely a man of that build. Seeing Lowen shirtless stirred her about as much as seeing a plucked chicken. Sam shirtless was... a different experience.

Sam had a good tan to him, making it clear that he often worked outdoors and shirtless. He had a smattering of dark hair in the middle of his chest, and a trail leading down from his bellybutton to his trousers.

Adrianna definitely made sure not to look at that, although she could feel heat rising to her cheeks.

To Sam's right was a nasty wound, like a bloody mouth from which seeped blood so dark it looked almost black. He grunted in pain, gritting his teeth, the muscles of his jaw bunching, and that pulled Adrianna right back to the situation at hand and away from her stupid, girlish mooning.

"Let's see what we have here, now," Mirabelle said, frowning.

"Will your magic work so close to the dragon?" Adrianna asked.

Mirabelle gave her a sad look. "The dragon is dead, pet, and therefore her magic has died with her." She turned back to Sam and waved her wand.

That was all it took. The wound closed up and healed, and in moments, it was as if Sam had never been hurt.

He whistled, looking down and examining himself with both hands, pressing and prodding the fresh new skin. "Impressive. I'm starting to see what all the fuss is about with regards to fairy godmothers. I also have another wound on my thigh. Not as deep..." He reached for his belt, beginning to unbuckle it.

"Stop right there, young man. There are young and impressionable ladies present," Mirabelle said at once. "Not that I would mind, but *their* innocence must be preserved."

She waved her wand, and Sam looked down with a frown.

"You can heal me through my clothes? Why did you make me remove my shirt, then?"

Adrianna rolled her eyes. Mirabelle really was incorrigible. The fairy, however, was the picture of innocence—not so much as a hint of embarrassment.

"While the young ladies must be preserved in their innocence, even fairy godmothers like to have something nice to look at while we do our work. And we do deserve compensation for all our toils, after all. We are so unappreciated in what we do, we receive so very little in the way of gratitude for our relentless, tireless—"

"All right, Mirabelle, we get it," Adrianna said.

"What are we going to do about the dragon?" Alinor asked.

"I don't know," Adrianna whispered. "And then there's the egg. We have to take care of the egg." The thought made her chest tighten, and she felt a sob rising up in her throat again. "Can you all just give me a moment?"

She took off the talisman from around her neck and let it drop to the ground. Then she walked over to the dragon's massive head. She needed that moment alone with the dragon, even though it was far too late.

She rested her forehead on the scales of the dragon's temple, right next to her eye. She wasn't sure how hot the dragon's body normally was, but the scales were still very warm to the touch, probably because she had died so recently.

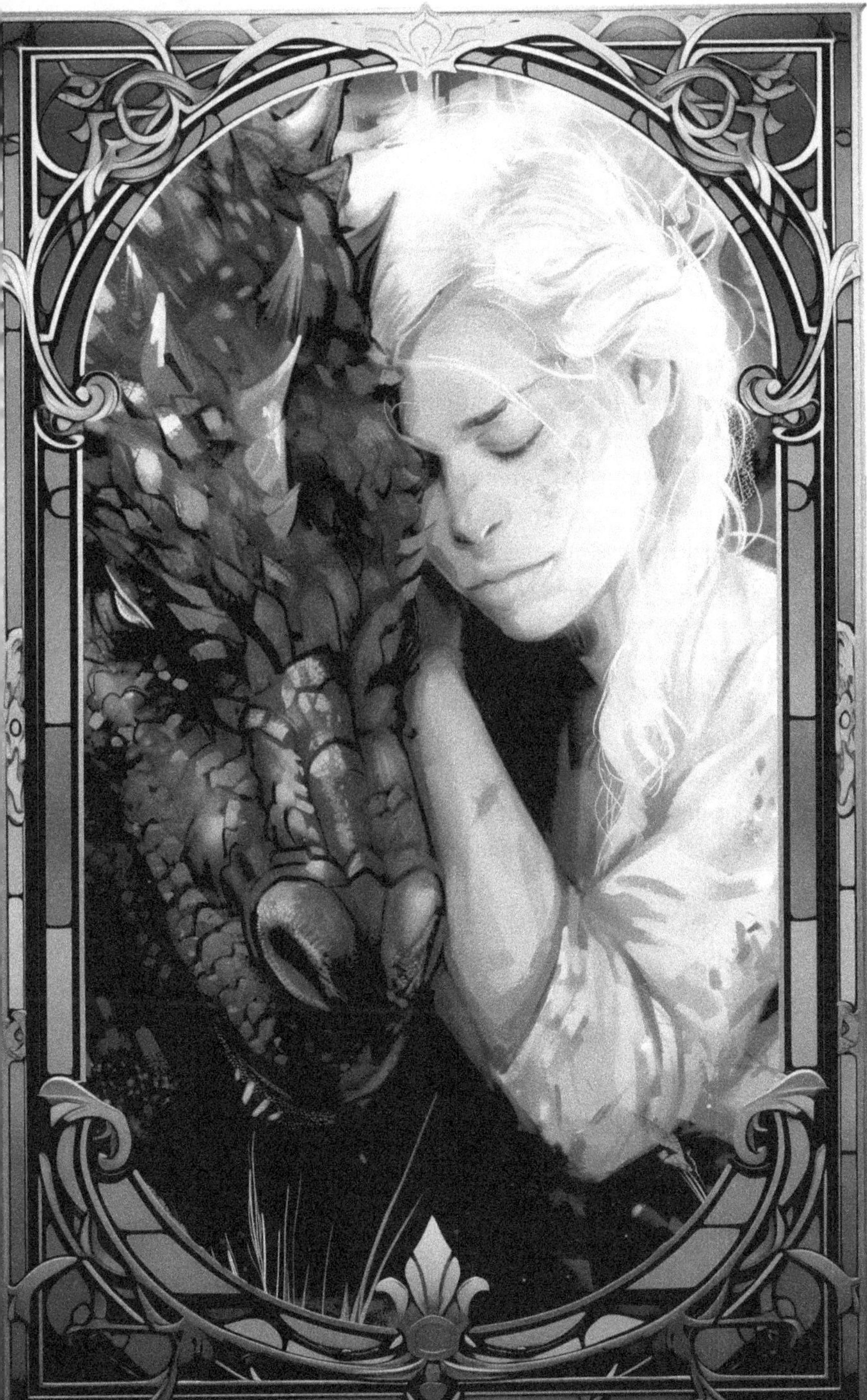

"I'm sorry, I'm so sorry," she whispered, placing both hands on the dragon. Her eyes filled with tears. "You were doing exactly what I was doing—protecting your family. I'm so sorry, I never meant for this to happen. I mean, I know I did, but that was before... But then after, when they took Alinor... It's all my fault, I screwed it all up. And I'm so sorry. I know I keep failing, and I failed you, and..." Adrianna was crying in earnest, now, tears pouring down her cheeks as she hiccuped through her words.

She clung to the dragon's head, crying, needing this moment of just being with her.

"I promise to look after your egg. I'll find a way to keep it hot, and I'll make sure it hatches, and I'll make sure that it's healthy and happy. It will be well-loved, your youngling. It will be become a strong dragon. And I promise—I promise—I will never let a single prince near it. Ever."

She took a final, shuddering breath. She kissed the cooling scales, feeling the warmth against her lips on which had mingled her tears. Then she straightened up, wiped her nose on her sleeve, and was about to turn back to suggest they tend to the egg, when she heard the dragon breathe.

It was faint and weak, but it was unmistakably there. Adrianna gasped. And then the dragon took another breath.

"The dragon is alive!" Adrianna shouted. "She's alive!"

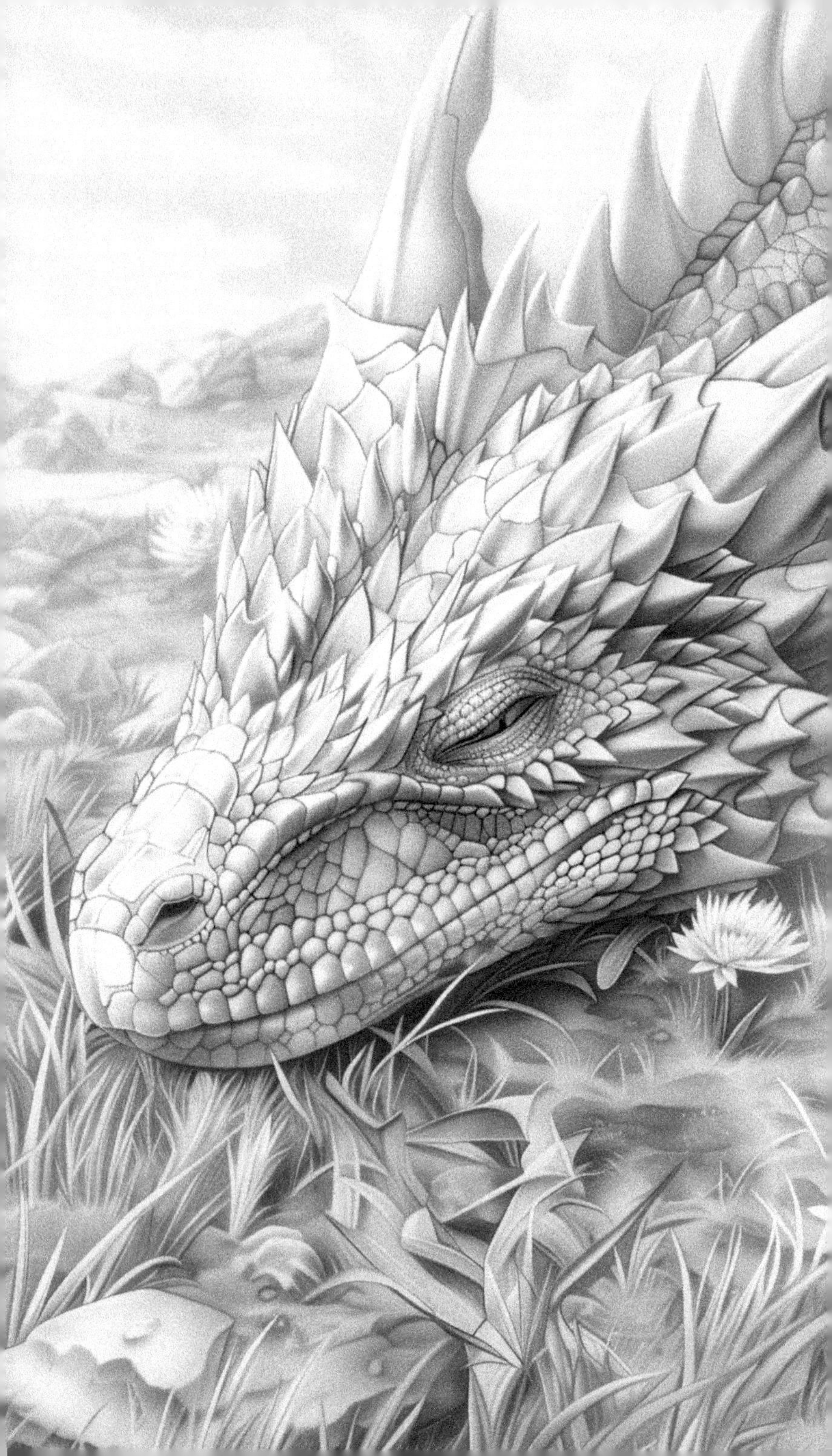

CHAPTER 28

Sam and Alinor hurried over to the dragon, but Mirabelle stayed cautiously back.

"You're right," Mirabelle said. "She's alive, but barely. There's only the tiniest flicker of magic to her."

"We have to get her out of here at once," Sam said decisively. "We can't risk her being out in the open when those idiots return."

Adrianna didn't need to ask him to clarify to which idiots he was referring.

"Should we pull out the swords and crossbow bolts from her?" Alinor asked.

"No," Sam said at once. "Once we do, the wounds will bleed, and we will need something to bandage them up. No touching the dragon until she is somewhere safe and we can actually deal with the wounds. But how the hell we're going to move her is the real question."

"Mirabelle, if the dragon barely has any magic, does that mean your magic can still work?" Adrianna asked hopefully. "Can you do anything to help us move her? Because otherwise… I have no idea how we would go about it."

"We'd have to build something," Sam said, running a hand through his hair. "But given the size of her, it would take time, and we'd need a lot of horses, and people..."

"Time that we do not have," Adrianna finished. "Not that we have materials, horses, and people, either." She turned to her fairy godmother, hopeful.

Mirabelle took a deep breath. "I... Might be able to finagle something."

"Oh yes, Mirabelle!" Alinor said eagerly, gripping the fairy's arm with both hands. "Finagle something. You can always make everything better. You're the best. We have to save her, we have to save the dragon."

Mirabelle cleared her throat. "Yes, well. The stories always fail to show that it is, in fact, the fairy godmother who saves the day. All the focus is always on the princes, when it is us doing all the work in the background."

"It is definitely you doing all the work," Adrianna said quickly, to stop the fairy going off into one of her favourite rants. "And we will all be hugely grateful to you and give you all the credit. But let's do what we can now, quickly, because once a prince comes back, we will be back in the same position as before, and I don't know that we will get another chance to save the dragon."

"I won't be able to move you all with her," Mirabelle warned.

"We can go back by horse," Sam said at once.

"Good. Now back away, all of you, back away." Mirabelle closed her eyes, knotting her brow in concentration. Adrianna wouldn't diminish just how grateful she was for her fairy godmother right now, but she also knew that Mirabelle would be absolutely loving this—the attention, the stakes, being the one coming to the rescue.

The fairy muttered something and waved her wand in complicated patterns. "Adrianna," she said, eyes still closed,

"You'll be travelling with the two of us. I'm not dealing with the dragon once we arrive."

"That's absolutely fine." Adrianna came closer. She looked back at Alinor.

"I'll bring Alinor back," Sam said at once.

"I'll be safe with Sam," Alinor said. "Don't worry about me."

Adrianna nodded.

Mirabelle waved her wand once more, and Adrianna felt a rush of wind and a buildup of pressure in the air.

"Hold on tight," Mirabelle said, although Adrianna had no idea what she was supposed to hold on to.

The world disappeared in a mad and blurry rush of air, and then Adrianna's ears popped, and she heard Mirabelle hiccup. There was a loud, thundering noise, like a boulder crashing to earth, and then they were at the castle.

Or to be more precise, the dragon and her egg had landed hard on top of one of the abandoned outbuildings, crushing it to matchsticks and gravel.

Adrianna stared for a moment, processing the carnage.

"The dragon's magic interfered with mine, which made it hard to navigate," Mirabelle said defensively. "And I got the hiccups at the wrong moment. Fairy godmothers are not designed for this. We are not designed to move dragons across distances. We are supposed to make princesses pretty and princes charming."

"Mirabelle, you did a wonderful job," Adrianna said. "This is *perfect*."

"Of course it is. Now, I need a stiff drink after all the day's excitement. I'm fairly parched and exhausted."

"You do that. And then we need to tend to the dragon's wounds and see what we can do to help her heal. And to keep her egg hot."

"Hmm, yes. I think I will leave you and Sam to deal with that. This is not a fairy's department, that. Dirty wounds and foul-tempered dragons—no, no, definitely not a fairy godmother's department. But I'm glad you're in better spirits, pet."

Adrianna gave a small laugh. "I might be in better spirits, but I'm still neck-deep in crap."

Mirabelle patted her arm, eyes twinkling. "Things will be fine. They will work out, you'll see. But for now, I have… things to attend to." She flitted towards the castle, calling Lowen's name, and then disappeared inside.

But it wasn't the gardener who came out but Petunia.

"Alinor? Alinor!" Petunia called, rushing down the stairs.

"She's fine." Adrianna updated her stepmother on what had happened. Petunia gripped Adrianna's hands the whole time, scanning her face anxiously—she looked like she might collapse at any moment.

Lowen appeared with a chair in hand, and Petunia sank gratefully into it.

"But she's fine? She's truly fine?" Petunia asked anxiously.

"Not a scratch on her. Being taken away and locked in a cell will have scared her, for sure, but she's fine."

Petunia covered her mouth with a shaking hand and nodded. She gave a big, shuddering sigh.

"And about…"

"That?" Adrianna pointed to the enormous dark teal and gold dragon lying on top of the wreck that had once been a building.

"Yes. That looks like a dragon…"

"It is. She's very hurt and we're going to try to heal her wounds."

"Right. Of course. And the prince who did this…"

"Princes," Adrianna said darkly. "We didn't manage to stop them."

"Stop them?" Petunia looked confused. "Why stop them?"

"I'm not marrying any of them, Petunia. And I'm saving the dragon."

To give her credit, Petunia took that in her stride. She nodded, still looking the dragon over. "Well, so long as it didn't crush my roses, and so long as it doesn't try to breathe fire on my garden, that's fine."

Lowen was hovering behind Petunia, looking like as much of a nervous chicken as ever, but there was a sense of expectation to him, too.

"Did you want news of Mirabelle?" Adrianna asked him.

"Just to know that she's not hurt," he stammered.

"She's fine. She brought the dragon here, and now she's gone inside in search of, er… brandy." Adrianna didn't want to terrify him with the news that Mirabelle had gone to look for him.

Lowen nodded and looked in the direction of the castle, both with fear and with a strange sort of longing. It really was impossible to know if he was attracted to or terrified of Mirabelle.

"Yes, yes, you can go," Petunia said with impatience.

Adrianna turned her attention to the dragon. She had more important things to do right now than to try to puzzle the mystery that was Lowen's mind.

She asked Petunia to have Helga bring blankets. Then she headed cautiously to the dragon, who was still breathing but unmoving. She carefully cleared some of the debris from around the egg.

Helga returned with the blankets, leaving them at the castle's door, too scared to come forward. Adrianna retrieved them and nestled the egg inside them, hoping it would keep it warm. Then she tucked the egg against the dragon.

That done, she hesitated. The truth was, she had absolutely no idea what to do now. She was so far out of the storylines, of the known. There was no script for a princess attempting to save a dragon after rejecting a marriage proposal from a prince.

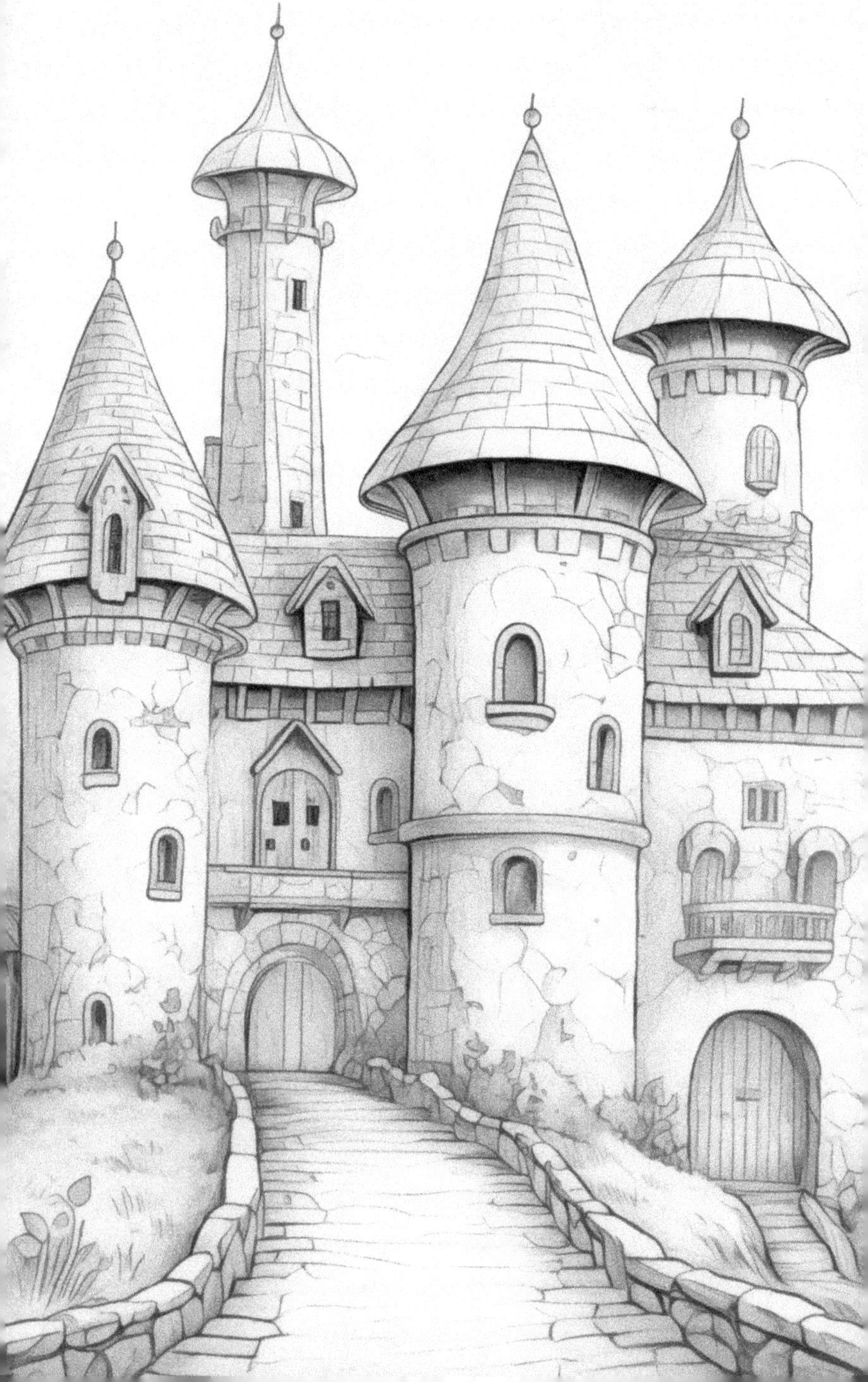

CHAPTER 29

It was a relief when Sam arrived and took control, giving orders for the supplies he would need to tend to the dragon's wounds. He was barely off his horse that he was listing out the things he would need, most of which were things Adrianna had never heard of. But Lowen—who returned after having found Mirabelle, although it wasn't clear if he was back to help or just to escape her—seemed to know all of it, rushing about the garden with his long legs and collecting the required herbs.

There was something truly reassuring about having Sam around. It made Adrianna feel like no matter what happened, they would figure things out. She kept hearing his voice in her mind—how he had told he would help her find a prince, that he would help her get Alinor back. That he wasn't just going to leave her in the lurch.

He had been there the way no prince had ever been. And he hadn't been there because he was interested in besting the Impossible Odds. Or for the glory of a big rescue. He had been there just for Adrianna.

Something that felt both wonderfully and uncomfortably foreign.

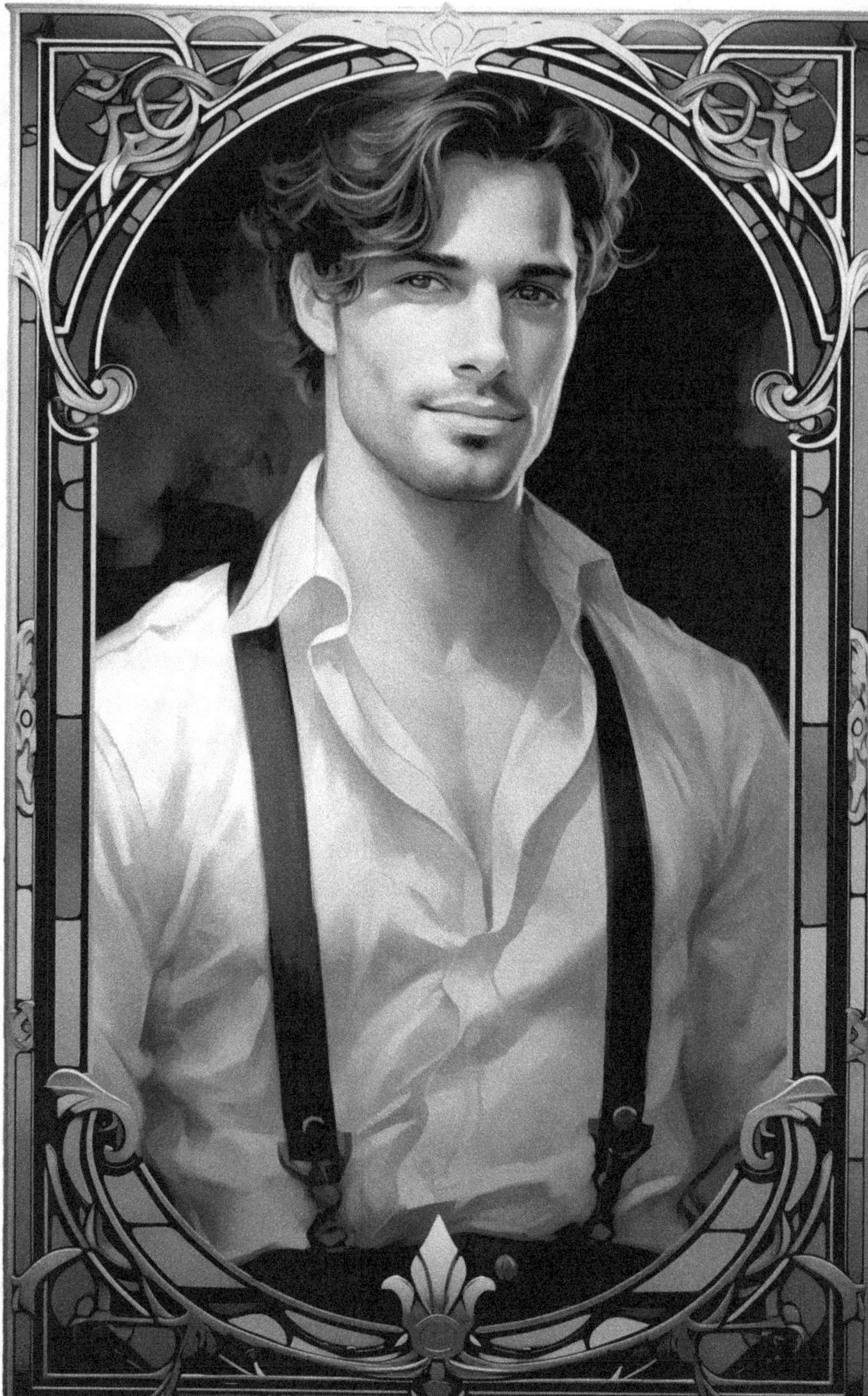

Petunia rushed out of the castle as soon as Alinor returned, to squeeze her daughter in her arms. She checked Alinor's face thoroughly, eyes brimming with tears of relief.

"I'm fine, Mama," Alinor told her quietly. "Nothing happened. I'm completely fine."

Adrianna turned away to give them a moment of privacy. Petunia was rarely given to emotional displays, and she was unlikely to want an audience.

Sam continued to calmly give orders to get everything ready to tend to the dragon. Approaching the dragon to tend the wounds was another matter. She had regained enough consciousness to snap in warning as soon as Sam went anywhere near her.

In fact, the only person she seemed willing to tolerate was Adrianna, which was odd. Even though Adrianna had stolen her egg and caused her to nearly die in the first place. And yet, the dragon looked at her with recognition and intelligence in her eyes. As if she had somehow heard what Adrianna had told her in the moments she lay dying or dead.

Adrianna still wasn't sure whether magic had taken place, bringing the dragon back to life, or if the dragon simply hadn't been quite dead. After all, kisses given with true love had a magic to them, magic enough to break curses and bring princesses back to life. Maybe that magic worked too when it came to dragons. Because in the moment Adrianna had kissed the dragon, she had truly loved her, and she still loved her now.

The dragon might have only just arrived at the castle, but it felt like she was already a part of this ramshackle little family. Adrianna fiercely wanted her to be better, and for her egg to hatch in the best possible conditions.

Since the dragon allowed Adrianna to come close, she was the one who worked to carefully remove the weapons that had been wedged into her body. Under Sam's shouted instructions from a safe distance, she tended to the wounds with the poultices and herbs that he prepared and gave her.

It was dirty, tiring work. The dragon's smell was powerful, and her scales were so hot, Adrianna needed gloves or her hands rapidly started to hurt. She pulled out the various weapons one by one, moving carefully but quickly to stop the flow of blood.

Bandaging the wounds required the use of most of the castle's bedsheets. Adrianna managed it all under the watchful eye of Sam, while next to him Alinor hovered, with Petunia close by. Both Adrianna and Petunia had forbidden Alinor from going near the dragon. Given that the dragon didn't seem to tolerate anyone other than Adrianna, they weren't going to risk Alinor getting hurt.

Alinor had sulked at not even being able to try, but the risk simply wasn't worth it. Especially not after having come so close to losing her. Petunia didn't take her eyes off her daughter—even her precious garden was forgotten for a time.

And so long as everyone kept away and only Adrianna came close to tend to the wounds, the dragon seemed content enough, breathing softly on her egg.

Adrianna worked hard, late into the night, until the dragon was fully bandaged and provided with water and a slaughtered sheep for her dinner.

"We need to name her," Adrianna decided, stretching her arms overhead against the ache she felt in her back.

Sam nodded. "Good idea."

"Ooh, ooh, Gabriella," Alinor suggested. "Or Sylera, or Eladora. No wait, Bellatrix!"

The dragon flicked open en eyelid at that and considered them. She breathed out a low rumble.

"I like Bellatrix," Adrianna said. "And she seems to respond to it as well."

"Bellatrix," Sam said pensively. "It's a good name. Very majestic."

Adrianna grinned. "Bellatrix it is, then."

Alinor gasped, looking the dragon over adoringly. "Beautiful, wonderful Bellatrix."

It took some convincing to coax Alinor indoors to sleep. Adrianna didn't want to risk leaving anyone alone with Bellatrix, certainly not Alinor, who was likely to be tempted to get too close.

Alinor helped Helga prepare a room for Sam, and since there was finally nothing left that needed immediate tending, Adrianna collapsed on her bed, too exhausted to remove her clothes. She had no bedsheets left, anyway.

The next day Bellatrix's bandages needed changing, so fresh herbs could be applied to help the healing. And the following days followed much the same rhythm. Exhausting work, tending to Bellatrix's bandages, and yet Adrianna was grateful for it. Grateful to make right the wrong she had done. Grateful that for now everything was all right—or at least she could tell herself that it was.

Alinor was safe, Bellatrix was alive, the egg was cared for. And it certainly didn't hurt that Sam was hanging around, either.

Everything was working out.

Except that, of course, nothing had worked out as it should. According to the storylines, everything was very, very wrong.

It was all far too good to be true to hope that it could

last. Adrianna did her best not to think about that. That was a problem for another day.

That day came when a carriage flanked by numerous guards arrived at the castle entrance.

Adrianna heard their arrival even before Petunia came to warn her. She grabbed a rag to wipe her dirty hands.

"It's them," Petunia whispered, her face twisted with fear. "It's *them*."

Adrianna's stomach plummeted. She knew who Petunia was referring to. Alinor paled.

"Keep Alinor back here," she told Petunia and Sam.

He nodded and put a protective arm around the young girl.

Adrianna entered the castle through the backdoor, quickly crossed it, and stepped out the front. She wished she'd had the time to change into something if not respectable, then at least more impressive than her dirty, smelly, blood-and-sweat-and-dirt-stained clothes.

She stepped out of the castle alone to face the arrivals.

The carriage was black and sober, but obviously expensive, and it was pulled by four gleaming black horses. The guards wore uniforms that matched the sentries who had been outside of the keep.

One man sat on his horse in front of the convoy, and he was dressed differently. Still in black, his expression dour, but his clothing was fine, as was his hat with a single, large and blood red feather. Obviously the man in charge.

Adrianna looked him square in the eye as she came down the four steps that led to the castle entrance. A far cry from the sweeping staircase that climbed up to the entrance of Charming's castle.

"How can I help you?" she asked haughtily, acting as much the princess as she could manage. "I suppose you are here about the damage the dragon did to the keep?"

"What? Of course not. That dragon did what it is in her

nature to do. She followed the right course of action. She is entirely as she should be. You, however, have interfered with a rearrangement procedure."

"There was no need for this rearrangement. My sister was doing nothing wrong."

"The rearrangement was not about her but about this entire storyline. Your evil *step*sister," and he put a strong emphasis on the word 'step,' "wasn't fulfilling her role. Neither were you, as the princess. Once her rearrangement had been taken care of, you were supposed to be next. Actually you were supposed to be first, but you happened to be away."

"But it's too early for that," Adrianna protested. "I still have time to find a prince and marry—"

"There are too many irregularities about this storyline for it to be allowed to continue."

Adrianna eyed all the guards. The pitiful attempts she and Sam had made to try to fight the princes made it clear that there was no hope of being able to stop them from taking anyone they wanted.

The man on the horse seemed aware of this as well. "You may either come of your own free will, or you will be dragged away like your stepsister was previously."

Adrianna's heart pounded hard.

"No, wait..."

"I will not wait. Please fetch your stepsister and your stepmother."

Adrianna felt faint. "No, wait, please. This does work as a storyline, don't you see? There were Impossible Odds—my sister being held captive in the keep. There was a daring rescue. There was a dragon. There was even, wait!" she gasped as she realised something. "There was even magic and True Love's Kiss—I kissed Bellatrix, the dragon, and she came back to life. That must count for something," Adrianna added desperately. "It's a full story, it's a proper story, and it can have a Happy Ever After."

"A princess can't do the rescuing," the man hissed. "And what on earth makes you think that kissing a dragon could qualify as True Love's Kiss? There isn't even a prince in your story, and he should be the one to surmount the Impossible Odds, not you."

Adrianna's mind raced, trying to find a way that she could weave the princes who attacked Bellatrix into the storyline she was desperately trying to cobble out of the mess that was her life.

"But there is a prince," a male voice said behind her.

Adrianna started, spinning around. Charming's voice sounded a little less like a frightened sheep's bleat than usual. He even looked a bit more impressive as he stepped out of the castle, shoulders squared back.

"Where did you come from?" Adrianna asked him.

"I've been hiding—I mean living here for the last couple of days." Charming cleared his throat and drew himself up straighter. "I came to be with my beloved."

He was so pale, with his blonde hair, his watery blue eyes. Yes, of course, his features were perfect, and he was immensely handsome, but the overwhelming impression he had always given Adrianna was of a damp sock, good looks or not. Except that now he no longer appeared like a damp sock. He appeared like a shy and retiring person who was pushing past his discomfort to wade into a messy situation and attempt to help.

Adrianna had never been more grateful for him, or for the tremulous authority that radiated from him.

Charming raised his chin. "I demand that you depart—"

The carriage door opened and a queen in all her regalia stepped out, complete with a golden crown on her head. She was beautiful—of course—but there was a hardness, a brittle coldness to her that was unappealing in the extreme. And between the poker-straight way she stood and her thinness, she gave the impression of being a beautifully dressed skeleton.

"Charming," she snapped, as if she were calling a disobedient puppy to heel.

The effect on Charming was immediate. He seemed to liquefy, as if he might dissolve in a puddle. His posture melted, losing all of its earlier confidence, and with his yellow hair and golden clothing, he now looked like a slab of butter that had been left out in the sun.

"M-m-mother."

"Cease this at once, Charming. You will come back to the castle, and I will choose your wife for you. Enough of this nonsense."

Adrianna expected Charming to slink to the carriage without protest, but he shook his head weakly.

"N-n-no, mother. I will not." Charming's voice was strangled, frightened, and more like the bleat of a sheep than ever, and yet beneath all the fear there was also a hint of determination. "I will live here. With my beloved." He gestured behind him to where Petunia was tentatively coming out of the entrance.

If spontaneously turning to ice was possible, the queen would certainly have frozen on the spot at the sight of her.

"There you go," Adrianna said quickly, before the queen could respond and cower Prince Charming into submission. "We have a prince. And there will be a wedding?" The latter she asked questioningly, glancing back at Petunia.

Adrianna had never seen her evil stepmother look so uncertain and scared, but the older woman nodded once.

"My beloved has accepted my marriage proposal," Charming said with a little more confidence. "We shall be married as soon as—"

"Queens cannot remarry," the man in black on the horse said coldly. "Only kings can remarry, once they are widowers. And a storyline without a wedding does not work."

Adrianna gulped. The answer was obvious—she would simply have to marry Charming. Although he hadn't proposed to her. If she announced that she wanted to marry him, would that ruin the storyline irreparably?

"Then I shall marry Adrianna," Charming said, with as much enthusiasm as Adrianna felt.

"I accept," she said at once, her voice as strangled as his, doing her best to ignore the shudder going down her spine.

"Charming has already proposed to another woman and been accepted," the man in black said. "He cannot marry you. Princesses do not get sloppy seconds. This remains a complete violation of the storylines."

Adrianna knew that he was right. If Petunia had refused Charming, there might have been something to work with, but she hadn't. No one heard of stories where a prince proposed to a princess's stepmother and then shifted to the princess, because that was more convenient.

"And without a wedding there can be no Happy Ever After," the man in black grated. "Without a wedding and a Happy Ever After, there is no story. So you and your stepsister will come with us for immediate rearrangement."

"Mirabelle and I are getting married," another male voice announced. Lowen's voice, in fact.

Lowen and Mirabelle came out of the entrance to stand on the steps alongside Petunia. Lowen's eyes were wide and terrified, his Adam's apple bobbing repeatedly. Mirabelle was looking at him with adoration in her eyes, and when he glanced at her, to Adrianna's shock, there was something that appeared to be tenderness in amongst all the fear. He took her hand shyly, like a small boy taking the hand of the girl he had a crush on.

Adrianna gaped. Lowen and Mirabelle were getting

married? But now was not the time to try to understand the inscrutable mysteries of love.

"There you go," she told the man. "We have a wedding. A Happy Ever After. We have a prince—"

"Who surmounted nothing," the man said icily. "He has not won his fair lady's heart."

"I faced the Motherly Wrath," Charming protested. "I faced the Motherly Disapproval, and I remained with my beloved, anyway. Those are Impossible Odds for me."

"Charming, how *dare* you speak of me thus," the queen snapped.

"Impossible Odds indeed," Adrianna said. "Given the nasty shrew that is his mother, the queen." A cheap shot, but it felt good. She hadn't liked the way the queen had caused Charming to cower. Adrianna counted out on her fingers. "So, to recap, we have a beautiful young woman who was taken, followed by a daring rescue. A dangerous keep was charged not once but twice. And then there was a battle to protect the life of another female—a battle in which blood was shed," Adrianna added, referring to the battle to protect Bellatrix. Adrianna was glad she could refer to Sam's fighting, and not to the ungainly scramble she had taken part in. "We then have a dragon who was slain by a prince. We have True Love's Kiss restoring life to said dragon. We have a prince who faced Impossible Odds to be with his beloved. And now, we will have a wedding and a Happy Ever After." Adrianna lowered her hands. "These are all the elements needed for a storyline to work."

The face of the man on the horse had been growing more and more sour the more Adrianna spoke. "None of this works, and you know it. You're not stupid."

"Look, it's not a perfect story," Adrianna said quietly. "It's not even a good story. I know it won't be told and passed down generations to inspire future princesses. It won't become a reference for future storylines. But it *is* a story, and it deserves to be allowed to continue to its end. Just let us have our happy ending. As imperfect as it is, it's our story, and it works. Please. *Please*. We're not harming anyone."

The man in black shook his head. "It's a disaster. A mess."

"You're right, it is. But then, so are people. We are imperfect and messy, and so our story is every bit as imperfect and messy. Just like us. Just like life. There's no point looking away and pretending things are otherwise. And you can't—you can't demand of us that we be perfect when we are not. No one is perfect, not even princesses. Especially not princesses. We're a neurotic, idiotic bunch, the lot of us."

"We *can* demand perfection of you because that is what you were born for," the man snapped. "You are supposed to be perfect. It is what you were *designed* to be. That is what you are blessed at birth to be."

"Then why was I born deficient?" Adrianna shouted, a lifetime's worth of anger and frustration and anguish bursting out of her. "Why make me so imperfect if you demand perfection from me? Why demand that I be gentle and feminine, but have me be born as none of these things? Why make my stepmother and stepsister so lovely and kind and then ask them to be evil? And Charming, who is a limp sock of a man, why make him a prince, when he clearly doesn't want that life for himself? In fact, why make *me* a princess when Alinor would be far more suited to that role than me? Because life is random and not fair, that's why. We do the best we can with the cards we are dealt, and that means that things don't always work out in the expected way. But they still work out, and that is *still* a storyline. It still works. It still has value." Adrianna clenched her fists, her voice rising. "We still count for something, even if we're different from what you people expect."

The man on the horse looked at her, nonplussed. He hesitated, glancing back at the carriage, obviously unsure what to do or say in response to Adrianna's rant.

The carriage door remained open, but a thin black curtain across the door prevented anyone from seeing inside.

"This is heresy," said a quiet voice from within the carriage. The voice was midnight soft, and yet something about it made Adrianna's skin crawl. She knew, knew in her bones, that this was the master the sentries had spoken of before.

"You speak of upending our whole order," the voice continued. "You question the very rules that make our world exist. You are a selfish, unfeminine princess who failed to capture the attention of a prince and dared to do her own rescuing. Your prince is a coward who fears his mother and is in love with an evil stepmother. Your evil stepsister is not evil, nor is your evil stepmother, who to add insult to injury is in love with her garden and not with the man who she is engaged to. Your fairy godmother is a drunk. Your hero cannot fight with a sword. The only one who is sticking to his role in all of this is your gardener, Lowen. The rest of you will have to be taken and re-arranged. *All of you*. Now."

Adrianna clenched her fists again. "Very well. You can try, but just know we won't go without a fight."

"And you have a stablehand on your side," a voice that Adrianna recognised at once said from behind her. Sam stepped out and came to stand next to Adrianna. He might not be able to fight with a sword, but he looked damn impressive holding one, his expression set, his jaw clenched in determination. In fact, he looked far more impressive than any of the princes who had galloped over to slay the dragon.

"And you have a prince," said Charming. "Even if I am a limp sock."

Adrianna felt a stab of guilt. "Sorry about that."

"No need," Charming said happily. "It's the truth, and I'm quite comfortable with it. I have no desire for heroics or adventure. The life of a sock suits me just fine. Indoor, quiet, comfortable. Cozy. It's perfect."

"And they have a fairy godmother on their side," Mirabelle said.

"And a gardener," added Lowen.

"And an evil stepmother and stepsister," Alinor cried out, tumbling out of the castle.

"Alinor, no!" Adrianna called, dismayed. "You were supposed to stay hidden inside."

"Charming, you will come to me now," the queen ordered. "You will come home with me right now—"

"He needs to be re-arranged," the voice inside the carriage sighed.

The queen paled and spun around to face the carriage. "No. That isn't—"

"You have no more say in this than anyone."

"But I was the one who called for the fixing of this broken story…"

"Indeed. And your son is a part of it, whether you like it or not. He will be re-arranged into a proper prince, and once he is suitable again, he will be returned to you. Now that everyone is helpfully gathered outside, seize them."

The guards dismounted, their weapons clinking. Sam clenched his fist tighter around his sword. Adrianna put her arms out to shield Alinor. She wondered if they had time to run back inside and bolt the door. Could they maybe get Bellatrix to spray fire, if she didn't move from her egg?

The guards approached.

But before they could get any closer, the castle let out a deep rumble, and the earth trembled.

The guards cried out in shock, and the horses whinnied in fear.

"What's that?"

The man on the horse had to get his steed under control, but he too looked around, nervous. The guards remained as they were, glancing about them fearfully.

And then a stone slab to the right of the door flew explosively out of the castle wall, pushed by a powerful spray of muddy-red water. It hit the guards so hard as to fling them back towards their horses, who ran off in fear. The guards flailed about, pinned to the ground by the water pressure. The queen had staggered back, her elegant grey dress splashed by the dirty water. The spray caught the black carriage, including the door, as well.

"What the..." the man on the horse gaped at the mess.

A second stone stab exploded out to the left, and a second geyser of water sprayed out.

"What's happening?" Alinor asked in a small, frightened voice.

Adrianna looked up. She could feel it. The castle. Somehow it was... not quite alive, but it was something, for sure. And it was on their side.

The water stopped then, and the castle rumbled again, the ground shaking hard. The air was thick with magic. It crackled with it.

Adrianna turned back to face the black carriage and the voice within it. "Like I said, we're not going down without a fight. We're all together in this, and we have a magical castle on our side. You can't take us."

For a moment, no one spoke. The master, hidden in his black carriage, remained silent. Water dripped from the carriage and from the soldiers. The man on the horse watched the carriage expectantly, as did all the guards, as did the queen—in fact, everyone watched the carriage.

"Leave them," the voice in the coach sighed at last.

"No!" the queen protested. "I summoned you to fix this situation, not—"

"You didn't summon me." The voice in the carriage turned even softer—menacingly soft.

The queen paled a little and swallowed.

"You alerted me to an irregularity. It, however, appears that this situation is beyond repair. The damages caused so far are already extensive enough—we do not need more mess to be created. That would create more problems to solve than simply leaving them all here. There are many other matters requiring my attention. I would prefer to focus my time and resources on situations that can be redeemed. Leave them to their disaster of a life. This storyline will finish, and they will sink into oblivion. No one will remember them. They will be a weird footnote in history, an embarrassment to be forgotten about."

Nothing had ever sounded so sweet to Adrianna.

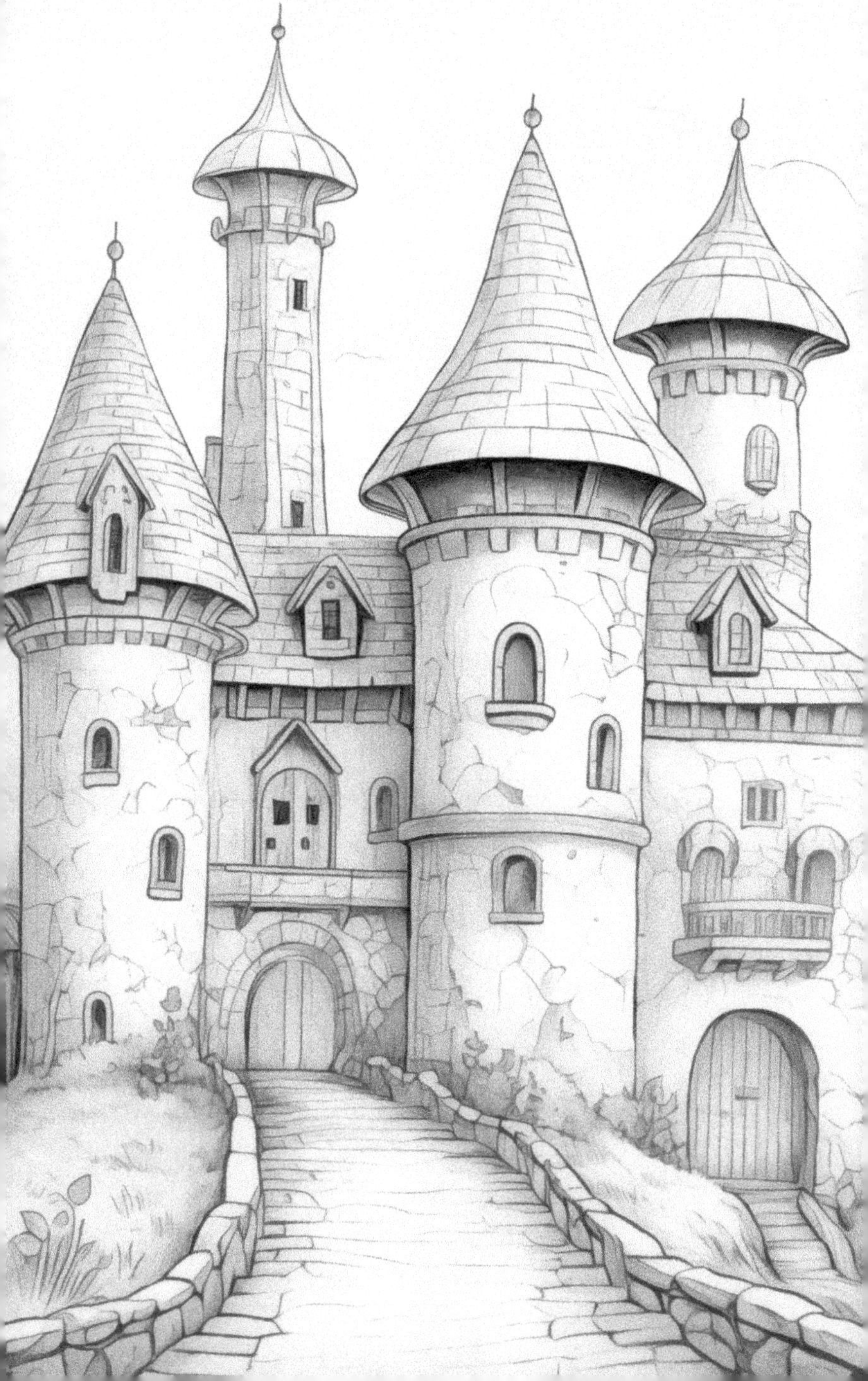

CHAPTER 30

Adrianna was walking past the library when she heard her evil stepmother's voice. She poked her head in to find Petunia looking remarkably agitated, pacing as she ranted at Charming with many impassioned gestures. She had on her gardening attire and from the smudge of dirt on her cheek and the soil and grass that clung to the hem of her skirt, it was clear she had come straight from the garden.

Charming was sitting in a chair, holding an open book, obviously not really listening to Petunia. He had given himself two challenges now that he officially lived in the castle. The first was to catalogue and organise the library, a task he seemed to relish, and the second was to find a way to improve on the castle's plumbing so that the water would run clear rather than reddish-brown.

He was every bit as pale and scrawny as when he had first arrived, but somehow, the limp sock impression he used to give Adrianna had gone. Maybe it was that she was growing accustomed to him. Maybe it was the energy that he was throwing into his research as he pored over her father's notes, trying to understand the mysteries of the castle's plumbing. Whatever it was, life here was clearly agreeing with him. He looked happy.

"And do you know what he told me?" Petunia was saying, stopping in front of Charming. "What he told me—*me*, technically the *queen* of this castle? That my hydrangeas were too crowded. Too crowded! Can you believe your ears?"

"No, dear." Charming continued his contented reading.

Petunia resumed her pacing. "I mean, what next, that my trees have too many leaves? Complete poppycock."

"Absolutely, dear."

"My trees are perfect as they are."

"Yes, dear."

"Lowen must have his head examined. Or his sight. Something is seriously wrong with that man." Petunia stopped and looked out the window, hands on her hips. "Yes, I believe there is something deeply wicked about this man. A kind of perversion. Probably due to his Cornish origins."

"You must be right, dear."

No one was actually sure what Charming and Petunia's relationship status was any more. There hadn't been a wedding, but they were still technically engaged. Charming agreed with everything Petunia said—although Adrianna was pretty sure he also didn't listen to a word she said. In their own weird way, they seemed happy. Adrianna had never seen them have a true conversation where they actually exchanged or connected in a meaningful way, but neither of them seem to require that. Petunia was free to monologue about her garden, and Charming was free to read and wander off in his thoughts. Petunia didn't require him to listen or reply to her, and Charming seemed perfectly content with this.

Petunia turned from the window. "Ah, Adrianna." She hurried over, and Adrianna braced herself for the inevitable torrent of garden-related information that was about to be foisted on her. "I needed to speak to Mirabelle. Your fairy godmother needs to do something about her husband. Lowen has frayed my last nerve."

"Hmmm," Adrianna replied noncommittally. This was far from the first time that Lowen had frayed Petunia's last nerve. Petunia had a lot of last nerves when it came to her garden. Adrianna also knew that Mirabelle refused to hear the slightest negative thing about her husband and so was unlikely to do anything about the current situation.

"A man's place is indoors, Adrianna, never forget it." Petunia turned back to give Charming a look full of tenderness. "I'm so glad this darling man knows his place in the world. I do declare, I don't think I ever see him leave the library, unless it is to attend to the plumbing—which is also a man's job."

Not that Charming did any of the heavy lifting when it came to the castle's plumbing. But he had come up with a rather impressive number of ideas and suggestions for things to try. He had also requested that the generous allowance his mother paid him—because it would have been an embarrassment for her son to be living in the genteel poverty Adrianna had known her whole life—be spent on the maintenance of the castle and the general expenses associated with running it.

In fact, Charming had asked that somebody take care of spending the money as would best benefit the castle and its occupants, because he didn't want to have to worry about it. His only requirement was that no other servant be hired. Adrianna had tried to explain that with more servants the library could be dust free, but Charming seemed to be horrified at the suggestion. So the castle continued as it always had been, a merry, disorganised mess where precious little worked as it was supposed to.

"It's hatching!" Alinor yelled, careening down the

corridor towards them. "The egg has started to crack—it's hatching!"

Adrianna gasped with excitement. "Let's go, quick! Petunia, Charming, are you coming?"

"Yes, and I'll take the opportunity to have words with Lowen," Petunia replied. Charming was already lost to his book again.

Alinor and Adrianna raced through the castle, taking the shortcut Alinor had created. They jumped through the hole in the floor down to the lower level, landing on the mattress Alinor had dragged there, what now felt like a lifetime ago. They ran all the way out into the courtyard where Bellatrix was settled with her egg. Her massive head was resting on the floor, watching the egg, eyes soft and tender. She looked relaxed, which was a hugely encouraging sign. If there was anything remotely wrong, she would have been tense.

Bellatrix was still in the place Mirabelle had brought her to, but Sam had built her a temporary shelter so she would be protected from the rain and the worst of the elements. It had been quite the complicated task, given that she didn't like anyone coming near her.

But somehow, she had seemed to understand Adrianna's explanations, and she had allowed Sam to come just close enough in order to build the shelter. As soon as it was done, though, she resumed her snapping and breathing little plumes of fire in warning any time he came closer than what she liked.

Sam stood at the edge of the courtyard, arms crossed, watching Bellatrix and her egg. His shirt sleeves were rolled up, displaying his thick forearms, corded with muscle. Considering how labour-intensive his work was, Sam's ability to remain clean was rather uncanny. Especially given that he was the one doing all the heavy lifting for Charming's attempts at modernising the plumbing. He displayed rather impressive levels of patience with the prince and seemed prepared to try all of his various schemes.

That was the thing Adrianna had noticed most about Sam in the weeks they had spent together at the castle. Sam was kind. Truly kind. He was matter-of-fact and down to earth, and he was kind in a way that none of the princes Adrianna had encountered at all the balls were. He was generous with his time and his attention, and not just with Adrianna, but with Alinor, with Lowen, with Petunia, with Charming. With people, in short, who didn't really have anything to bring him. He was kind for the sake of it.

Every couple of days he went back to his house to check on his brother's widow, and every time he left, Adrianna felt a pinch in her guts both of jealousy that he was going to see another woman, and of fear that maybe this time he wouldn't come back. But every time, he came back.

"There's a second crack," Sam told the girls as they came to stand next to him. He ruffled Alinor's hair and pointed. "Look." She squealed with excitement.

"I'm going to go check on Bellatrix," Adrianna said. Bellatrix was looking a lot better now that her wounds were almost completely healed. The steady supply of food and water made a huge difference as well.

"Hey, girl." Adrianna approached the massive head. She rested a hand on the scales briefly. Bellatrix was only just bearable to touch, far, far hotter than that day when she had nearly died, but Adrianna made a point of stroking and touching her every day to foster the connection between them. Bellatrix flicked her eyes at her before returning her gaze to the egg. She made a soft, deep rumble. Maybe it was Adrianna's imagination, but the dragon seemed happy. Adrianna hoped that was the case.

"Lowen came to get me as soon as he heard," Mirabelle said, stepping out of the castle with the gardener in tow.

He hovered behind her. They had gotten married—properly, officially married. Petunia had even come out of her gardening fog long enough to warmly congratulate Lowen and to demand that Mirabelle take good care of him.

That was when Adrianna had understood that despite how frustrated Petunia seemed to be with Lowen, she genuinely cared for him, as much as she was able to despite the enchantments that kept her gardening obsessed. And Lowen seemed to know this.

So Lowen and Mirabelle were married, and they seemed genuinely happy. A second couple that at first sight made no sense to Adrianna. At first she'd wondered if this was like when a captive fell in love with his captor. But Lowen, shy and terrified as he was, seemed to genuinely care for Mirabelle. Something that Mirabelle was thrilled about. They both spent most of their days in the garden, Lowen pottering happily among the plants, Mirabelle watching him. Until Petunia arrived to harass Lowen, of course.

To Adrianna, their relationship was as incomprehensible as Petunia and Charming's relationship, but who was Adrianna to judge? They were happy.

"A baby dragon, how wonderful!" Mirabelle clasped her hands to her bosom. "Do you think it will need a fairy godmother? Should I bless it with anything?"

"I thought your magic didn't work on dragons?" Adrianna asked.

"My regular magic, no. But a blessing at birth, that is too powerful for anything to resist. I will make it the handsomest dragon in the land, of course, but what else could I bless it with? With excellent fire, maybe."

"Bless it with the ability to repel princes," Sam said dryly. "Bless it with a safe, quiet life, devoid of attacks from any of those idiots."

"That's not very... Fairy godmothers are supposed to bestow more exciting gifts than a safe and quiet life."

"I think after everything Bellatrix has gone through, the best thing for her would be a peaceful life with her new baby," Sam countered.

"So, how is the hatching coming along?" Petunia asked, stepping out into the courtyard. "Ah, Lowen, just the man I was looking for. Now see here, about my hydrangeas..."

Lowen mumbled some vague excuse and hurried off towards the garden, Petunia trailing after him, her voice getting louder as she continued to monologue about her hydrangeas.

The egg cracked again, a third crack that snaked all along the length of it, and Alinor squealed again. Bellatrix breathed on the egg softly.

It took several hours, but finally a piece of the eggshell broke off, falling to the ground. Something moved in the little gap left behind. And then the top of the shell cracked away from the rest, and a little head poked up, blinking, the piece of shell balanced on top of it.

The dragon youngling was blue-green, same as its shell, with wide, green, slitted eyes, and little horns. It pushed its forelegs out of the shell and paused for a while, looking around. A little gunk stuck to its scaly skin, one longer thread connecting its snout to the edge of the eggshell.

Adrianna held her breath and next to her, Alinor muffled a little squeal. The baby dragon was adorable. Bellatrix lowered her head and gently snorted some warm air, causing the shell on top of its head to fall to the ground. The baby dragon made a little shriek and tumbled clumsily forward, breaking its shell completely. It picked itself up and shook itself, unfurling its little wings. It shrieked again and Bellatrix lowered her head to nuzzle it. It was one of the most touching moments Adrianna had witnessed. She fancied she could see the joy on Bellatrix's face. She was ever so glad that Bellatrix was here, safe and looked after, with no risk of some idiot coming along to kill her during such a precious moment.

"How will we know if it's a boy or a girl?" Alinor asked.

"From the colours, I'm pretty sure it's a female," Sam replied. "I'll check once she's a bit older if Bellatrix will let us near her. Best to keep our distance for a little while."

"I shall bless this baby dragon with the hottest of fires," Mirabelle announced, producing her wand from her corset.

Adrianna grinned as she spotted some chocolate still stuck to the base.

"I shall bless her with a long life," Mirabelle continued, "and with incredible agility in flight. And of course this shall be the prettiest—well… Maybe I should wait until we know for sure that it's a female. I wouldn't want to accidentally bless her with feminine features if it's a male."

"Maybe it doesn't matter if the dragon is pretty or not," Adrianna suggested.

"Nonsense, dear," Mirabelle scoffed. "Every fairy godmother worth her salt blesses a baby with good looks at birth. We've bucked enough rules, all of us. I think we can adhere to this one."

"She doesn't need blessing," Alinor said, staring at the baby dragon adoringly. "She's already perfect, just as she is."

"I second that!" Sam exclaimed.

"And me," Adrianna added more quietly. She briefly wondered what life would be like if princesses weren't blessed at birth, but instead were simply already considered to be good enough just the way they were.

Sam examined Bellatrix with a critical eye. "I'll go get her some food. She's been eating a bit less recently."

"I'll come with you," Adrianna said.

"I'm staying to keep an eye on the baby dragon," Alinor said at once.

"Of course you are."

"Don't get any closer than where you are now," Sam warned. "We don't want to take any risks to upset Bellatrix while the baby is so little."

"No, no, I won't move," Alinor replied, although her yearning to run up to the baby dragon was written all over her face. "Little baby dwagon," she whispered.

Adrianna and Sam headed over to the cold room. That was another benefit of having Charming around. They had enough money now to keep some livestock, which was a good thing as Bellatrix ate a lot. Sam took care of slaughtering goats, sheep, and chickens as needed, making sure that it was done humanely. Adrianna then brought the carcasses to Bellatrix using a trolley.

Bellatrix didn't seem to mind that her food wasn't living, although Adrianna suspected that once she was able to move again, she would go and hunt for herself. Adrianna wondered how long it would take for the baby to learn to fly. That was something to look forward to—like a human baby's first steps.

"I will probably need to go back to check on the farm soon," Sam said as they reached the cold room. He grabbed a goat, which he had already prepared, getting ready to heave it up onto his shoulders.

"Oh."

Sam turned to her. "What is it? You always make that face when I have to go."

"That face? What face?" Even as she asked, Adriana

could feel her traitorous face heating up, the red creeping up her cheeks.

"That look right there." Sam grinned. "What's that look for?"

"Oh..." Adrianna could have denied it—it was a bit embarrassing, after all. And yet, everyone else had their Happy Ever After—didn't Adrianna deserve one as well?

It occurred to her then that she had mocked Charming for his lack of spine after meeting him during the first ball, and yet he had dared to proclaim his desire to be with Petunia, whereas Adrianna was keeping silent about what she wanted. She took her courage with both hands and plunged forward.

"I'm always sad when you leave," she said. "Part of me always worries that maybe you won't come back." Adrianna was staring down at her boots, too embarrassed to look Sam in the eye, although in her peripheral vision she saw him release the goat.

"And you would mind that?" he asked. "If I didn't come back?"

"I would," Adrianna said in a small voice. She took a breath. "I would mind it very much."

And then a second pair of boots appeared in front of hers, darker and more scuffed. Sam shucked a finger under her chin and lifted her face until she was looking up at him.

"I would mind that too," he said.

"Oh." It wasn't so much a word as an exhale.

How had she not realised from the first moment she'd seen him just how devastatingly handsome he was? The way he smiled, the way his eyes gleamed, the way he moved. "Maybe... Maybe you could stay here, then," Adrianna said. "In Veridi. With us."

"I don't know. It depends. I'm quite particular about what I want, and what I need."

"Oh." Adrianna did her best not to feel crushed. It wasn't surprising—this had been the story of her life. Never quite right.

"You see, what I want is a princess who failed to capture the attention of a prince." Adrianna looked up at him. "I want a princess who dared to rescue her stepsister," Sam continued. His arm crept around her waist, pulling her to him. Adrianna found it hard to breathe but in a very, *very* good way. "I want a princess who gets dirty looking after a dragon and who really cares about the people in her life. I want a princess who can also sometimes be rude and annoying and a bit selfish and difficult when she's stressed and going through a hard time. I want a princess who's very imperfect and has flaws, and most importantly, who is unconventional. Do you know where I could find one of those?" He was smiling, now, widely.

Adrianna's heart was beating so fast, Sam had to be able to hear it. "I think I could maybe point you in the right direction... And that's really what you want?"

"Most definitely."

His words hung in the air. Sam pulled her closer to him, his arm tight around her waist until their bodies were as snug as two missing puzzle pieces finding each other. Their eyes were locked, the world receding to a distant background. Adrianna's breath caught in her throat as Sam dipped his head.

Their lips met, and the world burst into a symphony of sensations. Adrianna's entire body seemed to shiver with feeling, from the deepest depths of her stomach all the way to her toes and the back of her neck.

Sam kissed her gently at first, his arm tight at her waist, tangling the fingers of his other hand in her hair. The kiss slowly built in intensity. Waves of warmth cascaded through Adrianna's body, igniting a fire that burned brighter with each passing second. It was a kiss that spoke of hope, of unspoken promises, and of the desire to create a love story all of their own.

Adrianna realised that her failure to find a prince had brought her to something far better, far more profound—a real connection, built on authenticity. She'd found someone who wanted her for who she was, not for who she could pretend to be.

And as they kissed, it felt as though they were starting something, embarking on a journey. She didn't know if this was a Happy Ever After, and she didn't care. Sam's kiss held a promise—a promise to defy convention and embrace the courage to choose their own Happy Ever After. Whatever it looked like. However different it was from the damned storylines.

And wasn't that so much better than a regular old Happy Ever After.

THE END

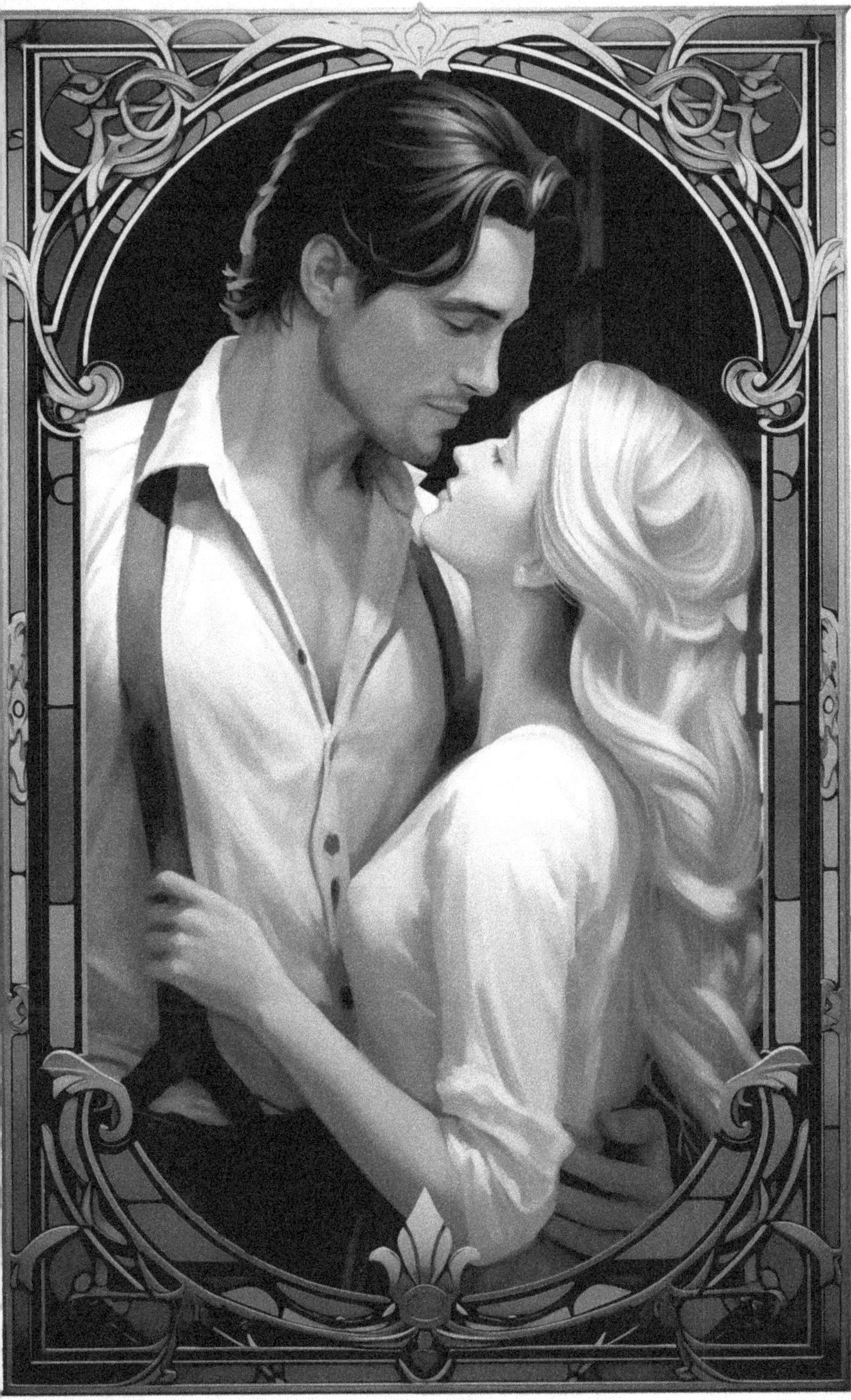

NOTE FROM THE AUTHOR

Dear reader,

I hope you enjoyed your adventure in the quirky world of Once-Upon-Thyme with all its wonderful misfits!

The sequel, Snow is White and the Seven Dragons will be launched on Kickstarter in the summer of 2025 in a similarly gorgeous special edition before being available to order on my site just like Once-Upon-Thyme.

Mirror, mirror on the wall... who's the most *accident-prone fairy godmother* of them all?

That would be Mirabelle, of course. And this time, she's really outdone herself.

After a *tiny* hiccup at a baby princess's naming ceremony (okay, she might have been a *little* tipsy), the poor baby ends up named **Snow is White** instead of just... well, Snow White. Unfortunately, names have power, and as

Snow is White grows up, her greatest talent becomes—quite literally—*stating the obvious.*

Whether it's describing the weather in excruciating detail or narrating situations no one asked for, Snow is White has a gift for driving potential suitors away faster than you can say "Once-Upon-Thyme."

And who's stuck cleaning up this enchanted mess? Her evil stepmother, the Wicked Queen, who, contrary to popular belief, is *so* over being wicked. She dreams of a quiet life filled with tea, cozy reading nooks, and an endless supply of books. But there's a catch—Wicked Queens can only retire after the **Happy Ever After.**

Since Snow is White's suitors keep fleeing, the Wicked Queen is forced to concoct increasingly desperate schemes to trap... er, *encourage* an unsuspecting prince to propose.

Can the Wicked Queen finally orchestrate a Happy Ever After and earn her long-awaited retirement? Or will Snow is White's knack for driving away romance leave them both trapped in this fairytale forever?

Come escape into another story that breaks the fairytale norms, where love is hard to find, villains just want to read in peace, and laughter is guaranteed.

You can find Snow is White and the Seven Dragons over on https://celinejeanjeanbooks.com/snow-is-white or by scanning the QR code below.

I just know you'll have a blast following Snow is White's Kickstarter campaign. It's a very fun and interactive process - you get to vote to choose certain aspects of the special edition (like the colour of the ribbon bookmark) and you also have the opportunity to get your hands on some cool extra bonuses and swag.

If the Kickstarter campaign hasn't launched yet, just click 'Notify me on Launch' to get an email as soon as the special edition launches. If it's live, then come join the fun!

Please note that if the Kickstarter campaign is already finished, you will be redirected to my website where you will be able to pre-order a copy of Snow is White and the Seven Dragons. The Kickstarter bonuses are exclusive to the campaign itself and aren't available once it is finished.

See you soon in Once-Upon-Thyme!

Hugs,

Celine

OTHER WORKS AVAILABLE AT CELINEJEANJEANBOOKS.COM

- OTHER SPECIAL EDITIONS -

Music & Mirrors

A gender-flipped Phantom of the Opera retelling that is, at its heart, a story about those who have spent their lives wearing a mask and who are searching for a place to belong.

I'm not a bookworm, I'm a book dragon

Special edition reading journals full of beautiful and adorable dragons

-REGULAR EDITIONS -

- THE VIPER AND THE URCHIN -

When a street-smart pickpocket blackmails a mysterious assassin for sword training, she steps into a dangerous game far beyond the streets she knows.

The Bloodess Assassin

The Assassins' Guild (a novella)

The Black Orchid

The Pick Pocket (a novella)

The Slave City

The Doll Maker

The White Hornet

The Shadow Palace

The Opium Smuggler

The Veiled War

The Rising Rooks

- THE RAZOR'S EDGE CHRONICLES -

A barber to the supernatural with weak magic faces a threat that frighten even the fae, and her only backup is a sarcastic cat.

Touched by Magic

Bound by Silver

Lifted by Water

Marked by Azurite

Hidden by Jade

Chained by Memory

Changed by Trust

Found by Rain (a novella)

- THE LONDON'S EDGE -

Acting on impulse, Priscilla rescues a hyena and stumbles into a magical turf war in London, only to discover her own unexpected magical abilities

Laughing at Magic

Hunting with Magic

Darkness in Magic

www.ingramcontent.com/pod-product-compliance
Lightning Source LLC
LaVergne TN
LVHW091044041125
824997LV00018B/77